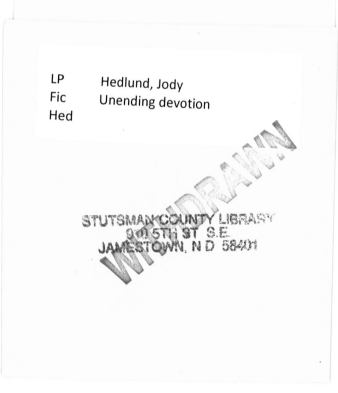

UNENDING DEVOTION

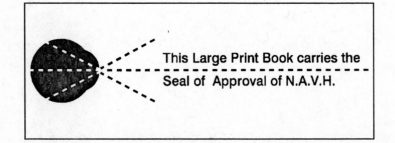

This Large Print Book carries the
Seal of Approval of N.A.V.H.

UNENDING DEVOTION

JODY HEDLUND

THORNDIKE PRESS
A part of Gale, Cengage Learning

GALE
CENGAGE Learning·

Detroit • New York • San Francisco • New Haven, Conn • Waterville, Maine • London

LIBRARY OF CONGRESS CATALOGING-IN-PUBLICATION DATA

Hedlund, Jody.
  Unending devotion / by Jody Hedlund.
    pages ; cm. — (Thorndike Press large print Christian historical fiction)
  ISBN-13: 978-1-4104-5330-3 (hardcover)
  ISBN-10: 1-4104-5330-8 (hardcover)
  1. Sisters—Michigan—Fiction. 2. Lumber camps—Fiction. 3. Corruption—Fiction. 4. Large type books. I. Title.
PS3608.E333U54 2012b
813'.6—dc23   2012030757

Published in 2012 by arrangement with Bethany House Publishers, a division of Baker Publishing Group.

Printed in Mexico
1 2 3 4 5 6 7 16 15 14 13 12

For all of the many women who are
helpless, hurting, and abused:

May you find a way out
of the coldness of winter
into the fresh spring
of freedom and hope.

CHAPTER 1

January 1883
Central Michigan

It was time. The drunk shanty boys were finally quiet.

Lily Young peered up through the shadows of the early morning darkness to the balcony that ran the length of the hotel. It was higher than she'd thought. Good thing she'd brought a rope.

She drummed her stiff fingers inside her mittens and lifted her gaze to the clear sky overhead. The last stars were fading. The lumber town would awaken with the first hints of light. And soon the woods would ring with the chopping and sawing of the shanty boys, who needed to make the most of each minute of daylight for their hard labor.

Which meant if her rescue was going to succeed, it was now or never.

But where was Edith?

Lily stepped away from the building and scanned the windows of the upper floor. Only yesterday, she'd looked the young girl in the eyes, watched the tears pool in their painful depths, and confirmed the escape plans.

Had the girl changed her mind so soon?

A window scraped open. Each halting inch up, the wooden frame rasped like a dying man gasping for breath. A bare foot poked through the opening followed by a slender bare leg.

Lily released a swoosh of air that made a white puff in front of her. "Good," she whispered. Another life rescued from the pit of hell. Yes, it was only one. And it wasn't her sister.

But it was a life that needed saving none-theless. How could she stand back and do nothing — especially when her own sister was suffering the same fate somewhere?

The young girl climbed out the window. She took one step forward then stopped and wrapped her arms across her camisole. Dressed only in her undergarments, the girl shook like twigs in a winter gale.

"Edith. Here," Lily called softly. "I'm over here."

The girl tiptoed to the edge of the balcony and leaned over, her eyes wide with fear.

"We're fine. Everyone's still asleep." Lily uncoiled the rope. "Tie this on the rail."

She tossed the rope toward the girl.

With shaking hands Edith wrapped the cord around a post, all the while casting glances over her shoulder toward the open window.

"You're going to be fine," Lily whispered. "Just focus."

The girl managed to hoist herself over the banister. With faltering movements, she snaked down the rope until Lily's outstretched arms reached her and supported her the rest of the way.

When the girl's feet finally touched the hard-packed snow, Lily grabbed the coarse sack she'd left in the snowdrift and dug through it for the items she'd brought for Edith. "Quick. Put these on." She handed Edith her only rubbers and then draped a blanket around the girl's shoulders.

"Curse the men who think women are no better than cattle," Lily muttered. The tavern owner had confiscated his girls' coats and shoes to keep them from running away. Of course, not all the prostitutes wanted to leave their life of degradation. But the minute she'd seen Edith, she'd known the girl was miserable, as miserable as her sister would be by now.

Lily slipped an arm around Edith. If only she could find Daisy . . .

During the past few weeks of living in Farwell's only temperance hotel, Lily had done the best she could to search for her sister among the dregs. And after questioning some of the prostitutes, like Edith, she was confident Daisy hadn't been in Farwell.

None of the shanty boys she'd talked to had seen anyone who fit the description of her sister. And she'd jabbered with plenty of the boys over the past month while helping photograph the lumber camps in the area.

The squeak of cutter blades on the icy road and the jangle of horse harnesses sent Lily's heart slipping downhill. Silently, she stepped to the side of the building and pulled Edith next to her. She put her mittened hand to her lips in warning.

"If Big Joe finds me, he'll beat me." The girl's voice wobbled.

"Stay right by my side," Lily whispered. "I won't let anything happen to you."

The cutter inched down the wide main street of the sleeping lumber town. In the predawn light, Lily could make out the hunched back of the driver. She released a breath and squeezed Edith. "Everything's all right. It's Oren."

Lily moved away from the hotel and waved at the oncoming cutter.

It slid to a stop, rattling the camera equipment that was piled high on the supply sled tied to the rear. Beneath a black derby hat, Oren's bushy eyebrows narrowed to a dark V. He shook his head and muttered, "What in the hairy hound do you think you're doing?"

"Edith needs a ride out of town," Lily said. "And since we're leaving, I figured we could give her a hand."

"Girl, you're going to be the death of me one of these days."

She was sure Oren was remembering the rescue from the previous month over near Averill that had resulted in a chase and several gunshots. "Well now" — she patted his arm — "if you stay quiet enough, we'll be able to get out of town before anyone hears us."

Oren grumbled again. Thankfully his walrus mustache muffled most of his words.

Lily helped Edith into the cutter and draped a thick buffalo robe across her. She brushed the girl's tangled hair out of her face. The heavy locks were in need of a good washing and brushing.

"You're going to be just fine now." She gave the girl the same smile and reassurance she used to give her sister on the many dark and lonesome nights when it had been just the two of them, when she'd been the only one to comb the tangles from Daisy's hair, hold her tight, and wipe the tears off her cheeks. She'd had to be both mother and father for as long as she could remember.

The ache in her heart squeezed painfully. Who was wiping Daisy's tears now?

A gust of frigid air slipped under Lily's collar and slithered down her back. She shivered and drew her coat tighter. But the cold tentacles of guilt gripped her insides and wouldn't let go.

How could she have let this happen? It had always been her job to protect her little sister and to make sure she was safe and happy. How could she have failed so horribly?

Lily climbed into the open sleigh and tucked the blanket under Edith's quivering chin. She grazed the girl's cheek. "It's all over now."

The girl nodded, but her focus darted to the open window of the hotel, where the edge of a tattered curtain blew through the opening like a crooked finger beckoning Edith to return.

"By the time the cookee blows the nooning horn," Lily said softly, "you'll be settled

12

safe and warm in your new home."

Home . . .

Tight anguish pushed up Lily's throat.

If only someone had rescued her and Daisy long ago . . . and if only she and Daisy could have had a real home . . . and a real family . . . then maybe Daisy wouldn't have had to run away.

Lily ducked her head to hide the sudden pool of tears that the bitter January air had already turned cold.

The slam of a door somewhere down the street echoed in the hollowness of dawn, and she quickly wedged herself into the tight space left on the seat.

"We best be going." She kept her gaze straight ahead.

Oren grunted. "Now that I'm packed in here like a dill pickle in a pill bottle, I won't be needing this." Before Lily could protest, he shoved aside his buffalo robe and tossed it toward her.

She caught the heavy fur, and a waft of sweet tobacco enveloped her. Of course Oren wasn't smoking his corncob pipe at such an ungodly early hour of the morning, but once the sun rose above the tips of the white pines, the older man was rarely without it.

"You'll be needing the blanket soon

13

enough." Lily pushed the robe back his way. Just because she'd covered Edith with hers didn't mean she expected Oren to suffer.

Oren ignored her outstretched arm and picked up the reins. "I've got more blubber than a bear in hibernation."

"This was my doing, and I'll bear the responsibility." She held her outstretched arm rigid.

He flicked the reins at his team and the cutter lurched forward. "If anyone's going to need the warmth this morning, it's you two bean poles. Especially now that I'll have to go out of my way to drop your new friend off at Molly May's."

Lily sat back and tugged the robe across her lap. A smile tickled the corners of her lips. Even though he'd grumbled like usual, she'd known he would help. He always did.

Oren caught her gaze above Edith's head. His eyes shone with admiration. And something else, gentler. He might never say the words, but Lily knew he understood her agony and would do anything in the world to help her.

"Thank you," she mouthed.

"Oh, don't thank me," he muttered. "I'll be making you work your hind end off at the next place to make up for this here delay."

"I always work hard. And you know it. Besides, if it weren't for me dragging those shanty boys over to the camera, you wouldn't have half as many customers."

He just snorted.

This time her smile broke free. She might not have a real family, but she had a good friend. And she couldn't forget to thank the Lord for that.

And she couldn't forget to thank the Lord that he'd helped her save another poor young girl. If He'd made it His mission to save lost sinners while on earth, then certainly she could do no less with her life. Besides, if she could steal Edith away, then she couldn't give up hope that someday, somehow, she'd find her sister too.

She'd rescue her or die trying.

Lily tramped up the plank step of the hotel and read the bold capital letters painted above the door: *Northern Hotel Est. 1881*. Out of four hotels in Harrison, the Northern was the only one with temperance leanings. She prayed there would be rooms available.

She refused to stay in any establishment that was "wet." She'd just as soon set up a tent and sleep in the woods before she supported the drinking and carousing that too many of the lumber-town hotels offered.

15

Even if that meant she'd have to freeze to death or face a pack of wolves.

Of course she was more than ready to get out of the subfreezing temperature. After traveling most of the day from Midland, where they'd left Edith in the capable hands of Molly May and her home for young girls, Lily was stiffer and colder than one of the long icicles hanging from the slanted eaves above her head.

With a determined set of her shoulders, she pushed the door open. A whoosh of warmth greeted her, along with the thick odor of woodsmoke and overcooked beans.

A gush of wind swept into the room with her before she wrangled the door closed. She swiped off her hood and used her teeth to tug snow-crusted mittens from her numb fingers. She stuffed the mittens into her coat pocket, and only then did she realize how silent the room had grown.

Several kerosene lamps hung from the ceiling and cast a smoky dim light over two long tables half filled with big burly men holding forks poised above their tin plates heaped high with beans, fried potatoes, and salt pork. A dozen pairs of eyes were fixed upon her.

She gave them a nod. "Evening." Then her gaze found what she sought — the proprietor or perhaps his wife — coming through the door from the kitchen carrying a steaming coffeepot in each hand.

"My, my, my. What do we have here?" The husky woman stopped short. Her face was as red as raw beef, likely heated from the six-hole range Lily glimpsed in the kitchen.

"Evening," Lily said, this time to the woman.

The way everyone was staring at her, she might have believed she was the first young woman they'd ever seen — if she hadn't known better. The fact was, there were too many women like Edith who lived and worked in the lumber towns. Lily knew she was rare, only in that she wasn't up on the table dancing in her skimpies.

"I'm checking to see if you have any rooms available for lease."

"If there aren't any, don't you worry," one of the men said. "I can make a spot for you in mine."

A chorus of guffaws rounded the tables, but Lily didn't bother to acknowledge the crude comment. After the past several months of living in various lumber towns, she was used to the depravation of the men.

The big woman ambled to the closest table and thumped the coffeepots down, sloshing some of the dark liquid onto the

17

oilskin table covering that looked like it already had plenty of spills. "Now, boys, you know Mr. Heller and I run a good Christian establishment here. My husband and I won't put up with any nonsense under this roof."

"But if the girl needs a bed," the man continued, "I'm just doing my *Christian* duty by offering to share."

"You don't get her in your room," another man growled. "If anybody gets the girl, it's gonna be me."

"I think you've just been itching for a fight all day, ain't you, Jimmy?" The first man pushed back from the table and rose to his feet.

"Boys, now don't you upset dinner." Mrs. Heller crossed her thick arms across her grease-splattered apron. "I won't stand for it."

But Jimmy was already rising. Before Lily could think to move, he'd come toward her and grabbed her. Within seconds she found herself in a tug-of-war between the two shanty boys.

"Let go of me!" she demanded, but they were too busy yelling at each other to notice.

Mrs. Heller abandoned the coffeepots and charged toward the men. She pulled a thick wooden spoon from her deep apron pocket and wielded it in front of her. "Boys, enough! This is just enough of this nonsense! If you don't stop, you'll force me to give you a whoppin' with my spoon." But they didn't pay attention to her either.

For an instant, alarm shattered the usual calmness of Lily's spirit. Maybe she'd been wrong to disregard Oren's hesitation when she'd first insisted he take her along during his itinerant picture taking among the lumber camps.

"Those towns are loaded with danger," he'd muttered. *"They're infested with graybacks and deadbeats. And if one doesn't get you, the other will."*

So far she'd avoided both the lice and any encounters with rowdy men. But there were plenty of shanty boys who had referred to Harrison as "Hell's Waiting Room." What if they'd been right?

"Take your hands off the young lady." A stern voice rose above the clatter.

The two men ceased their struggle, and silence fell over the room.

A broad-shouldered muscular man had abandoned his plate and risen from the bench. An unruly lock of blond hair fell across his forehead above dark green eyes. There was something commanding about his expression.

"I don't think this is any way to treat a guest," he said, "do you?"

None of the men said anything, but the two holding her made no move to unhand her.

"Connell's right." Mrs. Heller huffed. Her face was a shade redder than it had been before — if that were possible. "This one looks like she's a decent God-fearing girl. And even if she's not —"

"Oh, you can rest assured that I am," Lily said quickly, struggling to free her arms from the tight grip of the men.

Mrs. Heller pointed her spoon at the two men. "I've a mind to write home to your mamas about your foolishness. And you know as well as I do, my letters would bring those poor women to tears."

One of the men released her, but the other — Jimmy — just gave a short laugh, revealing a black space where he was missing a top front tooth on one side with only half of a jagged tooth on the other. His fingers dug into her arm, and his smile was hard with the lust she'd seen often enough.

But she'd never worried about the boys before. Oren had always been there to scare them away.

She glanced at the door. He was probably still across the street chatting with a couple of local business owners about the lumber camps in the area. Maybe she shouldn't have been in such a hurry to get inside and get warmed up. Oren was always warning that her impatience was going to get her into trouble eventually.

He would come looking for her before too long — of that she had no doubt. She could only pray it was sooner rather than later.

Connell took a step forward. "Let the girl get back to her business, and we'll get back to our meal before it gets cold."

He wore the usual short woolen mackinaw, a bright red-and-black-plaid coat that many shanty boys wore, allowing them to be better seen in the woods and protected against the many accidents that abounded in the camps.

He'd unbuttoned the light coat revealing suspenders stretched across a thick cotton shirt. He looked just as rugged as any other shanty boy she'd seen, but from the expectant way the men stared at him, he'd obviously earned their respect.

Except, of course, the respect of the man still holding her arm.

Lily gave a rough yank, trying to dislodge herself.

But Jimmy's pinch sank through her flesh and reached her bone.

She gave a yelp of protest.

Connell took another step forward. "Let go of her, Jimmy. Now." His voice turned ominous.

Jimmy jerked her against his armpit into the sour odor of a day's worth of hard labor. "And if I wanna keep her, what're you gonna do about it, McCormick?"

"You know I don't want any trouble," Connell said. "But you're taking this too far."

Lily just shook her head. She'd had enough. She wasn't the type of person to stand around waiting for help. She believed that if you wanted something done, then you better just roll up your sleeves and do it yourself.

"I don't take kindly to any of you shanty boys touching me," she said. "So unless I give you permission, from now on, you'd best keep your hands off me."

With the last word, she lifted her boot and brought the heel down on Jimmy's toes. She ground it hard.

Like most of the other shanty boys, at the end of a day out in the snow, he'd taken off his wet boots and layers of damp wool socks to let them dry overnight before donning them again for the next day's work.

Jimmy cursed, but before he could move,

she brought her boot down on his other foot with a smack that rivaled a gun crack.

This time he howled. And with an angry curse, he shoved her hard, sending her sprawling forward.

She flailed her arms in a futile effort to steady herself and instead found herself falling against Connell McCormick.

His arms encircled her, but the momentum of her body caused him to lose his balance. He stumbled backward. "Whoa! Hold steady!"

Her skirt and legs tangled with his, and they careened toward the rows of dirty damp socks hanging in front of the fireplace. The makeshift clotheslines caught them and for a moment slowed their tumble. But against their full weight, the ropes jerked loose from the nails holding them to the beams.

In an instant, Lily found herself falling. She twisted and turned among the clotheslines but realized that her thrashing was only lassoing her against Connell.

In the downward tumble, Connell slammed into a chair near the fireplace. Amidst the tangle of limbs and ropes, she was helpless to do anything but drop into his lap.

With a thud, she landed against him.

Several socks hung from his head and covered his face. Dirty socks covered her shoulders and head too. Their stale rotten stench swarmed around her. And for a moment she was conscious only of the fact that she was near to gagging from the odor.

She tried to lift a hand to move the sock hanging over one of her eyes but found that her arms were pinned to her sides. She tilted her head and then blew sideways at the crusty, yellowed linen. But it wouldn't budge.

Again she shook her head — this time more emphatically. Still the offending article wouldn't fall away.

Through the wig of socks covering Connell's head, she could see one of his eyes peeking at her, watching her antics. The corner of his lips twitched with the hint of a smile.

She could only imagine what she looked like. If it was anything like him, she must look comical.

As he cocked his head and blew at one of his socks, she couldn't keep from smiling at the picture they both made, helplessly drenched in dirty socks, trying to remove them with nothing but their breath.

"Welcome to Harrison." His grin broke free.

"You know how to make a girl feel right at home." She wanted to laugh.

But as he straightened himself in the chair, she became at once conscious of the fact that she was sitting directly in his lap and that the other men in the room were hooting and calling out over her intimate predicament.

She scrambled to move off him.

But the ropes had tangled them together, and her efforts only caused her to fall against him again.

She was not normally a blushing woman, but the growing indecency of her situation was enough to chase away any humor she may have found in the situation and make a chaste woman like herself squirm with embarrassment.

"I'd appreciate your help," she said, struggling again to pull her arms free of the rope. "Or do all you oafs make a sport of manhandling women?"

"All you oafs?" His grin widened. "Are you insinuating that I'm an *oaf?*"

"What in the hairy hound is going on here?"

She jumped at the boom of Oren's voice and the slam of the door.

The room turned quiet enough to hear the *click-click* of Oren pulling down the lever of his rifle. She glanced over her shoulder to the older man, to the fierceness of his drawn eyebrows and the deadly anger in his eyes as he took in her predicament.

A breeze of relief blew over her hot face. She was safe now — not that she'd been all that worried before. But she counted her blessings that Oren was on her side.

His heavy boots slapped the floor until he stood over her. With a growl, he lowered the barrel of his rifle and pushed it against Connell's temple. "Mister, you're a dead man."

CHAPTER 2

The steel pressed hard and cold against Connell's head. He'd been in plenty of dangerous situations, but this was the first time anyone had ever threatened to blow out his brains.

The twenty-four-inch-long rifle with its octagon barrel chambered fifteen ready-to-fire cartridges. But at this range, all it would take was one shot and he'd be a dead man.

"No one touches Lily" — the man jabbed the tip into Connell's temple, grinding it into his throbbing pulse — "and lives to tell about it."

The old man grabbed the rope that entangled them. He grunted and twisted it before finally pulling it free. Then he extended a hand to the woman and hoisted her to her feet. All the while, neither his Winchester nor his murderous eyes shifted so much as a thousandth of an inch from Connell.

Finally, in all of the shifting, the dirty socks fell away from his head and gave him a clear glimpse of the woman.

She untangled her skirt and smoothed down the folds of flowery calico, but not before he caught sight of her long knit socks, which strangely enough were striped in parallel rows of bright yellow and orange and green and purple.

"Now, Oren, there's no need to kill him." She patted the man's arm. "At least not tonight."

He muttered under the big mustache that hung over his upper lip but didn't move the gun.

"I agree," Connell said. "And really, I don't see that there's *ever* going to be a need to kill me."

"I decide who to kill and when." Oren jabbed the barrel again, and his finger on the trigger twitched. "And right now I'm in the mood to make someone eat lead."

Connell's mouth went dry. So this was it. He was going to die.

He'd already calculated the amount of time he spent in the woods and had given himself a twenty-five percent chance of dying from a lumber-related accident — being crushed by a falling tree or being buried by rolling logs. But a dining room brawl? Over a girl he didn't know? That had never entered any of his equations.

The fact was, he wasn't ready to die. Not yet. Not in the middle of the busiest time of the lumber season. Not when he had so much work to do.

"I wasn't doing anything indecent," he said. "In fact, I was just trying to help her —"

"And I suppose that's why your hands were stuck to her like a coon holding a coin."

"That's not true. She fell against me and we toppled into the socks. That's all." His focus darted to Vera Heller, still armed with her eighteen-inch-long wooden spoon. "Right, Mrs. Heller?"

The woman nodded. "Connell McCormick is one of my best boarders and one of the nicest boys in this town. If you wanna shoot somebody, then you take aim at Jimmy Neil over there. That boy is full of trouble."

Jimmy had already backed up to the stairway, and at Vera's words, he spun and took the steps two at a time, disappearing like he usually did whenever it was time to take responsibility for his actions.

Oren's finger stroked the trigger.

Connell swallowed hard. Did he dare

make a move for his knife? The hard leather of the scabbard rested underneath his shirt against his ribs, so close and yet so far away.

"I think you've taught him his lesson, Oren." The young lady pushed the barrel away from Connell's face. "I don't think he'll manhandle me again."

When she gave him a "so-there" look and then raised her chin, a spark of self-pride flamed to life in his gut. His mam had always made sure he knew how to treat a girl, but this was obviously no ordinary girl.

"If anyone was doing the manhandling, it was you." Connell rubbed the sore spot on his forehead. "I didn't ask you to sit on my lap."

Her eyes widened, revealing a woodsy brown that was as dark and rich as fine-grained walnut. The color matched the thick curls that had come loose from the knitted hat covering her head.

Oren stood back, tucked his gun under his arm, and tapped his black derby up. His eyebrows followed suit.

The girl opened her mouth to speak but then clamped it shut, apparently at a loss for words.

A wisp of satisfaction curled through Connell. After the way she'd let the old man humiliate him, he didn't mind letting her squirm for a minute.

But only for a minute.

Mam's training was ingrained too deeply to wish the girl ill will for more than that. He shoved himself out of the chair and straightened his aching back.

"Look," he said, plucking a last dirty sock from his shoulder. "Can we start over? I'm Connell McCormick."

She hesitated and then tilted her head at him. "And I'm Miss Young."

"I sure hope you'll forgive me if I've caused you any . . . discomfort."

Surprise flitted across her elegant, doelike features. "Well now. With that polite apology, how could I refuse to forgive you?"

He gave her a smile and waited. The polite thing for her to do was offer her own apology and perhaps even a thank-you for his attempts to save her from Jimmy Neil.

But she only returned the smile, one that curved her lovely full lips in perfect symmetry but didn't make it into the depths of her eyes.

She took a step back and thrust a hand into her coat pocket.

"Just make sure you don't lay even the tip of your pinkie on Lily again," Oren said, having the decency to look Connell in the eyes and nod at him. If the old man hadn't been so stooped, Connell guessed he'd add another three — if not four — inches to his height. Oren was gruff all right, but there was also something in his expression and about his fierce protectiveness of the young woman that Connell liked.

As if Oren hadn't scared the other men in the room enough already, he turned abruptly and swept the barrel of his gun across the wide eyes that stared at him. "And if any of you other shanty boys so much as thinks about touching Lily, I'll see it in your eyes and come hunt you down. Then I'll shoot you full of holes and feed you to the wolves."

Lily patted the man's arm and laughed, the sweet ring full of affection. "I don't know what I'd do without you."

Oren grumbled under his mustache. His gaze swept hungrily over the table and the plates of untouched food.

"Mrs. Heller, we'll need two rooms," Lily said, "and the use of your cellar for a darkroom, if it's available."

"Then you're planning on taking pictures while you're here?" Vera asked the question that was on the tip of Connell's tongue.

"That we are, among other things," Lily said cheerfully.

Oren snorted and shook his head. Then

he plopped himself down on the nearest bench and growled at Mrs. Heller. "How about serving me a meal before the food gets cold enough to grow legs and walk itself out the door?"

Connell made quick work of restringing the sock line and then situated himself back at his spot at the far table in the corner, where he could usually eat in solitude and work on recording and computing the day's figures in his ledgers. His books lay open and his pen was dry, with a half-inch ink splotch on the page where he'd dropped the pen and tossed his spectacles.

He stabbed the tip of his knife into a slab of salted pork. The greasy gravy had already cooled and congealed. For several seconds he twirled the meat and stared at it. The minute Lily Young had walked into the door he'd forgotten his hunger.

And now, he was ashamed to admit, he was much more interested in studying the vibrant Lily Young than doing anything else.

She'd slept too late. From the sliver of light between the thin curtains, Lily could see that morning was already chasing away the darkness of the long winter night.

Hurriedly, she tucked the last of her unruly curls into a knot.

She hadn't gotten used to the long winter nights of central Michigan, where the light disappeared at five in the evening and didn't show itself again until about eight the next morning. Even long after the rooster crowed, the skies were usually cloudy and dark, making it seem that night lingered forever.

If only the sun could break through the dismal covering more often.

She shivered and crossed the frigid unheated room to the window. She yanked open the curtains, letting in the dull light, longing for the bright sunshine that could warm her soul, if not her body. Oren claimed that it took a couple of winters for Easterners to grow thicker skin and adjust to northern winters. But after two years, her skin was apparently still as thin as the day she'd arrived from New York.

With her fingernail, she scratched a circle in the frosted pane and caught a glimpse of Main Street, mostly deserted. She didn't doubt the shanty boys were already hard at work. They didn't spare a single second of daylight in their quest to strip the earth of its treasures — namely white pine trees.

At the clomping of horse hooves on the hard-packed snow and the whistle of a distant train, Lily spun away from the window and crossed the room. Oren had probably been awake for several hours and was hard at work setting up his makeshift darkroom in the cellar.

And here she'd been, snug under heavy quilts, lazing the day away. She stepped over the pile of her discarded clothes and the grain-seed sack that held the rest of her earthly possessions. The contents spilled out of the bag, the result of her hurried attempt at her morning toilet in the freezing room.

The glint of silver stopped her, and she reached for the oval picture frame among the folds of her wearing apparel. She held the miniature portrait to her mouth, huffed a breath of warm air onto the cold glass, and with the edge of her sleeve, wiped away the smudges.

In the dim light, she glanced around the small room. A chair with blue-chipped paint sat in one corner. Two pegs on the white-washed wall awaited her clothes. Next to the sagging twin bed was a square bedside table holding a dusty lantern.

She stepped to the table, wiped off a layer of grime, and then gently set the frame on the clean spot, angling it so the picture faced the room.

Folding her arms across her chest, she stepped back and inspected her one attempt at making the room into the home it would become for the next several weeks. The silver frame was spotted with corrosion, but it outlined the dear faces of her mother and father. It was the portrait they'd had taken on their wedding day and was the only tangible reminder of the family she'd once had.

Lately, every time she looked at the picture, her parents' unsmiling faces seemed to accuse her of losing Daisy, of not doing everything she could to take care of her little sister, of not keeping her safe enough.

"I'm sorry," Lily whispered to the picture, her breath coming out in a white cloud. "I'm doing my best to find her. And once I have her, I promise I won't ever lose her again."

She swallowed the sudden lump in her throat. Her parents had every right to blame her. When the orphanage had told them they were getting too old to stay, she'd pushed Daisy to go with the Wretchams. She'd thought Daisy would be happy there, that she'd have a good life with a big loving family on a farm until she and Daisy could find a way to make a home of their own.

Lily had gone to Bay City with Oren, hoping to earn enough money to eventually afford a place. She hadn't known then that the grumpy old man and his sick wife would be two of the kindest people she would ever meet.

She'd faithfully written letters to Daisy, and Oren had even taken her to visit her sister on two different occasions. She'd always known Daisy wasn't happy, but she'd just assumed it would take time to adjust.

She'd never expected Daisy would run away. Until she'd received Daisy's last letter in October.

By then it had been too late. When she'd arrived at the Wretchams', Daisy had been long gone.

Lily gave one last nod at her parents' portrait. "I'm getting closer to finding her."

Silence was their only answer — just as it had always been.

With the weight of guilt pressing down on her, she lowered her head and exited her room. The second floor hallway was empty, and the tap of her footsteps echoed as she made her way down the long passageway to the narrow staircase that led to the dining room.

Today she would investigate Harrison. Find out all she could about the brothels. And try to discover if anyone had seen her sister.

She stepped into the dining room, and the

acrid scent of burnt coffee drifted toward her.

"There's the morning glory." Mrs. Heller paused in wiping a table, holding a dirty dishrag in midair.

"Oh no, Mrs. Heller. I'm most definitely not a morning glory." Lily glanced around the nearly deserted room. Only one man was working at a corner spot, his head bent over his books. "I'm really more like an afternoon crocus. I prefer daylight and sunshine, both of which are far too rare in these parts."

"But you're a burst of sunshine this morning." The woman gave Lily a smile that was the medicine she needed to chase the gloom from her soul.

"Why, thank you, Mrs. Heller —"

"You can call me Vera."

"And I'm Lily."

"Give me a minute and I'll rustle up a plate of pork and beans for you." Vera resumed her efforts at cleaning the oilskin covering, her large hindquarters wiggling in motion to the swirls of the rag on the table. "They won't be too warm anymore, but they'll be filling enough."

"Don't trouble yourself with me." The thought of a heavy meal for breakfast made Lily's stomach churn. "I'll be happy enough with a cup of coffee — if you have any to spare."

Vera stopped in midswirl and took in Lily's appearance. "Coffee? My, my, my. You need more meat on your bones, girl. You'll blow away with the slightest breeze. Don't you agree, Connell?"

Lily glanced to the corner spot, only to find the young man she'd met the previous evening staring at her above spectacles perched on the end of his nose.

He quickly looked back at the open book in front of him, but the slight reddish tint creeping up his neck above his collar was evidence that he'd been paying more attention to her than to his books.

"I'm sure Miss Young would appreciate whatever you're willing to provide." The young man pulled out his pocket watch and peered at it. "Especially considering the fact that breakfast has been over for exactly one hour and twelve minutes."

His hair was neatly combed, except for one sun-bleached streak that fell across his forehead. He'd shaven the scruff from his face, revealing skin that was rough and bronzed from long days outdoors.

"Connell McCormick." Vera thumped her hands onto her hips. "You sure don't seem to mind when I sneak you an extra doughnut or two. I think half the reason you loiter here in the mornings is because you hope I'll feed you more."

The faint red streaks climbed up to the base of his cheeks. He didn't say anything and instead dipped his head and scribbled something into one of his books, as if there were nothing more important at that moment than the page in front of him.

Vera winked at Lily. "I'll get you that coffee, but how about one of the doughnuts I fried up this morning too?"

Lily couldn't keep from smiling. "Well, only since you're already in the habit of sneaking them . . ." She had a feeling she was going to like Vera.

The woman disappeared into the kitchen, and Lily plunked onto the nearest bench. Too late she realized she had situated herself so that she was looking almost directly at Connell.

She fidgeted but refrained from rudely repositioning herself altogether, as she was tempted to do. She wasn't in the habit of staring at or making small talk with strange men — or really any men, for that matter. At eighteen she was old enough to begin thinking about a husband and marriage and that sort of thing. But she'd always been too busy worrying about Daisy to be even the slightest bit interested in romantic involvements.

Thankfully, with Oren scaring all the men away, she hadn't had to worry about anyone showing ongoing interest in her.

Anyway, what kind of man would be interested in her, a poor orphaned girl with no family, no money, and nothing to bring to a marriage except herself?

Connell barely lifted his eyes, as if trying to peek at her without her knowledge, and for an eternity of a second their gazes caught.

A spark lit his eyes, almost as if he were remembering their encounter of the previous evening and the draping of dirty socks they'd both worn.

An odd flush of pleasure wrapped around her middle, and she wanted to smile at the memory of how silly they'd both looked. But she shifted her gaze to the bare walls and drummed her fingers against the table. This time it was her turn to pretend nothing had transpired between them.

"Here you are." Vera ambled back into the room holding a pannikin in one hand and a coffeepot in the other. She dropped the pint-sized tin cup to the table, and inside was the promised doughnut.

Lily lifted out the doughnut before Vera

41

poured a thick brew of coffee into the pannikin.

"You're a dear." Lily lifted the cup, and out of habit she blew on the steaming liquid.

"Don't you worry none." Vera bustled toward Connell, sliding another doughnut out of her apron pocket. "I've got an extra for you too."

Connell reached for the doughnut, but Vera pulled it back and held it out of reach. She pointed to her ruddy cheek. "You know what you owe me first."

To Lily's surprise, Connell grinned, leaned toward the older woman, and planted a kiss in the spot she'd touched.

Vera handed him the doughnut and then gave the round flesh in his cheek a pinch. "You're a good boy, Connell."

Lily smiled at Vera's compliment. Connell was definitely no boy. His shirt stretched across his shoulders and around his thick arms. He had the rugged build of a man accustomed to cutting and hauling heavy logs. He might have earned the nickname of shanty boy, like all the other men who came north to work in the woods, but he was all man as far as she could see.

She took a sip of her coffee, only to find it was gritty and strong enough to choke a horse. She nearly dropped the pannikin on the table and couldn't keep from sputtering into her hand.

One of Connell's eyebrows shot up and his grin turned lopsided, as if he knew from personal experience just how awful the coffee was.

She swallowed the bitter mouthful and smiled back — a secret smile that gave her a strange sense that maybe this man had the potential to be a friend.

"Mrs. Heller sure does make the best doughnuts this side of the Tittabawasee River." He took a bite, easily chomping half the circle.

"You're only getting one from me this morning." Vera wagged her finger at him. "And no amount of flattery will get you more."

He shrugged at Lily, still grinning. "Doesn't hurt to try, does it?"

Vera pulled out the bench across from Lily, and her eyes danced from Connell's compliment. She sidled in, bumping the table and causing coffee to slosh out of Lily's cup.

Maybe with enough jostling, Vera would spill more and save her from having to drink it.

When she met Connell's gaze, his eyebrow quirked again.

Lily nibbled on her doughnut and tried to stifle a smile.

Vera fished another doughnut out of her pocket, brushed off a stray potato peel, and then took a big bite — a bite that rivaled Connell's.

"So tell me about yourself," she said with her mouth full. Her dark hair, threaded with gray, framed her splotchy face in a frizzy disarray. The woman had likely been up since the wee hours of the morning and had already put in a full day's worth of work. "Tell me where you're from. And all that good stuff."

Lily set her doughnut on the table. Where should she begin? How could she go about explaining the complexity of her past? And did Vera really care to know?

She looked into the woman's eyes and read genuine kindness there.

"Well . . ." Lily hesitated and then opted to give the abbreviated version of her life history. "We came up from Bay City. Oren has a photography studio there."

Vera stuffed the rest of the doughnut into her mouth and nodded at Lily to continue.

"He does good business during the winter months traveling around the camps taking pictures of shanty boys."

"And?"

"And I help him."

Vera brushed the crumbs off her hands and then folded them in front of her. "And . . . ?"

Lily smiled. She'd been right. She was going to like this woman. "And I'm trying to find my sister."

Vera swallowed the last bite of doughnut but didn't say anything.

"In her final letter to me she said she was heading north to the new lumber towns to look for work."

"Work?" Vera's eyes turned grave.

The ache in Lily's heart flared to life. "She told me it wouldn't be the kind of work I'd approve of. But apparently she'd heard girls could make a fortune during one winter season."

Vera shook her head and pursed her lips.

"She wrote that she wanted to earn money so we could afford a place for the two of us to be together again." Lily pressed the ball of her hand into her stomach to stave off the pain.

"Sounds like one foolish little girl."

"I have only myself to blame." She should have seen it coming, should have done more.

"Well, if you're looking for her among the spawn of the devil, you've certainly come to the right place."

Connell cleared his throat. "Don't you think you're being a little harsh, Mrs. Heller?"

The woman tossed him a glare that could have melted ice. "This town has less than two thousand permanent residents but over twenty taverns. And with all the sporting that goes on at almost every single one of them, I'm actually being kind in my description of this town."

"Twenty taverns?" That was more than any of the other small lumber towns she'd been to. She'd best start visiting them right away.

"And then there's the Stockade," Vera lowered her voice to a hush.

The name sent a chill crawling over Lily's skin.

"The place is on the edge of town, up on a hill, surrounded by a tall stockade fence. You can't miss it. And it's run by the devil himself in human flesh — James Carr."

Connell pushed away from the table, his bench scraping against the floor. "Harrison's like any other lumber town that's sprung up in these parts. It's got both the good and the bad. And that's just the way of things." He pulled off his wire spectacles and folded them closed.

Vera heaved a sigh and climbed back to her feet, bumping the table again and spilling more of Lily's coffee. "I don't like it. I wish we could do more to clean things up in this town."

"Why can't we?" Lily asked, pushing aside the odds. "I'm a part of the Red Ribbon Society in Bay City, and with enough publicity and pressure we got the Wolverton House to close its doors — and it was one of the bawdiest on the lower end of the Saginaw River."

In the spring after the river drive, most of the shanty boys ended up in Bay City, often spending every last dollar of their winter earnings on drinks and women. The port city had more than its share of debauchery. If she could help fight problems there, she could do the same in Harrison.

Connell shook his head. "The Wolverton was closed because it was falling apart and had become a fire hazard. Besides, there are still dozens of other taverns along Water Street that your Red Ribbon Society won't ever be able to close."

"In time and with enough effort, we'll make a difference." Enthusiasm sprang up like a spring blossom, despite Connell's negativity. "We can form a group here and hold meetings. We'll make the public aware of what's going on. And come up with a plan to help close the taverns."

Vera paused, as if weighing Lily's idea. "I wonder . . . maybe that's just what we need."

"If we try to rid the town of women, booze, and card playing," Connell said, "the men are going to try to sneak them into the camps. And we know how much trouble that will cause."

His words crashed into Lily, nearly knocking her from her bench. For a long moment she couldn't speak, but then finally managed, "I don't think I heard you right."

He stacked up his books and tucked them under his arm. "There's bound to be some evil in every town. It's just a fact of life."

She shook her head in utter disbelief and rose to her feet, her ire rising with her. "Are you telling me, Mr. McCormick, you're unwilling to do anything about the debauchery that runs rampant in this town, that you're content to turn a blind eye to the sin right under your nose?"

"If you were somehow able to miraculously close down all the taverns in this town, ninety-nine point nine percent of those owners would pick up and move to the next county and keep right on doing what they're doing."

"So why even try?"

"Exactly."

Too bad he'd missed the sarcasm in her voice. She thumped her fingers against the table in rhythm to the angry thudding of her heartbeat. "Your philosophy appalls me."

"I'm sorry. But I'm just explaining the reality of the situation."

"Well then, please don't say any more." She picked up the doughnut she'd hardly touched. She'd save it for Oren. "There may always be sin and evil, but that doesn't mean God wants us to sit back and turn a blind eye to the problems."

"Amen," Vera said.

"I, for one, refuse to give up hope that I can do my part to make the world a better place." Lily glanced to the big window across the dining room that overlooked Main Street. Where would she start her efforts?

Of course, she wouldn't neglect the work she had with Oren in the darkroom and all the pictures that still needed developing. But first chance she had, she'd begin her crusade to find Daisy. And in the process, she'd do everything she could to clean up Harrison.

How could she do anything less?

She squared her shoulders and shot Connell a look she hoped contained the contempt she felt toward his attitude.

"My sister is out in the middle of all that evil somewhere. And every night I get down on my knees and pray that it will be the last one she has to spend in her living hell."

CHAPTER 3

Connell blew a frustrated breath and leaned back in his chair. Perched on two legs, the old hickory creaked under his one hundred eighty-five pounds. He stared at the sheets of figures spread across his rough-board desk.

None of his three camps was cutting and hauling the number of logs he needed them to. With the newest narrow-gauge track they'd laid last summer to the farthest camp, they should have an increase of at least fifteen percent over last winter.

But the figures weren't adding up. In fact, he'd computed them enough times to know the camps were hauling less than last winter at this exact date.

He glanced at the wall to the large calendar, the only decoration in his sparsely furnished second-story office. He read through the familiar words printed across the top of the sheet in big black letters:

He'd already drawn *X*'s across the first ten days of January, which meant it wouldn't be long before Dad or his brother, Tierney, came up from Bay City to check on his progress. He never knew when one of them would show up. Neither had made the trek into the woods since before Thanksgiving, and Dad would be ready for an update by now.

Connell was determined to give them the kind of report they expected — the kind that reflected just how hard he and his men were working, the kind that showed McCormick Lumber coming out ahead of all the other companies in the area.

If only he could get his numbers to add up to more . . .

Connell let the legs of his chair slam to the ground. He jumped to his feet and tossed his spectacles onto his ledgers. "What am I going to do?"

He needed to figure out a way to increase production — from all his camps. But how could he require more of the men when they were already cutting and hauling from well before sunup to after sundown?

His boots clunked against the floor as he paced to the window, to the box stove, and then back to the window.

"Stop all that racket up there." From the office below, Stuart Golden tapped a broom handle on the flimsy boards that separated one floor from the next. "Some of us have work to do around here."

"That's right," Connell called with a grin. "Some of us *do* have work. So why don't you get to it?"

Over the past two lumber seasons, Connell had rented an office above the *Harrison Herald*. As chief editor, Stuart had been willing to part with the room in an effort to sustain his weekly paper. Even if the office wasn't fancy, it had sufficed. Not only did Connell have a private place where he could work on all the many details of his bookkeeping, but he could also conduct business with his foremen, timber cruisers, and all his other employees when they came to town to give him reports.

For all practical purposes, the office would serve as the headquarters for McCormick Lumber for the duration of their lumbering in Clare County. With all the other companies cutting logs in the area, Connell didn't expect to be in Harrison for more than another year or two before they'd gotten everything out of the land that they needed. Based on previous statistics, he'd calculated they had exactly eighteen months before all the white pine in the area was gone.

He already had a couple of cruisers out to the north scouting for fresh tracts of pineland and reporting back to him with estimates of the number of pine trees per acre. As soon as his cruisers located valuable land that wasn't already bought up, he'd make arrangements for McCormick Lumber to purchase it. Soon enough, he'd be busy planning for the new camps.

He liked Stuart Golden and the Hellers and several other townspeople who had become friends. But there was no sense getting too attached to a small town like Harrison when he wouldn't be there for long.

That's the way the lumber industry worked, the way his dad had run the business for the past twenty years. Through hard work and savvy, Dad had transformed himself from a poor, starving Irish immigrant into a millionaire.

And he expected nothing less than hard work and savvy from his sons.

A flash of color along Main Street drew Connell's attention back to the window.

Lily Young picked up her skirts and dashed

across the street like a schoolboy.

"That girl is something else," he mumbled.

She stopped in front of Johnson's Hotel. Wrapped in a heavy woolen coat, she stared at the big lettering across the front of the building. Her bright flowery skirt flapped in the wind, as out of place in the dull gray of winter as the girl herself was in the mostly male-populated lumber town.

She swiped aside a loose curl that slapped at her cheek and then stepped toward the double doors.

His muscles tightened. She couldn't possibly intend to go inside. Couldn't she see that the word *Saloon* was painted across the large front window, one bright red letter in each square pane?

There might not be much any of them could do to rid the town of the drinking and whoring that went on, but that didn't mean he liked it or supported it. And he certainly didn't think the establishment was the kind of place a decent young lady should enter — not at great peril to herself and her reputation.

Lily pushed open one of the doors and stepped inside.

"What? Is she crazy?" He spun from the window and clomped across the room, an anxious spark shooting through his gut like the snap of the crackling birch in the stove.

Without bothering to close the door of his office, he charged into the hallway and took the steps two at a time, hitting the bottom at full speed. He passed by the open door that led to Stuart's printing press and headed straight for the front door.

"Hey, where you going, you lazybones?" Stuart called, stepping into the hallway, wiping his ink-stained hands on a blackened rag.

Connell didn't take the time to answer but instead rushed outside, letting the cold morning reawaken him.

It had taken only two minutes after Lily's entrance into the Northern Hotel last evening for Jimmy Neil to grab hold of her. Of course, Jimmy would be down working at the loading docks all day and wouldn't be in any of the taverns to bother her. In fact, Connell doubted there were many men sitting around Johnson's saloon in the middle of the morning. But all it would take was one — one just like Jimmy — and Lily would be in big trouble.

Connell started across the street but then stopped abruptly.

Through the narrow rectangular window of the saloon door, he could see her outline.

One of her mittened hands pressed against the glass, almost as if she were prepared to run if need be.

His breath rose in puffy clouds in front of him.

"What are you all excited about?" Stuart joined him in the middle of the wide street. He carried his rag in one hand and a pica stick in the other. He glanced around the nearly deserted street as if trying to surmise what was wrong. "We don't have another *accidental* fire, do we?"

Halfway down the street, the charred remains of the new county jail glared from beneath a frosted covering of ice. Several weeks ago, the fire had started in the middle of the night, and by the time the fire bells had awakened the townspeople, they hadn't had a praying chance to save the place. Built entirely out of wood, the jail had burned to the ground within minutes.

Of course Stuart had his theory about who had started the fire. "And what's the use of having a jail anyway?" his friend would say. "The sheriff wouldn't ever lock anyone up, not when he'd have to lock himself up first."

"I'm not all excited. And no. There's no fire." Connell took a step back and glanced at the saloon door. Lily hadn't moved from her spot.

Stuart peered around. His eyes narrowed, his investigative mind likely already hard at work.

A gust of wind knocked into Connell, reminding him that he'd rushed outside without his mackinaw.

"So," Stuart said, "if we're not fighting fires, what are we doing out here freezing off our behinds?"

Heat crept up Connell's neck. What *was* he doing?

Apparently Lily didn't need rescuing from him this time.

Stuart focused in on the saloon door, and he squinted. "Oh, so *that's* what we're doing out here."

Connell shifted his attention to the sleigh coming down the wide street. He took a couple of steps backward, moving out of the way and nodding to the man driving the team.

Stuart grinned. "Or should I say, *she's* why we're out here."

Connell refused to give his friend the satisfaction of an answer.

"Word's going around town that she got the best of two big men last night. Jimmy Neil and another strong man, who happens to be standing in the middle of Main Street, ogling at her —"

"I'm not *ogling* at her." Connell looked far off to the south, to the puffs of black smoke billowing in the air, the distant signal that the train — a branch of the Flint and Pere Marquette Railroad — would make its daily appearance in Harrison. "And she didn't get the best of me."

Stuart slugged him in the arm. The point of Stuart's middle knuckle jabbed Connell hard enough to throw him off balance. Stuart wasn't a big man. In fact, everything about him was thin. His face was a narrow oval covered with a scraggly beard. His arms and legs were as skinny as the branches of a sapling. If Connell hadn't witnessed the man's enormous appetite on occasion, he would have guessed Stuart wasn't getting enough to eat.

"Sounds like she's got quite the spirit if she can get the best of you."

"I was rescuing her from Jimmy, and she fell on top of me."

"Rescuing?" Stuart gave a snort. "From the way I heard it, she did a pretty good job taking care of herself."

"No telling what could have happened to her if I hadn't stepped in when I did."

Stuart laughed. "Okay, big guy. Whatever you say."

The door of Johnson's saloon swung open, and Connell didn't have time to get irritated at his friend. Lily shifted to the crude board that served as a step and pulled the door closed behind her. She paused and sighed, lines of frustration etched across her forehead.

Apparently she hadn't found her sister at Johnson's. Even if her sister were there, Connell doubted Johnson would let her go. The brothel owners had a hard time attracting girls, and once they got them, they didn't like to lose them.

Lily straightened her shoulders and let the lines ease from her forehead. She set her lips with obvious determination and then stepped into the street. She glanced first one way and then the other. If she saw him and Stuart, she gave no indication.

Stuart muttered, "Why don't you say something?"

Connell wanted to, but his lips felt like they were frozen shut. He'd never been all that suave around pretty girls. And not only was this girl pretty, but she had enough spunk to knock a man off his feet — literally.

Stuart jabbed his ribs with his bony elbow. "At least go over to her."

Connell couldn't make his feet work either.

Lily stepped into the street and headed in the direction of the next closest tavern.

"You big chicken," Stuart said under his breath. Then he took off at a jog. "Miss Young," he called. "I'm Stuart Golden. Chief editor and owner of the *Harrison Herald*."

She stopped. She grabbed her flapping skirt and angled her head at Stuart.

He gave her a wide smile, one that froze Connell's insides like a lump of gravy on a cold tin plate. "And I'm a friend of Connell McCormick." Stuart tossed a nod his way.

She glanced at Connell for less than a second, but it was long enough for him to see that she was still holding him in disdain for the conversation they'd had earlier about the problems in town.

"Just wanted to introduce myself," Stuart continued, "and let you know that if you need any help — with anything at all — I'm the man for the job."

Her rich brown eyes were framed by lashes that were long and thick enough to sweep a man off his feet. And when she turned her attention upon Stuart, she seemed to do just that — sweep him off his feet and up into the air.

"Well now, that's mighty nice of you, Mr. Golden —"

"Stu." He regarded her like a puppy its master.

Connell wished he were standing next to Stuart and could sock *him* in the arm. Of course, he couldn't begrudge Stuart the attention of a woman, not after having lost his wife during the diphtheria epidemic that had ravaged Michigan back in '80. Stuart had lost his son too, and for all practical purposes had given up on the baby daughter he'd handed to the care of his parents who lived down in Saginaw.

If anyone deserved the company of a good woman, it was Stuart.

Why, then, did the sight of him going soft over Lily irritate him?

In a matter of seconds, Stuart had convinced Lily to accompany him into his office building. "I can tell you anything you want to know about any of the taverns in town," he said, ushering her through the door.

She stumbled but caught herself and raised her eyebrows at Stuart. "Why, Mr. Golden —"

"Don't go thinking I know from personal experience." He grinned and covered his chest as though wounded. "I'm an investigative reporter. It's my job to know everything and anything that goes on in this town."

Connell trudged behind them and kicked the door closed none too lightly.

"Besides," Stuart said, leading the way into his first-floor office that also sufficed as his printing room, "I get the inside scoop from Bass, my part-time assistant. He takes care of frequenting the taverns well enough for the both of us."

"Well in that case, how can I refuse your kind offer of help?" She gave him a smile, pointedly ignoring Connell. "Especially when it would seem that there are *some* in this town who are perfectly content to do *nothing* about the terrible problems that exist here."

Connell leaned against the doorframe of the newspaper office and bit back his response. What did Lily Young know anyway? Sure, she was just trying to find her sister. But she was also an overly idealistic young woman who knew nothing about the stark realities of lumber-town life.

He wasn't necessarily turning a blind eye to the problems — was he? He was merely allowing others who were more passionate and capable — like her — to deal with social ills. She obviously felt a strong calling from God to right all the wrongs. If she and others like her were doing the work, then God wouldn't need his meager help too — would He?

Besides, he'd already told her that some evils were there to stay. There was a zero percent chance of eradicating them.

But it wouldn't do any good to get into another spat with her.

Stuart lifted a twelve-inch stack of papers from his desk chair and plopped them onto the mounds of papers already strewn across his desk. Then he dragged the chair out and with a wave of his hand offered it to Lily, as if he were showing a queen her throne.

She sat and tugged off her mittens, not seeming to mind in the least that the room was a cluttered disaster. The job cases and accompanying metal letters were strewn over a three-foot-square table used for setting the type. Ink drums, sheaves of paper, and crumpled wads littered the floor. The Gordon platen jobber Stuart used for printing the weekly paper sat in the middle of the room, and it was a blackened, ink-stained mess, just like the floorboards around it.

Even though the jobber was operated by a foot treadle and fed by hand, it was still a sturdy machine that had served Stuart well not only for the weekly paper but for other printing jobs — pamphlets, posters, cards, and announcements — for local shops and businesses.

Yes. There were plenty of good businesses around town. But that didn't mean Lily was safe.

"You shouldn't be visiting the saloons by yourself," Connell said.

She pulled off her knit cap. "I didn't hear you volunteering to come with me earlier."

"If I'd known you were going to march around to all the saloons, I would have offered to tag along."

Her curly hair tumbled down around her face and framed eyes that widened. "I have a hard time believing you'd tag along with anyone."

"Next time try me."

She hesitated and her eyes flickered as if she wanted to believe him but couldn't. "For your information, I've been searching the dregs all winter, and I've been taking care of myself just fine."

Connell shook his head. "You're just asking for trouble."

"I'm not afraid of trouble."

"I can see that." He liked her spunk and her bravery. "However, while you're here in Harrison, I suggest that you use more discretion and caution."

65

She searched his face, apparently testing the sincerity of his statement. And he hoped she'd see it there. No matter their differences of opinion, she was a nice enough girl. He wouldn't want to see any harm come to her.

"Connell's right." Stuart perched on the edge of his desk. "Harrison isn't called 'Hell's Waiting Room' for no reason."

Lily stared at Stuart as if taking in the seriousness of his words.

"As I said before, I can help you too," Stuart continued, his thin face tight with earnestness. "Anytime you want to search, you just come on by. It'll give me an excuse to do some investigating of my own on the jail fire."

"If you're sure I won't be a bother."

"You won't be a bother at all," Stuart said too eagerly. "In fact, I'd count it a pleasure to go anywhere with you."

Connell almost groaned. His friend had fallen fast and hard for Lily. He didn't blame him. After all, there weren't many eligible women of decent character in these parts. He figured the ratio had to be at least two hundred men for every one upstanding woman, if not higher.

He supposed that's why he couldn't help his own fascination with her. Alone all winter with mostly men for company, he was letting the first pretty woman who came along turn him into a blushing schoolboy.

But the truth was, he wasn't a blushing schoolboy anymore. He'd learned his lesson the hard way two years ago. He'd gotten starry-eyed over a girl, had let her sweep him off his feet, and had floated on the clouds for a while. But eventually, reality had yanked him and he'd come crashing down, smashing the ground with a force that still ached in the deepest marrow of his bones.

He didn't need to make the same mistake twice in his twenty-six years of life.

"I suppose I'd better get back to work." He pushed away from the doorframe. It didn't sound like Lily wanted help. But if she did, Stuart was more than willing to give it.

"Work?" Stuart grinned at him. "Since when do you actually do any work, you lazybones?"

Connell forced a smile. "That's true. I can't work today, not after inhaling all of the deadly sock fumes last night. I'm still recovering."

The reserve fell away from Lily's face, and a smile crept up her lips. "I would have thought breathing in the odor of dirty socks was like smelling roses to a shanty boy like you."

He stopped. Did she think he was just a regular shanty boy? Surely she could tell he wasn't an ordinary man. After all, he was boarding in town instead of living at one of the camps.

Stuart's expression grew playful. "Yeah. Why don't you put on your smelly socks and get out there and cut some trees, you tough old shanty boy?"

For a quarter of a second Connell was tempted to explain who he was. He wouldn't mind watching her eyes widen in awe when she learned that he was the boss man of three of the area's largest lumber camps, the oldest son of Kean McCormick, one of the wealthiest lumber barons in central Michigan.

Instead, he merely tossed her a grin before turning to leave. As much as he'd enjoy impressing Lily Young, he wouldn't do it that way — not by boasting of his importance and wealth.

If he was going to win her favor, he'd do it like a man.

But of course he didn't care about winning her favor.

Not in the least.

CHAPTER 4

Lily had to admit, she liked the way Connell McCormick peeked at her over the rims of his spectacles. From his corner spot of the deserted dining room, behind his stacks of books, he pretended to work. But she could feel his gaze upon her, tickling her, making her insides flutter.

There was something about his intense green eyes and his attempts to hide his obvious fascination with her that warmed her and made her feel womanly in a way she hadn't experienced before.

At the last note of Mr. Heller's lively harmonica tune, Lily clapped, giving the hotel proprietor her biggest smile. "Your music makes me want to get up and dance with you."

The husky man ducked his head. In some ways, he was like a simple-minded child in a grown man's body. He kept mostly to himself in the stable, caring for the animals.

Vera hadn't wanted to talk about the logging accident that had taken her husband's wits from him, and Lily figured it wasn't her place to pry.

The strains of Mr. Heller's tune drifted away, leaving in its place the harsh plunking of the saloon piano across the street, drunken shouts, distant raucous laughter, and even a slamming door or two. There had already been one enormous fistfight in the middle of the street, and Lily had no doubt there would be many more before the end of the night.

All of the drinking and carousing served to remind her that she'd made so little progress over the past three days.

As if sensing the shift in her mood, Vera reached across the table and squeezed her hand. "It's like this every Saturday night. The boys coming into town from all the camps. All their fighting and wild activities would have their poor mamas in tears if they could see them."

Lily took Vera's offer of comfort gratefully and pressed the woman's hand back. It was the same in every other lumber town — the Saturday night revelry that preceded the one day a week the shanty boys had off from their hard labor.

She glanced at Connell, and his attention

70

flicked back to his book. Maybe he didn't want to fight against the evil, but at least he wasn't joining the other shanty boys in their debauchery. He seemed content to spend his evenings hiding behind his books doing whatever it was he did with them.

"You could always dance with Connell," Vera said, following Lily's gaze.

It was Lily's turn to feel embarrassed. "Oh no, I couldn't."

"Why not?" Vera smiled, a knowing gleam in her eyes. "I'm sure Mr. Heller won't mind playing another song. And I *know* Connell wouldn't say no to the chance to put his hands on your waist and twirl you in his arms."

She wiggled, her insides blushing. She highly doubted Connell would want to twirl her.

Connell lowered his head further into his book.

"And don't you dare contradict me, Connell McCormick." Vera wagged her finger at the man.

"What?" He sat up straighter and arched his eyebrows at them, as if it were the first time he'd noticed them in the room all evening.

Lily smiled at the feigned innocence on his face.

"Now, young man," Vera scolded, "you've had your eyes on Lily all week. Don't you deny it."

"I've been doing what I always do — sitting over here minding my own business and doing my work."

Vera shook her head. "You're in trouble now, boy. I was going to give you a couple more cookies, but" — she pushed the plate of treats toward Lily — "now only Lily gets more."

The sugary sweet scent of the freshly baked molasses cookies had bathed the room, driving out the lingering acridness of burnt coffee. Lily had already indulged in several in place of the usual fare of beans and salt pork.

She picked two more from the plate. "You're a dear, dear woman."

Connell snorted.

Vera's lips twitched with a smile she was holding back. "That's enough from you, young man. If you stopped all your nonsense, got up and danced with Lily like a real man, then maybe I'd give you the rest."

Connell sat up taller and eyed the plate that was still heaped with cookies.

Lily wanted to giggle but hid the smile behind her hand.

Then his eyes lifted to hers, the mirth

within them turning the green into the same shade as summer leaves fluttering in a warm breeze.

The warmth captured her and drew her in. For a long moment she basked in their private exchange of amusement over Vera's audacity. But then the green of his eyes darkened and the jollity of his expression faded, replaced with a determination that sent Lily's heart chugging forward like a locomotive.

Without breaking his eye contact, he pushed back from his spot and stood.

Would he really listen to Vera's silly challenge to dance with her?

Her heart picked up speed.

Everything in his expression said he would — that he wanted to dance with her more than anything.

Although she'd been in plenty of situations where she'd had to rebuff the advances of shanty boys, she'd never met one like this man — one she didn't want to rebuff.

Did she actually want his attention?

A tingle of fright pushed her off the bench and to her feet.

He stopped.

"I'd best be heading up to bed," she said, refusing to meet his gaze. Oren had long since gone up to his room. "I'm sure Oren will want to get an early start in the morning to one of the camps. For our first day of picture taking . . ."

Connell didn't say anything, and he didn't move forward to stop her when she said good-night to the Hellers and started toward the stairway.

She could feel the intensity of his gaze lingering upon her as she took each narrow step. She held herself rigid, hoping she wouldn't trip on the hem of her skirt or do something else that might embarrass her further. And when she turned the corner of the stairwell out of his sight, she leaned against the cool wall and took a deep breath.

What was wrong with her? Why was she reacting so strangely to Connell's obvious interest?

Of course he was very good-looking, having an odd combination of earthy and intellectual at the same time.

But she'd seen plenty of handsome and charming men that winter, and none had affected her quite like Connell just had.

The stairs creaked near the top, and she pushed away from the wall, flustered once again at the trail of her thoughts. She'd always kept herself pure, had prided herself over the years for her ability to stay away from boys when so many of the other girls in the orphanages had fallen into temptation.

She kept her head down and ascended with more speed. The clomp of boots coming from the other direction neared her, and she caught the acidic reek of whiskey.

"Well, well, if it isn't the little spitfire herself."

Lily glanced up with a start and found Jimmy Neil standing two steps above her. A slow grin spread across his face, and the black gaps where he was missing parts of his top teeth seemed to stare at her.

He'd leered at her several times that past week during the meals he'd taken in the dining room. But she'd made a point of ignoring him. And that's exactly what she planned to do this time too.

He moved one step closer, and the stench of the alcohol on his breath filled the space between them. He'd likely already been out at the taverns long enough to drink too much but would continue with the drinking as long as he was conscious. So why was he back at the hotel?

"Ran out of money," he said too softly, as if he'd seen the direction of her thoughts. "The night's still young, and I aim to get my fill of women." His eyes glistened with brittle lust.

A man like Jimmy Neil didn't deserve a response, not even the briefest acknowledgment that she'd heard his lurid words. She turned her head and pushed past him in the narrow stairwell.

But before she could get by, his arm shot out and blocked her path.

"Where you goin' so fast?"

"Get out of my way." She shoved his arm, but it didn't budge. She tried to duck under it, but he stuck out his knee.

He leaned into her. The sickly heat and sourness of his breath fanned her neck. "Maybe I don't need to go back out, not when I can have a little spitfire right here, right now."

She stifled a shudder and the shiver of fear that accompanied it. She might have broken free of him last time, but he was drunk now, and there was no telling what he was capable of doing.

Better for her to play it safe.

She spun and tried to retreat the way she'd come, but his other hand slapped against the wall, trapping her into an awkward prison within the confines of his arms.

"You ain't goin' nowhere except up to my room with me." He pushed himself against her in such a carnal way that she couldn't keep from crying out in alarm.

His hand cut off her cry, covering her mouth and smothering any chance she had at calling for help. A rush of fear turned her blood to ice.

For an instant Daisy's sweet face flitted into her mind. Was this the way men treated her sister? How could she possibly withstand such abuse day after day?

As if seeing the fright in Lily's eyes, his gap-toothed smile widened. "It's always more fun when there's some scratchin' and clawin'."

His hand against her mouth and nose was beginning to suffocate her. She swung her head, struggling to break free and jerked up her knee, trying to connect it with his tender spot. But he was pressed too close, and he only strengthened his grip.

She tried to scream and then bite him. But she was quickly losing strength in the dizzying wave that rushed over her.

Suddenly his smile froze and fear flitted across his face.

"Let go of her. Now. Or I'll shove this knife in all the way." Connell's voice was low and menacing.

Slowly Jimmy's grip loosened.

She caught a glimpse of Connell, one step down, his face a mask of calm fury.

Relief swelled with such force it nearly

brought tears to her eyes.

With a renewed burst of energy, she freed her mouth from Jimmy's grip. She sucked in a deep breath and then bit into his hand, digging her teeth into his flesh.

He cursed and released the pressure against her. The slackened hold was just enough for her to break away from him.

She scrambled up the steps, tripping and slipping, her heart racing too fast for her feet to keep up. It wasn't until she reached the top that she finally stopped and glanced over her shoulder.

Connell shoved Jimmy down the steps. "Go on. Get out of here." He held out a hunting knife and pointed it at Jimmy.

Jimmy half fell, half stumbled to the landing.

"And don't come back," Connell called.

Jimmy's eyes flashed with threats of hatred and the promise of retaliation.

"I'll have Vera clean out your room and put your bag outside."

Jimmy struggled to his feet. In a matter of seconds he was gone, and all that remained was the lingering odor of whiskey.

Connell straightened and looked up at her, his face full of concern. "Are you okay?" Somehow his knife had disappeared, almost as if it hadn't existed.

She swallowed the last traces of her fear and nodded.

He put a hand on the rail and took a step toward her.

With trembling fingers she brushed the loose curls from her face. There was a small part of her that wanted him to come to her, to reassure her. But there was another part of her that warned her against trusting him. After all, other than a few brief encounters, she barely knew him.

As if sensing her thoughts, he didn't make a move to draw any nearer. "I'll make sure Jimmy doesn't come back."

"Good."

"Even so, if I were you, I'd make sure I slept with my door locked every night."

"I do." But was a locked door enough to keep her safe?

Connell shifted, started to say something, and then released a gust of breath.

"I'll be fine," she said, praying she really would be.

For a long moment, he didn't respond. Instead, his questioning gaze penetrated her.

Somehow she managed to say good-night and walk to her room without shaking. But once inside, she crawled into bed, pulled the covers over her head, and shook uncontrollably.

She couldn't rid herself of the memory of Jimmy's body pressed against hers. And the thought of how close she'd come to ending up defiled . . . like Daisy.

Oh, Daisy. Her heart cried with all the torment of the past months. What had gone wrong? Why had her sister done the unthinkable?

Where was the little girl that had once snuggled against her in the bed they'd shared at the orphanage?

Lily had always been the one to stop Daisy's trembling — especially in the early days after relatives had given up caring for them and dumped them on the doorstep of the New York Foundling Hospital. She'd kissed away Daisy's frightened tears. She'd made sure Daisy was safe and fed — even when she'd had to go without. She'd given Daisy as much of her heart as she possibly could.

So why hadn't Daisy turned to her? Why had she chosen to sell her body and soul instead?

If Lily slept at all, it was fitfully, and when morning arrived, she had a hard time dragging herself out of the saggy bed to participate in a short worship service that Mr. Sturgis, the grocer, conducted in the dining room for a handful of sober and God-fearing townspeople. As in most of the new lumber communities, churches were scarce. Harrison didn't have a single one or a reverend.

By the time she and Oren arrived at the first lumber camp and set up the photography equipment later that morning, the usual low gray clouds had dissipated and glorious sunshine brightened the sky.

She turned her face to the warm rays and let the light caress her sun-starved skin. "Oh, beautiful sunshine," she said with a smile.

"Not half as beautiful as you," said one of the shanty boys standing in line waiting for Oren to take his picture.

She wanted to throw out her hands and twirl in delight at the rare day of delicious sunshine, but she was already the main attraction for the shanty boys, and they didn't need any more encouragement to stare at her.

Many of the men were still snoring in their bunks — probably sleeping off drunken stupors. But there were plenty who were taking advantage of the break from their regular lumber duties. One woodsman-turned-barber was giving haircuts near the bunkhouse door. Another man was sitting on a stump cutting patches for his pants from a grain sack. Still others were using the free day to launder their clothes.

Some of the camps had the rule that all crew members had to wash their underwear at least once every fortnight. Even in the dead of winter, boil-up day was a regular Sunday occupation — usually inside the cramped bunkhouse.

But today, with the touch of warmth, the men had dragged the scrub boards, wooden tubs, and yellow lye soap out into the trampled yard. Heaps of dirty clothing lay in piles on the slushy ground.

Steam rose from the hot water, which was already gray — almost black — from the flannel and homespun clothes the men were rubbing against the corrugated tin washboards.

Lily knew her clothes were overdue for a good washing. And Oren's were too. But the hard task was one she'd never relished, especially in the cold of winter, when the clothes took twice as long to dry and ended up stiff and difficult to put back on.

"Stop all your wiggling and foolish grinning," Oren called to the man who was posing with a cant hook that was nearly as tall as he was, counting the long steel hook at its end. "What do you think this is? A tryout for the circus?"

The man puffed out his chest and attempted to make his expression more serious and manly. Lily couldn't understand why smiling was discouraged. Sure, it was difficult to hold the smile for the length of time it took the photographer to capture the pose onto the dry plate. But still . . . if she ever had the chance to have her picture taken, she'd smile as big as she could. If she had to leave an imprint of herself for all time, she wanted it to reflect the happiness of her life, not the heartache.

Oren lumbered to the front of his Centennial perched on a tripod mount. The box camera was made of fine mahogany but had all the scratches and gouges that traveling brought. Oren wiped the glass of the brass lens with a soft cloth. Then he adjusted the faded red leather bellows that were creased and cracked with wear.

At a dollar a picture, he wasn't making a fortune taking pictures of the shanty boys. But it was good steady work all winter and supplemented the earnings from his photography gallery in Bay City, which he'd left in the capable hands of his partner.

"How much for a picture with the girl?" one of the men called, nodding at Lily.

Another man whistled and others

chortled.

Oren stiffened. He tipped up his derby, and his eyebrows narrowed into a scowl. "I've got two rules here today, boys."

Lily stifled a smile. She'd heard Oren's lecture plenty of times. She could only imagine what he'd say if he found out about Jimmy Neil's attack of the night before. He'd never let her go anywhere by herself again.

Oren pulled his corncob pipe out of his mouth and pointed the stem at the men.

"One — you keep your filthy hands off Lily, and I'll keep my hands off your puny chicken necks."

Except for the rhythmic ring of hammer on anvil coming from the crudely built log cabin that served as a shop for the camp blacksmith, silence descended over the clearing.

"Two," Oren continued, "you keep your shifty eyes off Lily, and I'll keep from blowing a hole through your pea-brain heads."

With that, he toed the rifle, which he always laid on the ground in front of the tripod. She saw no need to tell them Oren had never shot anyone, at least not yet.

Even if the men didn't stop looking at her, at least Oren's rules kept them from pestering her. In fact, she might even take a chance at going to the cook's shack to see if he would have a decent cup of coffee that she could have. After surviving on Vera's bitter brew the past few days, Lily was more than ready for a real cup.

She glanced around the camp at the scattering of log buildings. In addition to the bunkhouse and blacksmith shop, there was a log barn that housed the teams of oxen. The cook's shack connected to another large log building that was likely the dining hall. A smaller hut sat off to one side, and Lily guessed it was the van, the office and home of the camp foreman and his scaler.

The door of the van swung open, and her heart did a flip of surprise when Connell McCormick stepped out, deep in conversation with an older lumberman whom she guessed to be the foreman.

For a moment she stared at Connell, at the gold strands of his hair that the bright sunshine highlighted, the fresh cleanness of his mackinaw in comparison to the foreman's, and his purposeful stride.

The lines of his forehead wrinkled with seriousness as he talked with the foreman. There was a refined, educated look to Connell's face. And yet the strong lines of his jaw and nose defined him as a man worth reckoning.

Would he be surprised to see her? She swatted at the fresh mud splats on her skirt, hoping they weren't too noticeable. What would he say to her?

She waited for him to lift his head, for his green eyes to find her as they had in the dining room of the hotel. Her heart pattered faster with the thought of how he'd defended her honor against Jimmy Neil, how he'd watched after her and protected her.

But without casting even the slightest glance in her direction, Connell and the foreman headed toward the narrow-gauge tracks that ran through the middle of the camp. No longer were the lumber camps solely dependent on the snow and ice for transporting logs. The railroads meant they could carry on their lumbering operations year-round.

She could only shake her head at the piles of cut logs lining the track, waiting to be loaded and shipped to the main railway track in Harrison, the Pere Marquette line. She'd learned that from there, they were moved to the river-banking ground in Averill to await the spring thaw. Then the logs would be floated down the rivers until they reached the sawmills of Saginaw and Bay City.

The longer she'd traveled around central Michigan, the more saddened she'd grown to see the widespread destruction of miles and miles of forests and the devastation left in the wake of the lumber companies when they moved on.

Even though God had placed a burden on her heart to rescue lives, she'd begun to think that maybe the land needed some rescuing too.

As she continued her task of writing down names and collecting money from the men awaiting their pictures, she tried to focus on the task of asking about Daisy and whether any of them had seen or heard of her. But she couldn't keep from peeking at Connell and watching him at work.

The foreman followed Connell around, his hands stuffed into the tight pockets of his trousers, the weathered lines in his face growing more worried.

"Looks like the boss man is figgering out how he can get more work out of us," one of the shanty boys grumbled under his breath.

Boss man? Lily followed the man's narrowed eyes back to Connell.

Under the rising temperature of day, Connell had discarded his mackinaw and rolled up the sleeves of his shirt, revealing thick arms. With the help of another man, he lifted a log onto the back of a half-filled flat car, and his well-defined biceps bulged under the strain.

Her stomach fluttered with strange warmth. He was obviously a strong man and a hard worker. But was he the boss of the camp?

"I ain't gonna work on Sunday," another man muttered. "The boss man can if he wants. But I need my Sundays to catch an extra forty winks."

Surely Connell wasn't the one in charge of all the destruction and mayhem at this camp. The ruination of this beautiful forest.

But even as her heart fought to deny the accusation, her head told her it was true. It made perfect sense that he was the boss. He was too educated, too polite, too polished, and entirely too clean to be an ordinary shanty boy.

She didn't know why she hadn't realized it sooner.

A lump of disappointment lodged in her chest. She didn't know why the revelation saddened her, but it did.

At a tiny meow and a bump against her shin, Lily forced her attention away from Connell to a skinny kitten rubbing against her leg.

"Well now. What do we have here?" She bent and scratched the cat's head between its ears.

A tabby painted with the same streaks as a faint evening sunset peered up at her with hungry eyes.

"Oh, he's just the camp mouser." The shanty boy closest to her gave the cat a shove with the spikes of his boot, sending the tiny creature scurrying across the slushy clearing toward the edge of the forest and the fence of tall pines that hadn't yet suffered the sharp teeth of the crosscut saw.

"That was cruel." Lily scowled at the man and then started after the kitten. "Come here, kitty."

She patted her coat pocket and felt the bump from the two molasses cookies Vera had given her the night before. She'd wrapped them in a handkerchief, intending to have them for breakfast. But she wouldn't mind sharing some with the cat. The scrawny fellow looked like it needed the sustenance more than she did.

Following the cat's paw prints, she tramped toward the forest edge. Her boots sloshed in the mixture of melting snow and mud. "Here, kitty-kitty," she called as she ducked past a low pine sapling and over the rotting remains of a windfall.

She caught a glimpse of muted orange in the spiky tamaracks that grew among a confusion of vines and broken tree limbs. She darted after the cat, lifting her skirt to make the chase easier. Following the flashes of color, she headed deeper into the grove until she lost sight of the kitten altogether.

Sucking in a deep breath of the pine-laced air, she stopped. She'd be a fool to keep going and chance getting lost. Besides, even though Oren was used to her escapades — especially when it came to small helpless animals — she'd worry him if she were gone too long. He had always warned her not to stray too far.

Although she wasn't much of a worrier herself, she couldn't keep from glancing around with a shiver of fear. Only the wide trunks of the tall pine trees surrounded her.

The shadows swayed, and her body tightened with the thought that Jimmy Neil might spring out from behind one of the enormous trunks and pounce on her.

It was a silly thought, she knew. She hadn't seen him among the shanty boys back at the camp. He was likely nowhere near. But for a long moment, she stood absolutely still and listened.

The thud of her heart echoed through her head.

Finally, convinced she was alone, she glanced up the trunk of the tree closest to her. The rippled brown trunk towered high into the air. The tree was an endless pole rising into the sky to the top, where a canopy of green boughs formed a roof that blocked out the sunshine, except for shifting flecks that left quick kisses on her flushed face.

Even though she'd been in plenty of Michigan forests over the winter, the magnificence never failed to amaze her. Every time she stood in an undisturbed grove of white pine and gazed at the enormity of their beauty, she imagined she was in a cathedral — a natural God-made cathedral.

A breeze caught the boughs, and they began to awaken and murmur among themselves. In a few seconds they grew louder, humming like a choir beginning their warm-up.

She smiled and took a deep breath. The trees were glorious. She couldn't imagine why anyone would want to destroy this natural wonder.

At the snap of a twig behind her, her smile froze and fear shimmied up her backbone.

Her mind clamored for her to scream, to run, to get away from whatever — or whoever — was attempting to sneak up on her.

But before she could turn or make her getaway, a hand slid around her face and covered her mouth, cutting off the scream that clawed its way up her throat.

CHAPTER 5

Lily fought like a lynx caught in a steel trap. She scratched and bit and kicked with a force that took Connell by surprise. Her teeth sank into the sensitive flesh of his palm and forced him to let go.

"Calm down, Lily. It's just me, Connell."

The beginning of her scream died away, and she spun on him, her eyes flashing with fury. "Why did you sneak up on me like that?"

"I didn't mean to." He brought his smarting hand to his mouth and sucked at the blood she'd drawn. "When you didn't hear me approach, I thought I might startle you. And I didn't want you to scream — a sure way to get every shanty boy in the camp to come running."

The tempest in her eyes turned into a low gale.

He glanced at the teeth marks she'd left

in his hand. "You sure know how to greet a fellow."

"And you sure know how to scare a girl half to death."

"Why exactly were you so scared?"

"Because I thought you were someone else."

"And what if I had been *someone else?*"

She paused, her pretty lips stalled around the shape of her next word.

"Any number of the rough men from this camp could have followed you out here." He'd seen the way the men were looking at her, how they hadn't been able to take their eyes off her from the moment she'd arrived. "What would you have done then?"

When she'd run off into the woods after the stupid cat, he'd had to yell at several of the men to stop them from chasing after her.

"I would have screamed." She pulled herself up to her full height, which he estimated to be five feet six inches. "Since apparently I'd get lots of attention that way."

"I'm serious," he started. But then at the glimpse of the twinkle in her eyes, his ready lecture stalled.

He stuck his aching hand into his pocket and pressed his wound against the scratchy wool.

"I appreciate your concern," she offered with the hint of a smile. "But I'm a much stronger woman than you realize."

She'd be no match for any of his strong shanty boys.

"You were reckless to wander off by yourself." He tried to soften his accusation, but he wanted her to realize the constant danger she was in simply by being an attractive woman in a place populated by lusty men. "I strongly suggest you refrain from doing so again — especially if you hope to avoid any further run-ins."

He could see from the shadows that flashed across her face she was remembering the encounter with Jimmy Neil.

What would have happened to her if he hadn't seen Jimmy come back into the hotel? What if he hadn't gotten up to make sure she made it up to her room without trouble?

He hadn't been able to shake the gut-twisting fear at how close she'd come to being dragged off by Jimmy Neil and assaulted. He'd never trusted the scoundrel. Especially because the man was on James Carr's payroll.

Although Jimmy wouldn't be lurking in the hallways of the Northern Hotel anymore, Connell couldn't loosen the knot in his gut — the one that warned him Lily was going to get into big trouble sooner or later.

When she'd ridden into his camp that morning, bringing the sunshine with her, he'd told himself even if she wasn't any of his business, he could do nothing less than make sure she was safe.

So he'd spent the better part of the morning keeping her in his line of vision, all the while trying to work.

"Besides," she said, shaking her head as if to toss off any gloomy thoughts, "I always take a few minutes by myself to admire the majesty of some of God's finest creations."

She turned her attention back to the white pine next to her, and as her gaze traveled up the length of the trunk, her eyes widened with awe.

He had to admit, *she* was one of God's finest creations. After watching her all morning — and all week, for that matter — he couldn't keep from admiring the quickness of her smile, the sparkle in her eyes, and the pertness of her steps.

His focus lingered on the loose curls dangling against her ear. With her head tilted back, the long expanse of her neck taunted him. The rich shade of her complexion and the smoothness of her skin reminded him he'd gone too long without the affection of a woman.

But wasn't that what he'd wanted? To get away from women — and the pain and heartache they brought? At least that was one of the reasons he'd agreed to take the supervisor position for the Harrison camps when his father had suggested it. He'd needed to get away from Rosemarie and his brother and their treachery.

He shook his head at his own weakness, and before Lily could catch him staring, he shifted his attention to the tree. His trained eye quickly measured the hundred-fifty-foot length, approximately three-and-a-half feet in diameter. No hint of ring rot. No insect damage. No punk knots. It was one of the smaller pines, but still a perfect specimen.

"It's a beauty," he admitted.

"It's a natural temple," she whispered reverently.

He watched the way the slight breeze swayed the top and knew it would fall to the south if his boys were to chop it. He eyed the path of its descent. First they'd have to cut down a number of saplings that were in the way, and then make sure they left nothing else that could inhibit its thundering tumble to the ground. He'd witnessed too many accidents when a falling tree glanced off another object and threw it off course onto an unsuspecting man. The towering giants weren't called *widow-makers* for no reason.

"I'm guessing this one is about a hundred years old," he said.

"Then it's ancient."

He nodded. "If I'm lucky, I'll get twenty thousand feet of board out of it. Twelve feet long by an inch thick. Good solid board."

She took a step away from him, her face a mask of shock.

"What's the matter?"

"How could you even think about destroying this glorious, magnificent, beautiful tree?"

For a long moment he could only stare at her, baffled. "It's my job. What did you think we're doing out here? Digging for gold?"

"Oh, I know perfectly well what you're doing. You'll take all you can get from this land, and then you'll leave behind a chaotic mess."

"We parcel off the land and sell it to farmers."

"You know that's not happening."

"Maybe not everywhere."

She planted her fists on her hips. "I've traveled around enough of Michigan this winter to see what the land looks like after lumber companies pull out and head some-where else."

"Oh, come on, Lily." Exasperation tugged at him. "What would our country do with-out the supply of lumber we're providing? If we stop our operations, we'll deprive the average family of affordable means for building homes."

She arched her brow. "Affordable?"

"Compared to brick homes? Yes." She obviously didn't know anything about the industry. "As a matter of fact, hundreds of thousands of people in growing midwestern towns rely upon our boards and shingles for their homes. And on the other products that come from these trees." He patted the pine.

"I don't care." She reached for the tree, caressing it almost as if it were a living be-ing, trailing her fingers in the deep grooves of the bark. "These trees, this land — they don't deserve to be ravaged."

He sighed at her irrational thought pro-cess. He was tempted to keep arguing with her. Logically, if McCormick Lumber ever pulled out of the lumber business, there were a hundred other lumber barons who would continue to cut the trees until every last one was harvested.

The lumber companies were in Michigan to stay. And there was nothing he or anyone else could do about it, even if they wanted to — which he didn't.

But he bit back his response.

"Listen." The last thing he wanted to do was stand out in the forest and argue with her. Besides, he needed to get her back to the camp before his men started spreading rumors about them. "How about if we go get some coffee? Old Duff, the dough pounder here, makes the best coffee."

Her eyes lit up.

"I'm well aware it can in no way compare to the coffee our dear Vera makes."

Lily's lips curved into a ready smile. "Yes, I really don't know how anyone else can make anything quite like it."

He grinned. "I thought you'd agree."

She tromped behind him as he led the way back to the camp clearing. She stopped him once to admire several cardinals perched in a leafless shrub, pointing out how their flaming red contrasted with the dull gray branches among a backdrop of snow.

Another time she halted him so that she could watch a gray squirrel forage through a pile of dead leaves. She tossed it half a cookie and then laughed when it grabbed the piece in both front feet and began nibbling it. The tinkle of her laughter was like the warmth of a fire after a long cold day in

100

the woods.

They crossed the cleared yard, still littered with stumps, and passed Duff's pen of pet porkers next to the cookshack. Connell ignored the raised brows and hidden grins of the shanty boys but couldn't prevent strands of embarrassed heat from weaving up his neck. No doubt he'd be the talk of the bunkhouse later — he *and* Lily.

"Duff," he called as he ducked into the shack.

Through the haze of the smoke rising from the fry pans, Connell nodded at the old cook already hard at work on the noon meal. With one hand wielding a long iron fork, Duff moved thick slices of sizzling salt pork around the fry pans. With his other hand he used a cake turner to flip the chopped potatoes he was browning. He nodded back at Connell without missing a move.

"Don't let me bother you. I'll just help myself to the coffee." Connell sidled past a tub of lard, sacks of cornmeal, and crates of potatoes. He dodged the iron skillets and assortment of cooking utensils that dangled from hooks in the center ceiling beam. And he sidestepped the pork barrel, with its salt-encrusted meat hook hanging from the side. He attempted to avoid the puddle of slimy brine pooled around the base but stepped in it anyway.

He wanted to tell Duff to get his cookee to take better care at cleaning up and keeping the shack organized. But he clamped his mouth shut. He couldn't afford to irritate Duff. Good camp cooks were in high demand. He'd had several over the past couple of years who had nearly caused mutiny among his men with their unappetizing meals.

And with the way things were going lately with the statistics, he couldn't afford for his men to get upset about anything, including the camp fare.

A dozen dried-apple pies were cooling on the long worktable, and a half a bushel of cookies sat next to them. Spicy cinnamon lingered in air that was now thick with the scent of grease and pork.

"Last I looked, the thermometer read thirty-seven degrees," Duff said as Connell neared the cast-iron stove with two big kettles on the back burners.

"Thirty-eight now." Fresh discouragement slithered through Connell. He grabbed a couple of tin cups and a dish towel.

"Day or two more like this and the roads will turn to mud soup," Duff added.

Holding the hot handle with the towel,

Connell lifted the coffeepot and poured two cups. He didn't need a reminder of the changing weather. He'd seen the sunshine and felt the growing warmth all morning. An early thaw was the last thing he needed now, when he was working hard to figure out a way to increase production.

Even with all the advances the narrow-gauge railroad had brought to their lumbering efforts, he still needed the frozen roads for the teams to drag the felled logs out of the forest to the railcars. It would be too early to pull out the big wheels they used for the summer lumber season. The ten-foot wheeled skidders would only get stuck in the mud.

"Well, let's just hope the temps drop back down tonight and stay that way." Connell glanced out the grimy window of the cookhouse. Melting snow dripped from the roof like spring rain. "And let's pray the sun shrivels up and dies."

"Oh, how can you say such a thing," Lily cried behind him.

He spun, surprised she'd followed him through the cookshack instead of waiting by the door.

Her eyes widened with dismay.

At the sight of Lily, Duff's ambidextrous flipping came to a halt. He stared at her as if she were the first woman who had ever stepped foot in his kitchen.

But she had fixed her big eyes on Connell. "With as little sun as we've had this winter, how can you possibly wish it away?"

"Because we depend upon the ice and snow for production."

"You would begrudge us all the bright and beautiful sunshine so you can earn a bigger profit?"

Was he destined to clash with this woman on every issue — even something as insignificant as the sunshine? He sighed and handed her the hot cup of coffee.

She took it and wrapped both hands around it. "Not all of us are used to the dreary dark winter days of the north. New York winters weren't a picnic either, but they were never quite as cold and dark."

He took a swig of his coffee, savoring the dark roasted flavor.

She blew on hers and took a tiny sip. "Ahh. Now, that's good coffee." She gave Duff a grateful smile. "Thank you."

He beamed at her. But the blackened smoke rising from the skillets drew his attention back to the burning food, and he began flipping faster than before.

"If you dislike Michigan winters so much," Connell said, "why did you move here? Why didn't you stay in New York?" At least there she'd be away from wild lumber camps and towns.

The sunshine in her face disappeared. She took a longer drink of coffee before looking at him.

The heartache in her expression socked him in the stomach.

"I wish we could have stayed. Then maybe Daisy wouldn't have gotten herself into this predicament." Her voice was soft.

"If you find her, do you think you'll move back?"

"There's nothing left for us there. No one who wants us. No one who ever did."

She spoke so low, he wasn't sure he'd heard her correctly. And he couldn't help wondering what had happened to the rest of her family and how she had ended up with the cranky old photographer.

"*When* I find Daisy — not *if,*" she said, her voice growing louder and ringing with the passion he'd heard before. "When I find her, I'll never let her go. And I'll give her the kind of home she deserves — finally."

He took a slurp of coffee, not quite sure how to answer her. If he did the math, he could come up with the slim percentage she had of finding her sister, especially alive. But he didn't think she'd be too happy with the statistic.

"I'm old enough now that I'll be able to get a job and find a place for the two of us," she said, looking him directly in the eyes, as if somehow she could convince him. "I'll take care of her. We'll make it this time."

He prayed she was right. But he had the gut feeling she was in for far more challenges than she expected.

But who was he to contradict her and discourage her plans? He hardly knew her. In a few short weeks, she'd move on with Oren to another town and Connell would likely never see her again.

And yet, down in the dark depths of her eyes, there was a spark that drew him in, a flicker of loneliness and longing, and it tugged on him, pulling him deeper. . . . And he was afraid now that he'd already stepped into her life, he might not be able to pull himself back out.

CHAPTER 6

Five taverns down, fifteen to go.

Lily bunched up her skirt and squelched through the thick oozing mud that covered Main Street. The past several days of melting snow had turned the ground into a slimy marsh. But she didn't mind having to walk through it, as long as the sun continued to shine.

"Do you have time to visit one more this morning?" she asked Stuart, who stomped along next to her, not seeming to mind that his boots and trousers were caked with mud.

"I'm sure I have plenty of time." The newspaper editor didn't bother pulling out his pocket watch and instead grinned at her. "And if I don't, I'll make it."

She tried to form her lips into a smile. But she couldn't quite get them as generous as she wanted. Over the past several days he'd gone out of his way to help her visit taverns and was being awfully nice to her —

almost too nice. She didn't want to encourage him into thinking there was anything more between them than a plain and simple friendship.

"Besides," he said, "I'll take any opportunity to get out of the office and enjoy the sunshine and the warm spell we're having."

"Well, at least there are two of us enjoying it." She slid a glance at Connell McCormick, who was standing outside the butcher shop at the end of the street. He was leaning against a post and talking with the butcher, likely working out a delivery of meat to his camps. "There are *some* people around here who think sunshine is the tool of the devil."

Stuart followed her gaze.

It hadn't taken her long to learn that Connell was boss man of not just one camp in the area, but three. He'd proven himself to be a courteous and kind man. But she was disappointed to think that such a decent man would willingly participate in the mass destruction of the timberland. And not only participate, but orchestrate the mindless ruination.

Stuart grinned at Connell and waved.

She flipped her attention away, but not before Connell caught her staring.

"Connell McCormick sees everything in one of two ways," Stuart explained. "He either looks through the lens of dollar signs or the lens of mathematical symbols."

"Too bad he can't wipe off the greed and see things from a better perspective."

"You mean *your* perspective?" Stuart's voice was tinged with laughter.

"I'm only doing what any godly person would — taking a stand against the evil and fighting for what's right."

"Speaking of evil." Stuart touched her elbow, motioning for her to stop. "Here comes Maggie Carr."

A woman wrapped in a thin lacy shawl was making her way through the muck and heading in the direction of the train depot. The screech of steel brakes and a sharp whistle indicated the Pere Marquette was arriving right on schedule.

"She's the wife of James Carr, the biggest piece of scum that's taken up residence in Harrison."

The woman wore a scarf around her neck and had wrapped it so that it covered her mouth and nose.

"Carr keeps a pack of vicious bloodhounds up at the Stockade." Stuart inclined his head toward the edge of town. There on a rocky hill stood a wide two-story tavern surrounded by a tall log fence, the ends shaved to frightening points.

Lily stifled a shudder. She'd heard some of the shanty boys talking about the Stockade and boasting that James Carr had the best drinks and girls in all of Michigan. They'd also joked that a night didn't go by in which an unlucky shanty boy was tossed down the hill beaten and bruised — or worse. They'd called it Dead Man's Hill and had laughed about it, but she'd decided the Stockade would be the last tavern on her list to visit.

Stuart leaned closer and lowered his voice. "Rumor has it one of Carr's dogs bit off the tip of Maggie's nose."

Lily studied the scarf that concealed Maggie's face, and this time Lily couldn't hold back her shudder. The woman had reached the train and stood on the platform in front of the passenger car.

"She's in charge of Carr's girls," Stuart added.

Lily straightened, and her mind began to spin. This might be her chance to ask about Daisy without having to trudge up Dead Man's Hill and visit the Stockade.

"I'm gonna talk to her." Without waiting for Stuart, she hefted her skirts higher and sloshed through the mud. The sticky mixture tugged at her boots, trying to pull them off.

The passengers had begun to descend, the usual handful of shanty boys and businessmen. When a young woman stepped out of the passenger car and onto the platform, Lily stopped short.

Stuart bumped into her, his focus riveted on the newcomer too. "What in the name of all that's good and holy?"

The woman — who upon closer examination, looked more like a girl of fifteen or sixteen — glanced around the depot with wide frightened eyes. She wore a simple faded skirt and a tight coat that looked like it should belong to a girl much younger.

Maggie Carr wasted no time in approaching the girl, speaking to her.

The young woman braved a small smile.

"What's the devil's wife up to now?" Stuart growled, and his eyes narrowed on Maggie.

"Why?" Unease trickled through Lily. "You don't think she's recruiting the girl for her brothel, do you?"

"It's hard to believe a young, sweet-looking girl like that would come up here to work at the Stockade."

The trickle of unease swelled into a tide. *Was* it hard to believe? After all, Daisy had willingly done the same thing.

Lily could picture Daisy stepping off the train wherever she'd gone, her cheeks flushed, her hair mussed, her expression uncertain. She must have wondered if she was doing the right thing. She'd surely known Lily wouldn't approve.

Daisy had probably been just as frightened. Maybe when she'd stood on the train platform, she'd even wished someone would step in and force her to stop before she made a terrible mistake.

"I won't stand by and let that young girl throw her life away." Lily started forward with a surge of determination fueled by all the pain that flamed inside her.

"What are you going to do?" Stuart kept pace with her.

"I don't know."

He grinned. "Sounds like my kind of plan."

"You should know my motto is to act first, think later."

"I think I'm beginning to catch on to that."

Lily practically ran the rest of the distance down Main Street, not caring that she was splattering mud all over her skirt. By the time she reached the train platform, Maggie had taken the young girl's flimsy carpetbag and had linked arms with her, as if they were already old friends.

"There you are!" Lily cried breathlessly.

The girl took a quick step back. Her eyes were innocent and frightened, like those of a young girl who'd never traveled outside of her hometown.

Lily smiled at her. "I've come to help you." She sent up a prayer. She needed quick wits and as much heaven-sent help as possible.

"I don't know who you are or what you're talking about," Maggie said in a low muffled voice behind the gauzy red scarf. "But Frankie's here to work for me."

"Well now, Frankie," Lily said in her gentlest tone, "I know you don't really want to get started into the degrading life of prostitution. No one does. And I can help you."

"Prostitution?" The girl's face flamed red. "Oh no, ma'am. I'm here for decent work. Hotel work."

Maggie's eyes above the line of the scarf turned cold with calm fury. She yanked on Frankie's arm. "Come along, sugar."

"Not so fast." Lily grabbed on to Frankie's other arm.

"I ain't a loose girl," Frankie rushed to explain. "I'm answering the ad Mr. James

113

Carr placed in the Deerfield newspaper requesting help in his newly built hotel here in Harrison."

"Ad in the paper?" Stuart's voice rang with surprise. "What kind of ad?"

The girl reached into her pocket and pulled out a ripped section of a newspaper. Maggie lunged for it, but Stuart grabbed it first.

He scanned it, his thin face narrowing into a scowl. "Chambermaids and waitresses needed for the Carr Hotel in Harrison. Room and board provided along with excellent pay."

"Carr Hotel?" Lily said to Maggie, her voice laced with contempt. "You and your husband ought to be ashamed of yourselves."

Muttering oaths under his breath, Stuart folded the ad and tucked it into his pocket.

Lily patted the girl's arm. "Don't you dare go with Maggie Carr here. She'll lead you straight up that hill there yonder and put you to work bedding shanty boys."

Frankie followed Lily's gaze to the Stockade. It stood above the town like an ugly wart on a pockmarked face. The girl took one glance at the place and recoiled.

Maggie tightened her grip on Frankie. "Let's go, sugar. Don't pay any attention to these people. I've got a nice room for you, plenty of hot food, and a steady income. That's what you want, isn't it?"

Lily tugged on Frankie. "Don't listen to her. You don't want to end up dancing in your skimpies every night for shanty boys."

Horror widened the girl's eyes and filled every corner of her face. "Oh no, ma'am. Not at all."

"You'd best come with me, and I'll make sure you're kept safe."

The girl wiggled against Maggie's grip, trying to break free. Her thin coat stretched at the seams.

But Maggie didn't let go. "You're not going anywhere until you work off the price of your train ticket."

The determination in Maggie's narrowed eyes said she wouldn't relinquish her hold of the girl without a fight.

For an instant Lily despaired. How could she protect this young girl short of getting into a tugging match and pulling her into two pieces? The truth was, she was every bit as determined as Maggie to have the girl come with her.

"Now, hold on, Maggie," Stuart said. "If Carr is using false advertising to get young girls up here to Harrison, promising them work in a hotel when all along he's planning to enslave them in one of his brothels, then she shouldn't be held responsible for the price of her ticket, because she didn't know any better."

Lily shot him a grateful glance.

At her appreciation, he pulled his skinny body higher. "Now, you let the girl go or I might just have a new front-page story for the paper this week."

Above the scarlet scarf Maggie's eyes flitted with uncertainty.

The hesitation was the chance Lily needed. She jerked hard and pulled Frankie loose. The young girl fell against her with a pitiful cry.

Lily wrapped an arm around Frankie's waist and pulled her into the crook of her body. She didn't wait to see if Stuart could get Frankie's bag.

Instead, she propelled the girl off the platform and onto the muddy street, hustling her away from Maggie Carr as fast as she could.

It was only when she chanced a glance over her shoulder that she caught a glimpse of the sharp steel in Maggie's eyes — the glint said she'd find a way to stab Lily and inflict pain in one way or another. That it was only a matter of time.

Lily pulled Frankie closer. She didn't care.

With every life she saved from the pit of hell, maybe eventually she'd make up for losing the one life that had mattered the most.

CHAPTER 7

"I told you James Carr was the devil himself in human flesh." Vera thumped a bowl of beans onto the dining-room table next to a loaf of steaming bread.

Connell didn't have the appetite to fill his tin plate for the noon meal he took at the hotel whenever he wasn't at one of his camps. Not even the yeasty aroma was enough to tempt him. Instead, he glanced at the young girl sitting at the opposite table next to Lily, and his stomach gurgled with a sickening hollowness.

The girl crammed a slice of bread into her mouth as though it would disappear if she didn't get it in fast enough. Judging by the thinness of her cheeks and boniness of her fingers, it had obviously been a while since she'd had a decent meal.

"Do you think I ought to run the story anyway?" Stuart sat across from him and heaped four large spoonfuls of beans onto the mounds of pork and bread he'd already piled onto his plate.

"Of course you should," Lily responded, scraping a trail with the tip of her spoon through the scant serving of beans on her plate. "This community needs to hear the truth about what's going on."

Vera shook her head, the movement jostling her heat-flushed cheeks. "James Carr is completely despicable. Tricking young innocent girls by putting ads in the newspaper for his so-called hotel."

"What I want to know is how long he's been advertising." Stuart shoveled two bites of his meal into his mouth and seemed to swallow them without chewing. "I'm sure Frankie can't be the first girl Carr has deceived into working at his brothels."

"It doesn't really matter how long he's been doing it." Lily handed Frankie her piece of bread, and the girl took it eagerly. "All that matters is that we've discovered his deception. And now we need to find a way to make sure it stops."

Lily's eyes sparked like prisms, a brilliance of hot and cold. Her graceful features were sharp with all the earnestness of her heart spilled out, nothing held back, the emotions raw and clear.

For once he couldn't disagree with her.

Carr had gone too far. It was one thing for a girl to choose the harlot's life. But it was an entirely different matter to be forced into it.

"It's a shame," said Stuart between mouthfuls. "The girls who answer Carr's ad are the upstanding ones, the ones looking for decent jobs. If they'd wanted to join a bawdy house, they didn't need to come north to do it."

Connell knew full well Stuart wouldn't be able to run a story about Carr in the *Harrison Herald.* And he had the feeling his friend knew it too. Stuart couldn't print anything detrimental about Carr, not without putting his life in peril.

The door of the hotel opened and slammed against the wall.

Lily and Frankie jumped.

"Speak of the devil," Vera muttered.

Carr stepped through the doorway, his shiny black boots clicking an ominous rhythm against the plank floor. He swept off his hat and combed his fingers through his immaculately trimmed hair. Dressed as impeccably as always in a town coat, a matching vest, and a bow tie at his throat, he could have passed for a lumber baron.

But there was something about the hard set of his jaw that spoke of a life fraught with danger. The set of brass rings he wore above his knuckles shouted of the violence for which he was known.

The room grew silent, and Frankie shrank against Lily.

Carr's deep-set eyes went directly to the young ladies like a hound catching scent of its prey. With his forefinger and thumb he twisted the long curl at the end of his well-groomed mustache, and something just as twisted gleamed in his eyes.

Connell's hand slid to his hunting knife, sheathed under his shirt in the leather scabbard he wore strapped from his shoulder, across his chest, to his waist. He'd never had much time for James Carr, had always figured as long as the man didn't bother him, he wouldn't concern himself with what Carr did or didn't do.

But something deep inside told him Carr had overstepped the parameter this time — in a big way.

"What can I do for you, Mr. Carr?" Vera rested her fists on her wide hips, glaring at the man as if she'd like to cut him up and serve him for supper. Mr. Heller had come in from the stable and stood behind his wife.

"It seems to me there was a misunderstanding down at the train station." Carr's voice was much too soft for a man of his

121

six-foot height.

Stuart hunched over, stared at his plate, and stuffed spoonful after spoonful of beans into his mouth.

Carr pinned his stare upon Frankie. "And I've come to collect my newest employee."

Lily slipped off her bench and stood at her tallest. "Look, mister." She glared at Carr. "I don't know what kind of evil has possession of you. But you won't be taking Frankie out of here except over my dead body."

Stuart choked.

Connell fought back a grin. The situation was too dangerous for him to find even the slightest humor in it. But still he couldn't keep himself from wanting to smile — especially at the fact that Lily had been the first to stand up to Carr.

He should have realized she'd have no problem confronting the man and saying her piece.

Carr sized up Lily like he was calculating how much money he could make off her young flesh, and his gaze lingered on her face almost as if he recognized her.

Any humor Connell may have found in the situation evaporated like steam rising from a pot on a sub-zero day. Cold anger propelled him off his bench.

Carr's boots tapped increasingly louder as he crossed the room toward Lily. "Seems to me you're getting yourself involved in something that isn't any of your business."

"I've made it my business." Lily didn't flinch. "And I aim to keep doing the best I can to rescue helpless victims from tyrants like you."

Connell slipped his hand underneath his shirt and unsheathed his knife. If Carr tried to touch Lily — if he threatened her in the least — he'd give the man a scar to boast about.

Vera pulled her wooden spoon from her apron pocket, apparently unwilling to allow Carr to threaten Lily either. "Mr. Carr, if your mama knew what you were up to here in Harrison, she'd drown in her tears."

"Well, then it's a good thing she's already dead, isn't it?"

"Now, you go on and get yourself out of here and don't come back." Vera waggled the spoon in front of Carr's face. Mr. Heller backed away, his eyes wide and childlike.

"I'll be on my way just as soon as I get what's mine." He crooked one of his fingers at Frankie, giving her a wide view of the brass knuckles running the width of his hand.

She shriveled like a little girl being bullied

on a school playground.

Lily slipped an arm around the girl's waist. "Frankie's not yours. She never was, and she never will be."

"I paid for her train fare here." Carr's voice was frighteningly calm. "She's mine until she works it off."

"I'll pay for her fare."

Frankie glanced at Lily with surprise.

Carr's lips moved up into a smirk. But there was something dark, almost deadly in his expression that told Connell loud and clear the man wasn't playing a game.

"How much does she owe you?" Lily asked.

"Like I said, it's none of your business." Carr reached for the girl.

Lily jerked Frankie back. "And like *I* said, I'm paying her bill."

"And just how are you planning to do that?" Carr eyed Lily again in a way that made Connell's insides harden into ice.

"Don't worry. It might take me some time to get the money. But I will."

"I suppose you could come up to the Stockade in place of Frankie and work off her debt."

Vera gasped and Frankie followed suit.

Connell shook his head, disgust rolling through his gut. "That's enough, Carr."

Carr glanced at him, as if seeing him for the first time. His gaze flickered to Connell's side, to the knife partially hidden in his palm.

"Connell McCormick," Carr said softly, moving his hand to his waist and pushing aside his town coat, revealing the dark curved grip of his Colt. "I didn't take you for the kind of man who sticks his nose into problems that aren't his."

"I don't." Connell wasn't worried about Carr's pistol. With the fifteen feet between them, Connell calculated he could throw his knife into Carr's arm at least two seconds before the man could get the gun out of his holster.

"Then butt out of this, McCormick." Carr turned his attention back to Lily.

Connell fingered the dull edge of his knife. He couldn't afford to make an enemy of Carr, not when Carr could easily stir up trouble against him and his lumber camps. And with the warm weather causing a setback in production over the past few days, he didn't need any more trouble than he already had.

Carr took another step toward Lily. "I think I'd rather have you over Frankie anyway. With your looks, you'd earn me a fortune." He perused Lily's graceful cheeks too long. And when he raised his hand to finger her smooth skin, Connell's entire body revolted.

"You touch her and you'll find my knife in your hand." Out of instinct and years of practice, he'd lifted his knife and cocked it into throwing position. His muscles twitched, and he took aim, finding the center spot of Carr's hand, the place where his knife could penetrate the deepest.

Every eye in the room swung to the bright point of the blade.

"And don't worry," Connell said without taking his sight off the half-inch circle he'd mentally drawn on Carr's hand. "I never miss my target." At least he hadn't missed in the many years since Dad had forced him to perfect his aim.

Slowly Carr lowered his hand. "I told you to stay out of this, McCormick. This isn't your problem."

"Guess it became my problem — and the problem of everyone else in this town — when you decided you'd start making slaves of innocent young girls."

"You know as well as I do that my business is a necessity. The shanty boys wouldn't stick around if we didn't meet their needs."

Connell didn't want to admit Carr was right. He wanted to think that if there

126

weren't any taverns or illicit houses, the boys would still come north to work in the camps. But experience and statistics had shown that the camps were able to retain a larger work force when the boys were kept happy.

"I say let the boys go and good riddance," Lily muttered.

That was easy for her to say. But McCormick Lumber couldn't lose workers and expect to keep up with the other lumber companies in the area. "Listen, Carr. All we ask is that you stop bringing girls up to Harrison with the false advertising."

"That's not all I'm asking," Lily said quickly.

Carr glanced from Connell's raised knife to Frankie and then back, as if weighing whether he had enough time to grab her as a human shield and make his way out.

"And," Connell rushed, "I'll pay Frankie's train fee today. You send one of your men down to my office, and I'll give him cash."

"Well now." Lily turned wide eyes upon him. First surprise, then admiration flickered to life. "That's a very kind thing for you to do."

He nodded. "It's the least I can do for her."

Vera lowered her wooden spoon. "And

Frankie can help out around the hotel here until a more permanent arrangement can be made for her."

Lily smiled, and the brightness of it lit up the room. She gave Frankie an excited squeeze. Then she threw her arms around Vera and hugged her. "You're a dear."

For an instant, Connell reveled in the fact he'd not only made Lily happy, but that he'd stood up to Carr and won. Surely now everything would work out the way it should.

But then his gaze collided with Carr's. The edge in the man's eyes was sharp enough to chop through the hardest of wood.

It sliced into Connell's confidence, and the air swooshed out of him.

"I suppose if you're going to meddle in my business, McCormick, that gives me the right to meddle in yours." He didn't wait for Connell's reply. Instead, he crossed the room, shoved open the door, and stalked out, letting the door slam behind him.

The bang reverberated through Connell, and he stared out the window as Carr stepped into the street.

Maybe Connell hadn't won after all. He had the sick feeling he'd just made a huge mistake. But he refused to let himself calculate the percentage of men who had made an enemy of James Carr and lived to tell about it.

CHAPTER 8

Lily squelched the disappointment that had plagued her all day.

The feeling was unreasonable, she chided herself.

She tucked the tripod under one arm and hooked the bag of dry plates on her other. A glance over the sleigh told her she'd gotten everything.

With a sigh, she started across the yard in back of the hotel. The stable and outhouse sat a distance away from the main building, and several long clotheslines spanned the expanse. A lone pair of wool socks flapped in the growing darkness of the late afternoon.

The fresh breeze whipped at her hair with a sting that made her shiver and reminded her that even though the temperatures had been unseasonably warm that week, it was still winter.

She hated to admit how much she'd been

hoping she and Oren would end up at one of Connell's lumber camps for their second Sunday of picture taking.

Throughout the day, her gaze had inadvertently strayed, and she'd searched for him even though she'd tried not to. When at last they'd packed up their equipment, she'd given up hope he'd make an appearance as he had the first week.

It was silly to expect him to be at every lumber camp. But nevertheless, she'd surprised herself with how much she'd wanted him to be there today.

She hoisted the equipment bag higher on her arm. The warm light from the pantry door at the back of the kitchen beckoned her.

Of course, she'd only wanted to see him to tell him she was glad he'd done the right thing by confronting James Carr and helping bail Frankie out of trouble. That was it. After all, it was past time for him to start taking a stand against the evil that plagued the town.

She stepped onto the wooden plank that led into the pantry and pushed open the door with her hip.

The tangy scent of overripe apples wafted over her, along with the stinging bite of onions that had gone to seed. A glance down the cellar steps revealed the dim light from Oren's oil lantern against the dampness of the small underground cavern that he'd converted into his darkroom.

"There you are," Vera called from the kitchen. "Hurry up now and come get some dinner before it gets cold."

Lily deposited the camera equipment at the top of the stairs and then made her way past the crates that lined the floor, dodging a mound of dirty bed linens awaiting washday. She reached the doorway of the kitchen and stretched onto her tiptoes to peer beyond Vera's bulky form through the opposite door into the dining room.

"Any snow yet?" Vera asked. "My left foot hurts. That always means snow."

"Oh, of course there's no snow." Lily's gaze swept the eating area. "Your foot must be lying to you. It's been another gorgeous day."

She was only looking for Frankie, she told herself. She most certainly wasn't trying to see if Connell was already at his corner spot busy with his ledgers. But when she caught sight of his blond head and the unruly strand that fell across his forehead, her heart dipped with expectancy.

If she sat in her usual place, she'd leave him no choice but to sneak peeks at her while he attempted in vain to continue working. A ready smile touched her lips. She enjoyed watching him pretend he was laboring over his books when she knew very well he wasn't.

Vera stepped away from the smoking stove and raised an eyebrow at her.

Lily pulled back. "So how'd Frankie do today?"

Vera's other eyebrow quirked. "I thought Frankie was with you."

"Of course not." Lily eyed the dining room again and the assortment of men seated around the tables, but she didn't catch sight of Frankie. An odd, feathery worry tickled her insides. "I told you we were leaving Frankie here. It would cause too much trouble to take her into the camp with us."

Vera pushed a pan of half-browned potatoes to the back of the stove, away from the heat. The lines in her face tightened. "I haven't seen her all day. So I thought you changed your mind and took her with you."

Lily's heart clattered to a stop. Had Frankie stayed in their room all day? Maybe she'd been too scared to come out by herself.

But even as Lily clomped through the kitchen and dining room and made her way up to the room she had gladly shared with the young girl, the tickle of worry turned into a twist of dread. Over the past two days, Frankie had proven herself to be a hard worker, jumping in and helping Vera with any chores that needed doing.

In fact, Lily had been secretly hoping the Hellers would decide to keep Frankie there, give her employment, and make her into the child they'd never had. If they didn't, she knew Molly May down in Midland would take her. But she'd wanted her rescue efforts to benefit both the Hellers and Frankie.

Lily did a quick search of her room. Frankie's carpetbag was there and her personal items still neatly arranged among the disarray of Lily's belongings.

After scouring the hotel from top to bottom, the yard, stable, and every possible corner and closet, Lily finally returned to the kitchen.

"I can't find her anywhere." Panic had begun to stiffen each muscle in her body. "And nobody has seen her all day."

Vera paused above a tub of murky water, a tin plate in one hand and a greasy rag in the other. "I've got a bad feeling about this."

"Bad feeling about what?" Connell strode into the kitchen, his dirty dishes stacked into a perfect pyramid. He looked from Vera to her. And the concern that radiated from his eyes calmed the wild pattering of her heart.

"Frankie disappeared." Maybe Connell would be able to help her find the girl.

His brow furrowed. "Did anyone see James Carr around here today?"

Lily recoiled at the mention of the man's name. "You don't think Carr came back to get her? Not after you paid him?"

"I wouldn't put it past the man."

Vera shook the water off the plate in her hand and added it to the stack that had already received a dunking in the dishpan. "I didn't see Mr. Carr, but I had to give Jimmy Neil a good scolding this morning for showing up in the dining room half drunk."

Lily held in a shudder at the thought that Jimmy had dared to step foot inside the Northern Hotel. What reason could he have had for coming back?

Connell crossed the kitchen and dumped his dishes into the washtub. They sank past pork chunks, soggy bread crusts, and a scattering of half-smashed beans.

"I hate to say it," Connell said, "but I'm betting Carr came back and took what he thought was his."

When he lifted his eyes to hers, the regret she saw did nothing to reassure her. He wasn't planning to give in to Carr, was he? Not now. Not after they'd already stood their ground. "If you think Carr has her, then we best be on our way up to the Stockade to get her back."

Connell folded his arms across his chest and leaned against the tall worktable covered with piles of slimy apple peels. "We can't just march up there and get her back, Lily. It doesn't work that way."

"If Carr kidnapped her and is forcing her to prostitute herself against her wishes, then you better believe we can demand he let her go free. We'll get help from the sheriff —"

"Not in this town, you won't." Vera wiped her chafed hands on a soggy gray towel. "Mr. Carr has the sheriff tucked away in the itty-bitty pocket of his fancy coat."

"Vera's right," Connell said. "We won't get any help from the law. In fact, there's probably not much anyone could do to make Carr release Frankie."

"Well, we've got to at least try. Right?"

Vera's shoulders slumped. And Connell didn't say anything.

"You're not scared to go up there, are you?" Lily asked, frustration creeping in and tingeing her voice.

"Of course I'm not scared," Connell retorted. "But I can't chance hurting Mc-Cormick Lumber any more than I already have."

Disappointment wrapped around her like a heavy cloak. Apparently, if anyone was going to do something, she'd have to be the one to do it.

"I guess I'm left with only one option." She spun out of the kitchen into the pantry. "I'll have to be the one to go and get her." She stomped toward the back door and banged it open.

As she rushed outside, a gust of wind slapped her cheeks.

"Where are you going?" Connell caught the door before it slammed shut, and he followed her outside.

A hill of dark clouds had pushed in with the growing darkness. She pulled her coat tighter and started toward the front of the hotel, trying to ignore the long shadows of the evening that reached out to haunt her. "I'm heading to the Stockade to see if Frankie's there."

"You can't go up there by yourself," he called after her.

"I'm certain God would want me to do whatever I can to rescue the girl, even if it means going by myself." She picked up her pace, and her boots sloshed through the muddy snow that remained after the past week.

She made it only a half a dozen more steps before Connell's hand gripped her upper arm and dragged her to a stop. "I won't let you go." He spun her around so that she had no choice but to face him.

"How dare you? What right do you have to stop me?" She jerked her arm and tried to break away.

But his hold didn't budge. "I probably don't have any right to stop you."

She tugged again, this time harder. "Then leave me alone."

He wavered, almost as if he would let her go, but then with a growl he yanked her against his body. The strength of his grip held her captive. But the hard width of his chest against hers and the nearness of his face — only inches away — held her in greater captivity.

For a long moment she couldn't breathe, couldn't move, couldn't think. The crashing thud of her heartbeat and the soft rasp of his breath filled the space between them. His gaze lingered upon her cheek, her chin, her other cheek before moving to her lips.

Spring butterflies awakened in her stomach, and she couldn't keep from studying his mouth, so close, so warm, so firm. But the boldness of such an inspection sent embarrassed heat through her, making her want to duck her head.

"Lily," he whispered. His eyes turned into a forest at midnight. "I just don't want anything to happen to you. I can't let you go up to the Stockade. It's too dangerous."

The dreadfulness of what had likely happened to poor Frankie crashed over her again. "*Too dangerous?* Then all the more reason I need to go rescue her." The girl was probably shaking in absolute terror and praying to God for a deliverer — if it wasn't already too late.

Connell shook his head in protest.

"Imagine if Carr had kidnapped me instead," she said quickly. "I'm just as innocent as Frankie. What if he held me captive and forced me to do the unimaginable?"

Connell's breath was warm against her skin. His grip around her upper arms grew tighter.

"I made a vow to God long ago," she whispered, "that I would never turn away from anyone or anything that needed rescuing."

His dark gaze probed her, and the seriousness of his expression told her that he wasn't taking her words lightly, that he was trying to understand her position.

Could he see into her heart to her needs? Her passion? Her own losses?

She quivered. She'd never been in such close proximity to a man before. His body was solid and his arms strong. She could almost hear the pounding of his heartbeat against her own.

Her breath stuck in her chest. She knew she ought to back away and put a proper distance between them. But there was something exciting about being in his arms.

For an instant a light flickered in his eyes that said he was thinking the same thing. But just as quickly as the spark ignited, he wrenched her back and set her an arm's length away. Then he folded his arms across his chest and tucked his hands under his armpits, almost as if he were pinning them there in an attempt to keep from reaching after her.

A gust of cold wind struck her, and she hugged her arms against her body. A strange mixture of disappointment and relief swirled through her.

"I'll go up there," he said.

"You will?"

He nodded. "I'll see if I can find out what happened to her."

Hope sprang to life, along with something

else — something she couldn't define — something that made her want to throw herself back against him and feel the solidness of his chest and arms again.

"But only if you promise you'll stay here." He leveled his gaze at her. "Promise you won't go anywhere near the Stockade. Not now. Or ever."

"I promise I'll go back inside the hotel and wait for you."

He studied her face for a long moment.

She couldn't promise him she'd never go near the Stockade. Because the truth was, she'd go inside the pit of hell itself in order to find Daisy.

"All right, then." He glanced toward the Stockade. Through the growing darkness the sharp points of the fence were like fangs waiting to capture anyone who came near.

"I'll be praying for you," she said.

"Good. I'll need it."

CHAPTER 9

Lily paced back and forth across the dining room until Oren barked at her.

"Sit down, girl, before you wear out my last nerve."

She dropped to the nearest bench, perched on the edge, and drummed her fingers against the table. "He's been gone for too long. What if Carr did something to him?"

Oren pushed his empty plate aside and reached inside his vest pocket for his pipe. He muttered under his breath, his overgrown mustache muting most of what he said.

"Don't you worry about Connell." Vera swiped at the table covering, brushing crumbs onto the floor. The stale scent of her overused dishrag lingered on every surface. "He's strong. He'll take care of himself."

"I'm hoping he comes back with a broken arm." Oren packed a pinch of tobacco into the bowl of the pipe with his thumb. "Then I won't have to be the one to break it when he finally gets up enough nerve to touch Lily."

"Oren!" Lily scolded through a smile. Good thing Oren didn't know Connell already *had* touched her — even if it had only been brief.

"I see the way that man's been looking at you," Oren mumbled, adding another layer of tobacco. "Even a blind man could see that he can't keep his eyes off you."

Her inexperienced heart flushed with pleasure at Oren's words.

"Connell McCormick's a good boy." Vera wiped her arm across her forehead, brushing her frazzled hair into greater disarray. "I haven't met too many boys as good as Connell."

Lily had to agree. She'd never known a man like Connell — someone so thoughtful and considerate.

"All I have to say is he's lucky I haven't poked out his eyeballs yet for all the liberty he's takin' looking at Lily."

"He's attracted to her," Vera retorted, never afraid to give Oren the guff he deserved. "You can't blame the boy. Lily's probably the prettiest girl he's ever laid eyes on."

"Well, 'course she is." Oren packed a last layer into his pipe.

Mr. Heller shyly nodded from his spot near the fireplace, where he was whittling on his usual stick.

Lily ducked her head at the words of praise. She wasn't used to compliments. There hadn't been much of anything but harsh words where she'd come from.

And was Vera right? Was Connell really attracted to her?

A small flame, like the one in the oil lamp hanging above the table, flickered in her stomach. Why would a man like Connell be interested in a girl like her?

But even as she tried to silently deny the validity of Vera's declaration, she couldn't keep her heart from warming at the thought of their encounter outside.

The door swung open and Lily jumped to her feet.

Connell stepped out of the blackness of the evening, and a blast of cold wind burst in with him.

She scanned him from his hat to his boots. The tension in her muscles evaporated. He was safe — not a scratch in sight.

He shoved the door behind him, fighting against another gust of wind. When it was finally closed, he swiped off his hat and blew out a long breath.

That's when Lily realized he was alone.

Disappointment tumbled through her. "Where's Frankie?"

His brow crinkled. And the sadness in his face only made her pulse patter faster.

"What happened?" She crossed to him, rubbing her arms to ward off the sudden chill.

His fingers fumbled with the edge of his hat. "She's not there."

"Really? Are you sure?"

"I'm positive."

A whisper of hope wafted through her. "Then maybe she decided to leave Harrison. Maybe she took the train back to her home. Maybe she just didn't know how to say good-bye."

Connell didn't say anything. Instead, his chin dipped and he stared at the brim of his hat, where his fingers twisted at the hard felt.

A cold shiver chased away the tiny voice of hope and left in its place a blaring warning. Something had gone wrong. Terribly wrong.

She took a step back, not sure she wanted to hear.

It was then Connell lifted his gaze and met hers straight on. "I'm sorry, Lily."

Everything within her screamed to run to her room, bury her head in her pillow, and avoid the bad news. She'd had enough disappointments in her life, and she didn't want any more.

Vera stacked the remaining plates into a wobbly pile. "So tell us what happened to the girl. Did Mr. Carr sneak in here and steal her right from under our noses?"

"I'm not sure how Carr managed to get ahold of her." Connell's voice was low. "But he did."

"And?" Vera prompted.

"And he took her up to Merryville to the Devil's Ranch."

Vera whistled under her breath.

Lily could guess what the Devil's Ranch was. She had no doubt it was another whorehouse. But Merryville? Maybe there was still a chance to go after Frankie and rescue her. "Where's Merryville?"

"It's about six miles northeast of here," Connell said. "Won't be long before the Pere Marquette line runs all the way from Harrison to Merryville. And when it does, Carr will be ready for the boom the railroad will bring the town."

"Six miles isn't far." Lily's mind began to whirl. She and Oren often had to drive several miles to reach a camp for their picture taking. Surely they could drive six. Especially to rescue Frankie.

"Six miles is six too many for this time of year." Connell shrugged out of his coat.

"Not when an innocent life is at stake."

"I'm sorry to say that even if we went, we'd probably come away empty-handed."

"We won't know unless we try." Determination took root inside her. For a minute all she could think about was Daisy. By now her sister had surely realized her dreadful mistake. She was probably crying out and begging to leave her prison. But she was trapped, like most of the girls. And she would remain that way until Lily was able to find and rescue her. Frankie would be trapped too. Unless she helped her.

Connell hung his coat on a peg in the wall near the door.

"We have to do something," Lily said. "Now. Tonight."

Slowly Connell turned to face her. His face was solemn. "Even if I thought it would help save her, we couldn't go tonight."

"Why not? If we leave right now —"

"It's too dangerous at night."

She narrowed her eyes at him. "I think you just don't want to go."

He sighed. "It's a complicated issue, Lily. We're in Clare County. Carr knew that if he

147

took her up to the Devil's Ranch, which is right over the border into Gladwin County, we wouldn't be able to press charges against him — if we even tried to."

"So you're giving up? Just like that?"

He tossed up his hands. "What do you want me to do? March up there, force my way in, and take the girl back at gunpoint?"

"Yes."

"Now, now, children," Vera said. "Stop your squabbling."

Oren had lit his pipe, and the familiar sweet tanginess of the tobacco rose into the air with each cloud he exhaled. The fire crackled with a cozy warmth that didn't reach her.

"I'm sure we can figure out some way to help Frankie," Vera added. "But we won't be able to do anything more tonight."

Lily wanted to shout that it might be too late if they waited until tomorrow. She knew the desperation Frankie was feeling at that very moment as she waited for someone to save her. Lily had felt it once too. She'd waited day after day at the orphanage for someone to rescue her and Daisy, for anyone to take them away from the loveless sterile building.

But no one had ever come.

She couldn't let that happen to Frankie.

Especially when she was in a brothel.

"So you won't take me tonight?" She gave Connell her most pleading look.

"I already told you. It's too risky —"

"It's worth the risk." Frustration made her voice sharper than she intended.

"Sakes alive, girl!" Oren finally sat forward. He glared at her, but deep in his eyes was a gentle pride. "Get on up to your bed, and before the crack of dawn I'll drive you on up there and you can do one of your foolish rescues."

Lily smiled and her heart filled with gratefulness. She couldn't forget to thank the Lord for blessing her with a friend like Oren. Maybe he wouldn't take her right away like she wanted, but at least he was willing to help her.

"I don't think it's a good idea for the two of you to go up to the Devil's Ranch alone," Connell said.

"We'll be fine. The two of us make a good team." She crossed the room toward Oren.

"The place is at least ten times more dangerous than the Stockade," Connell added.

"Lily's done this rescue business a couple of times already," Oren retorted. "And she's fiercer than a mother wolf defending her pups."

149

She planted a kiss on Oren's derby hat.

He waved her away with his pipe. "Now, don't you go thinking I won't expect you to make up for the lost day of work — especially since I reckon we'll need to take the girl on down to Molly May's to keep her safe once and for all."

She turned away, and her smile faded.

Was Connell right? Was rescuing Frankie too risky of a venture?

Oren was a good man. She'd learned that in spite of all his grumbling, he would give his life to help others too. He'd put himself in danger for her already that winter.

But now — this time — if Connell *was* right, maybe the danger was too great. Maybe it was finally time to go alone, to do what needed to be done on her own. Over the months Oren had come to mean the world to her, and she couldn't bear to think of anything happening to him because of her.

There was no need to jeopardize both of their lives. Was there?

Besides, how could she wait . . . when every minute could make a difference in saving Frankie's innocence?

A rap on the door startled Connell awake. He jumped up from the corner chair and glanced toward his bed, still perfectly made.

He hadn't planned on dozing. He'd only wanted to rest and be ready whenever he heard Oren and Lily start out. Everything inside him protested the thought of them attempting such a foolish rescue mission on their own. He knew he could do nothing less than follow at a safe distance to make sure they were safe.

Another knock sounded at the door, this one louder.

He strode across the room, and instinctively his hand slid to the knife sheathed at his rib cage. He cracked the door and peered into the hollow blackness of the hallway.

Instantly the cold tip of a rifle rammed into his temple. "Where's Lily, you worthless piece of pond scum?" Oren growled at him.

"I haven't seen her." Connell shoved the rifle away and refrained from pulling out his knife. He wouldn't. Not on Oren. "I thought she was going with you."

Oren lowered his gun and muttered several oaths under his mustache.

"Isn't she in her room?" Connell had been listening for the squeak of the floorboards, for the click of her door down the hall from his room. How had he missed the sounds?

Oren muttered again.

Cold fear jabbed into him like the sharp end of a pike pole. "She didn't start off to Merryville on her own, did she?"

"That's what I'm afraid of." Oren's voice wavered, all bluster suddenly gone.

Connell's fear exploded into near panic. Without stopping to think, he grabbed the blankets from his bed and rolled them into a tight bundle. "What time do you think she left?" he asked, stuffing the bundle into one of his bags and then cramming in a pair of socks, his ax, and anything else he could find in his hurry.

"I'm guessing she had no intention of letting me drive her," Oren said. "She's too impatient."

"So she got a sizable head start?"

Oren didn't say anything. But his silence spoke volumes.

Connell shouldered the bag. Then without waiting to see if Oren followed, he headed down to the kitchen. Through the darkness, he rummaged through the food stores, stuffing as much as he could into the sack.

"Lily's gone." He heard Oren explain to Vera, who'd appeared in her nightgown. She wasted no time lighting a lantern and helping fill Connell's bag.

"There's already an inch of fresh snow on

the ground," she said, bringing him his coat. "And with the way my foot's been paining me all night, I'm guessing we're in for a lot more."

They all knew the urgency of the situation. Travel would have been dangerous enough for a woman alone in the wilds of the Michigan wilderness on a *calm* winter evening. Of course there was the cold and the possibility of getting lost in the darkness. But with a snowstorm brewing, the danger had quadrupled.

And then there were the wolves. In the dead of winter, they were more than a little hungry. Every winter a shanty boy or two disappeared. Sometimes in the spring after the thaw, they'd find a few scattered bones, all that remained after the pack's meal.

"You can take my sleigh," Oren said, his shoulders stooped at least three inches more than usual.

Connell pulled on his thick leather gloves. "I'll be able to go faster on my horse."

"Then take my rifle." Oren shoved the Winchester at him, along with a leather bullet pouch. The man had aged twenty years in twenty minutes.

Connell tucked the gun under his arm, slung his pack across his back, and with lantern in hand, stepped into the snow. It was already blowing sideways and pelted him in the face. The sharpness of the wind took his breath away.

He met Oren's gaze one last time. The thick furrowed brows drooped low. "I'll find her," Connell reassured him, praying he was right, that it wasn't too late.

Within minutes, Mr. Heller had helped him saddle his horse, and he headed toward the Pere Marquette railroad line. He figured Lily was smart enough to follow the tracks as far as they would lead her. But the snow was blowing hard, and if she'd left any footprints, they were long gone.

He quickly calculated that if Lily had left the hotel shortly after midnight, when all the lights had finally been extinguished, she'd likely gotten a two-hour head start. If she'd walked swiftly, he'd have to do some hard riding before he'd get within distance of her.

His gut pinched with growing anxiety. Since the snowstorm had just started, he hoped he'd make it to her before she suffered from frostbite, hypothermia, or worse.

He pushed his mare as fast as he could against the gusts of wind and heavy snow, but they made slow progress. Within thirty minutes, his fingers were so stiff with cold that he could hardly maintain his grip on the lantern. After another thirty minutes, he couldn't see through the swirling snow more than a foot in front of the horse.

"God," he whispered through chattering teeth, "I don't ever ask you for much." Come to think of it, he hadn't really asked God for anything since that night two years prior when he'd caught Rosemarie in Tierney's arms.

His pulse pounded with a fresh spurt of anger at the memory of his brother fondling Rosemarie — especially considering Tierney wasn't married to the girl. In fact, Rosemarie had been engaged to another man. Namely him.

Connell fought to erase the picture of Rosemarie that day and the passion displayed across her delicate features — a passion that she'd never shown toward him. Of course, he'd always regarded her with virtue, as Mam had taught him.

Apparently Tierney had forgotten that lesson.

"God," Connell tried again, "I haven't asked you for much. So if you could help me out now, I'd be grateful."

He held the lantern higher and strained to see through the curtain of blowing snow to the blackness beyond. He called Lily's name, but the wind carried it away into the abyss of darkness.

What if she'd wandered away from the tracks? With the growing snow and drifting, the tracks were well covered. In the denseness of the falling snow, it would only take one misstep to lose the ties, to get off course, and to get hopelessly lost.

His arm grew tired from holding the lantern and his voice hoarse with the effort of calling. Even though it was useless, he kept at it for the slim chance the wind would carry his voice to her.

After what seemed hours, but was only another thirty minutes, he slid off his mare. Frustration gnawed at his stomach like a bitter acid. The snow reached midcalf, and he estimated that an additional three inches covered the ground from when he'd left Harrison.

Although he'd been anxious for more snow after the past week, he couldn't find any joy in it now. Instead, he'd never wanted to curse it as much as he did at that moment.

"Lily!" he called again. He plodded forward, leading his horse with one hand and holding the flickering lantern with the other. His body was stiff from the cold and he couldn't bear to think how frozen Lily was — if she was even still alive.

The northern wind that had swept down from Canada had made it increasingly hard to breathe, and he finally pulled a scarf over his mouth and nose.

When the tip of his boot thumped against something, his heart crashed hard against his chest.

He bent down and dug through the drifting snow.

"Oh, thank you, God." His hands made contact with a body curled into a tight ball. He brushed the snow away and found his gloved fingers tangled in Lily's beautiful hair.

He dragged her limp body into his arms. Her face was pale, her lips blue, her eyes closed — almost as if she were already dead.

With an anguished groan he tore off one of his gloves. His red, raw fingers fumbled at her neck for any sign of a pulse. Too impatient and his fingers too cold to work, he brought them to her lips and waited for an agonizing moment.

Oh, God, let there be a breath, even a small one.

"Wake up, Lily." He shook her, suddenly desperate. "Wake up."

Her eyelids fluttered, a soft breath touched his fingers, and then her eyes opened.

An ache of weary gratefulness rose up his

throat and stung his eyes. "You're alive."

"Connell," she whispered, her eyes drinking in the sight of him in a way that sent warmth first to his belly and then to his arms and legs.

Her long thick lashes fell to her pallid cheeks, and her breathing faded. From the limpness of her body, the color of her skin, and the shallowness of her breathing, he knew he didn't have time to take her all the way back to Harrison.

He had to find a way to warm her body back up. Immediately. Her life depended on it.

A fresh spurt of panic ripped through him.

He tore through his pack for the blankets. With shaking hands he managed to bundle her within them. Even as he situated her in front of him on the horse, he knew his feeble efforts weren't enough. He turned the mare back toward Harrison, his mind scrambling to calculate exactly where he was and which lumber camp was closest.

Did he dare leave the railroad track and attempt to find a camp? What if he got lost?

The denseness of the blowing snow had the makings of a blizzard. Even if he stumbled across a narrow gauge and followed it to one of the camps, his gut told him Lily wouldn't make it that long.

But maybe there was someone or something else closer. A deserted Indian lodge?
An old trapper cabin?

For a long moment, his thoughts traveled
back over every inch of the Pere Marquette,
adding each mile, searching for anything.
"The Sweeny hut," he finally said with a
jolt of renewed energy.

If his estimates were correct, he'd come
exactly 4.3 miles. The old Sweeny hut would
only be another eight hundred feet up the
railroad and then fifty feet to the east of the
tracks.

He struggled to turn forward and urged
his horse. He clung to Lily with one arm
and his lantern with the other, hoping the
oil would hold out until he found the hut.
And he desperately prayed his computations
were correct. If he was off by just a few feet,
they would end up lost in the forest.

By the time he guided his horse off the
railway, his arms and back ached from holding Lily, and his thighs burned with the effort of gripping his beast. But he forced
himself to keep going, measuring each step
with precision, knowing their lives depended
upon it.

Finally, when he'd gone fifty feet he
stopped and slid down from the mare. He
held the lantern high but couldn't see

anything that even remotely looked like a hut.

A sliver of fear sliced through him. Had he made a wrong calculation somewhere?

Lily's limp body had grown heavier. She didn't move. And he couldn't tell if she was still breathing.

He was running out of time.

With a growl of frustration, he crunched forward through the heavy snow, working his way around a ten-foot radius until finally the flickering lantern light revealed a snow-covered hovel.

It was nothing more than a rudimentary shack, eight feet by eight feet wide, part dugout and part logs, not more than four feet high. The early land cruiser Bill Sweeny had constructed it when he'd first come to Clare County ten years earlier to scout for the best pine, pace off sections of land, and establish boundaries.

A quick inspection revealed a sagging roof and a door hanging half off the frame. It was in bad shape, but it was still something.

As Connell ducked inside and deposited Lily onto the cold earthen floor, he hoped he wasn't too late to save her life.

CHAPTER 10

Blessed warmth surrounded Lily.

She lay on the brink of heaven, knowing the warmth must surely come from the reflection of the sun, the golden streets, and perhaps even from the very presence of God himself.

Angel wings enveloped her.

She sighed with contentment.

Why had she been so afraid to die? Especially when paradise was so perfect?

She nuzzled her nose into the angel, catching the faint scent of pine and woodsmoke.

The strong wings developed hands that pressed against her, one spanning the place between her shoulder blades and the other splayed across the small of her back.

When the angel gave a soft moan, her heart lurched and her eyes shot open.

She found herself gazing at a wide expanse of a man's chest.

Her entire body froze with fear. And the

horror of her nightmare returned. Her numb feet that would no longer work to keep her walking. Her icy fingers that she couldn't keep warm no matter how many times she'd blown on them. The snow that stuck to her eyelashes, blinding her.

When she'd finally fallen to the ground in the absolute darkness of the snowstorm, she'd known she couldn't get up, that she was going to freeze to death, and that she would be buried in a coffin of snow.

And all she'd been able to think about was how foolish she'd been, that she should have paid more attention to the change in the weather and turned around when it started to snow. That now no one would rescue Frankie. No one would care about Daisy. If she died, the two girls would be trapped forever.

Lily shuddered.

The thick arms surrounding her pulled her tighter.

She couldn't make sense of where she was or what was happening. But then she lifted her eyes.

Connell's face was only inches away. His eyes were closed. Weariness creased his forehead. And his breath rose and fell with the steady rhythm of exhausted slumber.

He'd come after her. For the first time in

her life, someone had cared enough to rescue her.

A surge of gratefulness rose up swiftly and brought an ache to her throat.

She had the urge to lift her fingers to his cheek and brush the tips along the day-old scruff that had grown over his normally clean-shaven skin.

At the crackling of the fire behind her, she became aware of the heat against her back and the fact that she was warm — something she'd thought would never happen again. From what she could tell, she was lying on the floor, bundled under several blankets with Connell, and wrapped in his arms.

Her gaze dropped again to the view directly before her eyes, and her mind registered what it hadn't before: Connell was not fully clad. He'd stripped off his shirt and trousers and wore only a wool union suit.

Her body sparked with the acute reality that she was partially unclothed too, that Connell had taken off her dress and left her in only her camisole and drawers.

She knew why. Her coat and dress had been damp from the snow. And of course, being the considerate man he was, he'd shed it to save her. And he'd discarded his garments to give her his body heat, to warm her frozen body back to life.

But she sucked in a hiss anyway, knowing she was in a completely improper, indecent situation, and that she should move away from him as fast as she could. She was plenty warm now, and there was no reason to continue to lie next to him.

She began to wiggle away, but then stopped. He was likely exhausted. If she moved, she would wake him. For an agonizing moment, she held herself rigid, the uncertainty and embarrassment of the situation paralyzing her.

Through the dim light, she found herself gazing at the contours of his chest visible through the tight single-piece undergarment.

She closed her eyes, trying to keep from staring at him but found herself leaning in and breathing in his warm pine scent. The solidness of his body and the security of being so close to him sent a tiny shiver of pleasure through her.

She drew in another deep breath and then stopped.

What was she doing? Had the cold frozen her brain so that she couldn't think straight?

He gave a soft sigh and she pulled back, mortification dashing through her.

She held herself motionless for a long moment before daring to peek at him. His eyes were still closed, and his breathing even with the heaviness of his slumber.

A whisper deep in her soul told her she should move away while she had the chance, before she did something she would regret later. After all, she'd prided herself on her purity. She hadn't ever paired off with boys like so many of the girls at the orphanages had.

And now, she couldn't let the emotion of the moment control her.

Even as her soul warned her, she allowed herself one more look at the span of his chest. Her heart swelled with the longing to inhale one last breath of him before she moved away.

She bent her face toward him. At that moment he shifted and her nose bumped against the tautness of his chest. "Oh" came her nearly soundless gasp.

His hands against her back tightened.

Had she awoken him?

One of his hands slid up into the thick strands of her hair and dug through the curls. Gently he tugged her head back so she was forced to look into his eyes.

The green was dark, and when his gaze fell upon her lips, his pupils widened, making his eyes even darker.

Was he thinking of kissing her?

Sweet innocent anticipation wafted through her. She'd never been kissed by a man — never wanted to be kissed. She'd always kept herself far above any loose behavior.

With a groan, he closed his eyes, almost as if he were trying to block out the sight of her.

In one cold moment, he let go of her and rolled away.

He scrambled up and turned his back to her.

She shuddered from the blast of air that rippled across her skin.

Without looking at her, he grabbed his shirt, which he'd stretched out near the fire. His fingers fumbled to tug the garment over his head, his arms getting tangled in his haste to clothe himself.

"How are you feeling?" he asked without turning around. He jammed his arms into the sleeves.

The chill on her skin soaked into her flesh and worked toward her heart. What had happened? She'd seen desire in his eyes, hadn't she?

With his back toward her, he snatched his trousers from the ground and hopped on one leg and then the other as he worked them over the long material of his union suit. Hunched under the low roof, he snapped his suspenders over his shoulders and then finally chanced a glance her way.

She hadn't moved, hadn't the energy, hadn't the desire for anything but being next to him.

When his gaze landed upon her thin camisole, he hurriedly turned his eyes to the blanket. "Are you warm yet?" He reached for the blanket and draped it across her.

She couldn't get her voice to work but instead watched him, wondering why he'd pushed her away so quickly, wishing she didn't feel the sting of his rejection.

He hovered above her as if sensing her hurt. His fingers lingered on the blanket, and desire flitted across his face again.

"I'm sorry, Lily," he said hoarsely, ripping himself away from her. He glanced everywhere in the small hut but at her. "You have to believe me. I wasn't trying to take advantage of you. I was just trying to save your life. That's why we were the way we were . . ."

"It's all right," she whispered.

He cleared his throat and reached for a piece of wood out of the pile next to the door. "I didn't mean for things to get so . . . so intimate."

"It wasn't your fault." He'd only done what he'd had to. She couldn't fault him in the least.

He moved toward the fire, once again turning his back toward her. He added the log and used the blade of his ax to stir the coals. When he finally sat back, he'd put obvious distance between them.

"I won't take advantage of you, Lily." Again his voice was hoarse with emotion. "It wouldn't be right."

She grasped the blankets closer. She shuddered to think what could have happened if any other man had found her. And her heart swelled with gratitude that Connell was such a good man.

"You're an attractive woman." His voice was almost a whisper.

His words sent a fresh burst of warmth over her skin.

He stared at the flickering flames, and the muscles in his jaw worked up and down. Finally he spoke. "My mam taught me that I'd show my admiration best if I used restraint and respect. She told me a woman needs to be cherished, not used for the pleasure of the moment."

Was he telling her he admired her?

168

The warmth slipped into her blood and sent a different kind of tingle of delight throughout her body.

He'd always acted decently and honorably toward her. And even though part of her longed to be back in his arms, another part of her liked him even more for his strength and determination to show her respect.

She settled back against the hardness of the ground, and the strain eased from her limbs. She tried to adjust herself into a comfortable position, one in which she could still see him, but she noticed for the first time the crudeness of their shelter.

The roof was a sagging mess of rotten boards with holes that appeared to have been hastily patched with tree branches and pine-seedling boughs. The log walls were crumbling away, the gaps stuffed with a fresh mixture of leaves and boughs. Even the shabby door was propped closed with a large branch.

She could only imagine the hardship he'd endured to find her and get her to this place — wherever it was. And from what she could tell, he'd likely spent hours attempting to save her life while also having to make the shelter safe from the storm.

"Thank you for coming after me," she said softly, her mind beginning to comprehend the magnitude of what he'd done and the risks he'd taken — even putting his own life in jeopardy — to find her. "I don't know what I would have done without your help."

"You're welcome." A slow smile worked its way up his lips. The flames from the fire reflected on his face, highlighting his pleasure at her words. "After all the times I've had to bail you out of trouble, I have to admit, it's kind of nice to hear you finally admit you needed my help."

"*All* the times?"

"Yes, *all* the times." His grinned widened. "Starting from the first night you stepped into the Northern Hotel."

"If I remember right, I didn't do such a bad job taking care of myself." A smile twitched her lips. "But I suppose if it makes you feel like a knight in shining armor, I'll let you take the credit for saving me from doom."

"Oh, come on, admit it." His voice was low and edged with laughter. "You know for a fact I'm your knight in shining armor."

Her heart swelled. "Since you're forcing a confession out of me," she bantered, "then yes, I admit you're my hero." Little did he know just how much he was winning her heart.

"Well, then that's settled."

A gust of wind blew at the shack, rattling the walls and threatening to tear the roof away. A shower of snow blew in between several cracks, sending a dusting over them.

He glanced at the roof, and worried lines quickly replaced all humor.

"Sounds like it's still storming," she said. How many hours had elapsed since she'd left the hotel? "When I left I never expected it to start snowing or for it to get so cold so fast."

"Last time I went out we had ten and a quarter inches on the ground."

He was so matter-of-fact and precise she couldn't keep from teasing. "Are you sure it wasn't more like ten and a half?"

His eyebrow quirked.

She smiled. "I don't suppose you had a ruler to measure it now, did you?"

He ducked his head, but not before she caught sight of his grin. "I don't need one. I have one built into my brain."

"Built in?" This time her brow shot up.

"I'm good with figures."

The wind rattled again, whistling through the many crevices in the walls and down the narrow pipe that served as the chimney for the small dugout fireplace.

He stood, bumping his head against the ceiling. With a frown, he shrugged into his plaid mackinaw and then reached for his heavy coat.

"Is it time to go?" she asked, propping herself onto her elbow.

He tugged up the collar of his coat and slipped his feet into his boots. Then he looked at her with a seriousness that sent a jolt of fear through her. "We can't leave."

"Sure we can." She pushed herself up but was immediately overcome by a wave of dizziness.

"Even if you were up to leaving, which you're not" — he nodded at her weak attempt at sitting up — "I let the horse go last night. It was her only chance of surviving. Hopefully she made her way back to the stable."

"We could walk —"

"Not without snowshoes. The snow's too deep and the wind too harsh."

She leaned back again, suddenly weary and cold. "Then we're stuck here?"

"Until a rescue party comes for us." He pulled on his gloves. "Or until spring. Whichever comes first." He gave a half-hearted grin at his attempt at a joke.

But the shadows in his eyes gave testimony to the seriousness of their situation. "I'm going out to get more firewood."

When he opened the door, the overcast

daylight streamed in, along with a swirl of snow and wind. All it took was one glimpse of the blizzard that was still raging for her to realize he was right. They'd be foolish to attempt to go anywhere — as foolish as she'd been to set out in the first place.

He was gone longer than she'd hoped. And all the while the wind raged harder, squeezing between every crevice and slithering over her. She tried to sit up, then to kneel, knowing she couldn't lie helplessly while he did all the work.

She reached for her dress, and her body shook with the effort. As her fingers made contact with the damp material, she knew she wouldn't be able to put it back on yet, not while it was still cold and wet. She tried to spread it out to help with the drying but fell back against the ground, exhausted.

"Please don't let us die, God." Her heart cried out, just as it had when she'd fallen into the snow, unable to go another step forward. She couldn't die now. Not yet. Not when Daisy and Frankie still needed her so desperately.

Hunger gnawed at Connell's stomach. He handed Lily another slice of dried apple. "Come on now, one more piece."

She pushed his hand away. "I'm too tired

to eat any more."

He'd managed to stuff half a loaf of bread, a few dried apples, and a wedge of cheese into his sack, enough to tide them over for one missed meal, but certainly not enough to sustain them long term. And now, after just one day, their supply of food was low, even though he'd rationed himself to the barest minimum.

"You need to eat a little more," he urged, kneeling next to her.

"I'm not hungry."

"Bet you'd eat it if it were a cookie."

She managed a small smile. "Probably."

Worry gurgled with the acid in his stomach. She'd grown pale and listless as the day had worn on.

"*You* eat it," she said.

"No," he insisted, holding it out to her.

He'd taken Oren's rifle with him during one of his forays for firewood. But he hadn't figured on finding any game. With the intensity of the storm, every living creature was holed up, safe and warm where it belonged — unlike them.

Still, his stomach would have thanked him for a hare or even a squirrel.

Lily finally took the brown, shriveled piece of apple. "You need it more than I do. And you shouldn't have to suffer for my mistake."

"My mam taught me to take care of a woman's needs above my own."

Her lips formed into another protest.

"Besides, I wanted to help you," he said. "I made the decision to come out here of my own free will."

Her words died away, and she searched his face, as if trying to understand why he'd risked his life for her. But he couldn't find an answer for *her* any more than he could for himself.

What was it about her that made him rush headlong into doing things he normally wouldn't consider?

Certainly not just because she was an attractive woman.

He glanced at her lips, and his gut heated with the memory of lying next to her and how much he'd wanted to kiss her. He tore his gaze away. He couldn't let his mind dwell on the intimacy. He'd already had a hard enough time wrenching himself away from her earlier. If he let himself think of how soft and warm she'd been in his arms, he'd only feed his appetite for her — an appetite that didn't need any more fuel.

He reached for another log he'd split and tossed it onto the fire. Sparks flared into the air, crackling with power. If he wasn't careful, he could easily let the sparks he'd felt with Lily turn into out-of-control flames.

She situated herself on the blanket and took a nibble of the apple. "It sounds like you had a wonderful mother."

He nodded and sat back, putting a safe distance between himself and the temptation to pull her into his arms. "My mam is about as sweet as they come." The complete opposite of Dad.

"Tell me about her," Lily said wistfully.

"She probably would have joined a convent if she hadn't met my dad. But Dad was fresh off the boat and starving, like most of the other poor Irish immigrants fleeing from the potato famine. She took pity on him and helped nurse him back to health. And, of course, he convinced her to marry him."

Sometimes he wondered if she would have been happier at a convent.

Lily didn't say anything and instead watched his face.

"What about you?" he asked, ready to take the focus off himself and his parents. "What kind of mom did you have?"

She hesitated. Her hair was unraveled and lay in a glorious display of long dark curls around her face.

The muscles in his hands tensed with the

need to thread his fingers through the thick locks. Instead he grabbed his ax and poked the fire, sending more sparks flying.

"I don't remember much about my mother," she said.

He stared at the flames, trying to keep a rein on his thoughts about Lily.

"She died giving birth to Daisy." Her voice dipped.

"I'm sorry." He stilled and glanced at her again.

Her forehead crinkled above eyes that radiated pain. "My father couldn't take care of us, and for a few years we were shuffled between relatives. Until he got into an accident at work and died within a few days."

An ache wound around his heart.

"After that, no one wanted us anymore. I suppose without the money my father had provided them, they couldn't afford to take care of two more children — not when they struggled enough without us. So they dropped us off at the New York Foundling Hospital."

She paused, and he didn't say anything, although part of him wished he could curse the family that gave up two girls with such ease.

"We lived at the hospital in New York City until there was no longer room for us. Then we moved to other orphanages." She turned to look at the fire, embarrassment reflected in her face. "I made sure they never separated Daisy and me. I kept us together all those years, no matter where we were. And finally we had the option of moving here to Michigan. They said families needed boys and girls. We'd get to live in real homes."

The grip on his heart cinched tighter.

"When we got here, I thought I was doing the best thing for Daisy by giving her a real family to live with. The Wretchams seemed nice. They lived on a big farm. Needed some extra help —"

"So you and Daisy didn't stay together?"

"There weren't any families needing two almost-grown girls. But I consoled myself that it was only temporary, that we'd only be apart until I could find a good job and a place for us to live."

"That must have been hard on both of you."

"Letting her go was like ripping out a piece of my heart."

He wanted to reach for her, pull her into his arms, and comfort her. But everything within him warned him against even a move as innocent as that.

"When I learned she'd run away from the Wretchams, she ripped out the rest of my heart, and it hasn't stopped bleeding since."

No wonder she was so passionate about finding Daisy. "Why did she leave them?"

Lily shrugged. "From what I could tell the couple times I visited, they were taking good care of her. They had other children, and they made her feel welcome."

"Sounds like it was a good family."

Her face darkened and her eyes grew sad. "Since I never had a family of my own, I'm not very qualified to judge a family's worth, am I?"

"Whatever happened, you can't blame yourself —"

"I'll blame myself until the day I die," she said hotly. "I should have figured out a way to stay together."

"But you couldn't take care of her forever —"

"When I find her, I'll never let her go again." Her words rang with that fiery determination he was coming to admire. "I'm going to find a way to make a home for her the way she deserves."

And just what was Lily planning to do? What kind of skill or training did she have that would enable her to support herself and her sister? He bit back the questions, not willing to be the one to discourage her or make her face reality. But the fact was, there wasn't much a woman alone could do to earn a decent living except what Daisy was already doing — selling herself to men.

And he also wasn't going to be the one to remind Lily it would take a miracle to find Daisy among the hundreds of illicit houses littering central Michigan.

Besides, what kind of life would Daisy be able to lead if she left prostitution? No decent man would ever want to marry her. And respectable society would shun her.

Daisy would be an outcast. And Lily would end up one by association.

As hard as it was to admit the truth, he had the feeling she was better off not finding the girl.

CHAPTER 11

The second night in the hut brought a new chill, an arctic wind that penetrated every crack and forced them closer to the fire.

The firelight flickered over Connell's face, over the shadows of worry that he couldn't hide.

From where she lay on the floor, Lily's heart ached with the longing for him to gather her in his arms again.

But he'd done the honorable thing — he'd kept his distance. He'd shown her the utmost respect all day, as he'd promised he would. Without the slightest flicker of condemnation, he'd accepted her past, her homelessness, even her guilt over losing Daisy. He'd listened to her. She'd been able to bare her soul to him in a way she'd never been able to do with anyone else before.

Her admiration for him had only grown. As night crept in around them, she was certain she had never met a finer man than

Connell McCormick.

"So Dad saved up every dollar he made working at lumber camps in Maine, and when he'd saved enough, he decided to come to Michigan." Connell's voice was soft. He'd stretched his long legs out in front of him and leaned against the wall. "He'd heard there was enough timber in Michigan to build a house for every grown man in America."

A small part of her heart wanted to stay in the damp hovel forever — just the two of them.

But the other part of her knew the extreme danger of their situation. They were trapped. They'd eaten the last of the food. And there was no telling when a rescue party would be able start out or if they'd be able to find them.

"He started off as a land-looker for a mill owner downstate," Connell continued. "But he was also a freelancer. So whenever he scouted out pine for the mill owner, he'd usually do a little buying on his own account."

For once she didn't have the energy or heart to argue with him about the destruction the lumber industry had caused. Instead, she watched the loose hairs that fell across his forehead and the way the firelight

182

turned them to gold.

"One spring he located a fine stand of cork pine in the Saginaw Valley. But a rival lumberman was also looking at the same stand. Once my dad got the measurements and data he needed, he raced back to the nearest land office and registered his claim. The other agent showed up three hours later, but of course he was too late. My dad had won the race and established a small lumber camp there. Turned out to be a prime spot, the spot that turned him from a pauper into a very wealthy man."

"Sounds like he was an ambitious man."

Connell nodded. "And he's still ambitious. Sometimes too ambitious."

"Then you must take after him."

Connell snorted. "My dad didn't give me much choice. He's always demanded much of my brother and me. He taught us to work hard, but sometimes I think he's forgotten that we're not in Ireland, we're not in the middle of the potato famine, and we're not starving to death."

"I suppose he can't forget his past."

"Not when he had to watch every member of his family die of starvation in front of his eyes and not be able to do a single thing about it."

"It's hard when you want to be able to

help your family and you can't." She knew that feeling all too well.

"They had nothing but dirt and grass to eat. He watched his three youngest siblings die in a corner of their shack, lying there because they were too weak to rise, their limbs emaciated, their bellies swollen, eyes sunken, voices gone. . . . After they died, he left."

For a long moment he stared into the fire and didn't say anything.

"And now," he finally said, "nothing is more important to my dad than working hard and being successful."

"Is that what you believe too?"

"I guess."

"But you don't have to let his definition of success be yours." She tugged the blankets under her chin, but then felt a rush of cold air over her feet as the blanket slid off. Even though her dress had finally dried, she'd collapsed with weakness trying to don it on one of the occasions when he'd gone out. She'd had to give up and covered herself with her coat and blankets instead.

He leaned forward and tucked a blanket back around her feet. "When are you going to tell me about your striped socks?"

"Why, Connell McCormick." She gave a

mock gasp. "Have you been peeking at my feet?"

"I haven't meant to. But there've been a few times —"

"Few!" Again she pretended shock, but her smile gave away her playfulness. "So not only have you been peeking, you've made it a regular practice to glimpse under my hem."

"It's hard to miss those bright colors —"

"Come on. Admit it. You like seeing my ankles."

He poked at the fire and ducked his head.

She gave a soft laugh. Pleasure from his obvious attraction wove through her like a sweet summer breeze. She shifted her legs and let the blanket slide from her feet again, revealing them once more.

He glanced sideways for only an instant before focusing his full attention on the fire, prodding the logs and sending the flames higher — almost as if their lives depended upon how hot he could get them.

She laughed again.

A slow grin made its way up his lips.

"Well, if you must know," she said, "Oren's wife, Betty, made them for me."

"I didn't know Oren was married."

"He's not anymore. Betty died last summer."

He sat back on his heels and gave her his full attention.

Keen wistfulness washed over her. Even though she'd lived with Oren and Betty for only a year, the woman had become as dear to her as Oren had.

"How'd she die?"

"She was already sick when I went to live with them. Their only son went west back in the '60s, and they didn't have any other family around. Oren needed someone to help take care of Betty so he could do his work without worrying about her."

The distant howl of a wolf echoed through the night, which had finally grown calm.

"Betty was as sweet as honey. But I quickly realized Oren is just as sweet, once you peel back all those gruff layers."

Connell nodded. "Believe it or not, I actually like Oren. Even though he's threatened to blow my head off twice now."

"Twice?"

"When he realized you were gone, he came to my door —"

"He probably just wanted your help and didn't know how to ask."

"It's obvious the guy thinks the world of you."

She smiled. She thought the world of him too. "I was worried after Betty died that he might make me leave. I don't think he knew what he was going to do with me — especially once he left for his winter picture taking among the camps. But after I got Daisy's letter and begged him to take me along, he hasn't said another word about my leaving."

Another long howl carried through the windless night — this one closer.

She'd been too old to be sent back to the orphanage. If Oren had decided he didn't want her anymore, she would have had to make it on her own somehow.

She had no doubt she would. And when she found Daisy, they'd make a way together this time.

Something scratched against the door, and Connell sat to his knees.

A pattering of footsteps tramped across the roof, and a sprinkling of snow drifted down through the cracks.

Connell stared at the ceiling, and his eyes followed the trail of footsteps. Another scratch at the door was followed by a low whine.

She propped herself up on her elbow.

"Wolves." His voice was low.

Her heart skittered to a halt. She pushed herself to a sitting position. Her long hair swirled around her face in an unruly tangle. "Are we safe in here?"

His focus darted back and forth across the roof as if he were mentally following the path of each wolf. "I think there are at least six of them."

She shuddered.

The pawing at the door became more insistent. Suddenly, the old slab of rotting wood creaked inward, a long gray snout poked through, and a black tipped nose sniffed the air.

She sucked in a sharp breath.

Connell sprang to his feet and was against the door in an instant, ramming it closed with his shoulder.

A long chilling howl reverberated directly overhead, followed by several more.

"What do they want?" she asked, pulling a blanket around her as if she could ward off the frightening noise.

"Us." He shoved the tree limb back against the door to wedge it tighter. "For a meal."

"But they can't get in, can they?"

A shower of snow from the roof rained down on them.

He glanced back at the ceiling and reached for Oren's Winchester.

A flurry of pawing and digging sent another deluge of snow down upon their heads. A chunk slipped under her camisole and made a cold trail down her back.

"Move to the corner." Connell jerked to a spot next to the fireplace. The urgency of his tone sent her scrambling.

She dragged the blankets around her and crawled to the safety of the corner.

More snow poured into the shack until a paw reached through a hole in the ceiling and swiped at the air.

She huddled against the damp earth and breathed in the moldy scent of rotting logs from the wall behind her. Would the decaying structure be strong enough to protect them?

Connell pointed the gun at the ceiling and backed up until he was standing in front of her. Without moving his aim, he lowered himself to one knee, providing a barrier between her and the wolf.

The wolf retreated and began digging again. Snow fell through the cracks in another spot of the roof.

"I was hoping they wouldn't find the weak places." He looked from one area of the roof to the other as if he couldn't decide where to aim the gun.

"Did you know the wolves would come?" She shivered and wrapped the blankets tighter.

"I figured once the storm abated, they'd catch our scent. But I was hoping they'd leave us alone."

The scratching at the door started again.

He flipped the gun to the door. "Apparently they've decided to attack us with all they've got."

The branch against the door rattled.

Her body tensed, every nerve ready to fight, even though she doubted she could stand. "What can I do to help? Tell me."

"I need you to unsheathe my knife." He cocked his head to indicate the side where she'd find it.

She reached for the edge of his shirt and hesitated only a moment before slipping it upward.

"Hurry."

Her fingers fumbled to lift the flannel higher until she found the scabbard against his ribs. She worked the knife out, trying not to graze him.

Finally she clutched the handle and let the shirt drop back into place.

His chest deflated, and only then did she realize he'd been holding his breath. Did her touch affect him as much as his did her?

"Hold on to the knife and be ready to hand it to me when I ask for it."

"Don't you want me to use it?"

He shook his head. "Just have it ready."

If she hadn't been so weak, she might have

argued with him. As it was, she fell back against the wall, her body trembling with a wave of weariness.

The branch propped against the door scraped open a fraction. And the digging at the first hole in the roof resumed with a chorus of yips.

As the sliver in the door widened, splinters and branches from the roof caved in.

She didn't want to cower, but she had the awful vision of being cornered by wolves with no escape.

The door rattled and the branch slipped away. A slender head poked in. Golden eyes rimmed with black narrowed on them. In another second the wolf squeezed through the opening. It was thin enough she could see ribs protruding in its heaving sides. It dipped its head, laid its ears back, and growled, exposing a ridge of sharp yellowed teeth and fangs. Frozen saliva dangled from one side of its mouth.

The beast crouched lower and began creeping toward them.

Connell swung the gun toward the intruder, but a snarl at the hole in the roof drew his attention upward again. The roof was giving way to the wolf's scraping and in an instant the opening would be big enough for it to drop through.

She clutched the knife, her fingers stiff and numb with fear. How could they fight them all off?

"Get ready to hand me the knife," Connell said with a voice that was low and calm. He raised the gun to the ceiling and took aim down the long barrel.

"Now." Even as he said the word, he pulled the trigger.

In a blur of fear and hot dizziness, she held the knife toward him.

The crack of gunfire exploded in the air. At the same time his fingers gripped the knife, and before she could take another breath, he flung the blade with surprising swiftness and precision across the span of the hovel directly into the heart of the wolf creeping toward them.

The beast gave a sharp yip, took one step forward, and then crumpled to the dirt floor. A bright spot of red seeped through the thick grayish fur across its chest.

Connell stood, and with the smoking rifle aimed on the roof, he crossed to the door and slammed it closed. He leaned against it and studied the ceiling.

His jaw twitched and his finger cradled the trigger.

For a long moment they listened.

Silence descended around them, almost

as if the world had deserted them completely.

"Are they gone?" she finally whispered.

"For now."

She let out a shaky breath and let her body slump.

He shoved the wolf with his boot.

It didn't move.

With a swift jerk he slid the knife from the wolf's chest. Blood bubbled out across the fur and dripped into the dirt.

She stifled a shudder. "I wouldn't want to face you in a fight, not with the way you handle your knife."

"You can thank my dad for that." He stooped and brushed the blade against the carcass, wiping it clean. Then he tucked it out of sight under his shirt. "He wanted his sons to know how to fight — I suppose so that no one could ever beat us up and leave us for dead."

"I'm guessing that happened to him?"

"Twice. Before he left Ireland."

She protested when Connell went out into the black night to attempt to patch the holes in the roof. He filled the biggest spot as best he could, and all the while she couldn't help worrying that the wolves would return and attack him before he could get back into the shelter.

When he closed the door and shoved the weight of the dead wolf against it along with the branch he'd used before, she leaned her head back and closed her eyes, relieved but too exhausted to say anything.

She slept where she sat in the corner, waking whenever he shot the gun, realizing through a haze the wolves were attacking again. Off and on throughout the long night, the crack of the gun would startle her out of a fitful sleep.

Once he woke her, offering her a tin cup of water from melted snow. His tired bloodshot eyes were round with concern. He laid his palm across her forehead, the coolness of his touch soothing her.

She wanted to grasp his hand and hold it there. But she was too weak to move. She wanted to tell him how much she admired him, but she could only manage a small smile that she hoped conveyed her gratitude.

She wasn't sure how much time passed — it could have been hours — when something roused her.

With a start she opened her eyes. It took her a moment to realize Connell was sitting next to her and that he'd tucked her into the crook of his arm with her head against his chest.

The steady thud of his heartbeat echoed

against her ear.

His face was haggard with weariness, a testimony to the sleeplessness and danger he'd endured all night. She had no doubt it was well into the morning and that the threat of wolves was over for at least the time being; otherwise he wouldn't have allowed himself the luxury of breaking his vigilance.

Her parched tongue stuck to the roof of her mouth, and her body ached with feverish chills.

She was sick.

The peril of their predicament returned with a fresh wave of fear.

One glance across the shack to the door, to the dead wolf, to the blood now crusted brown, and the terror of the night crashed back through her.

How could they survive another day? Or another night?

"Please, God," she whispered through cracked lips. All those years growing up in orphanages, she'd learned to say her prayers, to honor God, and to follow the Ten Commandments. But it hadn't been until she'd met Betty, Oren's wife, that she'd ever heard anyone pray to God as though He was a real person and really cared about what happened.

Betty's prayers had always filled her with the whisper of hope that God wasn't so far off after all. That maybe He hadn't deserted her, as everyone else in her life had.

Lily closed her eyes and let the steady rhythm of Connell's heartbeat soothe her. She curled closer to him and dared to lay her hand on his.

Suddenly something shoved against the door.

Connell woke with a start, and his knife was out and positioned to throw before she could move.

She strained to sit up, but his arm tightened around her, pulling her closer.

Another shove against the door pried it open a crack.

"Don't move," he said in a voice slurred with leftover sleep.

She didn't know if she could move even if she tried. She was content to lean against him, into the safety of his arm, and know he would protect her, just as he had all night long.

Maybe her defenses had fallen away because she was sick. Maybe they'd crumbled because she'd come to realize that Connell was one of the most decent men she'd ever met. Whatever the case, she relinquished her need to always be the strong one, the one doing the protecting. For once, she could let someone else be strong enough for both of them.

A slam on the door, this one harder than the last, ripped the door from its tenuous hold on the rusting hinges. It crashed down on the dead wolf and tree branch, letting in a blinding stream of sunlight and a rush of frigid air.

"They're here!" someone shouted.

She blinked hard, her eyes watering from the glare.

There was more shouting, and before she knew it, a man bundled in a buffalo-skin coat shoved his way past the broken door.

Through the fog that weighed down her head, she glimpsed the anxious face of Stuart Golden. In one sweeping glance, he took in her position within the confines of Connell's arms and his eyes narrowed. She almost thought she caught a glimpse of jealousy in them before he forced a grin.

"What do you think you're doing out here slacking off, McCormick, you big lazy-bones?"

Connell's knife disappeared, and a tired smile hovered over his lips. "Oh, you know me. I'm always trying to get out of my work. Figured this was a good way."

"Yeah." Stuart peered at the gap in the

roof and then at the paw of a dead wolf dangling through the hole. "I'd probably have more fun out here fighting off wolves too."

"Yep. You don't know the rip-roaring good time you missed."

Stuart glanced again at her and then at Connell's arm that was wrapped around her. He shifted his gaze away and swallowed hard.

"Is she alive?" Oren's voice boomed from the doorway.

"Doesn't look like the wolves had a chance," Stuart said over his shoulder. "Not against Connell's knife."

Oren elbowed his way past Stuart. "Thank the good Lord."

Beneath the brim of his derby, his face was red and chapped from the cold, but his eyes brimmed with a warmth that brought an ache to her throat. His overgrown mustache drooped as much as his shoulders, as if worry had pressed down on him like a felled tree while she was gone.

"I'm sorry," she whispered, wishing she could turn back the clock. If only she'd waited for Oren to take her to Merryville instead of rushing off. At the time, she hadn't realized her rashness would nearly kill her and bring trouble to everyone else.

"How are you?" he asked, his gruff voice cracking.

"I'm fine —"

"She's got a fever," Connell interrupted.

Only then did Oren seem to take in the nature of her predicament. His gaze went first to Connell's arm around her. His eyes widened at the lace of her camisole peeking above the edge of the blanket where her coat had slipped away. And then he glanced at her dress puddled on the dirt floor where she'd left it.

"What in the hairy hound has gone on here?" Fury flamed to life in his voice and his face.

"It's not what it looks like." Connell slipped his arm away from her, leaving her suddenly chilled.

"I'm not blind or stupid."

"I know things don't look proper." Connell held himself rigid. "But you've got to believe me when I tell you that nothing happened between us."

"I think I remember telling you no one touches Lily and lives to tell about it."

"Then you'll be happy to know I treated her honorably."

"You had her sitting in your lap and were devouring her like she was your breakfast, lunch, and supper."

"Don't blame Connell," she said. If anyone deserved a rebuke for the indecency of their situation, she did. She was embarrassed to admit it, but she'd been the one who'd wanted to be close to him, while he'd done all he could to keep an honorable distance from her.

Oren's thick eyebrows came together in a furious scowl, one that would have scared the wolves away had they made an appearance.

"He saved my life, Oren." Everything within her rose up to defend Connell. "If it weren't for him, I'd be frozen like the ice on the river, and I'd be buried under several feet of snow. He did what was necessary to get me warmed back up."

Stuart cleared his throat, and when she looked up, two more men had ducked inside.

She tugged the edge of the blanket higher until it reached her chin. "Connell's a good man, and he treated me with the utmost respect."

Nobody said anything for a long moment, but it was obvious from the way the newcomers shifted their feet and looked everywhere but at her that they had assumed the worst too.

Embarrassment crashed over her, and she

sat forward with a burst of desperation. "Connell McCormick did nothing but put his life at risk numerous times to save me."

When Oren met her gaze, the anger had fizzled and was replaced instead with sadness. "He may have saved your life, but let's hope to high heaven he didn't ruin your reputation."

CHAPTER 12

"I'm going to make an announcement to the men at flaggins," Connell said to the foreman of Camp 1.

Herb Nolan didn't say anything and instead reached for the whiskey bottle filled with coal oil perched on a nearby stump.

Connell absently tapped the flat edge of his ax against the pine next to him, ignoring the growling in his stomach that told him the noon meal was fast approaching. "I've finally come up with a way to get us back on track with production."

Herb squirted a stream of oil onto the long crosscut saw his sawyers were jerking through the kerf. The wobbling blade stuck for only another instant before the few drops of oil did their job. The men resumed their practiced rhythm, the saw swishing back and forth through the felled tree.

Connell's trained eye measured the tree, checking the ax clips where the tree had been laid off, the places where the trunk would be cut into sections. Each was exactly twenty feet apart, just as he'd expected.

The swampers had already been over the tree, cutting off the limbs, throwing the tops and other waste into a pile. As far as Connell could tell, the log was an upper — a superior grade. Fortunately, about ninety percent of the logs from his three camps were uppers.

Unfortunately, they weren't getting enough of those logs into town to the main rail. They'd already been struggling with production, but the week of melting had thrown them back even more.

"I've had the icer out every night this week." The foreman stepped away from the sawyers. "I've even kept the contraption going during the daytime so we can haul as many logs as possible. The roads have never been smoother —"

"I know you're working hard," Connell reassured Herb. "But we've got to take advantage of this weather while we have it."

Herb nodded, but the crinkle across his leathery forehead was only the beginning of the resistance Connell knew he was going to get once he asked the men to start hauling at night. Maybe his announcement would help.

Just then the bugle of the cookee's nooning horn called to them above the echoes of chopping and sawing. The men straightened their backs and flexed their muscles before slipping back into the coats they'd discarded after becoming overheated from all their exertion.

They made their way to the swampy clearing where the cookee, the cook's helper, had brought them flaggins on his pung sleigh. He'd started a fire, and the men gathered around it to warm their hands in the bitter air that had poured in from the north and chased away every last hint of an early spring.

And while they did their best to stay warm, they ate the meal cookee served them. Some sat on logs and others stood, balancing their tin plates and pannikins in one hand and utensils in the other. They gulped the usual fare of beans, salted pork, and steaming tea, working fast to inhale the meal before it lost its heat.

Connell stood back and watched, knowing Duff would have a special mincemeat pie for him when he finally made his way back to the kitchen. He supposed it was one advantage of being the boss man. But it couldn't offset the fact he had to be the bearer of bad news. And from the scowls of some of the men, he figured they'd already guessed why he was there.

Once everyone was served, Connell moved to the front of the group. There was a part of him that wished he could walk away and let the men do their work. What difference would a few more thousand feet of board make? Especially when McCormick Lumber already had so much?

But the other part of him knew he had to stay and make sure McCormick came out on top of all the other companies. That was his job. Dad had trained him to work hard. And Dad was relying on him to help make McCormick Lumber successful. How could he do anything less?

"I've done an inspection of the camp," he started, drawing more frowns. "And from what I can tell, you're all doing the best you can."

Even after his investigation, he still hadn't been able to figure out why all his camps were falling behind on the logs they were delivering. From the reports his foremen were giving him for the trees felled and logs cut, they should have had more logs arriving in Harrison.

"But the fact is we're behind what we were producing last year, so now, especially after last week, we've got to pick up our pace."

A round of grumbling wound through the

group as they huddled near the fire, the raw January wind blowing down their necks.

"Yes, it's going to require some extra hours in the woods," Connell continued, pulling the collar of his coat closed to fight off the chill. "But I'm promising a bonus to whichever McCormick camp gets out the most logs over what the contract calls for. A nice bonus."

At the word *bonus,* the men stood taller and their faces glimmered with what Connell hoped was excitement. They tossed out suggestions and questions.

He did his best as always to present himself as a capable leader. But inwardly he exhaled a tense breath. Apparently dangling the possibility of a bonus in front of them had worked.

In a matter of minutes the foreman called the men to return to their duties.

"I sure wouldn't mind a woman for my bonus," one of the men said under his breath as he picked up his ax.

Another shanty boy mumbled back, "Yeah, and I wouldn't mind being stranded alone with a half-naked woman for a couple days. That'd be the best bonus I could think of."

The muscles in Connell's shoulders tensed. So the news was out. Ever since the rescue party had discovered them the previous morning, he'd kicked himself over and over for not doing a better job protecting Lily's reputation. He could have at least made sure she'd had her dress on, couldn't he?

He'd been secretly hoping that by some miracle he could spare her the gossip that was sure to get around. But from the snickers and sly glances the men were giving each other, the rumors had obviously spread as fast as typhoid fever.

The best thing was to ignore the insinuations. If he acknowledged them, he would only degrade Lily more.

The road monkey, the youngest of the shanty boys at Camp 1, stopped and joined the other two. "Heard his woman is a real looker." One of the teamsters yanked the young man and shook his head in warning.

But the youth wasn't paying attention to the old teamster or to the fact that Connell could hear every word he was saying. Instead the young man grinned at his friends. "Maybe when the boss man is done with her, the rest of us will get a chance to have a little fun."

There was something about the young man's comment that sent a hot slice of anger through Connell's gut. Out of instinct, his hand lifted to his knife. The heat pulsed through his fingers and he gripped the handle. For a long moment, all he could think about was throwing the blade into the youth's arm and making an example of him.

If he did, no one would dare speak about Lily that way again.

The teamster tugged the youth, his eyes fixed on Connell's hand and the knife that had somehow made an appearance.

The young man followed the gaze of the old teamster, and his grin froze faster than tobacco spit.

"Come on now," the teamster urged, pulling the youth along.

Connell had no doubt they'd also gotten word about how he'd killed the wolves.

The shanty boy stumbled after the teamster, casting frightened glances over his shoulder at the blade and tripping over his feet in his haste to get away.

The others disappeared just as quickly, and in a moment Connell was left standing with only the cookee and his foreman.

The cookee collected and dumped the dirty plates with a clatter into the pine soapbox fastened to the pole runners on the pung sleigh. He hustled about with an extra burst of energy that contrasted with his usual methodical trudge.

Herb looked off into the distance, his forehead furrowed.

Connell glanced at the knife and then slipped it away, wondering what had possessed him to unsheathe it in the first place. He wouldn't have thrown it at the man. The last thing he wanted to do was hurt one of his workers, especially a youth who wasn't strong enough to do much of anything but keep the iced roads free of horse or ox droppings.

Of course the youth hadn't known he was listening to them, that his ear was attuned to every crude remark about Lily, and that he was choked with guilt.

The cookee smothered the fire with ashes and snow and then sat on a log and began to strap on his snowshoes before beginning his haul back to camp. All the while he avoided making eye contact with Connell.

The men had to know he wouldn't have hurt the youth.

But the raw slice in his gut still oozed with anger. He only had to think of Lily's pale face when they'd finally arrived back at the Northern Hotel, and his frustration over the situation turned into a glaring wound once again.

Stuart had been the one to carry her inside to Vera's bed. And anytime Connell had tried to even look at Lily, Oren had scowled at him and forced him away.

Oren knew he hadn't taken advantage of Lily, that he'd treated her with the respect she was due. He could see it in the man's eyes. But it didn't change what had happened.

And now Oren was only trying to protect Lily from any further damage. He could understand that. That's all he wanted for her too.

Connell gave a long sigh that left a white wisp in the bitter air.

He'd tried to do the right thing by saving her, but somehow he'd ended up making a mess of everything.

Maybe he'd do them all a favor if he just minded his own business like he always had.

The feather pillow against Lily's head was like a cloud straight from heaven. And the warmth of Vera's quilts was like the heat of a glorious summer day.

If only the dear woman would stop insisting she take hog's foot oil, a homemade remedy Vera had concocted from boiled hogs' feet during butchering time. She claimed the oil had always cured her of any hint of cough or hoarse throat.

But the thick, slimy medicine had chunks

of who-knew-what in it. And the dead-animal stench made Lily gag just as much as the taste did.

"Maybe I could have another dose of the pine-resin syrup instead," Lily offered as Vera heated the bottle of hog's foot oil over the lamp, warming it so it would melt and slide out onto the spoon.

"I'll give you some of that too." She swished the bottle and peered through the narrow opening.

"But I'm actually feeling much better."

"Then all the more reason for another spoonful. That means it's working."

Lily stifled a sigh. After three days in bed with a fever and cough, she was past ready to be up and about. But Vera wouldn't let her set a foot on the floor and had hovered over her tirelessly, attending to her every need almost as if she were a princess.

She'd never had anyone wait on her before. And no matter how much Vera had insisted she lay in her bed, she couldn't keep the edge of discomfort from creeping in next to her, urging her to throw off the warm covers, get up, and stand on her own two feet like she'd always done.

Vera ambled over to the side of the bed. "Open up."

Lily struggled to rise. Time to count her

blessings and stop complaining. After all, she was safe and alive.

A knock on Vera's bedroom door sent a quiver of anticipation through Lily. She clambered to sit higher, combing her unruly curls away from her face.

Maybe it was Connell, finally coming to check on her.

As much as she wanted to deny the truth, she couldn't keep hope from rising inside her. She wanted to see him, had waited for him to visit, had lain on her bed straining to see into the kitchen, longing to get a glimpse of him in passing.

But in the past three days, she hadn't seen him. Not once.

Surely he would come. It was only a matter of time. He'd likely been busy trying to catch up on the work he'd missed. And when he finished, he'd stop by. Wouldn't he?

Her heart pattered faster. She longed to feel the warmth of his summer-green eyes upon her, as they'd been so many times since she'd met him.

"Can I come in?" a muffled voice said from the other side of the door.

"Only if you've washed your hands," Vera called, pouring the hog's foot oil onto the spoon.

The door opened a crack, but before Lily could see who it was, Vera lowered the medicine to her lips and forced it in.

Lily pinched her nose and tried to swallow the mucous-like mixture without it coming back up.

"And how's Lily this evening?" a cheerful male voice asked.

The medicine sank — along with her spirits. It was only Stuart. Again.

Where was Connell?

When Vera backed away, Lily peered beyond Stuart to the empty doorway. Why wasn't he coming? If she didn't know better, she'd almost think he was avoiding her.

Stuart followed her glance to the door, and some of the brightness of his smile faded.

She stuffed down her disappointment, knowing she wasn't being gracious to Stuart, who'd come faithfully every evening to see her. She pulled her attention back to him and forced a smile. "I need you to help me convince Vera I'm better and can get out of bed."

"I'll do no such thing." He crossed to the side of the double bed. "Vera's the best nurse in all of Clare County. In fact, she could open a pharmacy with all the medicine she has."

213

Vera chuckled.

"Too bad she wasn't here when we had the diphtheria epidemic. . . ." A gray cloud settled over his countenance.

"I'm not a miracle worker." Vera wedged the cork back into the bottle. "Besides, sometimes there's nothing we can do, even with our best efforts. As much as we'd like to think we can control everything that happens, we're not that powerful."

Sadness flickered in Stuart's eyes.

Lily wanted to reach out and comfort him, but she held herself back. He'd never told her about the wife and child he'd lost, but she'd heard enough to know the epidemic had hit him hard.

Vera patted the man's arm and then walked to her desk. She'd arranged quilt squares across the top of the desk over an assortment of combs, hairpins, scraps of material, and half-written letters. Each evening by the light of the oil lamp, she worked on piecing the quilt, sewing the colorful squares together with long but even stitches.

Lily could see a pattern emerging from the various diamonds and triangles, but it was still too soon to see the big picture of what it would become.

Vera pushed aside the edge of the quilt,

opened one of the drawers, and stowed the medicine bottle inside.

"When things don't turn out the way we want," the dear woman said softly, "about the only thing we can do is know God is still there piecing together all the scraps of the events in our lives the way He has planned." Her chapped fingers lingered on an intricate pattern. "He sees the big picture even when we don't."

The wistfulness in Vera's voice tugged at Lily's heart. What regrets could a strong woman like Vera have? Was she thinking about her husband's accident? She hadn't had to bury a husband, but surely she'd had to bury her dreams of a real marriage and family.

Maybe Vera was content to sit back and let God piece together her life in whatever way He saw fit, but Lily wasn't planning on waiting too long — if at all — for God to put the scatterings of her life together. She didn't figure God would mind too much if she helped Him get everything into a pattern they both liked.

For a long moment Stuart stared at his hat clutched in his hands. Then he cleared his throat. "Well, you might not be a miracle worker, Vera. But your medicine has worked wonders for Lily."

Lily shook her head. "My recuperation has nothing to do with the medicine —"

"Oh, yes it does." Vera wheeled around, her hands on her hips, her eyes blazing. "You wouldn't be doing nearly as well if it weren't for all my medicine. And you're going to take every last drop I give you."

"And I'll be right here to make sure she does," Stuart added.

"I thought you both liked me," Lily said with half a smile. "But now I can see you're just plain determined to kill me."

Neither of them laughed at her weak attempt at a joke. And she couldn't help wishing Connell were there. He would have peeked at her, and his eyes would have brimmed with laughter.

Her gaze stole to the open door and the kitchen beyond. Where was he? Was he sitting in his usual spot in the dining room? Wasn't he the least bit curious about how she was doing?

Vera lowered herself into the battered rocking chair next to the desk. It squeaked under her weight. "I won't hear any talk of you moving from this bed until you're completely better."

"I can't let you sleep in that old chair another night," Lily said, looking pointedly at the wicker back that was breaking away

216

from the frame. "Or making Mr. Heller sleep in the stables. Besides, it's past time for me to go to Merryville."

"You can't go!" Stuart and Vera exclaimed at the same time.

"I most certainly can." At their protest, she sat up straighter. All the worry and frustration of the past days pooled in her stomach. "Frankie is trapped at the Devil's Ranch against her will. And someone's got to do something about it."

"You're not capable of making that kind of trip," Stuart said in a calmer voice. "Not now. Not with the sub-zero temperatures and winds that have rolled in this week."

Every time she thought of the sweet innocence of Frankie's young face, of her naïveté, of the purity of the girl's youth, Lily wanted to weep over the cruel twist of fate that had swept the girl into a depraved life. Lily had no doubt by the time she got to Merryville and rescued Frankie, the girl wouldn't be innocent anymore. She'd likely have been degraded in all the worst possible ways.

But that couldn't stop Lily from helping. If she didn't, who would?

"We can't sit back and do nothing for the girl, can we? Not when we know she's been forced to do only God knows what —

against her will."

Stuart's face flashed with a burst of indignation. "You're right. We can't sit back and do nothing."

"Then you'll help?" She sat forward and grabbed his hand. "You'll go to Merryville tomorrow and bring her back?"

"Of course I'll help." He glanced at her hand on his, and his eyes widened. When he looked up at her, there was a gentle starry light in his expression that made her pull her hand away and tuck it under the quilt.

"Then you're not afraid of the danger? Of taking a stand against James Carr?"

"Of course not," he said too quickly. "I think it's past time to put the man in his proper place. He's gained far too much power in this county. And I for one would like to lead the way in exposing him and his evil deeds."

"You certainly have the power with your paper."

"I just need the cold hard facts to nail him on what he's been doing. And unfortunately I don't have that yet."

"If you were to write up what happened to Frankie, wouldn't that be enough?"

He shook his head. "It would be one poor little girl's testimony against his and everyone else he's got on his payroll — which is half the county. He'd probably bring charges against me for slander. And the sad thing is, he'd probably win."

The frustration in Lily's stomach ate against the tender lining. "We've got to fight. No matter what, we've got to fight against him."

"I agree. He's been like gangrene on this county since he first came. His evil is slowly rotting away all that's good."

"And I agree too," Vera said, jabbing a thread through her quilting needle. "But I don't want the two of you to do anything foolish and get yourselves hurt. Whatever you do, I want you to be careful."

Lily didn't say anything, because if she did, she knew she'd have to lie. There was nothing safe about what she was planning on doing. But since when was there anything safe about fighting hard for what one believed was right?

CHAPTER 13

Connell forced himself to look at the page of numbers in front of him. But every muscle in his body strained to get up, walk across the room, past the kitchen, and peer into Vera's bedroom at Lily.

Oren had come home from his Sunday picture taking and had gone up to his room early. The Hellers weren't back from their prayer meeting.

There was no one to stop him.

He glanced around the deserted dining room. He was alone. Most of the other men who boarded at the Northern spent their evenings at one tavern or another playing cards and drinking.

No one would see him.

He would make sure he stood outside the door. He wouldn't step a foot inside the room.

His pulse sputtered with sudden determination. He pushed back from the table and stood.

All he wanted was one glimpse of her. Then he'd come back to his spot and wouldn't think about her again the rest of the evening.

He yanked off his spectacles and tossed them onto the ledgers. He deserved to talk with her just as much as anyone else — especially Stuart. The man had tromped in and out of the Northern over the past several days, visiting Lily to his heart's content, and no one said a thing about it.

Why, then, couldn't he walk in and at least say hi to her?

He started around the table, stopped, and turned to the open fireplace and the lines of damp socks hanging to dry in front of it.

Sure, he'd overheard the shanty boys snickering and making all the usual lurid comments during his visits to each of his camps. But it was old news now. The rumors were dying down.

At least for Lily's sake, he hoped they were.

She didn't deserve the blemish to her reputation. And he held himself entirely responsible for the gossip. If only he hadn't unclothed her. At the time, he'd only been worried about saving her life. But he should have known better.

He supposed people would have talked anyway, even if she'd had her dress on. The fact was, he'd been alone with her for close to thirty-two hours. And in a town like Harrison, people would think the worst no matter what.

What difference would it make if he went to her bedroom door now and visited with her?

He made only three steps before the creak of the front door halted him.

"Ah, there you are!" came a muffled voice he knew all too well. The strident tone slammed into the spot between his shoulder blades and stiffened his back.

Slowly he pivoted. There stood his brother, muffled in an ankle-length sealskin coat with its collar turned up over his ears. He wore a fur-lined Scotch Windsor cap and heavy gauntlet gloves. Only his eyes showed between his collar and the brim of his cap.

"Tierney," Connell said as his brother kicked the door closed. But there was no joy in the greeting, not even a hint of warmth for his only sibling. That had evaporated completely two years ago — if it had ever existed in the first place.

"Should have known you'd be here." Tierney grinned and shrugged off his coat.

"You know me. I like to live it up."

Tierney's handsome grin widened. "Yes, you do."

Resentment sloshed in Connell's gut like fermented cider. But he ignored it, as he usually did. "How's Mam?"

"Busy." Tierney slipped off his hat and combed his fingers through his hair. "She's been helping Rosemarie with the new baby."

The new baby. The sourness in Connell's stomach rose up until he could almost smell it. "What did she have? A boy or a girl?"

"Girl." Unmistakable disappointment edged the word.

A twinge of satisfaction released the tension in his back. For once Tierney hadn't gotten something he'd wanted. And it served him right.

His brother had gotten Rosemarie. And after he'd married her, it had only made sense for their dad to give him the supervisor position over the sawmill so he could stay in Bay City near his wife. Of course, Dad had built them a big house. Now Tierney was living a life of luxury and ease, part of the wealthy circle of timber-rich families, going to dinner parties, dances, and the theater.

"It's too cold out there." Tierney tugged off his thick boots.

Connell ground his teeth to keep from saying anything. Little did Tierney know how difficult it was to work in the bitterly cold wilderness day after day, doing back-breaking work, eating the same plain fare for every meal, sleeping in a tiny unheated room in a hotel, and sharing a frigid out-house with the fourteen other men who boarded at the Northern.

Tierney had no right to complain about anything. Ever.

"I tried to convince Dad to let me wait to come up here until it warmed up," Tierney said. "But he was pretty adamant that I head out to check on you."

At Tierney's words, Connell stiffened and had the brief urge to wrestle his brother to the ground.

As much as he wanted to clobber his younger brother from time to time, he figured it wouldn't do any good. It wouldn't change what had happened.

He returned to his spot in the corner and picked up his spectacles.

"Besides, it was past time for an update on production." Tierney sauntered toward the fireplace.

Connell slid back onto the bench, his defenses rising like a wall. "You know we're behind after last week's thaw." Why was it that the visits from Tierney and Dad always made him feel like a little boy who couldn't live up to expectations?

Tierney tossed a log onto the fire. "We're confident you'll find a way to make up for the loss."

Connell didn't know which was worse, having Dad come and criticize him for every failure or having Tierney visit and act like the boss. Dad always said he'd leave the business to whichever of them worked the hardest for it. But Connell figured Dad was more likely to hand the reins to whichever son he liked the best.

And somehow Tierney always seemed to come out on top.

Tierney warmed his hands over the flames for a moment. Then he turned and gave Connell a wide grin, one that had a characteristic hint of devilish mischief. "Truth be told, Dad was in a hurry to send me up here because we got a report you were causing some trouble."

Connell sat forward. "Trouble? What kind of trouble?" But even as the words left his mouth, he knew what Tierney was going to say, and he didn't want to hear it.

Tierney's eyes glittered and his grin turned crooked with carnality. "We got word that you're living with a whore."

"That's not true." Connell jumped to his feet and hot anger tumbled through him, setting him off-balance.

Tierney laughed, but it was hard and crass. "Aw, come on, big brother. When I heard the news I was proud of you. I figured it was past time you made a man of yourself."

Connell clenched his fist, resisting the urge to go after his knife. "I'm not living with a woman."

Tierney only laughed again. "You don't have to deny it to me. You know I don't care."

And the sad thing was that Tierney really didn't care. That's why every time he came to Harrison on so-called *business,* Connell had to turn a blind eye to the fact that Tierney spent more time in the brothels than in his business office.

"The truth is, Tierney —" Connell started. But the hot words died on his lips. What difference would it make if he finally got up the nerve to tell Tierney the truth? That Rosemarie was a sweet woman. That Tierney was treating her dishonorably. That if Connell had been the one to marry her, he wouldn't have needed to find pleasure in the arms of any other woman. Rosemarie would have been enough.

What Connell really wanted to ask his brother was why he had wooed Rosemarie away from him when he hadn't planned to give her the kind of love she deserved. But of course, Tierney hadn't respected Rosemarie before they'd gotten married. Why would that change afterward?

"Look," Tierney said. "I know Dad is boiling mad about the whole affair, but you can be honest with me."

"Well, you can just take your sorry behind right back to Bay City and tell Dad there's nothing going on."

"Don't worry. That's what I was planning to do." Tierney winked. "But in the meantime, you've got to figure out a way to be more private with your affairs."

Connell growled out his growing frustration. "I don't have anything to hide."

The front door opened with a blast of evening air, and Stuart stepped inside. He rubbed his hands together and blew into them.

He greeted Tierney, who shook hands with him as if they were long-lost friends. That's the way Tierney had always been — charming. And it irritated Connell that Tierney could so easily sway women and men into liking him. Even Stuart, the one friend who knew the struggles he had with his brother, had fallen prey to the charm.

"I had to stop in Averill on my way up here." Tierney plopped down on the bench next to Connell. "Nothing like a couple drinks from the Red Keg to warm me up for the rest of the ride."

Stuart laughed, and Connell couldn't understand why.

"Stuart?" a soft voice called from the kitchen. Lily's voice.

Connell's heart flipped like one of Vera's johnnycakes. He jumped back to his feet. Was Lily finally feeling better?

Stuart straightened and rubbed a hand over the thinning hair of his head, slicking it back.

Lily peeked around the corner into the dining room. Her hair tumbled in wild abandon over her shoulders and around her face. Her honeyed skin was paler than usual, but her eyes were darker and more luminous than ever. They were clouded with the traces of sleep, as if she'd just awoken.

When those rich woodsy eyes collided with his, they knocked the breath from him. He could only stare at her, witless, sense-less, and completely speechless with the aching desire to be with her.

"Connell?" A welcoming smile curved her lips. "Where have you been?"

She stepped into the doorway then. She'd wrapped one of Vera's quilts around her, but it couldn't entirely conceal the white cotton nightgown she was wearing or the colorful striped socks upon her feet. "I've been waiting to see you." She tucked a stray curl behind her ear.

His heart did another flip. "I've been wanting to check on you, but —"

Stuart cleared his throat.

Connell rushed. "But every night Oren's been beating me away from your door with the butt of his rifle."

Her smile widened. "At least he's not threatening to shoot you."

Connell grinned. "That's a first."

"And who is this lovely creature?" Tierney asked, glancing from Connell to Lily and back, his eyebrow quirking into a roguish slant.

A fierce and swift protectiveness gripped Connell. He scowled at Tierney, wishing he'd stayed back in Bay City where he belonged. He didn't want Tierney meeting Lily. In fact, he didn't even want him looking at her.

As if sensing the turmoil inside him, Tierney's grin turned hard and his eyes brimmed with a lust that frightened Connell.

"It's none of your business." Connell moved into Tierney's line of vision, blocking him from seeing Lily.

"Ah." Tierney grinned up at him, almost laughing at him. "So this is your woman."

The way he said *woman* insinuated a relationship far more intimate than friendship. Connell clenched his teeth and fought the urge to swing his knuckles into Tierney's handsome face and disfigure him so that no woman would ever again fall under his spell.

"His *woman?*" Lily's voice rose clear and strong. She stepped forward, her face tense and sparking with anger. "I'm not any man's *woman.*"

Tierney's grin only widened. "And I see you picked a fiery one. They're the best kind."

"Don't say another word, Tierney," Connell growled. He stepped toward his brother and shoved him.

"It's no big secret anymore." Tierney laughed.

"I don't know who you are or what you've heard," Lily said. "But you're obviously misinformed."

"Is that so?" Tierney peered around Connell and appraised Lily again, seeming to take in every detail from her thick hair to the lacy edge of her nightgown.

"Who are you? And why are you here?" she demanded. The fury in her eyes only made her more beautiful.

"This is my brother." Connell narrowed his gaze at Tierney, hoping he'd take the clue to stop talking. "He's come up from Bay City for a few days."

The retort on Lily's lips died, and the thin line of her brows lifted in surprise.

"Sometimes he doesn't know how to take a hint and be quiet," Connell added.

"And sometimes Connell doesn't know how to speak his mind." Tierney winked at Lily, laying on the charm like he usually did.

Connell's fist tightened. His entire body revolted at the thought of Tierney attempting to woo Lily.

Lily regarded Tierney for a long moment, as though trying to see beyond his cocky grin.

Finally she looked at Connell. "He looks a little bit like you, but I'm guessing that's where the similarity ends."

She was right. He and Tierney had never had much in common.

"Now, Stuart." She glanced around the dining room. "Where's Frankie?"

Stuart shifted, and the mirth in his face dissipated. "I couldn't get to her."

"Why not?" Disappointment dripped from

her voice.

"She wasn't with the other girls," he said. "And when I asked about her, no one would say anything."

Connell wasn't surprised. When Stuart had told him yesterday of his plan to travel to Merryville to look for Frankie, he'd warned his friend he would come back empty-handed.

But Stuart had insisted on going anyway — claiming he was planning to track down a couple of potential eyewitnesses to the jail fire while he was there. Connell suspected his real motivation in going was that he wanted to become Lily's hero, for he surely would have earned heroic status if he'd returned with Frankie.

"Wasn't there any way to sneak in?" she asked.

Stuart shook his head. "There were bouncers everywhere — at all the stairways and at all the doors."

Lily's shoulders slumped and she leaned against the door-frame, almost as if she were too weak to stand another second.

Stuart darted toward her. "I think you need to get back in bed. You're still not well."

"I'm fine."

He offered her his arm, and when she took

it, Connell had the urge to rush over to her, sweep her off her feet, and carry her to her bed.

But if he did that, he could only imagine what Tierney would say.

Instead, he held himself back, and after she was gone, he spun on his brother. "Don't say anything more about her. Not one more thing."

Tierney shrugged. "And here I thought you'd finally loosened up a little."

"Just stay away from her."

"Fine. If it makes you happy, I won't interfere."

Somehow, Tierney's words only made him more uneasy.

"I won't say anything else." Tierney reached down and tugged off one of his thick wool socks. "Except . . ."

The word hung between them while Tierney pulled off his other damp sock. He tossed them over the line, heedless of the other socks that fell to the floor with the impact.

"Except," he said again, "Dad wants you to stop living with the girl, which means you'll have to find another place to board."

"That's ridiculous —"

"You've got to learn how to do this right, brother." Tierney pulled a silver cigar case out of his vest pocket. "You can see her all you want. Privately. But you've got to learn to keep the rumors to a minimum."

"And I suppose that's what you do every time you go out carousing." The sarcasm in Connell's voice couldn't compare to the acidity in his stomach.

Tierney clicked open the thin case and lifted out one of his custom-made cigars. "Nobody pays any attention to a man frequenting a tavern, even if it happens to have other amenities. But everyone notices when a man of your power and position fornicates publicly."

Connell could only shake his head.

"Dad's angry about what you're doing." Tierney snipped the cap from the head of the cigar. "He wants the rumors cleared up immediately."

The irony of the situation mocked Connell. He knew he shouldn't have been surprised by it, but he was, nevertheless. Somehow he'd ended up displeasing Dad when he'd done nothing wrong. And yet Tierney seemed to be earning more and more of their dad's favor, even though he made a regular habit of committing adultery.

Where was the fairness in that?

But then again, had there ever been any

justice when it came to Tierney or Dad?

There certainly hadn't been any with what had happened with Rosemarie. Connell had tried hard to do the right thing by keeping their relationship pure. All the while Tierney had been — he wouldn't let himself think about what Tierney had done.

And who had come out the winner? Who had ended up pleasing Dad?

Tierney sat back, lit his cigar, and took a long puff with an air of satisfaction.

Irritation curled through Connell. "Tell Dad he can believe what he wants. But eventually the truth is going to come out."

Connell could only pray that was true, that Dad would know he'd worked hard and lived with integrity the way he'd wanted him to.

And even if Dad never found out the truth, at least he could stand before God some day with a clean heart. Wasn't that enough?

Chapter 14

Lily glanced over her shoulder to the front door of the Northern, half expecting Vera to be standing there waving her wooden spoon, demanding she come back inside.

But the dear woman still hadn't noticed she was gone.

Lily took a deep breath of the bitterly cold air and fought back a cough. She huddled deeper into her coat and hoped Vera would forgive her for disobeying her orders to stay in bed.

The fact was, she had too much to do to waste another day lying around. Especially with Stuart's failed attempt to free Frankie over the weekend.

Lily's mind had been altogether too busy the past several days plotting how she could fight against the depravity that ruled Harrison. And it was time for her to get up and do something about it.

Her footsteps crunched in the icy layer of

snow, and the wind slashed her cheeks. But not even the cruelty of the north woods winter could hold her back. She was determined to meet with Stuart, lay out her plan, and enlist his printing press.

At midday, Main Street was nearly deserted. Like most of the lumber towns, Harrison didn't come to life until dark, when the men descended upon the taverns after a long day of work.

Most of the men who boarded in town were other camp bosses, businessmen, railway engineers, mill workers, and laborers who worked at the loading station — like Jimmy Neil — unloading logs the narrow gauges brought out of the various camps and reloading them onto the beds of the Pere Marquette railroad.

Very few of the men brought their families to the remote lumber town and so had little better to do in the evenings than frequent the places of debauchery.

Lily glanced in disdain to the many taverns she'd visited over the past several weeks. If only the town had more wholesome diversions — like a church or a school.

Ahead of Lily, the bell jingled on the pharmacy door as it swung open. Maggie Carr stepped out, tossing one end of her scarlet scarf over her shoulder. She carried a parcel wrapped in brown paper and tied with string.

When she glimpsed Lily, she stopped. Above the edge of the scarf that covered her mouth and nose, recognition flared in the woman's eyes.

Lily's footsteps faltered. "You had no right to take Frankie." The words burst out before she could stop them.

Maggie's cheeks rose and her eyes narrowed in the telltale signs of a self-satisfied smile. "You had no right to interfere."

Lily's insides curdled. "I had every right to step in. And I won't rest until I find a way to run you and your husband out of town."

"Don't waste your energy, sugar." Maggie's voice was laced with cold contempt. And before Lily could say anything more, the woman flipped the other side of her scarf over her shoulder and turned away.

Lily had the sudden urge to grab her, hold her hostage, threaten to pull off the scarf, and reveal her deformities unless she promised to let Frankie go. But instead, Lily watched with frustration as Maggie marched across the street, heading in the direction of the Stockade.

"Maggie Carr is a wicked woman," Lily said as she walked into the *Harrison Herald* moments later. The air was heavy with the metallic scent of ink and oil. The steady *thump-thump* of the hand-fed printing press added to the pounding of her determination.

Stuart lifted his foot from the treadle of the jobber, and all the various wheels whirred to a standstill. His brow lifted with surprise. "What are you doing here? You're not supposed to be out of bed yet."

Lily crossed the room to the only chair, which was piled with old newspapers. "If I have to stay in bed one more day, I'm going to wither up and die." She hefted the papers onto the already littered desk.

"You need a couple more days of recuperation, at least." Stuart's voice rang with worry.

"I've weathered worse." With her teeth, she tugged off her mitten. "Besides, I'm a strong woman."

Stuart grabbed a rag and wiped his ink-blackened fingertips. "Come on. I'm taking you back."

She dropped into the chair.

Haunted fear rimmed his eyes, as if he were seeing someone else instead of her. Was her illness bringing back too many memories of the wife he'd lost?

She wanted to tell him to stop worrying,

that she wasn't his wife and she wasn't going to die — at least anytime soon. "I promise I'll go back to bed just as soon as you agree to my plan."

"What plan?" Connell's voice came from the doorway.

Her heart skittered forward like a young colt learning to walk. She shifted in the chair, eager for another chance to see him. The encounter in the dining room the evening before had been too brief and had only left her longing for more of him.

He leaned against the doorframe, his arms crossed. Dark circles shadowed his eyes, and his fair hair was jabbed into an unruly mess, almost as if he'd spent a sleepless night in his office.

She gave him a smile, one that likely let him see all her desire. At the moment, she didn't care if he knew how much she'd missed him.

But he didn't smile back — not even to give her the barest hint of pleasure that he was as glad to see her as she was him, like he had last night. Instead, he looked tired, almost sad.

Her heartbeat tripped and stumbled over itself. What was wrong? Where was the sweet heat in his eyes that had recently reached out to caress her whenever they met?

"So what's your plan?" he asked again.

Her smile faded, and what was left of it felt brittle. "I'm ready to start a Red Ribbon Society here in Harrison."

Connell didn't say anything.

"I know you don't think it'll make much of a difference," she hurried. "But if we want to fight James Carr, we need to stir the public opinion against him. A Red Ribbon Society could be one way to do that."

Stuart rubbed his beard as though pondering her suggestion. But Connell's eyes only narrowed.

"Since we can't use the law to stop that villain," she said more emphatically, "our only choice is for all the God-fearing citizens of Harrison and the surrounding area to rise up and drive him out."

Both men were quiet. The only sound was the pop of wood in the corner stove.

Had she grabbed their attention? Would they go for her plan? Her blood spurted with a burst of anticipation. "Of course you'll still need to investigate Carr's dealings and see if you can find something concrete against him. But in the meantime, we can begin to expose his corruption to everyone in the county."

Stuart nodded. "Okay. I see where you're going with this. And it just might work."

"Maybe you could print up flyers announcing the start of the Red Ribbon Society along with the date and time of our first meeting."

"If we rally everyone against him," Stuart continued, "it'll be a lot easier to bring him down when we finally do have solid evidence."

"Exactly."

His eyes took on a spark that matched the fervor inside her.

Connell's tired expression only drooped. "Your idea has potential," he finally said. "But you have to remember Carr is a dangerous man, and he'll find a way to hurt anyone who takes a stand against him. I doubt you'll find many who will want to risk making an enemy of him."

"That's why we've got to band together against him," she said. "There's power in solidarity. And usually once a few people make a stand, the rest will follow."

"Good luck getting even a few," Connell said. "People are afraid of him."

"You mean *you're* afraid of him." Sudden irritation pushed her straighter in the chair.

Connell didn't say anything for a long moment. Then he sighed. "I'm not afraid of him personally. But he has the power to damage McCormick Lumber."

"Then you won't join in the crusade?"

"I'm not willing to jeopardize everything my father's worked for all these years just for the slight chance that we can raise public awareness and dislike of Carr. What good will it do?"

Anger needled her, driving her to her feet. "How can you say such a thing?" Her voice trembled. Even though she'd expected less enthusiasm from Connell for her plan, she'd hoped with all that had happened to Frankie that he'd had a change of heart about fighting against the evil.

"I want to see Carr brought to justice as much as you do," Connell said quickly. "But a bunch of angry townspeople won't be able to make a dent against him. We're going to have to wait until we have something big to use against him."

"I can't wait!" When she'd lain in bed and formulated her plans, she'd been so sure she was doing what God wanted. He was putting the pieces of her life together — like Vera had mentioned. And surely He wouldn't mind her stepping in and moving things along more quickly. Oren would finish his picture taking in another week or two. Her time in Harrison was numbered. "I need to do all I can right away."

"If we rush, we'll only bring trouble upon

243

ourselves. Haven't you learned that by now?"

"The lives of precious young girls are at stake. What's more important? Your father's bank account or saving lives?"

"Aw, come on, Lily. That's not a fair question."

She shot a glance at Stuart, hoping for his support.

He reached absently for a wooden box on the table next to the press. An assortment of lead type clinked together within the cases.

"Stuart knows how much trouble he'll bring down on himself if he faces off against Carr," Connell said. "Don't you, Stu?"

Stuart hesitated. Then he looked at Connell. "I understand what you're saying, but if Lily is brave enough to fight against the devil, don't you think we should too, no matter what it might cost us?"

"You could end up losing a lot of business," Connell said. "And if Carr gets mad enough, you'll risk losing the newspaper altogether."

"Maybe that's a chance I'll have to take." Stuart glanced at her as if seeking her affirmation.

She gave him what she hoped was an encouraging smile. "We all have to make sacrifices in the fight for what's right."

"Think about it, Connell," Stuart pleaded. "As a man with status in this community, if you join in the fight, you'll set a great example to many others and give them courage."

Connell was quiet for a long moment. Finally he sighed. "As much as I'd like to see Carr get what he deserves, I can't throw away everything I've worked so hard to build in the McCormick business for the slim chance you'll be able to stop the man."

Lily didn't realize she'd been holding her breath until it swooshed out, taking all her anger with it. All that was left was an empty ache — regret that Connell wasn't the man she wanted him to be, the kind of man who would sacrifice for things that really mattered.

As though sensing her frustration with him, he lifted his head. "Don't worry. You won't have to put up with me any longer. I'm moving out of the Northern today."

"You are?" she said at the same time as Stuart.

She didn't want to care where he went or what he did — but she did care. A whole lot.

"With all the recent rumors . . ." he started but then stopped and kicked a wadded paper across the littered floor.

Oren had been muttering under his breath all week about nasty rumors men were spreading about her and Connell, but she'd hoped he was being overprotective like he usually was. "Tell me what they're saying," she said. "I can handle it."

Faint streaks of red crawled up his neck.

She waited for a moment for Connell to elaborate. When he didn't, she turned to Stuart. "They better not be jumping to the worst kinds of conclusions. They know Connell's a good man and wouldn't take advantage of me."

Stuart dug his fingers around in the case of type and peered at the various pieces intently, as if nothing were more important at that moment than finding a particular letter.

"What are people saying?" she asked, glancing from one man to the other. But neither would meet her gaze.

Wariness settled in her stomach. "I guess that means people are assuming the worst?"

Finally Connell's eyes met hers. The apology in them only made her more uneasy. "The rumors are ugly, Lily. And I'd rather you didn't have to hear them."

"I'm sure I'll find out eventually."

Anguish mixed with the apology in his

eyes and wrinkled his brow. "They're saying that I'm living with you in sin — that you're my harlot."

Even though his words came as no surprise, they crashed into her anyway with a force that left her reeling with embarrassment.

His sad expression told her he wasn't exaggerating.

"Well then, we're just going to have to tell everyone they're mistaken."

"It's not that easy. Especially not when the rumor has already reached my dad over in Bay City."

A new kind of horror added to the chaos in her gurgling stomach. Connell's dad? Bay City? She reached a trembling hand for the chair behind her and lowered herself into it. How completely awful. She'd never expected to meet his parents, never even once considered it. But, even so, she didn't want them to know her as a prostitute.

A *prostitute*.

She shuddered and pressed shaking fingers against her temple. She'd always taken care with her reputation. Wasn't she fighting against the very thing for which she was now being accused?

"That's why I'm moving out," Connell said. "If I keep my distance from you, then hopefully the rumors will die down."

How could this have happened? Had she brought this upon herself with her foolish headstrong ways?

Her heart pounded against her chest. If the townspeople thought she was a prostitute, why would they join with her in trying to rid Harrison of Carr? They wouldn't trust her. They'd consider her a hypocrite. They'd hesitate to join her efforts to start a Red Ribbon Society — if they would give it any thought at all.

"I'm sorry, Lily," Connell said softly.

"It's not your fault."

"I take full responsibility. I should have moved out earlier in the week."

"Busybodies will always find ways to spread gossip." She pushed a hand against her heart, trying to fend off the pain and the shame. She'd never let discouragement defeat her in the past. She'd always stood strong against adversity.

Why should she do any differently now? She couldn't let a few bad rumors ruin her plans.

With a burst of heated passion, she shoved herself back to her feet. "I don't care what anyone thinks about me. I won't let the rumors stop me from starting the Red Ribbon Society." Her heart thudded forward, not with the usual fervor, but forward nevertheless. She might be having a slight setback, but she couldn't let it change her determination to do all that God was calling her to do.

She could feel Connell's gaze upon her, but she couldn't bear to look in his eyes, not when she knew what people were saying about them — that they were lovers, that she'd lain in his arms and shared intimacies with him.

A flush stole over her. It was a good thing no one had to know she really had lain against him. But even as another wave of embarrassment coursed through her, warmth followed in its wake.

She was ashamed to admit how much she'd enjoyed being with him. And the truth was she couldn't stop from dreaming about being in his arms again.

CHAPTER 15

From his second-story office, Connell stared down at Stuart and Lily standing together on Main Street in front of the *Harrison Herald.* They'd been in and out of businesses for the last hour, passing out the flyer Stuart had printed yesterday announcing the start of their Red Ribbon Society.

With cheeks flushed from the cold, Lily beamed at Stuart, apparently pleased with their efforts. And Stuart grinned back, adoration lighting his face.

Connell's fingers tightened with the need to run down and pull Stuart away from Lily. His friend obviously cared about her. From the way he rushed to do her bidding every time she uttered a word, it was clear he found great pleasure in being with her.

The question was, did Lily feel the same way about Stuart?

Connell's gut twisted at the thought. He didn't want Lily to care for Stu. He didn't want her to care about anyone — except for him.

Yet, what hope did he have of winning Lily's heart when they had such different goals and aspirations? On the other hand, she and Stuart seemed to work well together. And Stuart was such a decent guy.

He'd even invited Connell to move into his house with him — at least until Lily and Oren left Harrison.

Connell didn't have the heart to refuse the kindness of his friend, even though he'd had to wade through the clutter and disarray that covered every square inch of floor in Stuart's home. Connell doubted the place had been cleaned since Stuart's wife had last set about the task before she'd become ill.

The modest two-story home sat on the edge of Harrison with a cluster of other residences. When Connell had shoved his bag under the single bed in the room Stuart had pointed him to, he had to fight back a depressing shudder.

A wooden rocking horse sat in one corner, the red paint of the saddle chipped and peeling away. A child-sized cowboy hat and a hand-carved gun lay on the floor next to the horse.

Connell wanted to gather all the reminders of Stuart's past life and put them into a crate. It was time for the man to move on and find a woman who could make his house a home again, who could clear out the traces of pain and bring him new joy.

A weight pressed against Connell's heart. Yes, Stuart deserved a good woman like Lily. They were alike in so many ways. She would most certainly bring him joy.

Connell leaned his shoulder against the window frame and watched the way one of her curls tickled her pink cheek.

If only he didn't want Lily for himself.

"So I talked with Carr last night." Tierney sat at the desk, pretending to flip through the books and take an interest in the figures. It was the first time his brother had made any attempt to think about business since he'd arrived. Of course, he couldn't put it off any longer, since he was planning to leave in an hour.

Tierney's eyes were glazed from the past several sleepless nights of drinking and whoring. And Connell doubted he could even read the careful calculations within the ledgers, much less make sense of them.

"Please tell me you didn't go to the Stockade." Connell glanced in the distance to the tavern towering on the hill above town. "After all I told you about the way

Carr is tricking girls into working for him, I'd expect you to boycott him."

"You're exaggerating. As usual." The chair squeaked under Tierney's weight as he leaned back and combed a hand through his disheveled hair. What would Rosemarie think when Tierney returned home hung over, with bloodshot eyes and the sour stench of liquor in every pore? Would she notice? Or was she used to it by now?

"You know as well as I do that Carr is a scoundrel." Connell didn't care that his voice was testy.

"He's a powerful businessman." The legs of the chair thumped against the floor. "And according to him, you've been stirring up trouble lately."

"I'd say it's the other way around — he's the one causing the trouble."

"Stay out of his way, Connell." Tierney's voice was suddenly more sober than it had been since he'd arrived. "He said if you interfere again we'll have more than a few damaging rumors to deal with."

A gust of surprise whirled through Connell. Had Carr started the rumors about him and Lily? Had he made sure the ugly news spread far enough to reach Dad? It made sense. Dad, like most of the other lumber bosses, turned a blind eye to the

253

way the tavern owners operated their businesses. The taverns kept the shanty boys happy and ensured the wild behavior stayed out of the camps.

Besides, if a man like Carr didn't like a particular lumber company, he had the power to influence the shanty boys against the company. And Connell couldn't afford to lose shanty boys, especially during the busiest time of the season.

"Don't mess with Carr anymore." Tierney closed the ledgers with a slap. "That's all I have to say."

Connell couldn't keep his irritation from resurfacing, as it had many times over the past few days. He'd be glad when Tierney was gone. In his few sober moments, all Tierney had done was boss him around — as he was doing now.

Tierney tucked the ledgers under his arm and pushed away from the desk, letting the chair scrape the floor.

"You can't take my books with you," Connell said.

"How else am I going to show Dad what you've been up to?"

"Maybe if you'd actually taken the time to listen to my reports —"

"Aw, come on Connell." Tierney stood and stretched. "Stop being so uptight. You probably have the numbers all memorized anyway."

Connell wanted to rip the books away from Tierney and send him home empty-handed. What would Dad think of Tierney then?

"Guess I'll head out now." Tierney reached for his coat on the peg near the door. "That'll give me time to stop at the Red Keg again before heading for home."

"I can tell you're in a hurry to get home to your wife and new baby."

Tierney just grinned and then glanced out the front window. His grin widened. "Now I see what you've been looking at."

Connell peered outside again to where Lily still stood talking with Stuart. Her eyes sparked with all the passion that bubbled inside her. The pale sickness in her face was finally gone, replaced with the usual warm tones. She was flushed, and alive, and vibrant. And when she gave a bright smile to Stuart, a jealous twine slid around his heart and cinched painfully.

Tierney's glassy eyes narrowed and flamed with sudden lust. "She sure is pretty."

Connell silently agreed. She was beautiful. But he didn't need Tierney to say it. He'd rather Tierney leave. "You better get going."

"Her face is familiar." Tierney stared down at her. "I'm guessing I met her somewhere else. Maybe at one of the houses of entertainment in Bay City before she moved up here?"

"No. You've never met her. I guarantee it, one hundred percent."

Tierney was silent for a long moment but then shrugged. "Maybe I'm just confusing her with Bella."

Connell had heard the shanty boys talk about Bella, the young beauty Carr kept up at the Stockade. She was untouchable, or so they claimed. Apparently Carr only let his favorite friends see her and have turns with her. Or in the case of Tierney, those who paid good money.

"I'll have to find an excuse for Dad to send me up to Harrison again soon. Now that I've met Bella."

"Just stay home where you belong."

Tierney grinned. "So you want to keep Bella for yourself too?"

Protest rose swiftly within Connell. "I've never seen the girl —"

"Oh, that's right. You don't need Bella. You've got Lily." Tierney looked out the window down at Lily again. He studied her again and then whistled under his breath. "She looks enough like Bella that they could

256

be cousins or sisters or something."

Sisters? Connell tensed, and his gaze swung back to the Stockade. What were the chances that this Bella might be the sister Lily was looking for? Twenty-five percent? Fifty?

"She looks like Lily?" he asked.

Tierney's eyes sparkled with mirth. "So now you're interested?"

Connell shook his head, fresh irritation adding to the funnel cloud winding through him. "Is that all you think about? Bedding women?"

Tierney snorted. "What man doesn't?"

"I don't." At least he worked hard to keep his thoughts from swaying in that direction. He'd long ago decided if he didn't let his mind dwell on his lusts, he'd have a much easier time resisting the temptations when they came his way.

Tierney tugged on his hat. "The problem is you've always thought you're better than everyone else. And you're not. It's time for you to finally admit it."

"I'm not going to admit wanting to sleep with Bella when I don't. I'm just trying to figure out if she's the sister Lily's looking for."

Tierney's brow shot up and his grin quirked.

"Her sister disappeared back in the fall, and she's been looking for her ever since."

"Well, there's one way to find out if Bella's her sister." Tierney stepped toward the door. "I can describe her to Lily and see what she thinks."

"Wait a minute." Connell grabbed for Tierney, but his brother had already opened the door. "I don't think we should involve Lily yet." He didn't want to think what Lily might do if Bella was the girl she'd been looking for all these months. Lily was too impetuous. She'd likely run up to the Stockade the first chance she had and get herself hurt.

"Stop!" he called after Tierney.

But his brother was descending the steps two at a time, tossing a grin over his shoulder as if they were playing a game of tag.

"Let me tell her," Connell shouted, "after I've done my own investigation."

Tierney didn't look back. Instead he jumped the last four steps and darted toward the door, leaving Connell little choice but to follow him at full speed.

Connell raced outside, determined to wrestle Tierney to the ground and give him the thrashing he needed.

But Tierney skidded on the icy street away from him, nearly barreling into Lily in his haste. "Describe your sister to me."

She took a step away from him, out of his reach, letting him fumble to steady himself. Her brow lifted, and she regarded him without a trace of warmth.

At least Connell could console himself with one thing — Lily hadn't swooned over Tierney the way other women always seemed to. In fact, she hadn't shown the slightest interest in him.

"Why do you want to know about my sister?"

"Never mind, Tierney." Connell crossed his arms to ward off the cold air that was seeping through his mackinaw. "I'll deal with it later."

But Tierney was already speaking. "I think I might have found the sister you've been looking for."

She drew in a sharp breath, and her eyes turned to the size of the winter sun. "What do you mean?"

"Don't listen to him, Lily," Connell said quickly.

She'd already fixed her gaze upon Tierney, and the determination in their dark depths was strong enough to chain a man. Connell knew Tierney wouldn't be able to go anywhere until she got what she wanted from him.

And he knew Tierney was all too willing to divulge the information, especially now that Connell had asked him not to.

"I met a girl up at the Stockade this week," Tierney said. "And she looks a lot like you."

Lily's mittened hand fluttered to her chest. "A girl who looks like me? How?"

"The same dark curly hair and the same eyes."

"That could be any girl."

"And she had a beauty mark right here on her chin." Tierney pointed to a spot near the edge of his jaw.

Lily gasped and turned to Stuart. "It must be her. She's always had a spot on her chin, and she loathes it."

Stuart's gaze connected with Connell's. Hesitation filled his friend's face.

Connell shook his head, hoping Stuart would read the unspoken message: They couldn't let Lily do anything rash.

"Her name is Bella." Tierney tossed Connell a satisfied glance. And Connell pretended not to notice the immaturity.

"But my sister's name is Daisy."

Stuart cleared his throat. "Carr makes a lot of his girls change their names."

"Well now" — Lily's face lit with growing excitement — "if Daisy changed her name, that might be why no one knew about her."

"Carr usually reserves a couple girls for his special clients." Stuart glanced sideways at Tierney. "That means the ordinary shanty boys wouldn't know much about her other than hearsay."

"It must be her." Lily grasped Stuart's arm. "We need to go get her. Now."

"Right now?" Stuart asked.

"I can't wait another moment. If it's really her, then I need to go *now*." She tugged on Stuart's arm.

Stuart didn't budge.

Lily linked her arm through his and pulled him harder. "Come on. I've been waiting for this moment for months."

"You can't march up there and demand to see Daisy," Connell said. "You remember what happened with Frankie."

"That's the problem. *Nothing* has happened with Frankie." Her voice was edged with frustration. "Absolutely nothing. And I can't let that be true of Daisy too."

With that, she spun and began to stride away from them, her boots crunching in loud defiance, the white puffs of her breath coming in short bursts.

Tierney stepped back, crossed his arms, and watched them, his eyes sparkling with merriment — as if he were watching a scene unfold on the stage at the theater.

If Lily got in trouble, Connell was going to hold Tierney responsible. If only the scoundrel had minded his own business.

"Go home, Tierney!" Anger pounded through Connell's chest with a ferocity that rivaled what he'd felt the day he'd discovered Tierney with Rosemarie, both half clothed and flushed with their passion. "Just go away. And don't come back."

He didn't wait to see Tierney's reaction to his harsh words. If he never saw Tierney again, he'd count himself a happy man.

He sucked in a breath of air that froze his lungs and plunged after Lily, easily overtaking her. He circled his fingers around her arm and forced her to a stop.

"Let me go," she said between clenched teeth, holding herself as rigid as a hardwood beech. "I need to go get her. That's my baby sister. She needs me. I can feel it."

"You have to understand you can't go up there by yourself and expect Carr to let her go. Not Bella — his big moneymaker."

Along Main Street, faces peeked out of frosty windows. Some even opened their doors to watch the commotion. He didn't have to try to imagine what people were thinking. He knew the scene would only stir up more gossip.

"Go ahead and get mad at me," he half whispered. "But I'm not letting you go up there." Her safety was too important to let her run off to the Stockade. "After the way Carr kidnapped Frankie in broad daylight, I don't trust the man. Not in the least."

Her eyes wavered.

"I'm not the enemy, Lily," he said softly. "Believe it or not, I really do want to help you."

She trembled, just slightly, but it was enough for him to feel all the worry, excitement, and sorrow coursing through her.

"Let's come up with a plan together. Okay?" Even as he said the words, he knew he could do nothing less than help her. Maybe he'd regret the decision later when he was sane. But at that moment, with her heartache over Daisy so plain in every tense muscle, he couldn't resist. "We'll figure out something — some way to get her out of there. Together."

She hesitated and searched his face. "If you want to help me, then come with me now. I can't bear to think of her being in that place another minute. Even another second is too long."

"But Carr won't let her go without a fight. If we have any hope of getting her out alive, we'll have to do it in secret." If Daisy even wanted rescuing. But he didn't dare douse Lily's hopes.

She shook her head, impatience battling across the lovely features of her face. But then she glanced to the growing crowd they were attracting. She quickly broke free of his grasp and took a step back.

"I suppose as hard as it is, I'll need to tie up my impulsiveness?"

"If you tie it up, then you'll prevent me from having to tie *you* up." He hoped she could hear the banter in his voice. "And I don't think you want me wrestling you to the ground and hog-tying you in the middle of Main Street."

"Since everyone is already talking about us, why not give them something more?" The wry grin that tugged at one corner of her lips sent relief blowing through him.

"Then you'll wait?"

She nodded, but all trace of humor dissipated. The expression in her face said she'd wait, but it wouldn't be for long.

Tierney was still standing next to Stuart. Still smirking. Everything Tierney had just warned him about came careening back through his gut like a horse-drawn logging sled racing out of control on icy roads.

Tierney had made it very clear he wasn't supposed to interfere with Carr's business

264

again. If he did, Carr would find a way to punish McCormick Lumber.

He didn't even want to begin to imagine what Carr would do to anyone who helped steal one of his lucrative girls.

Connell swallowed hard.

How could he possibly help Lily rescue Daisy?

But how could he live with himself if he didn't?

CHAPTER 16

Under the dim oil lamp in the dining room, Lily stared at the rough sketch of the Stockade, trying to ingrain every detail into her memory.

"He keeps his dogs here." Stuart tapped the large piece of newsprint. "They're at the back entry of the compound."

"Does he keep them chained?" Connell peered over the edge of his spectacles to the *X* with the word *dogs* scrawled underneath.

"Bass didn't say." Stuart reached for another molasses cookie from the plate Vera had brought out from the kitchen when the men had arrived. In several quick bites, he devoured it.

Lily had lost count of how many he'd eaten — at least half of the heap. Of course Oren had helped eat a few but was now sitting in a chair in front of the fireplace, his feet propped on a crate and his pipe in his mouth.

"Good cookies," Stuart said again, as he had after each one he ate.

From her spot across the dining-room table, Vera narrowed her eyes on Connell. "At least one of you will go home with a full belly."

From the way Vera hovered over Connell every time he came into the Northern, it was clear she missed him.

Since the day he'd moved out, guilt had crawled in Lily's stomach and made a home there.

It was her fault for the upheaval, for the disruption to everyone's lives, for Vera having to lose her favorite boarder, for the drop in Stuart's newspaper circulation since they'd announced the start of the Red Ribbon Society. She'd even cost Oren some business the past Sunday, when one of the camps refused to let them set up and take pictures.

She'd caused them all unnecessary trouble. And if they helped her now, she'd make things even worse for them, much worse.

She traced a finger along the diagram of the Stockade. Well, it wouldn't be long before she'd be gone and out of their lives. With Daisy.

Her finger found the small square on the

map with the word *Bella* scribbled inside. Her pulse pattered with the same staccato as the ice-snow mixture that pelted the window. Daisy was there, in that very room.

Stuart's assistant, Bass, had willingly provided them with all the information they'd needed about the Stockade. He frequented the place often enough to draw an outline of the inside of the building, including the stairways and rooms, the livery, the distances to the palisade, and even the location of the outhouse.

And over the weekend, Bass had managed to get one of his regular girls to tell him more about Bella, where her room was located, and how to get to it. For extra cash, he'd even bribed the girl to deliver a note from Lily.

During the past several days since then, Lily had expected Daisy to try to smuggle a note out to her. She'd waited and hoped for some sign her sister had received her message and that she would be alert and ready for their rescue attempt.

But there had been nothing from the Stockade except silence.

And yet, Lily had decided she wouldn't let the lack of news discourage her. After all, how could Daisy manage a note without putting herself in danger? She was likely trying to stay safe and waiting expectantly for the rescue, as Lily had instructed her.

"What about the bouncers?" Connell pulled off his glasses. "If Carr's got them at every stairway and in each of the girls' hallways, we'll have a difficult time sneaking past them."

Stuart stared at the diagram and rubbed his hand across his beard, wiping away cookie crumbs. "That's going to be one of our biggest obstacles."

"According to Bass," Connell continued, "no one can get past the bouncers unless they're with a girl and have already paid for the time with her."

"Then each of us will just have to pay for girls —"

"Come on, Stu. You know that won't work." Connell's voice was punctuated with a frustration that only seemed to grow with each passing evening they met to discuss the rescue plans. "If either of us takes one step inside the Stockade during business hours, Carr will suspect we're up to something. He'll have his bouncers all over us."

Lily sighed and wished she could tell them to go back to Stuart's house, that she didn't need their help, that their plan to sneak inside was completely foolish. If she allowed them to carry through with it, they'd be walking into a deathtrap.

She stifled a sigh and tried to convince herself again that her decision to make the rescue by herself was right. She'd have a much easier time sneaking through the shadows unseen and unheard compared to the two of them.

Besides, hadn't she already successfully rescued several girls that winter?

Yes, her plan was much safer. It was the only one that would work, especially if she hoped to keep Connell and Stuart alive. But if Connell figured out she was going into the Stockade by herself, he'd tie her up and lock her in her room.

She studied the diagram again. She'd need to know every bump and corner so well that she could traverse it effortlessly in the darkness of night.

"So what do you suggest we do?" Stuart had asked that exact question so many times she'd lost count.

"We'll have to sneak in after visiting hours are over," Connell replied. "Next Saturday. After the boys are all passed out drunk."

"But we'll still have to get past the dogs and the bouncers, no matter what time we sneak in."

"I'll have my knife," Connell said, but there was something in his tone. Something that said he didn't think they really had much of a chance of succeeding.

Or maybe he hadn't dedicated his heart to the plans to begin with. Hadn't he told her that anyone who took a stand against Carr would face dangerous reprisals and loss of business? If he helped her free Daisy and lived to tell about it, he would make an enemy of Carr.

Sure, Connell said he wanted to help her. She'd sensed his sincerity when he'd stopped her from going up to the Stockade in broad daylight. But she also realized in spite of all her talk about sacrificing for what was right, she didn't want Connell to get hurt. Or Stuart. She didn't want to put either of them in danger.

"Your yap's been extry quiet over there, young lady," Oren said gruffly between puffs of his pipe. "As quiet as a fox sneakin' up on a hare."

"I'm just tired," she said. And she was. "I haven't been sleeping well the past few nights, thinking about Daisy."

"If you're not sleeping," said Vera, heaving herself up from the bench, "then I've got just the thing for you. A special sleeping tonic I made from motherwort."

Lily tried to suppress a shudder at the thought of having to take any more of Vera's medicines. "I'm sure I'll be just fine tonight."

She stared at the diagram of the Stockade again, not daring to meet Vera's or Oren's gazes. She wasn't planning on having any trouble sleeping. Mainly because she wasn't planning to sleep one wink.

"Now, no sass from you, girl." Vera crossed the dining room. "We can't have you getting sick again."

"I'm not going to get sick again."

The woman only snorted before she disappeared through the kitchen.

"So next Saturday night then?" Lily asked the men, knowing she needed to say something or she'd raise Oren's suspicions even more.

"Seems like it will be the best night." Stuart reached for another cookie. "Can you wait until then?"

She hesitated. How could she answer without lying? They all knew how anxious she was to get Daisy out of the pit of hell.

"It's an awful long time to have to wait," she finally said.

"It's only five days." Connell met her gaze head on. "One hundred twenty-six hours to be exact."

The intensity in his eyes probed her, and she quickly looked away. He was always too perceptive, and she couldn't chance his reading anything in her face. Not when so much was at stake.

"If Daisy's been there this long," she said, struggling to find honest words, "I don't suppose she'll die if she has to wait for the rescue."

"Here we are," Vera said, coming through the doorway. "I've got a vial of motherwort tonic and a tiny bottle of a special chamomile potion with enough power to knock out a pack of wolves for a week."

Lily started to shake her head, but Connell spoke to Vera first. "Too bad I didn't have your magic potion when I was fighting off the wolves a couple weeks ago."

"Aw come on, big guy." Stuart socked Connell in the arm. "Wasn't it more fun to have to fend them off with your bare hands?"

Connell grinned. "You're right. That was infinitely more enjoyable."

Vera held up a square bottle of yellow-tinged glass. It was filled halfway with a clear liquid. "All anyone needs is a couple drops of this, and you'll be asleep before you can whisper your prayers."

"I'll be fine without it," Lily started to protest but then stopped. What about the dogs? Would the potion work on them? They were still the biggest obstacle to her plans. Her *carefully* laid plans.

No one could accuse her of not learning her lesson from her attempt to rescue Frankie. This time she wasn't rushing off without considering every possibility and problem.

Vera pushed the two bottles toward her. "I won't take no for an answer."

Would the medicine sufficiently lull the dogs to sleep? Lily took the medicine and lifted the bottles to the light, peering at them more closely.

"One spoonful of the motherwort and two drops of the chamomile potion." Vera handed her a spoon.

"I suppose. But only if you insist."

"I insist." Vera put her hands on her hips. "I won't stand for you getting sick again. I'm sure your mother, God rest her soul, wouldn't have stood for it any more than I will."

Lily pictured the stoic face of her mother in the tiny portrait. She'd looked long and hard at the faces of both her parents that afternoon before she'd stuffed the framed photo into her sack. She'd seen the disapproval in their eyes again over her failure to protect Daisy. And she'd seen anxiety there too. They were waiting, just as she was, for the day of Daisy's freedom.

Before tucking the picture into the folds of her clothes, she'd kissed the frame and promised them she wouldn't fail again. She'd get Daisy back.

"How about a flour and onion poultice?" Vera asked, passing her a handful of cookies. "Soaked in a basin of hot water? That'll help too."

"Oh, Vera, you're such a dear." Lily almost choked over the words, suddenly realizing this would be the last time she'd see her new friend. She wanted to give the woman a hug but knew Vera wouldn't put up with a gushy display. So she tucked the cookies into one pocket, the medicine into the other, and reached for the woman's hand and gave it a squeeze.

Then she crossed to Oren in front of the fire. His brow cracked into grooves as deep as tracks left by cutters.

She leaned to kiss his head as she usually did but instead pressed a kiss against his scratchy cheek. The long curled tail of his mustache tickled her chin, and the tobacco scent that was uniquely his brought sudden tears to her eyes.

"What in the hairy hound do you think you're doing?"

"Just giving you a kiss good-night." She

spun away from him before he could see her sadness. Would this be the last time she'd see Oren too? After she had Daisy, she'd have to run far away someplace safe.

Her heart swelled with a painful ache. Could she really leave Oren? Now that he'd become like family to her? The family she'd never had? After he'd taken her into his home the way no one else had ever done? After he'd given her everything she needed and more?

Was she really doing the right thing?

Tears blurred her vision.

She hurried to the stairway before she started crying in front of them all.

"Wait, Lily," Connell's voice called after her.

But she skipped up the steps. She couldn't say good-bye to him. It was better to pretend she was going up to her bed like she did every other night.

"Lily." His voice chased after her.

She forced her feet to climb faster.

His footsteps clomped on the steps behind her.

She turned the corner in the stairwell and made it almost to the top before his fingers connected with hers.

He grasped her hand and immobilized her.

She twisted, trying to free her hand from

his hold.

"Stop. Please," he said. "Listen to me. Just for a minute."

The sincerity in his tone beckoned her to turn, and she couldn't resist. She wanted one more look at him, one last lingering gaze into his eyes, one final feast of being near him.

On the step above him, she found herself almost nose to nose with him.

"Lily," he started. His grip around her wrist slackened, but instead of letting go of her, his fingers slid down and intertwined with hers, the hard lengths capturing and fitting into each dip of her hand with an intimate tenderness that left her suddenly breathless.

"I wanted to make sure you're satisfied with all our plans so far."

If he was asking her, he must have sensed her resistance even though she'd tried to keep it from showing.

His lips were at the same level as hers, only a hand's stretch away.

Why hadn't he ever kissed her? Over the past month he'd had the opportunity — more than once. He'd wanted to kiss her — she'd seen his desire, like now. And he had to know she'd been more than willing to accept a kiss from him.

If she leaned forward, she could easily provide him access. She'd let him give her a good-bye kiss, for after tonight she'd never see him again.

"Lily?" he whispered, almost as if asking permission.

She didn't know how to kiss a man. She'd never done it before. But she leaned forward enough so that her lips pressed softly to his and clung there for a long breathless moment.

He grew absolutely still and silent. He didn't respond to her touch, but neither did he push her away.

Had she been mistaken? She'd thought he wanted to kiss her too. A twinge of embarrassment crept over her, and she began to lift her lips away from him.

But his breath came in a soft moan, and suddenly his lips caught hers in a powerful current that pulled her against him so that his mouth covered hers.

The grip of his fingers within hers tightened.

And she found herself drowning in his kiss, the sweetness of it, the sheer pleasure it.

She couldn't think of anything at that moment except that she wanted to be near him and have him wrap his arms around her.

"What have I done?" he whispered, wrenching his lips from hers. Agony laced his voice. He released her hand and took a step down and away from her. A tempest of guilt raged across the handsome lines of his face.

Was kissing her so wrong?

"I'm sorry, Lily," he whispered hoarsely.

"I'm not sorry," she whispered, pulling herself up.

He took another step down, his face growing taut. "It would be so easy to sweep you into my arms, Lily, and to go on kissing you till neither of us can think straight."

She touched her lips. It *would* be all too easy to let him go on kissing her.

"You're one of the nicest women I've ever met." He stuffed his hands into the pockets of his trousers, as if by doing so he could resist the temptation to reach for her again. "And I refuse to treat you anything like a loose woman."

Loose woman? The words slapped her in the face, jolting her to the reality of the situation. Had she really just thrown herself at Connell? Had she really just whispered that she wasn't sorry she'd kissed him? Had she so shamelessly wished she could go on kissing him?

"I don't want to give people any reason to

believe the rumors about us," he said, regret deepening the shadows in his eyes.

Fresh embarrassment tingled over her, and she backed up a step, wanting to disappear altogether. How easy it was in one small moment to lose all self-control and to lower her standards. When she'd always been able to resist thinking about men, how could she cave in so easily now?

What was happening to her? Perhaps she'd fallen prey to the depraved standards of the lumber towns. Since she was surrounded by so many people that had low morals, had she unknowingly begun to lower hers?

Of course, she'd never been in a situation that had tested the strength of her virtue. She'd never cared for a man. Never wanted to kiss one.

Was she just a weak woman in the face of temptation?

Whatever the case, she knew it was time to go.

"Good-bye, Connell," she whispered.

Then, without waiting for his reply, she spun and raced to the top of the stairs, to the dark hallway, letting the echo of her footsteps drown out the whisper in her heart that urged her to fling herself back into his arms.

CHAPTER 17

The stiff branches above Lily clattered like dry bones. With a shudder, she leaned her head against the trunk of the maple, the lone tree on the hill — one of the few trees left in Harrison, its hardwood unwanted by the lumber companies who fought over the soft wood of the white pine.

In the blackness of the early morning, the pale light from the tavern windows illuminated the barren, gnarled limbs. They reached toward her like claws of a devilish monster. She had no doubt they would snatch her and devour her if they could.

Every shadow, every dark moving shape was a demon. She'd heard the flap of their thin translucent wings. And she'd even seen the flash of fire in a pair of eyes.

She was sitting at the doorstep of hell itself. She'd braced herself for the pit, had told herself she was willing to enter hell for Daisy and to die if need be.

Even so, she couldn't keep from wondering — was she doing the right thing?

The question had only grown louder with each passing hour, swirling through her blood, chilling it, making it sluggish, until dread had reached every vessel in her body.

Should she have waited to attempt the rescue with Connell and Stuart?

The open gate in the Stockade's palisade whispered to her, urging her to slip back through it while no one was looking. She still had time to retreat down the hill to the safety of her room in the Northern. No one would have to know she'd gone.

She could wait for Saturday night as the men had planned.

"Get out of here, you good-for-nothing piece of scum!" The rear door of the tavern banged opened, and the shout shattered the eerie silence of the night.

One of the dogs in a pen on the opposite side of the yard began to bark.

Lily shrank against the trunk, trying to make herself invisible. The slight movement sent sharp pains into her cramped limbs and her frozen fingers and toes.

Though it was an early February night, the temperature still belonged to the deep freeze of winter. At least it had lost the arctic frigidness that had blown in with the last storm. The milder sleet and snow showers earlier that night had made the conditions perfect for an escape. Among all the other obstacles, they wouldn't have to battle blizzard conditions or frostbite.

Yes, she was doing the right thing. The men's plan had been foolhardy. If she'd gone along with it, she would have sent them to their deaths. She wouldn't have been able to live with herself knowing she'd saved Daisy's life at the expense of two brave, kindhearted men.

"You ain't nothing but a worthless drunk!" the same voice bellowed.

Lily peeked around the edge of her hiding spot toward the back door in time to see one of Carr's wide-shouldered bouncers carrying a shanty boy by his suspenders. The bouncer dug through first one pocket of the man's pants and then the other, likely emptying them of every dollar the man owned.

Then the bouncer made his way across the yard that was covered with shattered bottles, broken chairs, and refuse Lily couldn't begin to distinguish. When he reached the gate, he tossed the man outside the compound onto the rocky hill, discarding him like dirty dishwater.

The dog's barking grew more persistent,

and it lunged at the fence of its pen as if it would jump it in one bound if it could.

The bouncer muttered several profanities before closing the gate and turning toward the dog. "Aw, shut up and go back to sleep."

He grabbed a chain hanging loosely from the gate, wrapped it through the nearest stake of the palisade, and locked it.

Lily allowed herself a breath of relief. Her wait was nearly over.

The clink of the metal chain signaled the end of tavern business for the night. It effectively blocked anyone from coming in or leaving the Stockade. The yard would finally be deserted enough for her to come out of hiding.

When the bouncer made his way back inside, Lily waited until the twang of the piano ceased and the last strains of bawdy laughter faded before she pushed herself up. She winced and hoped her numb feet would hold her weight.

She needed to make her move now or never.

From several other rescues she'd orchestrated that winter, she knew she had only a brief window of opportunity. She needed to act while the majority of men were still inebriated but before dawn brought them out of their beds to start another workday.

She quickly shed the buffalo-skin robe. Oren's extra trousers hung like a tent from her waist over her thin legs. They were still stiff from the recent washing she'd given them, but her disguise in his clothing had worked. No one had paid attention to her entering the compound earlier.

With frozen fingers, she fumbled in her bag for her molasses cookies. She'd laced them with Vera's sleeping medicine and prayed the trick would work.

Cautiously she made her way out from behind the tree, hefting her sack onto her shoulder. Only one of the hounds was awake, sniffing along the slats of the fence. When Lily moved, it lifted its head, ears perking and nostrils flaring.

Even on her tiptoes, in the crunch of the freshly fallen ice-snow mixture, her footsteps sounded as loud as a heavy team of oxen.

The dog lowered its mangy head and growled. The jowls pulled taut, revealing sharp fangs.

If the beast started barking again, she was afraid to think what might happen.

Her heart plummeted into a wild dash, and her feet moved just as quickly. She had to silence the beast before it alerted the bouncer to her presence.

In an instant, she was close enough to toss

a couple of cookies into the pen. The dog's growl faded, and it turned to inspect the food. Two more dogs crawled out of the shadowed doghouses and approached the cookies.

The first dog growled again, but this time as a warning for the newcomers to stay away.

Lily threw the remaining cookies toward the other two dogs. "Eat 'em up, boys."

She didn't wait to see if the sleeping potion would really work. Instead, she made the most of the distraction to sprint to the building and duck into the shadows. She pressed her back against the siding and dragged in a shaky breath.

Her foot slipped in a puddle of slime. The overpowering bitterness of vomit assaulted her, along with the vinegary stench of whiskey.

She clamped her mittened hand across her mouth and nose and tried not to gag. She'd heard plenty of retching earlier in the night. If rumors were true, the tavern owners often developed their own nasty brew called forty-rod whiskey, named as such because after drinking a shot, the shanty boys claimed they couldn't walk forty rods without falling down. The concoction also made many of them violently ill.

Crouching low, Lily sidled along the

building. If Stuart's assistant had given them the correct dimensions for the Stockade, then Daisy's room would be on the front side of the building, the third window from the west.

When Lily reached the corner, she paused and glanced around. Her heartbeat skittered like a frightened hare. Dark misshapened shadows loomed long and thin.

More demons. A shiver crawled over her skin like maggots on dead flesh.

A low screech came from the opposite side of the compound near the livery. Even though the sound resembled the night call of a barn owl, Lily couldn't keep from wondering if maybe the winged devils were communicating with each other.

Maybe they were plotting how to foil her rescue attempt.

"Oh, God," she whispered. But her prayer stuck in her throat.

Why had she ever thought she could visit the pit of hell on her own?

Why hadn't she just waited?

She closed her eyes against the haunted shapes.

How easy the plan had seemed back in the safety of her room at the Northern. How easy to think God was waiting for her help in orchestrating the plan.

She'd imagined walking in, grabbing Daisy, and leaving town. She'd planned to take the girl to Molly May's in Midland and then head back to Merryville and rescue Frankie. She couldn't leave without getting Frankie. With every day that passed, guilt plagued her over the fact that she hadn't done anything more to try to rescue her.

Once she had both girls, she wanted to get as far away from Harrison and Carr as she possibly could. If she could save up enough money, maybe she'd even take them back to New York. At least there they'd be safe from Carr.

And maybe she'd eventually be able to start a shelter of her own, like Molly May's, where she could continue to rescue girls and give them a start at a better life.

But she hadn't counted on the demons of hell conspiring against her.

"Oh, God," she tried again. Was God close enough to hear her? "If I ever needed someone to be with me, I need someone now."

Even as the words left her lips, a slow burning of renewed strength trickled through her blood. She straightened and glanced around again. "If you'll use your angels to fight off the hordes of demons that live here, then I can take care of the rest."

She listened for a long moment, not sure what kind of answer she'd expected, certainly not anything audible. When a quiet sense of peace settled within her chest, she smiled. Somehow she had the feeling God had heard her and the peace was His answer. She had the distinct impression He was very close, even though she couldn't see Him.

"I can do this," she whispered, creeping around the corner to the front. The windows were dark, but she found the third one from the west. Daisy's.

Her heart pattered with new hope. She'd come this far. She wouldn't fail now.

She reached into the trouser pocket for one of the small stones she'd tucked there. Then with careful aim, she tossed it at Daisy's window. At the ricocheting ping, she crouched low and scanned the other windows, hoping no one else had heard the noise.

After what seemed like forever but was really only a few minutes, she stood and reached for another stone.

What if Stuart's assistant had misinformed them? What if the third window wasn't Daisy's room after all?

She lifted her arm to throw one more stone, but then stopped. There was a flash of movement in the window. She caught her breath. And when the window inched up a crack, then another, and another, her heart slammed against her ribs.

Through the darkness she could make out the fluttering white of a nightshift and the paleness of bare arms.

"Daisy?" she whispered.

"It *is* you." The return whisper brought tears to Lily's eyes. The beautiful face that peered down at her was framed by the usual tangle of dark curls and belonged to none other than Daisy.

Relief fell upon Lily with such force that she nearly crumpled to her knees and sobbed.

"I wasn't sure," the voice whispered again. "You didn't mention when you'd come."

"I didn't know." Lily glanced around, praying no one could hear them. "But I'm here, and we need to hurry."

With shaking fingers she found the rope in her bag and threw it up to Daisy. She instructed the girl on how to loop it through the headboard.

Then she shook one frozen foot and then the other as she waited for Daisy to secure the rope. Her gaze darted to the other windows, to the yard, and back to Daisy's room.

A sudden flapping over the roof sent Lily's heart into a crazy spin, and she crouched onto the ground, hoping to make herself invisible.

Had someone heard them?

Every muscle in her body tensed.

When Daisy finally tossed the rope back out the window and began the awkward descent, Lily silently motioned her to move faster.

In a thin nightshift, Daisy shuddered with the cold, hardly able to grip the rope. Her garment crept higher, revealing the glowing nakedness of her flesh beneath.

"Jump," Lily whispered once the girl was close enough. "I'll catch you."

Daisy let go and slid down the rest of the distance, her bare feet landing in the snow. Lily's arms enveloped the girl, bracing her fall and capturing her in a fierce hug, an embrace full of all the sorrow and pain of the long months of searching.

It was finally over.

Her throat closed with an overwhelming need to cry. "Oh, Daisy," she managed, breathing deeply of the girl's hair, rubbing her nose into the loose curls, remembering all the times she'd done the same thing when Daisy had been a little girl.

Daisy's arms wrapped around her in a

fierce hold, and she buried her face against Lily's coat. "I didn't think you'd ever come."

At the agony in Daisy's voice, Lily just hugged her tighter and pressed a kiss against the soft strands of her hair. Tears spilled over and made a frozen trail down her cheeks. "I missed you so much."

"I missed you too." The cold wetness of Daisy's tears mingled with Lily's.

She wanted to stop time and hold Daisy forever. Now that she had her, she didn't want to release her. She squeezed her sister harder, and Daisy clung to her as if she would never let go again either.

But the spit of fresh sleet against her face and the shudder of Daisy's thin body urged her into action. She pulled Daisy to arm's length and in one quick glance took in the girl's condition. Through the dim glow of light coming from the back of the tavern, Lily could see that her sister was as healthy as always and had apparently been well taken care of.

Only the bright fear glowing in her wide eyes testified to the nightmare she had lived through the past months. And the fact that she was standing before Lily practically naked, wearing a nightgown that dipped revealingly low and hardly reached mid-thigh.

"Quick, put this on." Lily shrugged out of her coat and draped it across Daisy's shoulders. Then she wrestled through her bag to find the extra boots she'd packed.

In a matter of seconds, Daisy was dressed sufficiently — at least enough to protect her from the winter temperatures for a short time.

Lily reached for her again, needing to hug her, needing to know her sister really was standing in front of her and that she wasn't just dreaming. But a light flickered in one of the upstairs windows, and the curtain swayed.

Had someone noticed Daisy's disappearance already?

"Come on." Lily grabbed the girl's hand and tugged her forward. They couldn't waste any time. Every second counted.

Daisy gripped her and squeezed hard, but resisted the pull.

"What's wrong?"

"I've missed you, Lily," she said in a broken whisper.

The ache in Lily's throat threatened to choke her with the pressure. She wanted to hold Daisy and tell her everything would be all right. She wanted to wipe away all the worries, all the horrible memories, and whisper that from now on they'd be together, that never again would she let anything or anyone split them apart.

But that would have to wait for the days to come, when they'd have plenty of time to talk. For now, she had to get Daisy out of the Stockade before anyone noticed them.

"I've missed you too." She brushed her sister's cheek, ready to cry all over again at the relief of finally seeing Daisy, of touching her, of knowing she was safe.

A long screech rent the air.

Lily's heart crashed against her ribs. "We'd best be going. We need to get out of here." They weren't safe yet. Not until they made it to the other side of the wall and down Dead Man's Hill.

She dragged Daisy along, leading her back around the building the same way she'd come. They crept low. And when they reached the back of the compound, Lily stopped and searched the dog pen.

The beasts were nowhere in sight. Had the sleeping potion worked?

She swallowed her fear. The only way to find out was to cross the yard to the gate. If the dogs were awake, they'd know soon enough.

"Run," she whispered to Daisy.

They bolted through the refuse. The sleet pattered louder, thankfully drowning the slap of their footsteps. Lily slowed down only long enough to grab a broken bar stool. Even with a missing leg, it would still be enough to boost them over the gate.

With pounding heart, she reached the gate, the only part of the palisade without the sharp points, and the only place low enough for them to attempt to cross over. Daisy fell against the wood slats next to her, her chest heaving. Lily flattened herself and pushed a hand against Daisy, warning her not to move.

For a long moment, they stood as silent as the empty broken bottles that were half covered with dirty snow.

The dogs didn't stir. And the tavern sat too quietly, the first-floor barroom windows still alight from the glow of a lantern or two within.

Had they really made it this far undetected?

Lily shoved the stool against the gate. "Climb up and I'll help you over."

Daisy hesitated.

"You're gonna be fine," she whispered. "I won't let anything happen to you."

"If Carr catches me, he'll kill me." Her frightened gaze darted around the yard, as if she expected him to jump out of the shadows.

"He'll have to kill me first." Lily patted the stool. "Now hop on up."

Daisy clambered up, fumbling to stand and reach for the gate.

"It's gonna be all right." Lily hoisted Daisy and at the same time used her body to steady the three-legged stool. She tried not to think about how she was going to manage getting over the gate by herself once Daisy was on the other side.

Shards of sleet pelted Lily, and a gust of wind pierced through her layer of shirts, sending shivers up and down her limbs. A sudden scurry of fur near her feet made her jump. She caught sight of the long skinny tail of a rat before it disappeared into a nearby pile of garbage.

"Hurry," she called hoarsely, stifling a shudder.

For what seemed an eternity, Daisy struggled over the top of the gate, first scraping her bare legs, getting her coat hooked on the edge, and then afraid to let go and fall the distance on the other side.

When Daisy finally made it over, Lily tried to climb onto the broken stool, but she couldn't keep it from tipping over. With mounting frustration, she returned to the yard and walked among the debris until she found a broken crate.

She jammed the crate under the stool in place of the missing leg. Even though it tilted at an awkward angle, it didn't budge. She managed to pull herself up, grab on to the top of the gate, and hook first one leg over and then the other.

Daisy stared up at her, shaking like a wild flower in a spring breeze. She didn't move to help her — not that Lily expected her to — not in her condition.

Just as she began to lower herself down the other side, a faint shout came from the tavern and another light popped to life in one of the upstairs windows.

Lily's stomach clenched into a tight ball. Someone *had* discovered that Daisy was gone.

Her pulse burst forward. She jumped, snagging Oren's trousers on one of the slats of the gate. She wrenched the fabric. It gave way with a sharp rip, and she fell to the ground with a thud that jolted her gut and knocked the breath from her.

"Let's go," she gasped, struggling to push herself up. They were going to have to run for their lives.

Would they have time to reach the livery behind the Northern?

When she'd done her planning the day before, she'd decided the best way to get

Daisy out of Harrison was to use Oren's cutter. She wouldn't steal it — just borrow it temporarily, like she'd done with his clothes. And even though he'd be stranded for a few days until she could return the cutter, she had the feeling he'd understand. At least she hoped he would.

Another shout broke the silence of the Stockade, this one louder.

Daisy's eyes widened. Her trembling fingers grasped Lily's, and she glanced frantically toward the rocky hill that spread out before them.

In the darkness the uneven shapes of the stones crouched like ghouls waiting to pounce on them.

Lily choked down her fear. They had no choice but to descend the hill, a barren, open stretch of land that separated them from the town and from anyplace they could take cover and hide.

With the echoes of more shouts on the other side of the palisade, Lily charged down the hill, pulling Daisy along behind her, dodging stones and shards of smashed bottles. When they reached the bottom, she didn't pause to look back at the Stockade. Instead, she stumbled onward toward the edge of town. Behind her Daisy's breath came in heaving gasps and her steps grew sluggish, slowing them down.

"I have to stop." Daisy choked out the words and bent over, holding her side.

Lily chanced a glance toward the Stockade. A man stepped through the gate and held up a lantern. The light cast gyrating flickers over the dark hill.

He was looking for Daisy. No doubt about it.

Lily's heart dipped with dread. "We can't rest now."

Daisy followed the direction of her gaze and gave a soft gasp. "Are they looking for me already?"

The man with the lantern had started down the long hill, holding the light high. The shouts of several more men behind him echoed in the stillness of the night.

"What are we going to do?" Daisy's voice trembled with panic. "I don't want to face Carr's brass knuckles. I've seen what he can do with them, and I wouldn't be able to bear it."

Lily's mind raced. How could she cross to the other side of Main Street to the Northern Hotel without being detected? And how would she be able to get Daisy out of Harrison tonight if she didn't get Oren's sleigh?

They had to make it out while it was still dark. At first light, if not sooner, Carr would have his men out searching every road leading to and from Harrison.

Lily clutched her sister's hand. She dragged the girl past overturned stumps left from the destruction of the forest in years past. Their roots swirled into the air like a thousand frozen snakes.

"Please, Lily," Daisy whispered, tears sliding down her cheeks. "Please don't let him get me."

The voices of the men grew louder and closer. The light from the lantern would soon reveal them. And how could they possibly run away from Carr's men — when Daisy was already tired?

Lily frantically scanned the nearby stumps and then she scrutinized the smattering of houses that edged the town.

"Don't worry. I'll figure out something."

Even as the words left her mouth, she prayed that she hadn't told her sister a lie, and that she hadn't helped her sister to escape only to put her in the worst danger yet.

CHAPTER 18

A thud at the front door woke Connell out of a deep sleep.

He sat up, the heavy layer of blankets falling away. The frozen air of the unheated bedroom rolled over him and seeped through his union suit like a winter storm.

A glance out the frosted window revealed the darkness of night. And yet his internal alarm told him sunrise was not far off — maybe two hours until the first hint of light.

Who would possibly have need of Stuart at five o'clock in the morning?

The door rattled.

Suddenly fully awake, Connell's fingers went to his knife, every nerve in his body alert. He swung his legs over the edge of the bed. The rusty frame creaked under his weight.

Was someone trying to break in?

His heart slammed against his ribs. He stood and made his way across the bedroom and down the narrow stairway. His bare feet turned to ice against the frozen floorboards. Even though he tiptoed, each step squeaked.

At the bottom, when he reached the door, he stopped and held his breath.

He could hear nothing but the distant howl of a wolf. Had the intruder heard him and gone away?

"Stuart" came a muted voice on the other side of the door.

"Lily?" Was it Lily? What was she doing out at this time of the morning?

In a flash, he sheathed his knife and swung open the door.

There stood Lily, without a coat, shuddering and hugging her arms across her chest. Next to her a young woman huddled into Lily's coat almost as if she wished she could disappear.

At a shout from Dead Man's Hill, both girls glanced over their shoulders, their eyes wide with fear.

His gut wrenched with anger. He didn't need to ask Lily what she'd done. It was clear. Her unusual acquiescence to his and Stu's plans, the silence of the night before, the hesitancy.

She'd been planning the escape. She'd intended to leave without any of them knowing it.

Even the kiss. It had been a good-bye kiss. He was certain of it.

And now, what had happened? Had she been hurt? Why was she turning to them now, unless something had gone wrong with her plan?

At another shout, this one nearer down Main Street, she shuddered. "We need a place to hide and fast."

Before he could speak, she pushed past him, dragging Daisy in her wake. "Hurry. Close the door before Carr's men see us."

Fear swirled with the anger roiling through his stomach. "What in heaven's name do you think you're doing?"

"Shh." She peered over her shoulder to the blackness of the night. "They're already out looking for us. They know we're nearby."

He clicked the door closed as quietly as he could. Then he grabbed hold of her arm and pulled her toward him. "Are you crazy?" His voice was a harsh whisper.

She squirmed under his grip.

He gave her a shake. "You could have gotten yourself killed."

A man's voice called out from across the street, and she jumped. Daisy gasped and grabbed Lily's arm. Lily quickly slipped her arm around Daisy and pulled her against her side.

Footsteps drew nearer and paused in front of the door.

They huddled together, not daring to move or talk or breathe.

Heavy breathing came from just outside.

Connell could only shake his head in frustration.

His mind conjured images of Lily in the hands of one of Carr's bouncers. Even worse was the thought of what Carr would do to her if he ever caught her. He'd witnessed the bloodied faces and bruised bodies of shanty boys who'd faced Carr's brass knuckles.

After several long moments, the footsteps moved toward the front window. Light from the searcher's lantern spilled through the window.

They shrank against the door, flattening themselves so that the light couldn't touch them. Except for Daisy's shaking, they stood in frozen silence.

Finally, the light and the footsteps moved away.

Next to him, Lily's body slackened.

"You should have waited for me," he whispered.

"And get you and Stuart into trouble?"

His heated response died.

The warmth of her breath hovered between them. "No. This was the best way. I'll take the full blame for Daisy's escape. Neither of you will have to suffer now."

"I was willing to help you, Lily." At least that's what he'd told himself over and over. But would he have carried through with the plans Saturday night? Would he really have been willing to sacrifice so much — even his life — if needed?

"I know you were willing," she whispered, leaning into him. "But you and Stuart wouldn't have been able to get her. Not your way. You would have only gotten yourselves killed."

"You could have gotten killed too."

"But I'm willing to die for her. She's the only family I have."

"She won't have anyone if you're gone."

"We'll be okay. I'll take Daisy far away, someplace where Carr won't ever be able to find us."

He wanted to tell her that he couldn't bear the thought of her dying. Or leaving. But he knew he had no claim to her, that she could do anything she wanted.

She trembled.

"You're freezing." He wanted to rub his hands over her back and arms and warm her up. But with a painful swallow, he stepped away from her. "I'll get you and

Daisy blankets."

"What's going on here?" Stuart's sleepy voice came from the stairway. He held up a lantern with one hand and rubbed his half-open eyes with the other.

"Put out the light," Lily said, glancing to the front window.

But Stuart lifted it higher, bringing the front room to life with its clutter of papers, the crooked sampler on the wall, and the scattering of mismatched dirty socks. The light seemed to shine directly on Daisy, illuminating Lily's coat, which couldn't adequately cover her bare night shift and long slender legs.

"Quick." Lily waved at the light. "Extinguish it before anyone sees it."

Stuart rubbed his eyes as if he were still half asleep.

"I've got Daisy." She reached for her sister. "And if Carr's men see the light, they'll know we're here."

Stuart's gaze locked on Connell. "What are you doing down here without your clothes on?"

Connell glanced down to his union suit. He hadn't stopped to think about pulling on a shirt and pants.

Stuart frowned.

"If you snuff the light you won't see him,"

Lily said, her tone laced with irritation.

At the distant bark of a dog and the shout of one of Carr's men, Connell took three steps toward Stu, grabbed the light, and with one puff blew out the flame.

Darkness descended over them.

"What's happening?" Stuart asked again, this time his voice more alert.

"I've got to get Daisy out of town." Lily edged toward the window and peered out. "But I don't want to chance trying to make it down Main Street — not now with Carr's men out searching."

"I don't understand." The perplexity in Stuart's question echoed the confusion churning through Connell.

He didn't know what was wrong with him, but he loathed the idea of letting Lily go, letting her ride out of his life. What if she went someplace where he couldn't find her?

In hushed tones she explained how she'd managed to get Daisy out of the Stockade and how she'd planned to borrow Oren's cutter.

"If one of you will go get it for me," she said, "then we can be well on our way before dawn."

"If Carr's men see one of us riding through town," Connell said, "they're going to know we're up to something."

Lily gave an exasperated sigh. "What do you suggest then? That we walk through town in broad daylight and catch a ride on the Pere Marquette?"

"Oh, Lily," Daisy said softly. "Maybe this is all too dangerous. Maybe I should just go turn myself back in."

"No!" Lily's whisper was harsh. "Don't even think about going back. I'll keep you safe. I promise."

"Carr might be a cruel bastard," Daisy whispered. "But he didn't hurt me as long as I did everything he asked me to do."

"You're not going back. Not now — now that you're finally free."

"Maybe I can tell him you forced me to it."

"Daisy! Stop! How could you even say such a thing? Don't you want to get away?"

"Yes."

Connell's insides twisted like the logs going through the giant circular saw blade at the mill. How could he keep Lily safe?

He knew one thing. He wouldn't let her step a foot outside the door by herself. And he certainly couldn't let her ride out of town in Oren's cutter. Carr would track her down within the hour.

What other choice did he have besides driving her out of town himself and taking her somewhere safe?

"What about one of your horses?" Lily asked. "If you get us a horse, we'll take that instead."

Stuart looked out the window to the livery down the street. "I'll go get mine." But even as Stuart said the words, more footsteps echoed in the street outside the house.

Lily jerked Daisy back with her against the door. Connell crouched and prayed Carr's men weren't coming back to break down the door.

The footsteps and voices passed by, but Connell's fingers were at his sheath nonetheless.

After several minutes of silence, Lily finally whispered to Stuart. "Go now. If you bring the horse around to the back of the house, we'll meet you there."

Connell buried his face in his hands. Stuart would throw himself onto the point of a dagger if Lily asked him to.

Cautiously Stuart peeked out the window again.

Connell shook his head. "It won't work, Lily. You won't be able to make it out of town. And if you do, they'll be on your trail before you're halfway to Clare."

She turned to Stuart. "Do you have a gun?"

"Sure —"

"Then we'll be just fine." She lifted her chin in defiance. "I've had to outrun bouncers before."

The razor-sharp saw blades in Connell's gut whizzed faster. He had to do something to save Lily. And now. But if he did, what would that mean for his future? For McCormick Lumber? For everything he'd worked so hard to achieve for the company?

"Let's go," she said. "We can't waste any more time."

With a groan, Connell stood and reached for her. Through the dark his fingers found hers, and he captured them within his.

She stopped, and this time she didn't try to pull away from him.

"I'll take you," he whispered.

Her fingers trembled. "Take me?"

"I'll drive you and Daisy out of Harrison."

"You will?" Her question was breathless.

"Yes."

Her grip tightened.

The strength from her touch seemed to move up his arm and through his body. It swirled through the sawdust of his insides and finally landed in his heart, infusing it with resolve. And with something he'd never felt before. He didn't know what it was. All he knew was that he couldn't let her ride out of his life. Not yet. Maybe not ever.

"I'll make sure you and Daisy are safe. I'll take care of everything."

At his soft promise, she sagged against him as if the weariness from her long night and the dangerous escape had finally settled upon her.

"You and Daisy stay here until I come for you." Even as his mind went to work formulating an escape plan, he tugged Lily's knitted hat from her head, letting her long hair spill in disarray down her shoulders.

She didn't resist.

He combed the curls away from her neck, letting his fingers revel in the silkiness. He bent his face into a handful, breathing in the scent, as sweet and thick as maple sap after a boiling. "While I'm gone, please don't do anything impetuous."

"Me? Impetuous?" Her voice had a hint of a smile.

He might have grinned if the situation hadn't been so dangerous. As it was, he tugged her closer. "Promise me you won't try to do anything more on your own."

"I promise."

"I'll be back later." With the firm self-control he'd cultivated over the years, Connell let go of Lily, dragged his fingers from her hair, and took several steps away from her.

Now wasn't the time to hold her again. He'd only end up thinking about the kiss they'd shared and how much he'd liked it.

Nothing good would come of dwelling on the intimacy. Especially not when he needed a clear mind, keen instincts, and solidness of purpose.

There was too much at stake for him to fail.

He couldn't bear to think what would happen to them all if he did.

CHAPTER 19

Midmorning, Connell drove his team of horses hitched to the box sleigh around the back of Stuart's house. He'd filled it with the usual weekly supplies from Sturgis's Grocery and General Store — sacks of beans, cornmeal, potatoes, and barrels of flour. He hoped no one besides Mr. Sturgis would realize he was three days early for his usual pickup and delivery to his camps.

He jumped from the high seat of the sleigh and glanced around to the scattering of other houses with the same weatherworn, peeling paint. They'd likely been white several years ago when they'd first been built. But now the boards were a dirty gray — the same color as the slush mixture that sat in lumps along the dirt streets.

He hadn't noticed before just how shabby and sleazy Harrison looked.

With narrowed eyes, he surveyed the Stockade. From the outside, everything was placid and silent — just as it always was during daylight hours.

But every place he'd gone that morning, everyone had talked about how Bella had run away during the night. And Carr was apparently handing out favors to anyone who could give him information about the girl or Lily. Apparently he'd put the rumors together and figured out Lily's involvement.

Connell had no doubt Carr's men were still out searching.

He tossed a canvas over the load of supplies and then turned toward Stuart's house. His muscles were tight, and he prayed no one would suspect him.

"Where have you been?" Lily met him at the back door, her brows wrinkled.

At least she'd kept her promise and stayed in the house as he'd asked.

"I couldn't rush anything and draw attention to myself," he said, stepping inside and closing the door behind him. "And of course I had to calm Vera and Oren down without giving away my escape plans. They'll be safer not knowing."

She nodded, and the worried lines on her forehead eased.

"Are you ready to go?" He peered past her through the kitchen to the front room, where Daisy lay curled on a faded settee.

"Stuart found an old skirt and blouse that belonged to his wife." Lily followed his gaze and her expression softened. "At first Daisy didn't want to wear them. She thought they were too big and unfashionable. But I finally convinced her to put them on."

"No need to worry about fashion at a time like this."

"I offered her mine too, but apparently what I wear is even less fashionable."

He'd never paid much attention to her attire. "It doesn't matter what you wear. You're always beautiful." The words slipped out before he could stop them. He ducked his head, but not before he caught sight of the smile that tugged at her lips.

Fingers of heated embarrassment grabbed his neck. Why had he gone and said something like that? What was coming over him?

"We need to be on our way," he said quickly, starting across the kitchen, hoping to hide the color that was making its way to his face. "Before anyone sees the sleigh outside and starts to wonder why I'm here."

She followed him into the sitting room and bent over Daisy. "Connell's back, my dear." She smoothed Daisy's hair away from her face, revealing features that were as smooth and pretty as Lily's. It was a wonder Carr or Maggie or some other shanty boy hadn't made the connection between the two sisters — that Tierney had been the one to see it.

Daisy stirred.

Lily combed her fingers through the girl's hair. "Wake up, Daisy. We need to be on our way."

After a bit of coaxing, Lily finally managed to rouse the girl. In no time they were bundled in buffalo-skin blankets and ready to go.

He hid them under the canvas among the supplies, tied down the covering, and started on his way, doing his best to act like he was on a regular ride out to one of his camps to deliver supplies.

He took the tote road north out of Harrison, knowing he had to stay as far from the main roads as possible. The indirect route would make a longer ride for the women, but heading north around Budd Lake was the safest.

His heart didn't stop pounding in tempo to the horse hooves until after they made it over the border into Gladwin County. Even then he didn't allow himself to take a break until they'd gone ten miles east of Harrison.

He found a wayside tavern and refilled the coal warming box he'd brought along for the women. Briefly, he let them get out and stretch before starting on their way again.

There was only one safe place he knew to take Lily, only one person in the world he trusted to take care of her as well as he would. He'd pushed the horses hard, trotting them at a brisk pace all day. And when they finally reached the outskirts of Bay City, night had fallen.

"Where are we?" Lily's voice was groggy. Thankfully, she and Daisy had slept most of the long day.

Daisy was still asleep and snuggled between them on the front bench of the sleigh where he'd finally agreed they could sit.

"We've only got five more miles now." The soft jingle of the Swiss bells that hung from the horses' collars kept an easy rhythm with the swish of the blades in the snow. A quarter mile to the east, past the edges of the few remaining pines, lay Saginaw Bay and beyond that Lake Huron. It was frozen and lifeless now. But once it thawed, it would teem with ships from far and near coming to transport the bounty of the lumber camps and sawmills to ports in Chicago and the East.

Lily sat straighter. Through the darkness in the distance, they could see the first flickering lights of the city. "Are we safe?"

"Carr wouldn't dare come this far after

you." At least he hoped.

She didn't say anything for a long moment. Then she reached across Daisy and found his gloved hand underneath the blanket on his lap. She squeezed it. "I know you've risked a lot today, doing this for us. Thank you."

He'd tried not to think about how much trouble the rescue was going to cause him. He'd told himself that Carr wouldn't find out about his involvement, that no one needed to know why he left Harrison in the busiest part of the lumber season. He'd consoled himself with the instructions he'd given to Stuart to tell anyone who asked: He'd had to leave for a family emergency.

But his insides had frozen into crusted ice, leaving an unshakable chill in the depths of his soul. He reminded himself he hadn't done anything wrong, that he'd only stood up for what was right. If Daisy wanted to leave her life of prostitution, she should have the freedom to walk away from it without anyone trying to stop her.

Carr had gone too far once again. And Stuart and Lily were right. It was past time for someone in the community — someone influential like him — to let Carr know he couldn't get away with his vileness or his tight-fisted control of Harrison.

Now that he'd taken the first step, surely others would follow. Wouldn't they?

And even if they didn't, was it possible that God was nudging him to stop sitting back and to begin doing more to deal with some of the problems that surrounded him?

When Lily started to pull away, he captured her hand, not wanting to break the connection with her. "Did I really hear a thank-you?" He tugged her playfully. "I'm shocked."

"I can be grateful when I choose to be." Her voice was light. "And I can also be quite admiring."

"I'd like to see that." Little did she know exactly how much he wanted her admiration.

"I have been a little rough on you at times, haven't I?"

"A little?"

"Or a lot." She laughed softly. "Maybe I can make it up to you."

"And just how do you propose to do that?" The banter warmed his insides.

"I promise you won't have to rescue me again."

"I like that promise." He grinned.

"And no more middle-of-the-night scares."

"That would be nice."

"I'll do my best to focus on taking care of Daisy now."

"Sounds like you're going to start having a normal life."

She grew quiet. "I don't think I really know what normal is."

His own thoughts turned sober. What would she do now that she had Daisy? What kind of life could she possibly make for herself and the girl?

They rode in silence, the chill of the night slithering around his feet and legs, sending a shiver over his skin.

"Have you ever thought about having a normal life, Connell?" she finally asked.

"With all your dangerous rescues, mine seems tame compared to yours."

"No. I mean a real life. Away from the lumber camps."

A real life? What was *real* anyway? A big home with a wife and a baby and a job as the supervisor over his father's sawmill like Tierney? Was that real? That could have been his life — would have been his — if Tierney hadn't stolen it all away from him.

Instead, he lived with Stuart Golden in a cluttered house, ate his meals at a hotel, and had nothing to show for his work. He calculated numbers day after day, always with the stress of trying to make those figures add up to something bigger.

But deep inside he knew it was a losing battle. Eventually McCormick Lumber would cut down every profitable pine and be forced to move on. The hunger for more would never really be satisfied, and he would always have to race to find more fuel to feed that insatiable appetite.

"What would you do if you didn't work in the lumber camps?" she asked.

He shrugged. "Lumbering is all I've ever known."

"Didn't you ever want to do anything else?"

"It's never been about what I wanted. It's always been about the business. McCormick Lumber. And what's best for the company."

"You've never really thought about doing anything else?"

Had he? He honestly couldn't remember that he'd ever had one thought about pursuing any other ambition except the lumber business. From his earliest memories, Dad had drilled into him the importance of succeeding, of working hard, of doing his part. And he knew Dad was counting on him or Tierney to someday take over the business.

"There has to be something else you'd like to do besides lumbering," she persisted.

"Something you've secretly dreamed of doing."

He shook his head. "In a family like mine, the only dreams that matter are those of my dad."

Daisy stirred.

Lily pulled her hand back into her lap, leaving him wishing he could hang on to her and her passion for life just a fraction longer.

"Maybe it's time for you to start making your own plans and having your own dreams," she said softly.

Daisy pushed herself up from her resting place against Lily's shoulder. "I'm so cold and hungry."

Lily lifted the blanket off her lap, shifted it onto Daisy's, and tucked it around the girl.

"I don't think I've ever been so cold in my life."

"We're almost there." Lily lifted her sister's feet back onto the warming box.

"And I've got a horrible headache."

Connell clamped his lips together to keep from saying anything. The girl's complaining had worsened as the day had progressed. She was likely experiencing alcohol withdrawal. From what he'd heard, most prostitutes drank heavily. Some even drank themselves to death.

Even so, his frustration had mounted with each passing mile. The girl obviously took Lily for granted and expected her to take care of her every whim — and probably always had.

"Where are we going?" Daisy asked as Lily tucked her under the crook of her arm like a little girl.

"We're in West Bay City," Connell said. They were no longer passing the small farmhouses that dotted the countryside but had entered the residential neighborhoods of the western side of town.

Through the darkness of the evening, the lamplight from the windows of many new houses cast a glow on the snow-covered dirt road. Most of the houses were simple two-story structures made of scrap lumber. Brightly painted, they sat close to the streets and belonged to immigrants — Germans, Poles, French Canadians — who provided cheap labor to the many mills, lumberyards, and factories along the river, including McCormick Lumber Company.

Every time he returned, the city sprawled larger. No longer was business confined to the Saginaw River waterfront and Lower Bay City on the east side. Industry was booming everywhere — restaurants, hotels, clothing stores, boardinghouses, churches, new schools.

As the lumber industry had expanded, so had the city. The problem was that eventually Michigan was going to run out of white pine, and when it did, what would happen to the city that had relied upon the logs for its life?

"And where exactly are you planning to take us?" Daisy's voice was irritable, as if she needed someone to blame for her misery and decided Connell should be the scapegoat.

Only then did he realize Lily had never once asked him where they were going. She trusted him. Believed in him. Had utterly and completely placed her life in his hands.

The thought frightened him and made him marvel at the same time. When he glanced across Daisy's head and met Lily's gaze, her brows lifted, no doubt waiting to hear the answer to the question.

"I'm taking you home," he said.

Her brows arched higher.

"You'll be safe there." And if she were in his house, she'd still be very much a part of his life. Maybe then she'd forget her idea of taking Daisy someplace far away. Maybe she'd like his home. Maybe she'd stay.

The fact was he couldn't bear the thought

of losing her. And he was sure he'd do just about anything to keep her from slipping away.

CHAPTER 20

"This is your home?" Lily was utterly unprepared for the enormity of the residence.

Connell had jumped from the sleigh and was already around to her side, holding out a hand to help her down.

But she couldn't move. She could only stare at the tall Queen Anne–style mansion that seemed to sit on a throne of lattice and reign amidst the sprawling block-long grounds. Each of the dozens of various sized windows was lit — big bay, round arched, small square, diamond, and even stained glass. In the darkness, the interior lights illuminated the elaborate details of the grandly built home, almost as if the owner had planned to display it like a museum piece.

Connell followed her gaze. "Dad had it built three years ago."

She'd guessed that McCormick Lumber

was prosperous and Connell's father was a wealthy man. But she'd never really thought about Connell belonging to a completely different class and way of living. She'd only seen him in his shanty-boy attire and thought of him as a backwoodsman.

She hadn't pictured him in an elaborate home — not one like this with terra cotta brick, pretty gables covered with decorative patterns, and steeply pitched roofs. The prominent circular tower with its conical peaked roof made it look almost castle-like.

"I'm not really sure why he decided he needed a home this size," Connell said, "especially since it's just my mam and dad — and the servants."

"It is rather large." Her mind couldn't even begin to comprehend why two people would need to live so extravagantly. In fact, she couldn't understand why a family of *any* size would need such a large house — not when she'd grown up living with dozens of other children in sterile brick buildings that rivaled the McCormick mansion in size.

Her memory of living in a real home had faded — until Oren had brought her to his second-floor home above the photography studio. His few small rooms had seemed like paradise at the time, compared with anything she'd ever known.

But Connell's family home was like an entirely different world.

"I suppose Dad just wanted to keep up with what all his friends were doing." Connell reached for her hand again, and this time she allowed him to help her down.

He nodded to the house across the street, which was not as large, but still a finely designed Victorian-style home. "He had a house built for my brother and his wife as a wedding gift."

"That's a big gift," Lily said.

"Especially for someone who doesn't appreciate what he's got." Bitterness edged his voice as he assisted Daisy from the sleigh.

Connell greeted a man who had come around the house from the livery. He handed over the reins with instructions to take care of the team and supplies. Then Connell guided her and Daisy up a plank walkway to the front door.

Delicate leaves were carved into the panels of the door, and equally intricate carvings adorned the swan brackets above the porch posts. If every little detail of the outside of the home spoke of a style of living that was far above her own, what would she find on the inside? And how would she ever hope to fit in — not that she wanted to — but how could she take one step inside without feeling like a foreigner?

When he reached for the door handle in the shape of a lion's head, she touched his arm and stopped him. "Are you sure this is the best place for us?"

He quirked his brow.

"I mean, look at us." She lifted the faded material of her everyday skirt — made over from one of Betty's old dresses after she'd died. "What will your mother think of you bringing two homeless girls into her beautiful house?"

"Mam will love you." His eyes radiated confidence.

"Do you think so?" Suddenly she wanted his words to be true more than anything. She wanted Connell's mother to like her and to approve of her. Not just as a charity case. But because of Connell. For Connell.

"Don't worry," he said.

"But what about the rumors she heard about us? What will she think of me?"

"She'll think you're a special woman." His voice softened. "Just like I do."

Daisy smiled. "I think I'm beginning to understand what's going on."

Lily was relieved to see Daisy's smile, the first she'd given her since the rescue. Even if it was more of a smirk, it was still something.

"You and Connell are . . . you know . . ." Daisy wagged a finger back and forth between them, and her eyes took on a knowing glint.

Lily shook her head, fighting back a flush of embarrassment. "We're just friends."

"You're falling for Connell."

"Now, Daisy, that's enough." She tried to make her voice stern.

Daisy's smile crept higher.

Connell looked from one to the other, his expression full of curiosity.

"It's true," Daisy persisted. "I can see it in your eyes."

"Let's just go in." Before Daisy could say anything more to embarrass her, Lily stepped to the door, hoping Connell wouldn't see the same thing Daisy had noticed.

Connell grinned, reached past her, and opened the door.

Warm light spilled over them as they walked into the wide front entryway. Lily stopped short and gazed at the long spacious hall in wonder. A welcoming fire crackled in a tiled fireplace with a curved settee positioned in front of it. A wide winding staircase rose at the far end. And a crystal chandelier dangled from the high ceiling.

She had the urge to slip off her boots lest she soil the bright hues of the lush oblong carpet that covered the polished hardwood floor. The luxury of the long hallway was everything she had expected and more, from the mahogany wood paneling and vibrant patterned wallpaper to the scrolling frieze. Though it was just the entrance, it was the fanciest room she'd ever seen.

She had the urge to step back outside, to demand that Connell take her and Daisy somewhere else, but he closed the door behind them with a thud that echoed of finality.

"Who's there?" a voice called from the parlor.

"Just me, Mam," Connell replied.

"Connell?" In an instant, a woman in an elegant evening dress glided into the hallway. The narrow plaitings of silk and the large bustle on the back of her skirt rustled with each graceful step.

"Hello, Mam." Connell grinned.

The woman's beautiful face registered first surprise, then delight. She rushed toward Connell, smiling in return, leaving a lovely rose-powder scent in her wake. Connell held out his arms to her, and she swept him into a crushing embrace.

Something joyously painful lodged in

Lily's throat. She'd never known a mother's love — had never seen a display of affection like the one Connell's mother was showering upon him. And even though she didn't begrudge Connell his happiness, she couldn't deny the keen longing for all she'd missed.

He pressed a kiss against his mother's stylish coils of hair. The golden strands — probably once the shade of Connell's — had begun to fade to the dimness of winter sunlight.

"It's so good to see you." Her voice had a slight Irish brogue. She stepped back and examined him, her eyes searching his face, as if she could read there all that was written in his heart.

The longing inside Lily swelled. What would it have been like to have a mother? To have had a real home? How different things might have been for her and Daisy.

Mrs. McCormick reached for Connell's hands and squeezed them. "You look well."

His grin faded, as if he sensed the depth of his mother's probing and the unasked questions about what was happening. For surely from the second she'd heard his voice, she must have guessed something was dreadfully wrong for him to have left his work unattended to make the long ride home.

"Don't worry," he said. "I'm all right."

It was only then that Mrs. McCormick turned toward Lily and Daisy. Her kind eyes, so much like Connell's, regarded them without judgment.

"Mam, this is Lily and her sister Daisy."

Lily nodded. "Evening."

Daisy murmured a shy greeting.

"I'm pleased to meet you both," the woman said, and from the sincerity in her tone, Lily could almost believe the woman meant it.

"Everything you've heard," Connell rushed to explain. "None of it's true."

Mrs. McCormick smiled gently. "Of course it's not, son. And I know in due time you'll explain what's going on."

He nodded. "It's a long story. And the short of it is that I need you to take care of Lily and Daisy for me."

"I would be honored to."

Lily didn't know if love at first sight was possible, but she was suddenly overwhelmed with the woman's kindness. She wanted to throw her arms around her and hug her.

"Connell?" A young woman appeared in the wide arched doorway of the parlor. She juggled a fussing baby against the silky pale blue and silver of her dress. The front of the skirt was trimmed with several ruffles below the waistline and embroidered with pearls. She wore a double strand of matching pearls around her slender neck and appeared every bit as refined as Mrs. McCormick.

At the sight of the woman, Connell stiffened and took a step back toward the door.

Mrs. McCormick laid a hand on Connell's arm as if to stop him from leaving. "Tierney is working late tonight, and I invited Rosemarie to spend the evening with me."

The muscles in Connell's jaw flexed.

"She's brought their baby." Mrs. McCormick's voice had a soft pleading quality to it. "Your niece."

Rosemarie took a step toward Connell and then stopped. The graceful lines of her face were creased with uncertainty.

Lily's heartbeat came to a slow and pattering halt. Who was this woman? And why was Connell having such a strong reaction to her?

Mrs. McCormick squeezed Connell's arm, and her gaze gently admonished him.

He nodded curtly. "Good evening, Rosemarie. Congratulations on the birth of your baby."

She gave a hesitant smile. "Thank you."

"I hope you're both in good health."

"We're doing as well as can be expected."

Connell didn't meet the woman's gaze, even though her eyes practically begged him to.

A twinge of something new pricked Lily. Had Connell harbored feelings for this woman at one time?

She had the urge to reach for his hand, to capture it and lay claim to him, although she had no right to. She didn't want him looking at anyone but her or thinking about another woman. She wanted to be the only one.

In Harrison, she had been the only single young woman for miles around. Connell hadn't had any other options. But here? Even if Rosemarie was his sister-in-law, there were other women who would vie for a man of Connell's winsome character and wealthy status — not to mention his clean-cut handsomeness.

What chance did she have to win Connell's affection against other women? And why did she even want to win it?

Mrs. McCormick summoned the maid to serve them dinner. Even though Connell's mother apologized for the simplicity of the fare, the meal of fluffy biscuits, fresh oranges, mini sausages, and sliced cheese was one of the most delicious Lily had ever eaten.

Or maybe sitting in the fancy dining room made the meal seem that much nicer. The light from the wrought-iron chandelier and from the large fireplace made the polished black oak dining-room table gleam like the clear surface of a lake. Every piece of furniture, from the matching sideboards to the mantel, was elaborately carved. And everything that could be covered in velour or silk was — the curtains, pillows in the box seats of the bay windows, and the cushions on the chairs.

When they finished their dinner, Mrs. McCormick ushered them up the winding stairway, past dozens of colorful oil paintings, past the vast rooms on the second floor, to the third story. She led them down a hallway beyond the glittering ballroom to the guest rooms.

The moment Mrs. McCormick opened the door to the first guest room and waved them in, Daisy collapsed on the bed and was violently ill. Mrs. McCormick was ready with the basin she had grabbed when she had noticed Daisy's coloring earlier. She retched until she could hardly moan.

Much to Lily's surprise, Mrs. McCormick stayed by the girl's side. She helped Daisy undress and slide under the covers, bathed the girl's face with a cool cloth, and held the basin for her whenever she retched.

"How's Daisy?" Connell's voice startled Lily as she stepped into the dimly lit hallway and closed the guest room door behind her.

Connell pushed away from the wall, where he'd obviously been waiting.

Lily brushed a loose strand out of her face, hoping she'd left the stench of vomit behind.

Connell approached her, his brow wrinkled with concern.

"She's got the chills and can't stop shaking. Your mother is sending me to fetch more chamomile from the maid."

"I'm sorry, Lily." He lifted an arm as if to reach for her, but then stuck the tips of his fingers into his small trouser pockets. "I sent the stable hand after the doctor. Maybe he'll have something to ease the withdrawal."

"Do you think she's addicted to liquor?"

"I'm fairly sure." His expression was sober.

As much as she supported temperance, she knew it wouldn't do any good to get upset at Daisy for imbibing. "I suppose the liquor took the edge off the horror and pain of what she went through."

He nodded. "Many prostitutes resort to

337

drinking in order to survive. Daisy will be miserable for several days, but she'll get through it."

Lily rubbed her arms, wishing she could take away all of Daisy's pain and make it her own.

"How are you doing?"

His question was soft and it wrapped around her, warming her heart. "I'm overwhelmed by your home."

"It's not mine."

She smiled. "And I'm overwhelmed by your mother. She's amazing."

Connell grinned. "I won't disagree with you on that count."

"She's just what Daisy needs right now."

"Then you promise you won't run off? That you'll stay here?"

His tone stopped her playful answer. She cocked her head. "You're not leaving tonight, are you?"

"Tomorrow."

"That's so soon. Why can't you stay for a few days?"

He didn't answer. He didn't need to. The dark shadows that flitted through the pine green of his eyes were only the beginning of the storm that would pour down upon him once Carr learned of his involvement in the escape.

"Do you really need to go back and face Carr?" She didn't want to think about the danger that might await him upon his return.

"Not face him? Weren't you the one who said I needed to join in the fight against him, regardless of the cost?" He grinned but the humor didn't make it into his eyes.

She leaned against the wall. "But maybe you did what you needed, and now maybe it's time to get out of Harrison."

"Get out of Harrison?"

Her fingers grazed the raised abstract pattern of the wallpaper, its coolness and smoothness a contrast to the hot bumpy pace of her pulse. "Leave Harrison for good. Leave lumbering. Find something else to do with your life. Something *you* want to do."

He didn't say anything for a moment.

"You're so good with numbers. Maybe you can find a job that involves working with figures."

He stretched out his arm, leaning his palm against the wall near her head. "I already have a job that involves figures."

The nearness of his hand sent a shiver through her. "I mean a job that doesn't involve the destruction of the forests."

"I think you're just going to miss me," he said lightly. But there was a hard set to his jaw that frightened her. "That's why you don't want me to go. Admit it."

She sighed. And before she could stop herself, she reached up and laid her hand against his cheek. "I admit it."

His breath hitched. The shadows in his eyes darkened, but this time with something more like desire.

Her fingers grazed the scratchy stubble of his unshaven cheek. Her heart quivered at the texture of him against her fingertips.

He leaned closer, and the sweet tang of oranges lingered between them.

"Connell?" a voice at the entrance of the hallway made her start.

She dropped her hand.

But he didn't move — except to stiffen.

"I was just coming to tell your mother good-night."

She glanced past Connell, and there stood Rosemarie. She'd donned a velvet bonnet trimmed with chenille and feathers and a jacket that glittered with fanciful beads. The woman's eyes widened as she took in Lily's unladylike proximity to Connell.

A twinge of embarrassment prodded Lily to straighten. She didn't want to begin her visit with the McCormicks by making a poor impression, especially when she already had a sullied reputation.

She tried to slip away from Connell, but he boxed her in with his other arm.

"Connell, please," she whispered.

But his eyes had taken on a spark of anger, and instead of moving away from her, he dipped closer.

"I'll be sure to tell Mam you said good-bye." He tossed Rosemarie a slight glance, all the while brushing his cheek against Lily's.

The scruff skimmed her sensitive skin, and the scratchy sensation sent a shiver through her.

Rosemarie didn't say anything, but she couldn't seem to tear her focus away from Connell. There was a painful longing in her eyes that pleaded with him.

"You better get home to Tierney." His voice was hard. "I'm sure he's waiting for you."

Lily didn't know what was going on between Rosemarie and Connell, but she was certain there was something. She knew she ought to break free from Connell and give the two some privacy, but the touch of his cheek against hers and the warmth of his breath held her prisoner.

"Besides, I'm saying good-bye to Lily." With that he seemed to dismiss Rosemarie. He leaned into Lily's ear. The rasp of his breath there captured her with a strength that left her powerless, weakened her muscles, and made her dizzy.

The heat of his breath bathed the skin of her neck. And when he pressed a kiss into the hollow of her ear, she found herself clinging to him to keep from falling.

Only Rosemarie's gasp brought her out of the drowning swirl of his nearness.

Lily tilted her head away from him, breaking the contact. Out of the corner of her eyes, she saw Rosemarie spin away and retreat toward the stairway, the sharp click of her heels growing more distant.

Lily pushed against Connell's arms, but he didn't move.

He dragged in a ragged breath.

The curling warmth in her stomach stretched tighter. And as embarrassed as she was that Rosemarie had witnessed their intimacy, she didn't want to pull away from him. Would he kiss her again, a real kiss like the one they'd shared in the stairwell of the Northern?

But, as he had the last time, he tore himself away from her and stumbled to the other side of the hallway. With a groan, he rubbed his hand across his eyes. "I can't believe I just did that."

The regret in his tone sent a chill through Lily.

He put both hands over his face. "What was I thinking?"

"That you wanted to say good-bye?"

He shook his head. "I'm sorry, Lily."

The cold chill rippled over her skin, and she folded her arms across her chest trying to fight it off. "Who is she to you, Connell?"

He didn't respond for a long moment. Then finally he straightened and looked directly at her. "She was my fiancée."

The words blew into her blood like the north wind.

"But now she's married to Tierney."

"Why?" She forced the question out, even though she wasn't sure she really wanted to know. "What happened?"

"Two months before the wedding, I caught them together, down in the library." The dimness of the hallway shadowed his face, but nothing could hide the pain in his voice.

"Were they kissing?"

"They were doing a whole lot more than kissing."

At his insinuation, she sucked in a startled breath. "Not Rosemarie. She seems like such a lady."

"Apparently it wasn't the first time they'd

been together."

"I don't understand why she would give you up for your brother."

"Tierney has a way about him that women like. And I guess he was more persuasive than I was."

"You mean he's a lying, cheating double-crosser who uses women, and you're a gentleman, trying your hardest to be honorable?" Connell had always treated her with the utmost respect. She had no doubt he'd done the same with Rosemarie.

"For all my efforts to treat her honorably, I lost her anyway."

"Then it was her loss."

"When I see her with the baby and the house across the street, it's hard not to think about how much I lost too."

The honesty of his words pierced her. She didn't want him to long for Rosemarie and the life he could have had with her. She didn't want him to think about anyone else.

She wanted him to love her.

The truth spun through her aching heart. For the first time in her life, she'd met a man she desired, a man whose love she craved.

Was it possible she was falling in love with him?

"Did you love her?"

With the tip of his boot, he dug into the plush rug that ran the length of the hallway. "Dad had arranged my marriage to her. And as the daughter of one of his wealthy friends, it was a good match for both our families."

"Then you didn't really love her?" She held her breath. From the guest room, she could faintly hear Daisy's agonized retching again.

"I've known her all my life and always thought she was a sweet girl. When my dad told me of the plans, I was more than willing to do what was best for me and our family. Especially with Rosemarie. She was easy to love."

Lily pushed away from the wall and stepped toward him. Her body was tense with the need to know how he felt about Rosemarie, about her, about everything. "Do you still love her, Connell?"

She looked deep into his eyes, unwilling to let him hide from her. Her heart demanded the truth.

"Maybe I was in love with the idea of being married, of having a family, of settling down. And if we'd gotten married, I would have done my best to devote my life to her and to love her."

The ache in her heart swelled. He was such a good man. He would have made

Rosemarie a very fine husband. Had the woman guessed how much she'd lost when she'd given up Connell for Tierney?

"But how do you feel about her now?"

Connell finally grinned. "You're sure nosy tonight."

"Just tell me. Do you love her or not?"

"Do I detect jealousy?" His grin inched higher.

She was terribly jealous. It was pouring through every vein in her body, tightening every muscle, making her want to pound her fists into his chest and demand his answer. "I just want to know whether she stole all of your love. Or if you still have some left that eventually you might be able to give to another woman."

"Rosemarie doesn't have my love — not anymore." The green of his eyes lightened to the shade of meadow grass. "I think whatever she stole has finally been recovered."

The warmth in his eyes spread through Lily, and she allowed herself to breathe again.

His smile seemed made just for her. "In fact," he said, his voice turning to a whisper, "I'm beginning to wonder if maybe someone else is stealing my affection."

Hope unfurled in her middle like a wild flower.

She smiled in return and reveled in the beauty of his words. And she ignored the doubts that buzzed in and out among the flowers — the nagging thoughts that told her no matter how much he cared for her, their differences were too great and love could never fully blossom between them.

For now, she wanted to believe anything was possible.

CHAPTER 21

Connell was trapped. With Dad at one end of the dining-room table and Tierney at the other, he couldn't escape.

Dad took a puff of his cigar and blew out a thick cloud of spicy smoke. It swirled in a haze around the angry lines grooved through his forehead. "Ye better start thinking with yer head instead of yer pants."

"I *have* been using my head," Connell retorted, hating that he felt like a twelve-year-old boy instead of a twenty-six-year-old man.

Tierney took a slurp of coffee. His eyes were bloodshot, his shirt wrinkled, his cravat askew — as if he'd spent the night at the tavern instead of home in bed with his wife.

The ticking of the silver clock on the mantel echoed through Connell's mind. He'd been sitting listening to Dad and Tierney cuss him out for the past fifty-two minutes for stealing one of Carr's prostitutes and bringing her to their home. Not only did Connell want to avoid arguing with them, he needed to get back to Harrison.

In the early hours of dawn, he'd meant to sneak down to say good-bye to Mam. But somehow in the process, she'd convinced him to have a cup of coffee and fresh buttermilk pancakes and bacon and bread with jam. And then of course, he'd wanted to tell her about Lily and all that had happened so she would believe his innocence. The last thing he wanted to earn was her disappointment.

Then Dad had joined them, almost as if he'd anticipated Connell's early morning escape. Not long after, Tierney had shown up.

Of course Dad had nodded for Mam to leave the room, taking away any hope of support.

Dad dug into the pocket of his jacket. He pulled out a crisp stack of hundred dollar bills and slid it across the polished table toward Connell. "Deliver this to Carr and tell him I'm compensating him for his losses."

Connell's gut twisted. Part of him wanted to take the money and pay Carr for peace. But another part of him wanted to stand up to him once and for all. Why did they have to bow to a man like Carr?

"Tell him ye won't interfere again." Dad sat back in his chair and took another puff of his cigar.

"Can't we get along without having to grovel at Carr's feet?"

"Are ye daft?" Dad shoved away from the table and rose to his feet. With his broad shoulders and thick arms, he was an intimidating man — just like he'd always been. It didn't matter that his once dark hair was now completely gray. He was still as strong as a team of oxen. "We rely on men like Carr. They feed our camps. The saloons and illicit houses are a necessity."

"But he's crossed the line this time. He's forcing girls into prostitution."

"I don't care what he's doing." Dad slammed his hands onto the table, rattling the dainty cups and saucers. "As long as he keeps our men happy, that's all that matters."

"He shouldn't prevent his girls from leaving." Connell slapped his hands against the table. If Dad could rattle the china serving, why couldn't he? "If they want to get out, they should be free to come and go."

Dad took a step toward him and clenched his fist. "Where are ye coming up with this? Since when do ye care about what happens in the illicit houses?"

Tierney snorted. "Since he got himself a whore of his own."

Anger exploded in Connell. The burst propelled him out of his seat to his feet. "She's not a *whore*. And I don't want to hear you call her that ever again."

"Or what?" Tierney's grin taunted him.

Connell's muscles tightened with the urge to put a couple of bruises on Tierney's pretty face and knock out a few teeth.

"I don't want to know what ye do in your personal life. Keep it to yerself." Dad shoved him. "But don't go messing things up in me business. Do ye hear?"

Connell braced himself. He knew what was coming. A punch in the gut followed by the usual lecture.

Sure enough, Dad swung his fist into his stomach.

The impact would have doubled him over in years past. But all the months working in the camps had hardened his muscles. He let the fist bounce off his solid abdomen and forced himself not to flinch.

"Ye know how hard I've worked to get what I've got?" Dad grabbed Connell's chin and pinched it like he had when he was a boy.

Connell yanked away. The trouble was, he

wasn't a boy anymore. "I realize you've worked hard —"

"I didn't have a penny in me pocket when I stepped off the ship." Dad continued as if Connell hadn't spoken. "And I was so hungry, I could count every bone in me body."

He'd heard Dad's stories a thousand times. And when Dad let go of his chin and returned to his chair, Connell eyed the clock and then the door, wishing he could make a getaway.

"Sit down," Dad barked. "I'm not done with ye yet."

"I don't have time to listen to any more."

Dad hit the table again. "Sit down."

Connell's muscles tightened. Did he dare defy Dad and leave? Could he?

"I had to sweat for every single cent I've ever earned."

"I know, Dad." Slowly he lowered himself to the edge of his chair.

"I've never asked either of me sons to work harder than I work. I only expect of ye what I demand from meself."

Connell could recite Dad's words in his sleep. Yet for once he wanted to interrupt Dad's tirade and ask him if all his success had made him happy. Was he satisfied with life?

Even more than that, didn't he have the least remorse for the ruthlessness with which they operated? How could they live with themselves if they continued to over-look crime and injustice and evil, just so they could heap up more wealth they didn't need?

And how could they live with themselves if they didn't start taking better care of their workers?

Mam had told him about one of Tierney's sawmill workers who had fallen in the path of a large circular saw and been cut in two. Mam had been taking food to the wife and child left behind. McCormick Lumber didn't offer any compensation to the mill workers or to the shanty boys, not for injuries or for death.

But he couldn't help thinking that maybe they wouldn't have to worry about Carr or other men like him stirring up problems with their workers if they provided an environment where the workers were treated with common decency.

Connell ran his finger around the silver rim of his coffee cup. His mind filled with numbers — the low wages and the long hours — and he blocked out his father's angry voice. Numbers had always been his escape.

The clearing of a throat from the entryway of the dining room brought his head up.

His gaze landed upon Lily — but not the Lily he'd come to know. Instead, somehow she'd been transformed. She wore a deep red silk dress that was slim fitting, outlining her womanly curves. The skirt was fashionably layered with a mound of ruffles in the back. And the bodice was equally flattering with velvet trim and braided cuffs.

He quickly pushed back his chair and stood, his heart clattering with wild admiration.

She gave him a shy smile. "What do you think? Your mother insisted I wear one of her gowns today while mine is laundered."

The dark red of the dress brought out the rich walnut of her eyes and the creamy honey of her skin. Even her curls had been brushed into submission and coiled up onto her head with short ringlets dangling by her ears, as if to entice him to kiss her there — again.

"You look lovely." His words came out more breathless than he'd intended.

Her thick lashes fell against flushed cheeks. "Your mother fixed my hair too."

"She did a fine job."

When her lashes lifted, they knocked him off his feet and swept him into the air. There was no doubt about it, she'd captured his heart and stolen his affection.

He may have bantered with her about it, but the truth was he'd never so thoroughly and completely cared about a woman before — not even Rosemarie.

"Son." Dad had risen from his chair. The angry lines had disappeared, replaced by a calm façade. "Ye are forgetting to introduce us to yer guest."

For all his ambition, Dad had the decency to be respectful toward women — at least when they were in his presence.

"This is Lily Young." Connell smiled at her. "She works with Oren Evans, a photographer with a shop over on Washington Avenue. She came north with Oren to help him take pictures among the camps and to look for her sister."

Dad nodded at her. "Nice to meet you, Miss Young." And even though his eyes narrowed with the frustration of Connell's involvement and all it had cost him, he was polite enough not to say anything more about it.

"I'm pleased to meet you too, Mr. McCormick."

Connell shuffled around the table toward her.

But Tierney sat back, pushing his chair

into Connell's path. "Don't forget to tell Dad Lily's the whore you were living with up in Harrison."

Lily gasped softly. Her face paled and she took a step back, her eyes widening with horrified embarrassment.

Dad's jaw clenched and his eyes darkened.

Tierney grinned up at Connell and then took a slurp of coffee.

Fury set Connell's blood on fire. He grabbed Tierney by the front of his shirt, crunching the wrinkled cotton into a fist. "I told you not to call her that ever again."

"Or what? You gonna beat me up?" Tierney's face held no fear — only scoffing.

Suddenly Connell saw himself reflected in his brother's eyes — a weakling. He was the first to give in to pressure, the responsible one who did what was expected, the kind one who never fought back.

Tierney thought he was weak.

Was he?

Connell gripped Tierney's shirt harder, pulling him up and suspending him above his chair by at least two inches. "I oughta give you the licking you deserve."

"I'm so scared." Tierney's grin crooked to one side, daring Connell to do something.

Lily took another step back out of the room. The pain in her face reached out and gripped his heart, wrenching and slicing it so that her pain became his.

How could he stand back and do nothing? Especially when Tierney was attacking her honor?

"Good ol' Connell," Tierney said. "Go ahead. Hit me. I dare you."

Connell lifted Tierney another inch.

"Or are you too nice to fight me in front of your whore?"

"She's not a whore!" Fury tore through Connell again, and he knew he could do no less than fight for Lily's honor.

He slammed his fist into Tierney's gut with all the strength he'd developed lifting logs and cutting trees.

Tierney grunted at the unexpected blow and fell into his chair. Surprise flitted across his face.

But before his brother could stand up and swing back, Connell pounded his fist into him again, his resentment finally unleashed. He knocked Tierney backward in his chair so that he crashed against the floor. Tierney rolled and tried to scramble away, but Connell jumped on him. And this time he swung his knuckles into his brother's face, clobbering him first in one eye and then the other, then in the mouth.

Tierney roared with sudden rage and took

a swing at him, his fist connecting with Connell's eye.

At the jolting pain, Connell reared his head. But Tierney's other fist slammed into his mouth with the force of a man well practiced in the art of brawling.

Pain radiated through Connell's jaw, and the sting of his tooth slicing into his lip took his breath away.

The sticky metallic taste of blood oozed onto his tongue.

For an instant Connell feared the fight would end in his humiliation, that Tierney might overtake him, and that Dad and Lily would witness the defeat.

But he only needed to picture the humiliation in Lily's face at Tierney's insult and his strength returned with renewed effort. He couldn't let Tierney win. Everything within him demanded that he avenge Lily's honor and teach Tierney never to insult her again.

He struck his brother again and again. The heat of his anger blinded him to anything except the fact that Tierney needed to suffer.

"That's enough, son." As if from a distance, Dad's voice broke through the fury.

But Connell couldn't stop himself from slugging Tierney in the stomach, only faintly realizing his brother wasn't fighting back anymore.

"Enough." Dad's hands gripped him. With a strength that belied his age, he heaved Connell off Tierney and tossed him away like good-for-nothing cull lumber.

Connell bumped into a pedestal. The Oriental vase toppled and smashed to the floor. His shoulder slammed into a porcelain plate mounted on the wall. It too crashed against the hard wood.

He caught and steadied himself, his breath coming in heaving gasps.

Tierney lay sprawled next to his over-turned chair — unmoving.

Fear spurted through Connell. Had he killed his brother?

Dad shoved Tierney with the tip of his boot.

Tierney groaned.

"He'll survive," Dad said.

A sick load dumped into Connell's stomach. What had he done? What had come over him to resort to such violence?

"The boy needed a good kick in the pants." Dad leveled a look at Connell that contained a hint of admiration — or the closest thing to admiration Dad could muster. "It was long overdue."

Connell swallowed a rise of nausea. Was

Dad proud of him for beating Tierney senseless? After he'd tried all his life to do the right things, to work hard, to make Dad proud, he'd finally earned the coveted favor by getting in a fistfight?

He shook his head, disgust adding to the heavy weight in his middle. He pressed the coarse sleeve of his mackinaw to his busted lip and winced at the pain.

"Get up." Dad nudged Tierney.

His brother rolled to his side and groaned again.

A flash of red in the door caught Connell's attention. He blinked through the painful swelling in his eye in time to see Lily turn away.

"Lily. Wait."

But she dashed across the hallway and disappeared.

He shoved away from the wall and skirted past Tierney.

"Good fight," Tierney croaked.

Connell stopped and stared at his brother.

Blood trickled from Tierney's nose and dripped onto the thick Turkish rug. He cracked one eye into a narrow slit, and a corner of his mouth lifted into a grin. "Guess you're gonna marry that woman."

Connell's heartbeat slammed to a halt.

"You never fought like that for Rosemarie." Tierney edged himself up onto his elbows, cringing with each slight movement. "Guess that means you've finally found someone worth fighting for."

Tierney's words were like a fist in his gut, knocking the wind out of him. Tierney was right — at least about not fighting for Rosemarie. The day he'd found her with Tierney, he'd walked away. Sure, he'd been outraged and devastated at Tierney's betrayal. But he'd retreated like he'd always done. He'd opted for peace and safety.

What had happened this time to push him to fight for Lily?

He'd grown to care about her. He wouldn't deny that. He glanced to the hallway, and his heart resumed beating at double the speed.

But he couldn't marry Lily. Could he?

"Don't worry," Tierney mumbled. "I won't try anything on her while you're gone."

If Tierney had meant to reassure him, his promise had the opposite effect. With a growl, Connell stuck his boot onto Tierney's breastbone and pressed down.

Tierney cried out as Connell twisted his heel deeper.

"If Lily tells me that you so much as look at her the wrong way, I'll make you wish you were blind."

Tierney gave a weak laugh.

"And leave Daisy alone too. Stay away from her. Stay away from them both."

He gave Tierney a last shove before stepping away from him. He didn't know when he'd have the chance to return to Bay City to see Lily, not during the busiest time of the lumber season. Of course Mam had reassured him the girls could live there as long as they needed.

But if he wasn't around to make sure Tierney stayed away, how would he be able to keep them safe?

"Just go home." Connell's tone was as hard as his muscles. "And start being a good husband and father."

He started toward the door, but Dad shoved the stack of bills against his chest. "Take this. Clean up the mess ye made. And leave James Carr alone."

Connell hesitated. He'd stood up to Tierney. Could he stand against the pressure of Dad too?

Dad slapped the wad harder.

Connell took it and stuffed it into the inside pocket of his mackinaw. "I'm taking the cash, but I'm going to handle the situation the way I think is best."

Then, without waiting for Dad's reaction,

he exited the room.

"Lily," he called softly. His footsteps echoed in the deserted entryway. He strode toward the parlor and peeked in.

She was standing near a big bay window and staring through a crack in the thick curtains.

"Lily?"

She didn't turn. Instead, she lifted her chin.

"I'm sorry about what Tierney said." Connell stepped into the room and made his way around the love seat.

"I promise he won't demean you like that again," he said, coming up behind her.

She stared outside at the snow-covered lawn and the wide muddy street beyond.

He waited for her to turn. The lacy collar of her dress covered most of her neck, leaving only the long graceful curve behind her ears exposed. The soft creaminess beckoned him to bend and taste, even though he knew he wouldn't, or he'd unleash the passion that was growing each time he kissed her.

Her shoulders and back were rigid.

"Lily," he whispered, daring to touch a hand to her waist.

She didn't resist him.

Slowly he spun her around until she faced him. And he tipped her chin up until she had no choice but to look at him.

Her eyes glistened with sadness. "I wanted your family to like me."

"They do like you."

"They think I'm a loose woman like Daisy."

"Don't listen to what Tierney says."

"I'm from a completely different class altogether, and now the rumors only make it worse."

"You're not from a different class. My parents started as nothing more than poor Irish immigrants." He released his hold on her chin. "Besides, I didn't take you as the type of woman who cares what others think about her."

"You're right."

"We don't have anything to be ashamed of." At least mostly. He couldn't help feeling slightly guilty for the moment of intimacy he'd shared with her in front of Rosemarie. He'd reacted out of anger and hurt. But still, he shouldn't have done it.

She lifted her fingers to his face and poised them above his eye. "Your face is a mess."

"That's very kind of you to say." He tried to grin, but winced at the pain in his lip instead. "I defended your honor and got myself battered in the process."

She smiled. "You were really brave."

"It was a first. I've never fought anyone like that before."

"Well, you handled it as well as any shanty-boy fight I've ever seen." She skimmed her fingers over the puffy skin next to his eye.

His breath hitched in his chest.

She was standing less than six inches away and was altogether too beautiful. When she lifted her fingers to his swollen lip, his entire body ignited with the touch.

The softness of her graze reminded him of the gentle sweetness of her lips.

He could probably sneak another kiss. They were alone. No one would know. He was leaving. What harm could come from kissing her again?

The dimness of the room, the crackle of the fire in the hearth, the faint scent of lavender soap on her skin — his senses reeled with the enticement of being intimate with her.

Flee from temptation. His mother's teaching sounded in his head, almost as if she were in the room instructing him, as she had so many times when he'd been a young boy. She'd trained him to trust God's guidelines above his own desires. *Do not lust in your heart after her beauty. Instead may you rejoice in the wife of your youth.*

If he had any hope of resisting the temptation to drink of her beauty, he had to stop putting himself in situations where they were alone.

God help me. He took a step away from her. He cared about her too much to use her for his own momentary pleasure. And he'd long ago vowed he'd keep the pleasures of the marriage bed within the marriage bedroom.

Her eyes widened, and the desire within them chased after him.

Stifling a groan, he turned away from her and crossed the room. He positioned himself behind the love seat, putting a barrier between them.

"I can't seem to control myself when I'm alone with you." His voice was hoarse.

Her lips curved into a shy smile. "I think you're doing a mighty fine job."

"And it's past time for me to be on my way."

The longing deep within his soul threatened to drag him back around the love seat toward her. But he grabbed on to the carved oak scallop to anchor himself. He wouldn't take advantage of any woman, especially not a special woman like Lily. She deserved so much more than a quick tryst in a deserted room. She deserved a man who would do the right thing and marry her.

Marry her?

What if he were to marry her? Today. At that very moment. His mouth went dry at the thought of making her his wife and taking her to bed that very night.

Tierney's words echoed through him. *"Guess you're gonna marry that woman."*

What was stopping him? He cared about her more than he'd ever cared about any other woman. He'd never been in love before, but he suspected that what he felt for Lily came pretty close.

"Do you really have to go?" she asked, almost as if she'd read his mind.

"So, does this mean you can't live without me?" he teased softly, holding his breath in anticipation of her answer.

A flush stole over her cheeks, and she twisted one of the ringlets by her ear. "I admit, it's hard to imagine my life without you a part of it."

Her confession sent a shiver of delight through him. "Since we're being honest, then I admit I don't want to live without you either."

He could send the stable hand for the preacher. They could have a wedding in the parlor. And then tomorrow he could head back to Harrison.

"What if you were to stay here?" Her voice was low.

His heart rammed into his ribs. If he married her and stayed an extra day, it wouldn't make much difference when he got back to Harrison, would it?

Did he dare to do something so impulsive? So uncharacteristic?

"I might be able to squeeze in an extra day," he said.

"Just a day?"

Maybe he could take her back to Harrison with him.

As soon as the thought entered his mind, he tossed it out. She'd be in too much danger there — at least until he could pacify Carr. And he doubted she'd want to leave Daisy so soon after being reunited. No, she'd be better off staying with Mam. And maybe after the spring river drive, he could ride back home to visit her.

She slid around one of the chairs and approached the front of the love seat. She narrowed her eyes like a cat about to pounce on a mouse.

Suddenly he couldn't see anything but the rounded curves that the elegant gown outlined. If he was going to marry her today, surely he could let himself feast upon the sight of her just a little.

"I don't want you to go back to Harrison," she said. "Ever."

"You know I have to go back." His focus dipped to her waist, and he pictured his hands spanning the circumference.

"Just to rescue Frankie," she said. "Then you could bring her here and never go back."

Maybe he could use the money Dad had given him to buy Frankie's rescue. "I'll do my best to get Frankie out. But I can't stay here."

"You could if you found some other way to earn a living."

His gaze snapped up to hers. "I can't do that, Lily."

"Why not?" She kneeled on the edge of the love seat. "You're a talented man. You could do anything you wanted."

"I already told you that lumbering is all I've ever known."

"But after everything that's happened lately, I thought you were beginning to see the problems and you'd be ready to leave them behind."

He scrambled to make sense of what she was saying. "Yes, I can admit there are some aspects to the business that aren't the best —"

369

"Aren't the best?" Her voice rose an octave. "How can you see anything good, especially after all that's happened with Daisy and Frankie?"

"Now, that's unfair, Lily."

"You know as well as I do that lumbering lays waste to the land and feeds an appetite for lust and greed among the men for money, whiskey, and women."

"Aren't you being judgmental? It's an industry like any other — like salt works that line the river or the commercial fishing out in the bay."

"I've witnessed for myself just how depraved the lumber industry is. And you can't convince me otherwise."

He stifled a groan of frustration. "Look, I don't want to get into another argument with you over this today. McCormick Lumber is in my blood. It's what I do. It's who I am. I can't just walk away from it."

"You can't? Or won't?" Her voice turned low.

Uneasiness lodged in his gut. "If I walked away from it, I'd have to turn my back on my family — and my dad. I can't do that."

"And you know after all that's happened that I can't go back to the debauchery, especially not with Daisy." Her eyes flashed with determination.

His stomach rolled. He wanted to defend himself, to remind her of all that he'd already done to stand up to Carr, the risks he'd taken to help in Daisy's rescue. But he clamped his jaw. He had the feeling all the defense in the world wouldn't satisfy her. She'd only want more sacrifices from him than he could give.

Her jaw was set with a firmness that indicated the strength of her passion in the issue. Her passion was one of the things he loved about her. How could he ask her to change who she was for him? And what right did she have to expect him to give up everything that was important to him?

"Maybe we're just too different," she finally said. "Maybe we're destined to live two separate lives."

He nodded. He didn't want to agree with her, but he couldn't add up the situation any other way. He couldn't stay in Bay City, and she couldn't live with him among the lumber camps.

"It's probably best for us to just go our own ways."

Her words sliced his heart.

For a long moment, she gazed at him with wide expectation, almost as if she wanted him to contradict her.

But how could he disagree? They were as

different as summer and winter.

He didn't say anything.

A shadow fell across her features, and he turned away from her before he could read the disappointment in her eyes.

"Good-bye, Connell." The finality in her voice pierced his heart again.

"Good-bye," he whispered through a tight throat.

And when the swish of her satiny skirt moved away from him out of the room, he ached to run after her and fight for her, fight for them and what they could have had together.

But he lowered his head and let her walk out of his life.

CHAPTER 22

The ache in Lily's heart pressed against her lungs and made breathing difficult. She had no desire to speak past the constriction in her throat.

Thankfully, Daisy was in one of her talkative moods and hadn't noticed how quiet she'd been all morning.

Lily stretched out next to Daisy on the bed and stroked a silver-handled brush through the girl's hair. The curls turned into waves under her deft hand, just the way they always had when Daisy was younger.

Lily's toes grazed the large flat stone at the end of the bed. Even with the heating stone and the thick quilt for warmth, she couldn't keep from shivering.

Or from thinking about Connell.

"I've never seen lovelier gowns than those Maggie purchased for all the girls," Daisy said, lying on her side and staring at the flames in the marble fireplace. "The dresses were always gorgeous colors."

Lily slid a hand over the satiny fabric of the garnet gown Mrs. McCormick had so generously presented to her earlier in the morning. Connell's eyes had lit up when he'd seen her in it, just the way she'd hoped.

"And Maggie sure knew how to fix our hair." Daisy's voice was wistful.

"Sounds almost like you're fond of Carr's wife," Lily said, swallowing past the ache and trying to push aside all the pain raging through her heart.

Connell had told her he didn't want to live without her, but when faced with the choice to return to his work in Harrison or stay with her, he'd chosen his work, the family business, the success of McCormick Lumber.

She'd hoped he'd changed, that he would want to keep on doing the right thing — fighting against injustice and evil. But instead, he'd fled back to Hell's Waiting Room, ready to get back to business as usual.

Besides, even if he had a mind to fight against the problems, how could they possibly make a relationship work if they lived in two different places? She couldn't move back to Harrison — or to any of the lumber towns — not with Daisy, not now after all that had happened with her.

"Maggie was always nice to me." Daisy rolled onto her back and gazed at the ceiling, papered in a print that coordinated with the walls. "She was like a mother to many of us."

Lily pushed herself up and sat against the tall headboard, the raised wood carvings pressing into her back. Mrs. McCormick was the kind of mother she'd always dreamed about — the sweet considerate mother their own would have been.

"Did you know a lot of the girls at the Stockade were orphans, Lily?" Daisy peered at her with wide trusting eyes.

Lily swept her fingers across her sister's forehead and then down her cheek, tracing her beauty spot above the edge of her chin. For all the pain she felt over losing Connell, she couldn't forget to count her blessings. She had Daisy back again. They were together. And they could start over building a new life.

It didn't matter that Connell was gone. She didn't have room for him in her life anyway. Not now that she had Daisy to take care of. They would be busy getting work and looking for a place to live.

"Most of the girls are really good girls at heart," Daisy continued.

"I can't imagine how hard it must have been for each of you to have to degrade yourself night after night."

"It was hard at first." Daisy's voice grew faint, and pain flashed through her eyes.

"I'm sorry." Lily smoothed the fair cheek of the girl, wishing she could as easily wipe away the painful memories.

For a long moment, the crackle of the fire was the only sound in the cozy bedroom. The dark mahogany of the bureau and armoire, along with the thick draperies closed against the light of day, deepened the shadows of the room. The dim light from the lamp on the bedstead table reached out to touch the silver decorations around the room and made them glitter — the leaf-patterned edge of the pedestal mirror, the tall candelabras on the mantel, a tiny decorative box.

The room couldn't even begin to compare to the cramped, barren bedrooms of the orphanages they'd lived in for so many years, with rows of beds made of sagging, urine-stained mattresses and rusting metal frames.

She didn't doubt Mr. McCormick had worked hard over the years to accumulate his wealth and the beautiful possessions she'd seen in every room and hallway of the house. But at what cost? The destruction of thousands upon thousands of acres of prime forestland? The callousness to the vile way of living that had accompanied the devastation?

And now Connell had chosen to follow in the same footsteps as his father. Apparently the success of the business was more important than anything else — including her.

Pain swirled through her again, as it had since she'd left him in the front parlor hours ago. As the morning had passed, she'd finally given up hope he would barge through the bedroom door and tell her he'd changed his mind.

He was gone.

If there had ever been a whisper of anything between them, it was gone now too.

Daisy gave a long sigh and stared at the ceiling, as if gazing into her past.

"Why did you do it, Daisy?" The question slipped out before Lily could stop it. She didn't want to scold the girl. And she didn't want to make her feel any worse than she already did. But the question had nagged her all winter, and she wouldn't be at peace until she knew why Daisy had sold herself, body and soul.

"I told you in the letter I sent you last fall." Daisy flipped away from her.

Lily reached for a strand of the girl's hair, but then hesitated. "I know you wanted to earn money so we could be together again. But why didn't you come to me first before you ran away?"

She shrugged.

"I would have figured out some way for us to be with each other."

Daisy was silent.

"We could have gotten factory jobs or we could have gone back to New York — or something. Anything besides . . . giving your innocence away."

The idea of her sweet little sister lying with countless strange, dirty men made her stomach ache. The pounding fist of depression threatened to overwhelm her every time she allowed herself to think about it.

Daisy's innocence was gone. And now she could never get it back.

"Oh, Daisy," she whispered, wishing she could turn back time and keep her sister from making such an enormous mistake.

"I didn't *give* my innocence away," Daisy said sullenly, as though sensing the condemnation that Lily was trying so hard not to place upon her.

"It's okay." Lily combed the girl's hair with her fingers, but Daisy stiffened under her touch and pulled away.

"Someone *took* it from me."

Lily froze. Her heartbeat slowed like wagon wheels in slush, and her fingers became tangled in Daisy's hair. "What do you mean?"

"The nice, normal, wonderful Mr. Wretcham? He wasn't so nice after all."

"What?" Dread crashed through Lily.

"Apparently orphan girls are good for something, huh?"

"What happened? What did he do?" She wasn't sure she wanted to know, but anger pushed her up to her knees, and she grabbed Daisy, forcing her to turn over and face her.

"From the very first day, he made me uncomfortable with his attention and his too-wide smiles." Daisy twisted away from her, as if she were ashamed to look at her. "Eventually, he started touching me. Not openly — almost like the bumps and brushes were accidents."

Lily wanted to scream at her to stop. She didn't want to hear anything more. She couldn't bear to think she'd pushed Daisy to live with the Wretchams. If she hadn't, none of the heartache would have happened.

But Daisy continued in a monotone. "Finally one day, when Mrs. Wretcham was gone visiting neighbors, he found me alone in the barn. One of the cats had just had kittens. They barely had their eyes open . . ."

Lily closed her eyes to block out the scene. But suddenly all she could see was Daisy kneeling in the warm hay with the earthy scent of freshly harvested wheat all around and sunlight streaming in one of the windows. The downy fur of the kittens, their rumbling purrs and soft mews comforting her.

"He tried to kiss me. And when I wouldn't cooperate like he wanted, he pulled me into one of the empty stalls, and . . ."

Revulsion swelled in Lily's throat, and for a moment she had to fight a wave of bitter nausea. She wanted to weep at the picture of her sweet little Daisy being hurt in that way. How had she let this happen to her? How had she failed to protect her sister so horribly?

"After the first couple of times, I didn't fight him anymore," Daisy said weakly. "But I didn't want to stay there —"

"Why didn't you tell me?" Lily's voice caught the edge of a sob. "Why didn't you come to me? I could have helped you."

"What could you have done? Taken me to live with the sick woman and grumpy old man you were staying with? And let him have his way with me too?"

380

"Oren wouldn't have dreamed of defiling you." If only she'd let Daisy live with Oren and Betty in the first place. "He protected my honor more times than I can count."

Daisy shrugged, as if she didn't believe her — or care. "When I heard about how much money girls were making in the taverns in the lumber camps, I figured I could go for a few months, make my fortune, and then come get you."

The pressure of the stifled sobs in Lily's chest threatened to cut off her breathing. She could only imagine how dirty Daisy must have felt after losing her innocence to Mr. Wretcham, how defiled, how violated. Had she also felt hopeless? Had she decided that since one bad man had used her, she was unworthy of any good man?

"Oh, Daisy." Lily squeezed the words past the tightness in her throat. "I wish you would have let me help you."

Daisy didn't say anything. Instead she reached for the oval picture frame on the bedstead table — the miniature portrait of their parents, the only thing either of them owned to connect them to the family they'd once had so briefly.

Lily had taken it out of her sack earlier and placed it where they could both see it. For all they'd been through, they were still a family. And from now on, they'd never be apart again.

Daisy ran her finger around the corroded silver edge. The unsmiling faces of their parents stared at them.

Lily had wanted to show her parents she'd found Daisy, and maybe they'd be happy with her again. But for some reason, their eyes were still as accusing as always.

With a sigh, Daisy placed the frame gingerly back onto the table, facedown.

Did she feel their censure too?

"I want you to know I still love you," Lily whispered. "You're still precious to me."

Daisy reached for her hand and slipped her fingers into it.

Lily squeezed. "I'll make sure no one ever hurts you again."

"I'm okay, Lily. Really I am." The color had come back into the girl's face, and she hadn't vomited that morning. She'd even been able to eat a little breakfast from the tray Mrs. McCormick had brought.

"Maybe you'll be able to take a bath later," Lily said, only because Mrs. McCormick had already offered to have the maid draw up hot water for them. "They have a real bathroom with a big tub."

Daisy's eyes lit. "I've never had a bath in a real tub."

Lily thought back to all the years they'd had to stand in line for baths. Only the first few in line had ever gotten anything but cold, dirty water. "We might not have had much, but we always had each other."

"Remember when we'd lie on our bed together at night and play the 'what if' game?"

Lily smiled. All those years in the orphanages, before falling asleep each night, they'd snuggle together in their narrow bed and one of them would start the game by saying "what if . . ." and fill it in with something they longed for.

"Do you remember when I said, 'What if we could have our own room, with a big bed, with warm blankets'?"

A sudden lump lodged in Lily's throat. She nodded.

Daisy gazed around the luxurious suite, taking in every elegant item. "*What if* this were really ours?"

The lump in Lily's throat pushed higher.

"What if we never had to leave this place?"

"I promise things will be different from now on."

"Will they really?" Daisy's voice was soft, but the doubt in her tone rang loudly.

"We're older now. We'll be able to find work. And we'll be able to find a place to live — not as nice as this, but we'll get our own home."

Daisy's eyes locked with hers, and in the depths Lily could see that her sister wanted to believe her. But the specks of too many past disappointments floated in the murkiness.

"We'll go somewhere safe." Lily tried to infuse more hope into her voice.

Daisy shuddered. "Preferably somewhere far away from Carr."

As soon as they could get Frankie, they'd go. "You know he's been kidnapping innocent girls and forcing them to work for him?"

Daisy nodded soberly. "I've seen him beat several of the girls until they were nearly unconscious. He's vicious and cruel. And he never let us keep any of our earnings. Not even the extra cash men leave on the bedside table." Daisy's voice turned bitter. "One of the girls hid a few dollars, and a few days later Carr found it and bloodied her up with his brass knuckles."

"Someone ought to use those brass knuckles on him and see how he likes it."

"He's untouchable."

Lily's thoughts returned to the flyers she and Stuart had handed out in their effort to start the Red Ribbon Society. Not many of the townspeople had been interested, especially when she'd explained her desire to rise up as one against Carr.

"I don't understand why he's so untouchable," she muttered. "Seems like everyone could stand up to him if they really wanted to."

But Carr wasn't her concern anymore. Nor was the Harrison Red Ribbon Society. Stuart would have to carry on without her.

"I can't tell you how many shanty boys Carr's killed or had his bouncers kill," Daisy said. "Nobody really knows, except that men disappear all the time, never to be seen again."

A tremor of fear wound through Lily. What would happen to Connell when he got back to Harrison? What if Carr found out about his part in Daisy's escape?

Carr would unleash his fury on Connell. And Carr would want to kill Connell once he helped rescue Frankie from the Devil's Ranch.

Lily shivered and slid under the quilt. As much as she wanted to deny her heartache over losing Connell, she knew she couldn't. Deep in her core, she cared about him more than any other man she'd ever met. The thought of anything happening to him terrified her.

He might have disappointed her and rejected her. But she couldn't bear the thought that Carr might kill him.

Her cold toes pressed against the heating stone, and she pulled the quilt around her tighter. She closed her eyes to block out the image of Carr pounding his brass knuckles into Connell's face. The damage from Tierney's fists wouldn't begin to compare with the broken bloody mess Carr would make of Connell.

Why hadn't he just stayed with her, as she'd begged him to do?

Her fingers dug into the quilt against the stitches that formed into a complex pattern. The quilt was large and colorful and intricate — just like Vera's quilt would be once she finished.

What had Vera told her about the way God worked? When things didn't turn out the way they wanted, they could know God was still there piecing together everything the way He had planned. Was it really true? Or did it just mean she needed to try harder to help make things happen?

She wrapped her arm around Daisy, drawing against the girl to feel her warmth and to stop the trembling in her limbs.

At least she could find comfort in one thing. Even though Connell wasn't a part of the quilt of her life, Daisy was. And that was all that really mattered.

Wasn't it?

CHAPTER 23

Upon seeing the front office of the *Harrison Herald,* Connell's blood ran cold.

He jumped from the sleigh, stiff and frozen after the long hours of traveling. Through the darkness of the evening, the bright light from the tavern across the street illuminated the ghastly pallor of the newspaper office — the smashed glass of the front window, the door hanging from its hinges, and the printing equipment strewn through the entryway.

During the entire ride back to Harrison, Connell had tried to convince himself everything would be fine, that his life could continue as normal, that nothing needed to change.

But one look at the *Harrison Herald* told him everything had changed. Nothing would ever be the same again.

With a glance at the dark shadows that lurked around the building, his fingers found the smooth handle of his knife and unsheathed it.

He pushed his way through the broken door and stepped gingerly across the disarray of papers, broken cases, and lead type.

No doubt about it. Carr had been there. He must have learned of Stuart's part in Daisy's escape. And if he'd learned of Stuart's part, then he'd know of Connell's.

"Stu?" he called hoarsely. Every nerve in his body was poised for an attack, his ear attuned to every sound, his fingers on his knife and ready to fight.

The overpowering scent of ink assaulted him. The crunch of broken glass under his boots forced him to a halt.

"Stuart," he called again, louder, straining to see through the dark shadows.

With a thudding heart, he backed out of the room and ventured up the creaking stairs to his office. The door was wide open, and through the hazy moonlight drifting through the window, his last breadth of hope fizzled as he took in his overturned desk, the ripped books and ledgers, and the broken desk chair. His organized files were dumped on the floor; even the calendar had been ripped from the wall.

He let out a long tense breath and his shoulders sagged.

He'd been holding on to a slim margin, the one percent chance Carr wouldn't connect him with Daisy's disappearance. But now he was one hundred percent certain Carr had pegged him as an accomplice.

The moment he'd decided to help Lily take Daisy out of town, he'd cast his lot against Carr. For better or worse, he'd made an enemy of the man.

And he doubted even Dad's money would buy peace now.

He kicked one of the ledgers, its pages torn in half. He wasn't sure he wanted peace — not with a man who thought he was above the law in every way. It was bad enough that Carr was forcing young girls into prostitution and keeping them penned up in his brothels like slaves.

But now . . .

He clamped his mouth shut to keep from giving life to a curse.

Now Carr was destroying those who dared to stand up for what was right. He'd destroyed Stuart's livelihood. And only heaven knew what he'd done to Stuart.

He spun out of his office and retreated down the steps. In seconds he was back on his sleigh. And in less than a minute, he pulled up in front of Stuart's house. One glance told him Carr had ransacked Stu's home just like he had the newspaper office.

Connell made his way cautiously through the wrecked house, dreading what he'd discover as he went from room to room. Finding only more of the same mindless destruction and with no sign of Stuart, he finally returned to the sleigh. He turned in the direction of the Northern Hotel, praying as he drove that Carr had left the Hellers alone.

A rumble of anger rolled through his chest at the thought of Carr hurting Vera and her husband or in any way damaging their business. If he'd touched them, Connell didn't know what he'd do.

Was God trying to get his attention and send him the message that he needed to do more to join the fight? If so, it was working.

For once, he was grateful for the crass laughter and obnoxious piano music of the taverns, the coming and going of the shanty boys, and the usual brawling and shouting that punctuated the frigid night air. At least he could ride undetected and buy himself a little time before Carr realized he was back in town and sent his men after him.

Connell stomped up the step of the hotel and knocked the mud and slush from his boots. Through the front window, nothing appeared amiss. But his breath wobbled in short white puffs, and he opened the door slowly.

The dining room was deserted. The fire was low and in need of feeding. And only one of the oil lamps hanging from the ceiling was lit.

He closed the door and put his hand to his side, feeling the hard length of his knife.

"Who's there?" Vera's voice called from the kitchen.

"It's just me. Connell."

In an instant she appeared in the doorway, wielding her large wooden spoon, as if ready for battle.

When her gaze landed upon him, her spoon slipped from her fingers and fell to the floor with a clatter. Tears pooled in her eyes. "Connell. Oh, thank goodness you're alive."

He crossed the room toward her. "I'm just fine. What about you and Mr. Heller?"

"We're scared. But mostly for you boys."

He stopped in front of her, examining her for any signs of injury.

Her cheeks were as red as always, and frizzy tendrils of her speckled hair framed her face. Her grayish apron was splattered with the day's work. Only her eyes were different — filled with sadness instead of the merriment he'd come to expect.

"I've been so worried about you." She reached for his cheeks and squeezed them between her palms. "Looks like they beat you up too." She frowned first at the cut on his lip and then at the puffy discolored skin surrounding his eye.

"I got in a fight with Tierney. That's all. I'm okay —"

The cold butt of a rifle pressed into the back of his head.

"You won't be okay when I'm done with you."

Vera slapped her hands on her hips. "Now, you put that old thing away, Oren."

The barrel dug into Connell's scalp.

"I should have blown your brains out the first day I saw you," the gruff voice of Oren came from behind him.

"The boy is cold and hungry," Vera huffed. "Just you leave him alone."

"I'll leave him alone as soon as I'm done pounding lead into his head."

"Don't mind him." Vera reached up and patted Connell's cheek again. "He's been worried near sick about Lily. That's all."

"Where in the hairy hound did you take her?" Oren demanded.

"She's safe."

"Where?"

"I can't tell you here. Not out in the

393

open." They couldn't take any chances on Carr finding out where Lily and Daisy were.

The pressure of the metal slackened but only slightly.

"She and Daisy are being well taken care of. They have everything they need and want." It had been only ten hours and thirty-five minutes since he'd left Lily, but it felt like ten years.

He pictured her again standing before him in the parlor. She'd been so beautiful and so passionate and so bent on saving the world, as always. And he adored her for who she was.

Leaving her and riding away from his parents' home had wrenched his heart in two pieces. And he felt like he'd left the bigger half with her and now carried only a sliver of what remained in his chest.

He tried not to think about the finality in Lily's voice when she'd walked away. But the fact was, he couldn't just leave everything — his job, his family's business, and all that he'd worked so hard to accomplish. She had to know that he couldn't walk away. And he couldn't ask her to join him in Harrison or any of the lumber towns — not now. Maybe not ever.

His shoulders slumped and defeat mocked him again as it had the entire ride back.

They were just too different.

"You sure she's someplace where Carr can't get her?" Oren's voice was gentler.

"It's not the moon. But hopefully Carr will stay away."

Oren didn't say anything for a long moment.

The barrel trembled. But Connell wasn't afraid of the old man. He could only imagine Oren's worry over the past days and didn't blame him for needing someone upon whom to take out his frustration.

"If anything happens to her, I'll hunt you down like a buck, shoot you, and skin you."

"You don't have to worry," Connell said, turning to face the old man and pushing aside the rifle.

Oren's shoulders were stooped more than usual, if that were possible. And under his bushy gray eyebrows, his eyes were bloodshot, as if he hadn't slept in the two days Lily had been gone.

"If anything happens to her," Connell said, "I'll come straight to you and *let* you shoot me."

Oren's sad eyes locked with his and seemed to peer deep into Connell's soul.

He wanted to tell Oren he cared about Lily just as much as he did. But the words stuck in his throat. He hoped Oren could see the truth. Even if he and Lily could never be together, he'd still do everything he could for her. He didn't want anything to happen to her either.

"Ah," Oren finally muttered. With a shaking hand, he reached for the edge of the table and slowly lowered himself onto the nearest bench.

Vera bent over and picked up her wooden spoon. She stuck it in her apron pocket and then patted Connell's arm. "Give me a minute, and I'll rustle up some dinner."

"What happened to Stuart?"

She shook her head, clucked her tongue, and then started toward the kitchen.

Fresh dread battered Connell's gut. "He isn't —"

"Of course he's not dead." Vera disappeared into the other room. "Not with me doctoring him."

Connell wasn't sure whether he should feel relief or worry. "How bad is he hurt?" He trailed after Vera.

She lifted a long iron fork from a hook on the grease-splattered wall near the stove. "He's plenty bruised up and has a few broken bones, but he'll live."

Anger once again sizzled through Connell like salt pork in a frypan.

Vera lifted the lid off a large pot on the

396

back burner. The earthy odor of simmering beans made his stomach gurgle, reminding him he hadn't eaten since the breakfast he'd shared with Mam early that morning.

"He won't have the use of his arm for a while, and his ribs are cracked." Vera stabbed the fork into the pot and emerged with a thick piece of pork dripping in bean juice. She flopped it onto the closest plate still covered with a film of dishpan water from the after-dinner dunking. Then she poked the fork into the pot again.

"Where is he?"

She nodded toward the closed door of her bedroom. "He's asleep for the night. You can visit him tomorrow."

"Think he's safe here?"

"Not any safer than you'll be." She slapped another piece of pork onto the plate.

"What about you? Has Carr threatened you or Mr. Heller?"

"A couple of his men came in this morning and said that any man who stays at the Northern isn't welcome at the Stockade anymore."

"He has no right to intimidate your boarders like that."

"Well, it worked. Now we've only got a handful of men left." She reached into the bread box and pulled out a couple of slices of crumbly bread.

"I'm sorry for bringing all this trouble on you."

She added a fistful of cookies to his plate and handed it to him. "I'm not sorry." She wiped her hands on her apron. "I'm glad that we're finally starting to do something to oppose that evil man."

Were they really opposing him? Or were they merely stirring up a hornet's nest?

Connell bit into the bread. It stuck at the back of his throat.

No matter what might happen, one thing was certain.

He was in the thick of the hornets now. And it was only a matter of time before he got stung.

CHAPTER 24

"How many boys are gone?" Connell asked his foreman, bracing himself for the bad news.

"At least twenty."

Connell jabbed the end of one of the logs already loaded onto the flat sleigh at the skidway and bit back an oath aimed at Carr.

Twenty was one-fifth of the crew at Camp 1.

"And there's more talking about leaving." Herb Nolan spoke quietly, his focus unswerving from the growing pyramid of logs on the sleigh.

The experienced loader at the top of the pile used his cant hook to maneuver another log up a pair of slanting poles. He straddled the logs already in place, the spikes in his caulk boots giving him traction. The snorts of the big workhorses, the grunts of men, and the jangle of chains filled the air around them.

"Not our best workers?" Connell didn't want to ask, but he had to take stock. He had to see how much damage he'd brought to McCormick Lumber.

"So far it's been the boys more partial to fat pork and sundown."

"Good." He couldn't afford to lose anyone, but he'd much rather lose his swampers and road monkeys. If he lost his best loaders, sawyers, or teamsters, he'd be ruined for sure. He had to find a way to shut the door on Carr's scare tactics and stop the exodus from his camps. And he had to do it fast.

Connell cupped his gloved hands around the tin cup of coffee he'd picked up from Duff in the cookshack when he'd arrived. Steam rose from the dark liquid, and the wind twirled it away, giving him only a lingering waft of the freshly ground aroma.

He took a swig and already it was lukewarm.

A winter storm was blowing in and would bring fresh snow.

At least the weather was cooperating — although with spring only five weeks away, there was no guarantee they'd have much time left to get the largest share of the logs out of the forest to the banking grounds.

"The fact is," Herb said, "that devil Carr

is scaring the stink out of everyone."

"Well, you can let the men know that anyone who stays with me through the river drive will get double the bonus." He had the sick feeling that not only would McCormick Lumber fail to come out on top in lumber production at the end of the winter, but they might actually go into the red.

"And you can let them know I'll be sending out Charlie from Camp 2 to do some hunting for all the camps. Hopefully, you'll have fresh meat more often."

The foreman pinched at one of the little icicles hanging from his mustache. "The boys have been lookin' funny at Duff's porkers. I know they've got a hankering for something besides the usual."

Connell took another slurp of his coffee. He'd slept a grand total of fifty-one minutes the previous night. His body had been too keyed up, anticipating Carr's men barging into the room he'd taken at the Northern. And his mind had been too full of plans for how to save the business from complete devastation.

He'd been more than a little surprised he'd made it through the night without a confrontation. And he'd been even more surprised that he'd made it out the door and all the way to Camp 1 without an altercation.

He knew it was only a matter of time before Carr came after him, especially since Carr had already battered Stuart. In the dark hours of the morning, Connell had slipped in to visit his friend. The low light couldn't conceal the deep bruises and lacerations on Stu's face.

As prominent as Stuart was in the community, they hadn't dared to kill him. But Stuart wasn't so sure about Bass, his assistant. They hoped Bass's disappearance meant he'd fled town. But they both knew if Carr had gotten hold of him, they'd never hear from Bass again.

According to Stuart, Carr had figured out every detail of how they'd helped Lily and Daisy and was now determined to ruin McCormick Lumber, to set an example of what would happen to anyone who defied him.

Connell gulped the rest of the coffee, draining the cup.

"Tell the men I plan to reward everyone who's loyal to McCormick Lumber."

He quickly calculated the diameters of each of the logs already in place on the sleigh awaiting transportation to the camp decking ground near the narrow-gauge train. Most were cut in twenty-foot lengths and weighed six tons. He could see that his sawyers were working hard.

And the icers were too. From the deep icy ruts in the road, it was obvious they were still making several tours each night. Their diligence was allowing the horses to transport the heavy sleighs of logs with more ease and speed.

They were moving out prime lumber. But they couldn't keep it up if they lost any more men. Would the lure of a bonus and fresh meat be enough to keep the rest of the men from leaving? What reason had McCormick Lumber ever given their men to remain loyal to the company?

Shouts and the clomping of horse hooves on the iced roads echoed through the brittleness of the clearing. The frantic pounding was not the usual even pace of the team returning on a go-back road for another load of logs.

Connell's muscles tensed. He tossed aside his tin cup and grabbed the foreman's ax from a resting spot against a Norway maple — one of the trees in the stand not worth cutting. At the same time he unsheathed his knife.

An instant later, the cookee came careening around the bend in the road on one of the blacksmith's horses. Clouds of vapor billowed from the beast's nostrils.

Cookee's eyes were wild and his face red. "Carr's men are here!"

"Where?" Connell asked.

"They're tearing apart the van!"

"My office?" the foreman roared.

Cookee nodded. "And the store."

Connell's mind flashed to the needless destruction he'd witnessed at the newspaper office and at Stuart's home. Heated anger spurted through his blood at the picture of Carr's men tearing through the small building where the foreman and scaler worked and slept, where they also kept a small inventory of store goods — mittens, socks, tobacco, and medicines.

"How many men, Cookee?" Connell's grip on his knife tightened.

"Three."

Herb had already started forward.

Connell threw him his ax, which he caught by the handle and wielded like a weapon. The hardness of the man's face confirmed he'd fight alongside Connell. He was angry at the destruction and intimidation too.

"Anyone care to loan me his hunting knife?" Connell glanced around to the others. "I think I'll have need of one or two more."

The men had paused their work and were

staring at him. What did they think? Would they support him or not?

"I won't put up with Carr bullying any of my men or my camps."

When several of the men nodded and a few others muttered oaths about Carr, the tightness in Connell's chest eased. And when two of the send-up men handed him their knives, a jolt of confidence propelled him forward.

He nodded his thanks and then took off at a sprint after Herb.

After running at top speed the half mile back to the camp, they arrived in front of the van with their breaths puffing into the air like bursts of steam engine smoke.

The blacksmith, waiting in the doorway of his log shop, joined them, a hammer in one hand and a sledge in the other. His shiny black apron pulled taut across his wide girth. He lifted his hammer. "Some of us around here are fed up with how James Carr can do whatever he wants and get away with it."

Connell stopped at the sight of the wrath boiling in the blacksmith's eyes. Would the people of Harrison, the men of the camps, and the residents of Clare County be willing to fight Carr? Had he been wrong to assume everyone was afraid of him?

"I brought Carr's anger upon myself," Connell said to both the men. "You don't need to do this —"

"We think you did the right thing," the smith said. "We're in this together."

"Anyone who threatens this camp," Herb added, "threatens me."

The two men didn't back down.

The shattering of the glass window on the side of the tiny log building was followed by the crash of a chair against the hard-packed snow.

Connell raised one of the knives and then kicked the door. The force flung it open and slammed it against the wall. The usual musty odor — a lingering scent of kerosene and tobacco — swelled over him.

"Well, look what we got here, boys" came a voice from within the dusky interior.

One of the men, in the process of tearing the pages out of Herb's tally book, paused. A half page fluttered to the floor. Another man rummaging through a spilled carton of cigars straightened.

"Get out." Connell drew mental targets on the two men in places that would hurt but not cause death.

"We've been waiting for you to get back to town." Another man stepped closer to the door, the daylight revealing his face.

"Jimmy Neil?"

The man smiled, exposing the black gap in his cracked top teeth. The smile was followed by the glint of a pistol.

"So Carr's got you doing his dirty work now?" Connell's body tensed. He wasn't sure he could fling his knife into Jimmy's hand before he pulled the trigger.

"Putting a bullet in your heart isn't dirty work," Jimmy sneered. "It's chopping your body into tiny pieces and tossing them into the well that gets messy."

"Carr can't kill me." At least he was gambling upon the fact that Carr wouldn't have him murdered in broad daylight.

Connell took a step toward Jimmy, but his heart quivered with the uncertainty of how to proceed, how to actually fight against Jimmy or anyone. Sure, he'd pounded Tierney until he was nearly unconscious, but how would he fight against three men?

"We've got orders to take you to Carr." Jimmy's aim didn't budge. "Today. Now."

"You can tell Carr I've been meaning to pay him a visit." Connell flung one of his knives toward the bouncer with a stolen cigar in his mouth. The knife came within two inches of the man's face and sliced the cigar so that only the head remained between his lips, dribbling tobacco to the floor.

With a twang, the knife embedded into the shelves behind the man — the shelves barren of all the camp-store supplies, which were dumped across the floor.

Connell had another knife in place and ready to throw before the man could even blink.

"Let Carr know I'll make sure he's more than compensated for the girl." With a flick of his wrist, he threw the next knife into the center of the tally book the other bouncer was holding, missing his fingers by a mere half inch.

The man cursed and dropped the book as if it were glowing hot metal straight from the smith's forge.

Connell aimed the last knife at the hand Jimmy was using to hold the pistol. "Now, go on and get out of here before I decide to do a little more target practice."

Jimmy didn't move. His eyes narrowed on Connell.

"You heard him," Herb bellowed. "Get out of my camp and don't come back."

Jimmy looked at the foreman and then the blacksmith. He lowered the pistol. "Carr doesn't like you, McCormick."

"You can tell him I don't like him either." Connell's dad had told him to clean up the mess he'd made and to make sure he didn't anger Carr again. But how could he sit back and let the man bully him — and anyone else who opposed him?

Why did they need to cave in to Carr's wishes and demands? Maybe they'd somehow inadvertently given him control over their county. But that didn't mean they couldn't take it back from him, did it?

"And you can tell him we're tired of him intimidating and bossing everyone around."

Jimmy tucked his pistol into his holster. "I'll be sure to relay your messages. They'll make him real happy." Something dark lurked in the man's eyes — something that sent a shiver of trepidation through Connell.

"Then let Carr know I'll make it my duty from here on out to make him as *happy* as I possibly can."

Jimmy flashed a gap-toothed grin — one as cold and sharp as the angles of broken glass remaining in the windowpane. "You're a fool, McCormick. A big fool."

Maybe he was a fool. Maybe he was going to end up getting hurt or even killed in the process. But deep inside he could feel God shifting him away from apathy to a solid foundation where he could plant his feet and start acting like a real man.

After Jimmy and the two men were gone, Connell stepped outside and leaned against the log building. Through the layer of his cotton shirt the chinking of moss and clay was cold against the sticky sweat on his back. His legs felt weak and his fingers trembled as he sheathed his knife.

The blacksmith finally lowered his hammer and turned to Connell, his eyes alight with admiration. "You're a good man, Boss."

Herb's cussing from within the van penetrated the silent gray air of the morning.

"It ain't easy to take a stand against Carr," the blacksmith continued. "But I'm glad to see you putting that man in his place."

Connell wasn't sure that he'd put Carr in his place. In fact, he probably hadn't accomplished much of anything, except to anger Carr all the more.

One thing was certain, however. Lily would have been proud of him for not caving in to Carr's demands, for being willing to fight against the man. He could picture her wide smile. She would have been jumping up and down with excitement at the sight of him tossing knives at Carr's men. Her brown eyes would have lit up with passion, and she wouldn't have been afraid to give Jimmy Neil a piece of her mind.

His gaze strayed over the stumps scattered around the camp, the tobacco-stained snow, and the frozen slop puddles. For an instant he saw the camp the way she did — the barrenness, the ugliness of the landscape, the destruction. He and his workers were like the blades of the saw, ripping through the land, cutting down everything in their path, leaving behind slashings and stumps and waste.

The devastation they were wreaking wasn't a pretty picture. In some ways it reminded him of the way the van now looked after Carr's men had rampaged through it.

Lily had wanted him to walk away from the business.

Everything within him had resisted.

And still did.

He couldn't agree with her that the lumber industry was evil and worthless. It was a business like any other, and along with the many good things it was also bound to have problems. But could he do more to not only stand up and fight against Carr, but to also stand up and fight against some of the problems within the business?

Maybe there was more he and the other companies could do to help take care of the land so it didn't look like a burned-out war zone by the time they moved on.

One pure white snowflake floated softly in front of him, followed by another and another.

He'd never been a fighter. He'd always been content to float through life.

But since the moment Lily had walked into his life, something about her had kicked him off his behind and propelled him into action.

And now that he'd started fighting, he had the feeling he wouldn't be able to stop.

CHAPTER 25

Lily swatted the edge of the basket against the spindly insect that seemed to appear out of nowhere and skitter across the surface of the table.

She pressed down until she heard the telltale crunch letting her know she'd rid the widow's one-room apartment of another cockroach.

Holding back a cringe, she hefted the baby in one arm and used the basket to sweep the ugly rust-colored bug onto the littered floor.

"I will be praying for you, my dear." Mrs. McCormick rose from the only chair in the room and reached for the widow.

Tears trickled down the young woman's cheeks, and she embraced Mrs. McCormick with a fierceness that spoke of her gratefulness more than words ever could. The contents of the now empty basket were strewn across the sagging bed: packages of fresh food wrapped in brown paper, diaper cloths, and other necessary items.

After losing her husband to a sawmill accident, the widow had no money and no easy way of earning a living — especially with the responsibility of a young child. Mrs. McCormick's gifts wouldn't last long, but they would provide the woman with some stability until she could find a means of caring for herself and her infant.

The baby reached sticky fingers for the wide velvet laces of Lily's bonnet — one Mrs. McCormick had loaned her. Trimmed with ostrich feathers, it was far too extravagant for Lily and out of place in the boardinghouse. But Mrs. McCormick had encouraged Lily to wear it.

Lily repositioned the baby on her hip and pressed a kiss absently against the child's grainy hair. The sourness of the baby's soiled diaper and clothes had seeped into her smooth deerskin gloves and the fashionable but heavy tweed jacket Mrs. McCormick had insisted she don to match another of the lovely skirts she'd loaned her.

But she didn't mind — not when she could help alleviate the widow's suffering — even if just for a few minutes.

"I wish we could do more for her," Lily said as they closed the door behind them and began descending the narrow stairwell.

"I wish we could do more too," Mrs. McCormick said wistfully, pausing to retie the big lacy ribbon under her chin.

The putridness of rotting garbage that littered the floor underneath the rickety stairs rose to gag them. Lily tried to breathe through her mouth and made an effort to hide the disgust that swirled through her stomach — especially because several small urchins at the bottom of the steps had turned wide eyes upon them and were watching every move they made.

Except for the click of their boots on the steps and the faint wail of a baby in one of the apartments, the tenement was mostly deserted and quiet.

The boardinghouses near the sawmills were common two- or three-story establishments that charged five dollars a week for room and board. But from what she'd seen, they weren't worthy of five cents. They were poorly built, run down, and rat infested. She'd killed at least a dozen cockroaches in the widow's sparsely furnished room. And no doubt there were hoards of bedbugs and lice as well.

The orphanages she'd grown up in had been cleaner and safer.

When Lily pushed through the front door

and stepped onto the muddy street, a burst of bitter air slapped her cheek, as if reminding her that but for the kindness of Mrs. McCormick, such a building — or worse — might become home for her and Daisy.

She'd promised Daisy that she would take care of her and make things better for them. But where else would they be able to afford to go, besides a boardinghouse like one of the many along the river?

With a determined set of her shoulders, she climbed into the waiting carriage and refused to look at the dilapidated building again. She had to keep believing she could provide Daisy with a better life now. She couldn't allow herself to think they would end up like the widow.

Mrs. McCormick followed her into the carriage and sat across from her, her eyes never once leaving the apartment complex, not even after their conveyance began rolling away. Only when they'd turned the corner and begun the short ride back to the McCormick mansion did the older woman tear her gaze away with a sigh.

"Someday I would like to have a home of refuge to help young women like her." She smiled faintly.

Lily reached for one of the woman's hands and squeezed it. "You're wonderful and kind, Mrs. McCormick."

The woman pressed her hand in return. "Thank you, my dear."

"Someday I'd like to have a safe place for young women too," Lily admitted. And once the words were out, she wished she could take them back. Who was she to think she'd ever have the means to provide such a place for scared and helpless women?

Mrs. McCormick didn't scoff at her. Instead she wrapped both her hands around Lily's. "All God needs is a willing heart. If we desire to serve Him, He can take care of the rest of the details."

Lily was half tempted to argue with Mrs. McCormick. Surely they had to do more than have a willing heart. They had to work hard to make things happen. At least that had always been her philosophy. But something in the wise depths of Mrs. McCormick's eyes stopped her response.

The ride home was over in a matter of minutes, and as Lily walked into the lavish home, she shrank back, overwhelmed with guilt. How could she live in this comfort and splendor — even if only for a short time — knowing that four blocks away families lived in squalor and filth?

"How can we live like this" — Lily waved her hand at the entryway into which the widow's apartment could have easily fit — "when there are so many people who have so little?"

As the words left her lips, Lily cringed at the brashness of them. Mrs. McCormick was one of the most generous people Lily had ever met. And she certainly didn't want to lose the woman's favor. Even though Connell had walked out of her life, there was still part of her that clung to the hope he would see the error of his ways, change his mind, and come back to her.

The woman laid her gloves on the tall polished side table and glanced into the oval mirror that hung above it. She began unbuttoning the tight-fitting jacket that matched her striped silk visiting dress. A crease formed in the gentle contours of her forehead.

"I'm sorry," Lily said. "It's just that all winter long as I've traveled through the lumber camps, I've witnessed mile after mile of ruined forestland. And even worse, I've seen lives ruined by the evil and greed that the industry fosters."

Mrs. McCormick nodded.

"I've seen young girls lured into prostitution. Some are even forced into it against their will." Lily pushed aside the twinge of guilt she felt every time she thought about

Frankie and the fact that she still hadn't done anything to rescue the girl.

They'd been in Bay City only four days. She told herself that she couldn't leave Daisy quite yet. Besides, Connell had promised to go after Frankie, and despite their differences, she believed he would keep his word.

A chill snuck under her jacket and up her back. She could only pray Connell was still alive and that he'd escaped harm. If anything *had* happened to him, surely someone would have sent news to his family by now.

"My dear," Mrs. McCormick said softly, "I can't even begin to imagine the vileness you've witnessed this winter. But as you saw this morning, the effects of the wickedness are not limited only to the camps. They're all around us here in Bay City too."

"That's my point." Lily's voice rose with passion. "Your husband, and other lumber barons like him, have grown wealthy and successful, but at the cost of land, and life, and decency for the common laborer. Is it right for us to live this way, when it has come at such a high price?"

Mrs. McCormick sighed and glanced around the opulent hallway. "I have thought of this too. I've lived at one end of the spectrum — in a place very much like the

419

one we visited today. And now with my husband's hard work, I'm at the other end of the continuum."

"Then you must see the injustice of it all."

Mrs. McCormick's eyes filled with warm understanding. "As long as man lives and breathes, there will always be sin in this world and consequently injustice."

"But that doesn't mean we should give up, sit back, and do nothing."

"You're right. Nor can we fight against everything. We must instead discover where God wants to use us."

Lily's heart pulsed faster at the woman's words.

"I may not be able to rebuild the company boardinghouse to make it safer and more livable," Mrs. McCormick continued. "That isn't within the scope of my influence or control. But I can offer comfort to those who live there. That *is* something I can *choose* to do. And of course, I keep praying that someday I'll be able to do more."

Mrs. McCormick lifted her hand to Lily's cheek. Her rose-powder fragrance swirled in the air. And Lily couldn't keep from leaning into its warm caress, longing swelling deep inside.

What would her mother's touch have felt like? What would it have been like to have a mother giving her advice?

In the presence of this lovely woman, experiencing her goodness, her wisdom, and her sweet touch, buried needs pushed through the tough winter ground of her heart. For so long, she'd had to be strong so she could be both mother and father to Daisy. She'd had no one to turn to, no one to take care of her, no one to lean on.

Just for once, she wanted to know what it would have been like to have a mother.

As if sensing Lily's need, the woman reached for her and wrapped her arms around Lily, drawing her against her bosom.

Lily couldn't resist. She slipped her arms around Mrs. McCormick, falling into the embrace, relishing the gentleness of the woman's arms and the firmness of the squeeze.

"You are a brave and strong young woman," Mrs. McCormick said. "And you amaze me."

An ache pushed up Lily's throat. Sadness pressed at her chest, making her want to weep at what she had missed all those years without a mother to turn to.

And now, in Mrs. McCormick's tender but strong arms, she couldn't keep from wishing for more — a real family, a real home.

Mrs. McCormick pressed a kiss into Lily's hair and pulled back.

Reluctantly, Lily let go.

"You're already choosing to fight the battles God is giving you." Mrs. McCormick gave her cheek another gentle pat. "But be patient with those who are still discovering where God wants to use them."

Mrs. McCormick's eyes held Lily's. Reflected in the kind depths she saw Connell. And she couldn't help wondering if somehow Mrs. McCormick had learned of the quarrel she'd had with Connell and was asking her to be patient with him.

After Mrs. McCormick left, Lily started up the broad winding staircase. Her footsteps were slow and her mind swirled with bittersweet emotions. Was it too late to wish for a real home for her and Daisy?

With a sigh, she paused on the landing of the second floor. As much as she wanted a woman like Mrs. McCormick for a mother, she and Daisy couldn't impose on the woman's good graces indefinitely.

At some point she would need to find a job and a place for them to live. And when that time came, she could only pray their new home would be better than the boardinghouse she'd visited.

The tinkling of Daisy's laughter came

from the second-floor hallway.

Lily started forward in surprise.

Daisy had declined going with them earlier upon complaint of one of her headaches. In fact, she hadn't left the house since their arrival. And even though Lily wanted to encourage Daisy to put her shame behind her and move on with her life, she hadn't wanted to push her to go anywhere before she was ready — especially before she had the chance to get the alcohol out of her system.

The laughter came again — playful, almost teasing.

Lily smiled.

She hadn't heard Daisy laugh much during the past few days they'd spent together. When Daisy wasn't feeling sick, she had despaired over her future.

"Who will like me now?" she'd say between sobs. "I'm nobody and nothing."

And when Lily would try to reassure Daisy that eventually she'd meet a nice young man who would love her and want to marry her, she would only say, "Nice boys won't want a girl like me."

Lily prayed Daisy wasn't right. They would have to work hard to put the winter behind them, forget about it, pretend it never happened. Eventually, the memories would fade. And when the right man came along for Daisy, maybe he could forgive Daisy for her time at the Stockade.

A squeak of a desk chair and the thump of a book falling to the floor came from the library.

Lily moved toward the door with a new lightness of step. Whatever could bring Daisy from her room and fill her with fresh laughter was worthy of capturing and using again.

Another soft laugh came through the crack in the door, followed by a gasp.

Lily didn't bother to knock. She pushed the door open with a ready smile, breathing in the heavy scent of varnish and musty books.

But her entire body came to a crashing halt at the sight before her. Her blood chilled into a frozen river. And her smile turned to ice.

Daisy was perched on the edge of an enormous oak desk flanked on either side by floor-to-ceiling bookshelves. Sitting in the chair in front of her was Tierney. Daisy's skirt was bunched up, revealing her stockingless legs. And even worse, her bodice hung loosely, exposing her.

Much to Lily's dismay, Tierney leaned his face toward the girl. As his lips made contact, Lily expected Daisy to push him away and to utter horrified words of protest. But she didn't move.

Lily took a step forward. She had to help Daisy put a stop to Tierney's advances.

But Daisy closed her eyes and gave a soft sigh.

Did Daisy enjoy Tierney's touch? Surely she didn't. Surely she was only putting on a show.

But a deep part of her soul wrenched with pain at the realization that perhaps Daisy had become more tainted through her experiences than she wanted to admit.

Lily took another step into the room and shook her head. This was all wrong. Tierney had obviously cornered Daisy and forced her to debase herself.

"What do you think you're doing?" she demanded, her voice trembling.

With a gasp, Daisy sat up and scrambled off the desk, tugging her bodice with trembling fingers.

Tierney leaned back in the chair, its creak echoing in the tense silence. He crossed his hands behind his head and grinned. "Well, hello there, Lily. How are you today?"

The purplish half moon beneath one of his eyes was all that remained from Connell's beating.

Did he think this was a game? He was a married man. Daisy was vulnerable and hurting. "How dare you do this to my sister!"

He shrugged and perched his feet on the edge of the desk, crossing them at the ankles. "What can I say? Your sister is the most beautiful woman I've ever met."

Daisy dipped her head. But Lily could see the flush of pleasure his words brought the girl.

Angry flames seared Lily's insides. "You know we're trying to make a new life for ourselves. Leave Daisy alone. For the love of all that's good and decent, let her try to put her past behind her."

Her plea rang through the library, against the dark paneled wainscoting of the walls to the bright bay window in the front and the dark billiard room in the rear.

"Daisy's a grown woman. She can decide what she wants."

"No, she can't." Lily glanced around the room, her fingers itching to grab something — anything — to throw at Tierney's mocking face. She spotted a knit blanket draped across one of the cushioned chairs near the fireplace.

With determined steps, she retrieved the covering, draped it across Daisy's shoulders, and then propelled the girl toward the door.

Daisy didn't resist. She hung her head, letting her long hair fall into her face, refusing to meet Lily's gaze.

"Daisy is the only family I have left." Lily spat the words at Tierney, hating his grin that rose higher. "She's my responsibility. I won't let you hurt her. I'll do whatever I have to in order to stop you."

Tierney lifted his hands in mock surrender. "Whoa! Don't crucify me."

"You're nothing like your brother."

"I try hard not to be."

She didn't stop to analyze the bitter edge to Tierney's voice. Instead, she circled her arm around Daisy and hurried her back to their bedroom. Once the door closed behind them, she brushed Daisy's hair aside and began to fasten the buttons at the back of the dress. Lily's throat ached and her fingers trembled.

"Stop, Lily." Daisy shrugged her hand off and walked toward the large window. She yanked open the curtain, letting light spill into the dark room. For a long moment, the girl stared out the window, tears sliding down her cheeks and the knit blanket drooping down one bare shoulder.

Anguish tore through Lily's stomach. She wanted to go to Daisy and pull her into an embrace, comfort her, and reassure her that everything would be all right. But there was a stiffness to Daisy's stance that stopped her.

"Stop treating me like a child," Daisy finally said, swiping at the tears.

"But you're only sixteen —"

"And stop acting like my mother."

"I've always taken care of you."

"I don't need you to anymore."

Lily sucked in a breath. What was Daisy saying?

"I can take care of myself just fine."

"How can you say that? Especially after the way Tierney just accosted you —"

"He didn't accost me." Daisy lifted her chin and turned to look at Lily. "I like him."

Lily shook her head. "He took advantage of you. He knew you'd be weak and vulnerable."

"I don't care." Daisy's eyes flashed with sudden defiance. "When I'm with him, he makes me feel special and pretty."

"He's using you."

"He cares about me."

Lily wanted to cross the room and shake sense into Daisy, but she held herself back. "All he cares about is your body and how he can satisfy his own lust."

Daisy pulled herself up and tossed her hair

over her shoulder. "And I care about him too."

"His wife and baby live across the street."

She shrugged and the blanket fell from her other shoulder. Her bodice had slipped down and her hair tumbled about her shoulders in wild abandon, providing a thin veil. But Daisy didn't seem to notice or mind her indecency.

Desperation rose inside Lily. This was her sweet baby sister. What had happened to her?

Lily had the urge to cry out and stomp her feet and demand that Daisy stop acting so foolishly.

Instead, she took a deep breath. Daisy's emotions were as fragile as a thin coating of ice on a pond. She had to remember it was going to take time for Daisy to heal and move past all that had happened.

And apparently it was going to take more time and effort than she'd realized.

As hard as it would be to leave the McCormicks, she knew she couldn't put it off any longer. They needed to find a place of their own, a place where Tierney wouldn't be able to find Daisy.

A place where they could finally be a family together.

CHAPTER 26

Connell brushed the wet snow off the four-inch-thick round slab of pine. Clear as a summer day, the McCormick log mark, a smaller *M* inside a large *C,* was stamped onto the sawed-off end.

"Where did you find them?" Connell's fingers traced the grooves of the company sign, anger settling into the crevices of his heart.

Charlie looked around at the group of men at the dock who'd stopped their work and gathered near. They brushed the sweat from their foreheads and donned the coats they'd tossed off earlier.

"I was checking one of my traps and found them shoved underneath a stand of cedar near Camp 1. Not too far from the narrow-gauge tracks."

A miserable mixture of rain and snow had been spitting at them all afternoon, but nobody was paying attention to the cold, wet weather anymore. The moment Charlie had ridden up to the loading ground at the Pere Marquette, Connell had known the young man wasn't bringing good news. So did all the others. Any time a shanty boy had a need to ride into town in the middle of the day, the tidings were bad.

"There's more than just McCormick Lumber that's been robbed." Charlie tipped a large grain sack upside down and a dozen round slabs fell to the muddy ground.

Several other camp bosses stepped toward the pile and kicked the ends, examining them for their company marks.

"From the looks of it," Charlie added, "whoever's been stealing has been doing it a little bit at a time all winter."

All the logs were stamped with a specific mark that belonged to each lumber company in order for them to keep track of their logs among the flow of all the others. Even so, log piracy was a common problem.

That was one of the reasons each camp hired watchmen to protect their logs during transport, especially as the logs were transferred down the Pere Marquette to Averill to await the spring river drive.

"Looks like we've got a thief in the midst of us," Connell said, searching the faces of the other bosses.

The anger slanting across their features reflected the frustration that had made a home inside him. They grumbled and began speculating who was to blame.

Connell gave a weary sigh. At least now he knew why his numbers hadn't been adding up. The foremen at each of his camps had been giving him the correct totals of logs leaving their camps. But somewhere between leaving the camps and arriving in Harrison, someone had been tampering with the logs, sawing off company marks, and likely remarking the logs with their own stamp.

It appeared that the thieves hadn't just been targeting McCormick, but had been sawing the marked ends from a variety of the camps. The strategy made sense. Taking a little bit from each of the camps would make the theft harder to discover.

The unbalanced ledgers had caused him plenty of headaches. But they were the least of his concerns now.

In the week since he'd returned to Harrison, he'd had forty shanty boys demand their paychecks and defect to other area camps or mills.

A few had come back when they'd learned of the extra bonus he was offering. But those who remained were getting threats from Carr's men whenever they went into town, and he had the feeling it wouldn't be long before more of them left.

He'd decided Carr didn't deserve the payoff money Dad had given him. If anything, Carr ought to be the one paying him for all the losses he was causing McCormick Lumber.

"What do you want me to do with the slabs, Boss?" Charlie finally asked.

Connell didn't know if he had the energy to think of a plan to catch the thieves. He'd obviously have to hire some men to guard the loads coming out of his camps on the narrow-gauge trains. But at the moment, he didn't know if he even cared.

All week he'd slept poorly, waiting for Carr's men to strike again when he least expected. So far they'd stayed away. But he knew his days were numbered. It was just a matter of time before they caught him unaware and alone.

And with the way he was stirring up the hornet's nest lately with Stuart's help, he knew a fight was coming. It wasn't a matter of *if*. It was a matter of *when*.

Under the guise of Lily's Red Ribbon Society, they'd held their first meeting two days ago. Even though the turnout had been small — only nine men and one woman,

Vera — he'd begun to see that more people were tired of Carr and his lawlessness than he'd expected.

At the racing clomp of horse hooves and the shout of his name, Connell straightened his sagging shoulders and wiped a hand across his eyes, fighting off the weariness.

Stuart came charging toward him, one arm in a sling and the other gripping reins. His face was still a patchwork of yellowish-green and purple bruises and cuts.

Connell stepped away from the group of men now arguing about who was to blame for the thieving. "Thought you were working on our project in Merryville today," he said as Stuart reined next to him.

"I was." Stuart's face was grim.

Although the thought of riding up to Merryville in the black of night and breaking into the Devil's Ranch was one of the last things he wanted to do, he figured if Lily could rescue Daisy, he and Stuart could get Frankie.

It was past time.

Besides, since he'd already made an enemy of Carr, what difference did it make if he stirred up more strife?

Stuart had decided to ride up to Merryville for the day to get word to her that they would come after her in two nights.

Connell pulled his watch from his coat pocket. It read two-thirty. "You're back early."

Stuart slipped from his horse, wincing as his feet touched the ground. "We won't need to rescue the girl," he said softly so that none of the men could hear their conversation. His eyes brimmed with a sadness that set Connell on edge.

"What happened?"

"From what I could gather from various witnesses, Carr beat her up about a week ago. With his brass knuckles. Because she refused to get out on the dance floor and strip for the men."

Connell shook his head. He'd heard the tales of the pails Carr put out on the dance floor. The men tossed coins into the tin containers to entice the girls to perform. As the pails began to fill, the girls would expose more flesh and the dances would turn more lurid.

He couldn't imagine a sweet young girl like Frankie dancing in front of a roomful of drunken shanty boys. Why had Carr demanded it of *her* of all his girls? He could have made one of his other women do it — one of the women there by choice.

Stuart's brow furrowed into deep lines. "Dr. Scott said he examined her and tried to help her. But she was so severely beaten and covered with bruises that she would've had a hard time surviving. If she'd had a will to live, which apparently she didn't."

The news hit Connell's gut as painfully as if a log had come loose from the top of a banked pile and crushed his middle. "Then she's dead?"

"She died yesterday."

Sick guilt added to the weight that pressed against Connell's gut. They'd waited too long.

Neither of them said anything for a long moment. The accusing shouts of the men behind them punctuated the air. The discovery of the sawed-off log ends would only add dissension during a time when they all needed to unite against Carr.

"And what's worse," Stuart said, as if things could get any worse, "is that nobody is doing anything about her death. Nobody cares. In their minds, she's just another worthless prostitute."

Connell knew what the majority of townspeople thought — it was the same thing he'd always told himself: What was one more dead prostitute in a community where fighting and beatings and death were a daily occurrence? Why bother trying to change anything when the problems looked insurmountable?

God was obviously whacking him across the head in His efforts to show him how apathetic and uncaring and fearful he'd been. *I get it now, God.* He lifted his eyes heavenward. *You can stop the lesson anytime.*

If only they could get a little help . . .

They wouldn't get any sympathy from the Clare County sheriff, not when the man operated off Carr's payroll, like most of the county.

"What about the Midland County sheriff?" Connell asked, trying to renew his quickly fading desire to fight. "What if we were to ask him for help?"

"He can't do anything. This isn't his jurisdiction," Stuart said. "What we need to do is to elect a new sheriff and a new county prosecutor who will support reform."

"I agree. We've got to have men who aren't being paid off by Carr to do his bidding." But county elections were largely a sham, especially when no one dared to run or vote against Carr's approved men.

Even as Connell spoke, Stuart's face reflected the hopelessness wedged in Connell's heart. "The only thing I can do is finish fixing up my jobber, write up this story, print it, and get it out to as many people as possible."

They'd spent the last few evenings trying to clean up the newspaper office and salvage what they could. They were fortunate that amidst the destruction, the printing press hadn't been damaged too badly.

"At least you have enough witnesses that Carr can't accuse you of libel."

"I'm sure he'll try, but what harm will it do me now?" He grinned, but Connell could see past the false bravado to the fear flitting in Stuart's eyes.

"He could break a lot more than your arm this time."

"I can't back down now — not when I've been looking for a way to frame him for his crimes. I thought I could nail him on the jail fire. But murder is even better."

They would do all they could. But would it ever be enough?

Stuart rubbed his broken arm, as if thinking the same thing. Then he sighed. "I'd hate to be the one to tell Lily the news about Frankie."

A fresh wave of weariness washed over Connell. "I'd hate to be the one too." But he had a feeling he would have to break the news to her eventually.

She was going to be devastated.

And would likely despise him all the more.

■ ■ ■ ■

Lily didn't want to leave Daisy alone for any length of time while she went looking for a job. It wasn't that she didn't trust her sister, she told herself. It was that she didn't trust Tierney.

Even though he'd stayed away the rest of the week — or at least she thought he had — she had the feeling it was only a matter of time before he came back and tried to ensnare Daisy again.

Lily wanted to make sure they were long gone before that happened.

With a pattering heart, she stopped on the second-floor landing and listened, every nerve in her body alert for the sound of the two of them together.

For a second she imagined she heard Daisy's soft laugh of pleasure, and the unbidden picture of her sister's passion filled her mind.

Lily couldn't keep from thinking about the pleasure she'd found in the brief moments of closeness with Connell. Warmth spread through her stomach.

She shoved it aside, the shards of embarrassment and guilt slicing through her.

Who was she to condemn Daisy for taking pleasure in Tierney's touch when she'd relished each instance with Connell and longed for more?

She didn't want to admit she was a hypocrite. After all, she hadn't allowed Connell to ravish her so intimately. They'd kept their distance even though the attraction had been strong between them. She liked to think she would have stopped him if he'd wanted more from her when they'd been stranded alone during the snowstorm.

But the truth was, her curiosity and longing always made her lose reason when she was with him. His strong commitment to purity had kept them both from indulging in intimacies they would have later regretted.

Through the dumbwaiter in the wall of the hallway, she could hear Mrs. McCormick speaking to the maid in the kitchen on the ground floor. Other than the rapid thump of her own heartbeat, she couldn't hear anything else. The house was silent.

She bounded up the steps the rest of the way to the third floor. All the way she tried to tell herself she was different from Daisy, that she was strong and pure and virtuous. But with each step, she couldn't keep from thinking the line that separated her from Daisy was much thinner than she cared to acknowledge.

At the doorway to their room she paused. Hopefully, they'd have their own place soon, away from the McCormicks. They could both start fresh. Tierney wouldn't be a temptation for Daisy, and Connell wouldn't be one for her. She'd never see him again.

With a long sigh, she tried to breathe out the disappointment that came whenever she thought of Connell and how much she missed him.

"Daisy?" she said softly, opening the door. "What if we moved to Saginaw?"

Lily stepped over the girl's untouched lunch tray, still on the floor where the maid had left it.

"I'm not having any luck finding work here. And I heard someone say there are more factories in Saginaw."

She wouldn't tell Daisy what else she'd heard — that there weren't many jobs available for single women. In fact, everywhere she'd gone, she'd been told the saloons were hiring pretty waiter girls. She'd have no problem locating work down on Water Street.

But she knew most of the time "waiter girl" was just another term for prostitute. And she knew as well as any other decent citizen that Water Street was "Hell's Half

441

Mile." She'd heard the rumors of the catacombs, a winding labyrinth of rooms and tunnels that existed in the bowels underneath the saloons and hotels. Just the reference to the crimes and illicit activities that took place within the dark, damp hallways was enough to make Lily's skin crawl.

She couldn't — absolutely wouldn't — take Daisy into such an environment, not even if they became desperate.

"What do you think?" she asked, dodging the piles of discarded clothes on the floor and making her way to the window. "We could start fresh in Saginaw, where no one will know us or anything about the past year."

She yanked open the curtains, letting daylight into the room. She hadn't given up hope — she *wouldn't* give up hope — that everything would work out for her and Daisy.

"Come on. Time to get up, sleepyhead." She turned toward the bed, and even before the words were completely out, fear pricked the back of her neck.

The bed was empty. The quilt and sheets were unmade and in disarray — which wasn't unusual, at least until the maid came in to tidy the room. What *was* unusual was that Daisy had gotten out of the bed, something she hadn't done except to meet with Tierney that day in the library.

"Daisy?" Lily's gaze swept around the room, and dread pooled in her stomach.

Tierney. She was with Tierney again.

"No!"

Where had that lying, cheating, no-good grayback taken her this time? To a secluded part of the house where Lily wouldn't be able to find them?

"You won't be able to hide from me." She walked to the bed, her footsteps choppy and her mind formulating the hot lecture she would sling at Tierney once she found him. With a jerk, she tugged the knit blanket loose from the tangle of sheets, praying she could catch them before Daisy bared herself to Tierney again.

A piece of folded paper on the bedstead table caught Lily's attention. She reached for it, and at the sight of her name in Daisy's scrawled handwriting, her heart ceased beating.

She flipped the paper open and read.

Dear Lily,

I'm leaving. I want to live my life the way I want. I'm a grown woman now, and I don't need you to tell me what to do or how to live anymore. Please, just let me go and don't try to find me.

That was it. No "I love you." No "Thank you." No "I'll miss you."

"Oh, Daisy." Lily pressed her fingers against her lips to hold back a cry.

She dropped to the edge of the bed and read the note again, hoping the words would say something different this time.

But the same cold message slapped her and brought stinging tears to her eyes.

"How could you?" After all she'd done for Daisy, how hard she'd tried to make things right, how much effort she was putting into trying to give them a new life.

And Daisy repaid her by running away again?

With a groan, Lily buried her face in her hands. She'd put her own life at risk to rescue Daisy. So had Connell. There was no telling what kind of trouble he was in with Carr now — all because of Daisy.

Sobs of anger and disappointment tore at Lily's throat, begging for release.

Why had Daisy done it? Didn't she love her? Didn't she want to be with her?

She swallowed through the tightness of her throat. With a burst of determination, she stood. She wouldn't let Daisy run away again. Not now. Not after she'd just found her.

With a shake of her head, she brushed away the nagging thought that maybe she was trying to take too much control of the plans for her life, that she'd taken over completely and wasn't leaving room for God's bigger plans.

All she needed to do was work harder, didn't she?

A quick glance around the room revealed that Daisy had taken all of her dresses, even the ones Mrs. McCormick had loaned her. The silver-handled brush was gone. The decorative silver box. The candelabras.

Lily's heart sank. Had Daisy turned into a thief too? How could she so thoughtlessly take the belongings of someone who'd generously opened her home and provided for their every need? What kind of girl would do that?

Certainly not the sweet little girl she'd raised.

Lily's gaze landed upon the bedside table. The miniature framed picture of their mother and father was gone too.

Her body constricted.

"No!" She dropped to the floor and scrambled to find the photograph, the last connection she had with her mother and father, the only tie to her past.

A search under the bed, through the sheets, and around the room revealed nothing but the selfishness in Daisy's heart.

"You had to take it, didn't you?" Lily yelled at the rumpled bed, as if by doing so she could bring Daisy back. "You knew it was important to me. But you didn't care!"

The pressure in her chest made her want to weep.

"You foolish, foolish girl!" She pounded a fist against the bed and caught the edge of a sob before it could escape.

"You don't know what you're doing." Where would Daisy go? What could the girl possibly do besides return to a life of prostitution? And that was unthinkable. She couldn't let Daisy make that mistake again.

Daisy had told her not to find her. But Lily had no choice. The girl couldn't survive on her own. She needed Lily whether she thought so or not.

Lily raced from the room, down the winding staircase, and into the front hallway. She paused only to retrieve her coat before plunging out the front door into the wintry afternoon.

Large fluffy snowflakes were coming down thick and fast. The snow had formed a fresh blanket over her earlier footprints and covered any tracks that might lead her to Daisy.

But Lily didn't care. She fixed her gaze on the redbrick Queen Anne home across the street. With its steeply pitched roofs, conical tower, and numerous gables, it was an elegant home, a smaller version of the one she'd just exited.

As she reached the end of the walkway and stepped onto the wide muddy street that was immune to the fresh snow, she ignored the others passing by.

Each footstep slapped louder against the muck in the street and each breath puff whiter in the frigid air. She couldn't find the energy to complain about the fact that another winter storm was blowing in, that it was nearing the end of February and spring felt like it would never arrive.

The only thing she wanted was to get her hands around Tierney's neck and squeeze until he confessed Daisy's whereabouts. He would know. Daisy would turn to him first.

When Lily stepped off the street onto the snow-covered plank walkway that led to Tierney's home, fingers suddenly gripped her forearm and the tip of a knife poked through her coat and the layers of her clothes into her back.

She gasped.

"Don't say nothin'. Don't scream" came a hard voice from behind her. "And maybe you'll live."

Lily froze.

"Walk nice and slow to that carriage there." The point of the knife was painfully close to piercing her skin, and the strong grip propelled her toward a carriage parked along the side of the road. A team of horses snorted as if waiting for her.

Fear pulsed through her. "Who are you? What do you want?" She tried to yank her arm free and twist around to identify the man. But he pushed the knife deeper, this time cutting into her skin.

She cried out at the sudden burning.

"I said not to say nothin'." The man pushed her faster toward the open carriage door.

The driver was perched, reins in hand, ready to go. "That ain't Bella," he growled.

"I couldn't find her," said her captor, shoving her upward, giving her little choice but to climb into the carriage. "Figured this one could help us."

She couldn't think fast enough or move quickly enough, and before she knew it, the man had tossed her against the hard, cold seat. She struggled to untangle herself from her skirts and sit up.

But he shoved his way into the cramped space after her, pushing her down and towering over her. He yanked the door closed with a finality that sent chills over her.

The odor of dust and decaying leather lingered in the cracked seat. And as he lowered his face to hers, the strong scent of onions and tobacco on his hot breath choked her.

He gave a short laugh. "I've been waiting to get a taste of you."

Through the dark shadows of the boxy interior, she caught a glimpse of his face and the black gaps in his grin. "Jimmy Neil from Harrison."

"That's me." His hand crept over her bodice, sending new horror through her.

The worst was happening. He was going to defile her.

"Get off me." She struggled against him, scrambling to get out from underneath his heavy weight. She kneed him and scratched his face, and fought with all the desperation welling inside her.

The jerk of the carriage as it started forward sent him crashing against the rear-facing seat.

She used the brief respite to pull herself onto the bench and move as far away from him as possible. She cowered in the corner, trying to still the trembling in her limbs, knowing she couldn't put enough distance between them, and he could easily over-power her if he chose to have his way with her.

But that didn't mean she wouldn't fight him. She'd rather die fighting than let him violate her.

He cupped his hand, cursed at the edge of the seat, then yelled at the driver.

She balled her fists, ready to swing should Jimmy come at her again.

But he lifted his hand and blood gushed from a deep tear in the flesh of his palm.

"What have you done with Daisy?" she asked. Maybe he'd already captured Daisy and was planning to make her return to the Stockade.

"That's funny." He reached for a rag next to him on the seat. "I was about to ask you the same."

"Did you kidnap her too?"

He bit down on the edge of the rag, and despite the bumping and jostling of the vehicle, he used his teeth to tear a long strip. "I figured when I couldn't find her that you took her and hid her someplace new."

Lily glanced out the carriage window as best she could through the smudged and frosted pane. They were moving fast.

Jimmy wrapped the strip around his wounded hand. "Tell me where Bella is."

"I don't know." Her fingers moved toward the door lever. "And even if I did know, I wouldn't tell you. Not even if you stuck your knife into me and cut out my heart."

Jimmy snorted. "Oh, believe me, you'd tell me if I stuck my knife into you. I'd make sure of that."

Lily shuddered and inched her hand higher. She needed to get away from him and find Daisy before he did.

"My boss told me to bring Bella back to him or he'd kill me."

"You'd best tell your boss you won't be bringing Bella back to him. Ever. I won't let it happen."

"Then I guess you're gonna have to take her place." He finished tying the bandage around his wound, but a dark spot of blood was already seeping through the material. "Because I'm not going back empty-handed."

Her fingers made contact with the metal handle. Her heart whirred in a frenzy. She couldn't let him drag her back to Harrison. She'd jump to her death before she let him take her to the Stockade.

She flipped the latch and the door swung

open. She lunged for the opening. The swirling snow and cold air hit her face. She glanced down. The crunching of the wheels in the ice and mud made her hesitate for just a moment.

But it was a moment too long. Jimmy grabbed onto the fancy bouffant skirt and yanked her backward with the strength of a man who wrestled logs for a living.

She fell back against him, and this time his arm slid around her neck, pinning her body to his.

"And just where do you think you're going?" His voice rasped against her ear as he leaned forward and slammed the door closed.

"I'm leaving." She fought to free herself from his grasp. "And you can't stop me."

"Oh, yes I can. Watch me." His arm around her neck tightened, cutting off her breath. He reached for the rag again and brought it to her face.

She tried to lean away from the filthy, streaked rag, but he pinned her harder. A rotten odor assaulted her, and she could only gasp for breath, sucking in the fumes that saturated the damp rag.

He shoved it against her nose and mouth, cupping it over her so that she had no choice but to breath in the mind-numbing chemical.

She flailed her arms, as if she were sinking underwater and trying to reach the surface, where she could finally gasp for air.

But Jimmy's hand pressed harder.

Her vision grew blurry and her head dizzy.

She pounded at Jimmy but felt like she was beating against a pillow.

God, help me! her heart cried.

Then the world turned black.

CHAPTER 27

Twenty men and three women. That was thirteen more than the last Red Ribbon Society meeting. Connell jotted the number onto the open ledger on the table in front of him and then pulled out his watch.

Seven thirty-two.

In his usual neat print, he added the time to the meeting minutes.

He'd agreed to act as treasurer and secretary. But he'd deferred the hands-on leadership to Stuart.

Besides, most of the newcomers were there because of Stuart's article about Frankie's murder. His friend had stayed up all night getting the jobber back into working order. By midmorning, he'd had the paper ready to go, citing all the details of Carr's kidnapping Frankie, forcing her into prostitution, and then beating her to death when she didn't cooperate.

Connell had helped him with the delivery,

riding the country roads to get the news out and announce another Red Ribbon Society meeting.

And now, the dining room of the Northern Hotel was fuller than it'd been in a long time. The air was charged with angry conversations about Carr — exactly the reaction they'd hoped the newspaper article would generate. Stuart had invited the bosses and foremen from some of the other lumber camps. Surprisingly, several had shown up, including Herb Nolan from his own Camp 1.

Vera maneuvered past him, a coffeepot in each hand. She stopped and poured more into his cup, adding to the grainy lukewarm liquid that remained. Some sloshed onto the tablecloth, reminding him of the first morning after Lily had arrived at the Northern and how they'd shared a smile over Vera's awful coffee. Her smile had soaked into him like bright rays of sunshine on the first warm day of spring.

What he wouldn't give to turn back the clock and see her sitting across the room from him again.

"Looks like you could use the whole pot," Vera said, moving past him. "Are you getting any sleep these days?"

He shook his head. Exhaustion made

every bone in his body ache. It had been at least two weeks since he'd slept more than an hour or two at a time.

"I wish you'd let me give you some of my motherwort tonic to help you sleep better."

"I'll be fine."

"I insist," she called over her shoulder as she refilled another man's cup. "Now, be a good boy and don't go to your room tonight without it."

He didn't have the heart to tell her he went to bed every night wondering if it would be his last. Now that he'd made an enemy of Carr, he doubted he'd ever get a good night's sleep again.

He glanced at his watch. Two more minutes had elapsed. Through the mingling crowd, Connell caught Stuart's eye and tapped his watch. They were now four minutes behind schedule.

Stuart nodded and called the meeting to order. "There is a glimmer of good news amidst all the bad," Stuart said once the room had quieted.

For a moment, the only sounds were the blowing and drawing of the men slurping coffee. The yeasty fragrance of the doughnuts Vera had made for the morning couldn't compete with the thick heavy aroma of freshly brewed coffee.

Oren rested in a chair near the fireplace, his stockinged feet propped on a crate that sat near the glowing white coals. He puffed on his corncob pipe, his eyebrows scrunched together in a perpetual scowl.

Even though Connell had reassured Oren that Lily was completely safe at his family home in Bay City, the man hadn't stopped worrying.

Connell's heart begged him to take the next Saturday off and ride home to visit her, to hold her in his arms again. But what had changed between them? How could they ever hope to make things work? If he went to her, she'd probably just push him away. Especially when he gave her the news of Frankie's death.

Besides, his head told him he couldn't leave again, not when the whole business was a chaotic mess.

He'd spent hours lately adding up the numbers, trying to figure out a way to get McCormick Lumber back into the black. But he couldn't see any way to bring in a profit after losing logs all winter to a thief and after losing ten percent of his work force to Carr's intimidation.

Stuart cleared his throat and continued. "The good news is that D. E. Alward of *Clare Press* is going to run the story about

457

Frankie. And the editor of the Farwell paper might run it too."

The men murmured among themselves, nodding at the news.

"And the other good news is —" Stuart paused and glanced around as if making sure he had everyone's attention — "I think I've discovered who the log thief is."

Connell's gaze snapped to Stuart and riveted there. From the absolute silence that descended, he was sure the other boss men had done the same.

"After doing some investigation, I learned that Carr has registered a log mark."

"What does he need a log mark for?" called one of the bosses.

But even before Stuart spoke again, Connell knew what the scoundrel had done.

"Turns out," Stuart continued over the murmuring, "after I did some poking around down at the banking grounds in Averill, I discovered that Carr has a substantial number of logs bearing his mark."

"I ain't seen him cutting any logs," started the boss. But then he stopped, understanding dawning on his scruffy face. "He's been sawing the ends off our logs and stamping them with his mark."

Stuart nodded. "I don't have solid proof yet. I haven't actually caught any of his men in the act of stealing —"

"I'm sure they've been sneaking around at night," called Herb Nolan. "No doubt they've been sawing off the end of a log here and there, nothing noticeable, nothing to alert any of us. But enough for Carr to build up a steady supply of logs so that at spring river drive he'll turn a nice profit."

For several minutes the room was filled with the speculations and plans of the men. Connell sat back and nodded at Stuart, whose eyes shone with the self-satisfaction of a job well done. If they could implicate Carr in the thievery of the logs, they'd be one step closer to driving him out of Harrison.

If nothing else, they'd at least turned the other lumber-camp bosses against Carr. There was no way they'd support a man who was stealing from them and undermining their efforts.

Stuart finally cleared his throat to get the attention of the crowd. "Hopefully, when the rest of Clare County hears the truth about Carr, they'll decide they've had enough."

"It's past time for reform," called Herb.

"Here, here," said another man.

"Time to make a decent place of Harrison," said Mr. Sturgis, the grocer. "A place where we feel safe bringing our wives and children."

"We need a church and a school."

Once again, the men began calling out their suggestions — this time with excitement in their voices.

Many of the business owners had left their families behind in the bigger cities, not wanting to bring their children and wives into the lumber town's dangerous and unwholesome environment. Apparently, the idea of cleaning up the town and establishing law was something most of the men wanted but had been too afraid to voice.

Connell didn't know what to jot down in his meeting notes. His mind whirled with the possibilities. If he could help facilitate the reforms in town, he could certainly bring about a few reforms within the lumber industry too, couldn't he?

What would Dad think if he started demanding changes?

The muscles in his stomach hardened. He could almost feel Dad's fist pounding into his gut, telling him all too clearly not to do anything that might jeopardize his business.

But what about what *he* wanted to do?

Lily's words came back to him. *"Maybe it's time for you to start making your own plans and having your own dreams."*

A sudden bang of the front door jolted him off his bench. A shanty boy barged inside and then doubled over at the waist, gasping for breath.

The room grew silent again.

"Boss McCormick," the young man managed between heaves. Connell recognized him as one of the road monkeys from Camp 1.

Connell stepped forward and only then realized he'd pulled his knife and had it ready to throw. He quickly sheathed it, berating himself for being so jumpy.

If Carr's men were going to come after him, they wouldn't pick the Northern during a meeting full of angry men.

"Boss," the man said, straightening and giving him a look that sent chills over his skin. "Just ran into some friends leaving the Stockade."

The young man glanced around the room at the other men. He took another deep breath before turning to face Connell again. "Thought you might want to know Carr's saying he's got your woman."

"My woman?" Connell's pulse sputtered to a stop.

"You know." The man glanced at his boots, making a muddy puddle on the dining room floor. His voice grew softer as if

461

he were afraid to say the word again. "Your *woman*."

Oren was on his feet with a speed that belied his age. His chair fell backward with a clatter. "What in the hairy hound are you talking about?" His voice boomed with the ferocity of a roaring bear. "You better be drunk, or I'll be tying you up and roasting you like a Christmas goose."

Connell couldn't move. He didn't want to ask any more questions. He just wanted the young man to disappear, to head back out into the darkness of the evening, and to take his terrible rumor with him.

"I ain't lying." The man backed toward the open door. "Just thought you'd want to know."

"But she's in a safe location," Connell said, starting toward the man. Fear gusted through him, freezing his steps into slow motion. "There's no way Carr could get her."

But even as he said the words, anguish crashed through his heart. A painful cry swelled deep inside and rose in his throat.

The shanty boy was telling him the truth.

Carr had finally found a way to destroy him. He'd taken the one thing that mattered to him most.

Lily.

The only woman who'd ever come into his life and challenged him to think beyond himself and to live with intention and purpose.

Suddenly he knew with complete clarity she was more important to him than the business, than Dad's approval, than success. She meant more to him than his own life.

She was the kind of woman whose smile he wanted to see first thing in the morning when he woke up, whose zeal for life would follow him throughout each day, and whose passion would fill his arms all night long.

He loved her. Deeply and completely.

And now Carr had captured her and made her a prisoner in the very pit of hell itself.

Rage burst through him.

"Where's Carr holding her?" He stomped toward the door. He had to go get her. Now. Before it was too late, before Carr hurt her or forced her to do anything against her will. Just the thought of any other man touching her soft skin or claiming the lips that were meant for him alone sent his anger spiraling out of control.

"Where is she?" he yelled, grabbing the young man, blind to anything but the fact that he needed to find her.

"Heard he's got her locked in a room upstairs at the Stockade." The man cowered under Connell's grip, his eyes wide, almost as if he feared Connell was going to kill him.

Connell shoved the shanty boy away and reached for his coat. He'd go find her, and he'd kill anyone who got in his way — including Carr.

"Where are you going?" Stuart asked, starting toward him, his face mirroring the fear in Connell's heart.

"I'm going to get her." He tossed his coat over his shoulders and reached for the door.

"You can't go by yourself." Stuart lunged for him and grabbed his arm.

Connell shrugged his friend off. "I'm going now." He couldn't wait. He'd waited to rescue Frankie, and it had been too late. He couldn't take that chance with Lily.

"You can't just march up to the Stockade by yourself."

"Sure I can."

"But that's exactly what Carr wants." Stuart socked him in the arm with his bony knuckles. "He's just looking for an excuse to kill you."

"I don't care if he kills me." Connell lurched and broke free from Stuart. He only made it two steps before Stuart slammed into him and wrapped his good arm around his neck, choking him. Quick as a fall frost, Stuart yanked Connell's other arm behind his back.

Connell roared with frustration. But his friend, though wiry and thin and having a broken arm, was stronger than he looked.

Stuart gave a painful yank that brought Connell to his knees.

"You're acting as impetuously as Lily." Stuart was breathing hard from the exertion, but his grip was solid and tight.

"Let me go!" A fresh wave of desperation crashed through Connell. Every second they wasted brought Lily further danger.

"I'm just as worried about her as you," Stuart said. "And so is Oren. But we can't go tearing out of here without first coming up with a workable plan to get her back."

He knew his friend was right. But the rage inside him was storming like a blizzard.

"I'm sure we could get any number of these men here tonight to help us." Stuart cocked his head toward the men who were watching them.

The room was silent except for the melting snow dripping down the chimney and sizzling in the smoldering fire.

Oren was already slipping into his coat and had his rifle under his arm.

For a long moment, no one said anything. But then benches scraped the floor, and one by one the men stood.

" 'Course we'll help," said Herb Nolan. "We need to teach Carr a lesson once and for all."

"We gotta show that man he can't get away with this kind of nonsense anymore," said another angrily. "Who's he gonna kidnap next? Our wives and daughters?"

Several of the men nodded and voiced their support.

As much as Connell despised the thought of waiting to rescue Lily, he knew he'd have a better chance of freeing her with the help of the men. What good would he do Lily if he stormed into the Stockade alone without a plan?

Vera laid a hand on Oren's arm. He muttered under his mustache and then his shoulders slumped, as if coming to the same realization that they needed the help of the men. His face fell with a sadness that jerked at Connell's heart.

Oren had trusted him to keep Lily safe.

And he'd failed.

Connell stiffened. Well, he wouldn't fail this time.

If he did, he'd finally let Oren pump a bullet into his head.

Lily crouched in the corner of the closet. The blackness pressed down on her. The

466

rag tied around her mouth gagged her. And the rope around her ankles and wrists burned her skin.

The damp coldness had turned her fingers and toes numb. And having been stripped of all but her camisole and drawers, her body was rigid with the chill that had seeped to her bones.

Maggie Carr had opened the door several times during the day. Each time she'd asked her the same question, "Are you ready yet?"

And in the blinding sliver of light, Lily had shaken her head violently and hoped her eyes conveyed what her words couldn't — that she'd never *ever* subject herself to prostitution.

They could kill her first.

When Maggie had locked her in the closet upon her arrival the previous evening, she'd told Lily she had to agree to cooperate before she could come out or have any food.

Lily figured the scare tactic worked on most girls — young, sweet girls like Frankie — who would eventually give in, especially when the pangs of hunger and parch of thirst became overwhelming.

But Maggie didn't know her. She wasn't like other girls. She'd never give in.

"If you aren't cooperating by tomorrow," Maggie had said during the last visit a couple hours ago, "then my husband will join me in your training."

Lily didn't care. Carr could beat her black and blue if he wanted. She still wouldn't give in.

Through the darkness, she'd explored the narrow cell as best she could with the tips of her fingers. There wasn't a way out except the door, which Maggie kept locked.

Lily knew she was trapped. She may have helped orchestrate the escapes of others that winter, but she couldn't have pulled off one like this.

Not even Connell could get her out.

Had news of her predicament reached him? Surely by now Mrs. McCormick had realized she and Daisy were gone. But the dear woman wouldn't know what had become of them. She'd likely assume she'd stolen the silver with Daisy and had run off before they could get caught. There was little chance the woman would report Lily's disappearance to Connell — not when she believed Lily was a thief.

She was stuck.

Lily leaned her head back against the cold wall. The rag in her mouth was torturously dry against her swollen tongue.

Better her than Daisy.

Loud laughter and the twang of the piano

sifted through the floorboards. The debauchery of the evening was well under way.

And where was Daisy? Had she gone to a brothel somewhere?

Lily squeezed her eyes closed at the possibility that Daisy had gone to Hell's Half Mile. The very thought of her sister selling her body in the dark catacombs underneath Bay City made her stomach lurch with nausea.

The question resounded through her mind as it had over the past day since she'd found Daisy's note: Why? Why had Daisy done it? Again?

Lily couldn't accept that Daisy liked prostitution. The idea was too repulsive.

Her heart radiated with pain.

What hurt more than anything was knowing Daisy had willfully left her, that she hadn't wanted to be with her.

Oh, God, why? The ache moved up her throat. *Why my baby sister?*

She'd already lost her parents. Wasn't that enough? Why Daisy too?

All her life she'd wanted to keep Daisy safe and for them to be a family — the two of them and the tiny portrait of their parents. She'd tried to raise her sister as best she could, doing everything she thought their mother and father would have wanted.

What had she done wrong?

The agony pushed up into a choked cry, but the tight rag in her mouth prevented any sobs.

She'd been bent on saving the world — everything and everyone. But she hadn't been able to save the one person who mattered most.

Tears welled in her eyes.

Oh, God, are you there? A trickle of cold wetness rolled down her cheek. She had no one now — not even the image of her parents that she'd clung to for so many years.

She shuddered, wishing she could wrap her arms around herself. But with all her efforts earlier to free herself from the binding, she'd rubbed her skin until it was painfully raw. And she was still no closer to loosening the ropes than when she'd arrived.

Did God still care about her?

Could she trust that He was creating a beautiful quilt — a bigger plan for her life — even when the pieces didn't look so pretty at the moment?

She'd been trying so hard to put together her life the way *she'd* wanted. Was it possible God had other plans for her that didn't fit the pattern she'd tried to create? Maybe it was time to stop trying so hard to be in control.

The questions swirled through her. And suddenly she didn't feel quite so alone. She almost had the feeling God was near enough to hear her desperate cries. That He was listening. That He was trying to tell her that even if everyone else left her, He never would.

Footsteps clomped in the hallway, growing louder as they neared her closet.

Was Maggie coming again?

The steps halted in front of her door.

Lily sat up straighter. Sudden resolve poured through her. Maybe it was time to start asking God what His plans were instead of always taking matters into her own hands.

Okay, God, what do you want me to do?

She listened intently, hoping for a voice, for some audible direction, but all she heard was a key in the keyhole rattling and then the door squeaking open a crack.

Maggie peeked in, lifted her lantern, and cast brilliant light on Lily.

After almost complete blackness during the past twenty-four hours, Lily blinked hard.

"Are you ready yet?" Maggie's voice was muffled by the bright scarf that covered her mouth and nose.

Lily started to shake her head as adamantly as she had the other times, but then stopped.

How would she escape if she didn't get out of the closet? If she pretended to submit to Maggie, maybe the woman would remove the binding and let her leave the black hole.

She'd go along with the woman for a little while and buy herself some time to try to figure out what God had in mind for her. This time she would try to trust Him.

With a choked breath, she nodded her head and tried to make herself look as broken and humiliated as possible.

Maggie's eyebrows shot up, and she stared at Lily for a long moment, as though trying to grasp the sudden change in Lily's attitude.

"Fine," Maggie said slowly. "We'll get you dressed up real pretty, and then you can show us what a good girl you're willing to be."

Lily hung her head, but inside she was standing up tall and fighting with all her might.

"But don't think you're going to find a way to leave."

Maggie's warning jolted through Lily. She shook her head and hoped the woman would read it as submission.

"One wrong move, sugar, and you'll be back in this closet faster than you can blink." Maggie reached for her arm and dragged her into the deserted hallway. "And if that happens, I'll make sure you learn your lesson. I never, never put up with lying. Never."

Lily tried to ignore the fear swarming through her.

She could only pray that God would provide a way of escape. And soon.

CHAPTER 28

They would kill him if they recognized him.

Connell slouched, his stomach tight and ready for the first punch or shot of lead.

The bouncer at the door eyed him up and down, then nodded and moved aside to let him enter the saloon.

He ducked his head, pulled the borrowed derby low over his eyes, and stepped into the crowded, smoke-filled room. The room reeked of dirty socks and flesh that hadn't had a good scrubbing in months.

The drunken laughter and piano music drowned out the loud chopping of his heartbeat. He'd never been good at playacting, but he forced his feet forward, trying to exude the swaggering confidence of a man who frequented such establishments on a regular basis.

He lifted his chin long enough for a quick glance around the room. Two more bouncers. One standing at the bottom of the stairway. And another by the money pail at the bar.

That brought the total to four so far, including the one at the gate and the one he'd just passed at the door.

If Bass's map of the Stockade was still correct, there would be two more bouncers — somewhere upstairs. For a total of six.

Connell scuffed his boots in uncharacteristic laziness and headed toward an empty chair at one of the round tables where several shanty boys were drinking and playing cards.

"Deal me in the next hand," he said in a raspy voice that he hoped disguised his own. He didn't wait for their acknowledgment. Instead, he scraped the chair across the floor and lowered himself into it, making sure to jingle the coins in his pocket as he sat.

Their frowns of protest smoothed into eager acceptance. One of them chortled and called out to a girl at the bar. "Bring this fella a drink, sweetheart. And bring more for the rest of us too."

The scruffy faces of the shanty boys at his table didn't look familiar. But that didn't mean they wouldn't recognize him. He was too well known, even among other camps, to get by for very long without someone figuring out who he was, even in disguise.

His foreman at Camp 1 had been more than willing to loan him his work clothes. And now his odor was as sour as any other shanty boy. The shirt was stiff with dried sweat, and the stains and grime of many days' hard work were ingrained into every fiber.

Vera had darkened his hair with soot from the stove. She'd blackened his fingernails and had added a smudge or two to his face for good measure. She'd even brought out a foul-smelling concoction of hers she claimed would change the color of his day-old scruff. But he'd had to draw the line some-where.

The disguise would only buy him minutes. And he wouldn't fool Carr, especially because the good-for-nothing scum was no doubt expecting him.

Connell had asked the other men to hold off storming the Stockade — to give him fifteen minutes to locate Lily, to have her safe in hand before the battle began. There was no telling what Carr would do to Lily if they didn't have her before the fighting started.

But he had a feeling rescuing her first was wishful thinking. He didn't know where she was and had no way of searching. Even so, the men had reluctantly agreed to let him go in alone for fifteen minutes under disguise, urging him to be cautious. If Carr caught him too, then he'd have two hostages. The men would likely be helpless, unable to do anything except what Carr demanded to get him and Lily back.

Connell's heart rammed against his ribs, just as it had done since he'd climbed Dead Man's Hill. The clock was ticking, and he needed to make every second count.

He had to find out where Carr was keeping Lily. That's the only thing that really mattered anymore — the only thing he could think about.

"Heard Bella's back." He chanced another glance around the tavern. Half a dozen girls in their fancy silk dresses sashayed with swinging hips through the room. Some delivered drinks from the bar, while a few others were hanging on the arms of men or sitting on laps giggling and flirting.

He'd wager the low-cut dresses exposing the creamy flesh of their bosoms was enticement enough for most of the shanty boys. The girls surely didn't need to do much more to interest a man in going upstairs.

He forced his eyes away from the temptation. He couldn't imagine how any man could stay strong against lust when he was surrounded on all sides by such scantily attired women.

The dealer across the table from him gave a short laugh. "Naw, Bella ain't back." His fingers arched against the cards, sending them cascading with a snap and speed of a seasoned gambler.

"But Carr's got something better tonight." One of the other men grinned. "He's breaking in Bella's sister."

The blood drained from Connell's body, leaving him breathless and weak. Was he too late to protect Lily from rape? He rose from his chair an inch, eyeing the bouncer at the base of the stairway. Could he overpower the man and make it upstairs?

"The man who puts the most money in the pot," the dealer said, nodding toward the tin pail next to the bar, "gets the first chance with her."

"Hope you're ready to lose some money," said the third man, " 'cuz I'm aiming to take that pretty little spitfire to bed first."

The man nodded in the direction of the bar. At that moment, the woman turned, two mugs of beer in each hand.

Her rich woodsy brown eyes glowered with fiery sparks.

Lily!

His heart crashed forward.

Her brows shot up, and she stopped so

suddenly that some of the foaming amber liquid sloshed out of the mugs. Her lips began to curve into a smile, and she opened her mouth.

He gave a quick shake of his head, warning her not to say anything, not to acknowledge him, hoping she'd understand the need to play along with his charade.

Her smile withered before it had the chance to bloom. She promptly forced a scowl back to her countenance, one fierce enough to ward off any man who might grab her as she passed. But her eyes were still wide and questioning, and — dare he say — filled with happiness to see him?

He wanted to stand up, hoist her over his shoulder, and make a run for it. But he knew he'd only get a gunshot in his back and would put her in danger as well.

No, he'd have to stay calm, somehow get ahold of her, and make sure she was tucked securely by his side before the other men barged in.

"I'm here to win, fellas," he said picking up the cards the dealer shoved his way. "Especially if the winner gets Bella's sister."

Lily neared the table and plunked the mugs down, spilling more of the beer. But the men had turned their gazes on her and didn't notice anything except the low neckline of her bodice and her exposed cleavage.

"There she is," one of the men said, grinning like an idiot.

Connell's fingers went to his knife, and he fought the urge to get up and cut out the ogling eyes of each of the men. Nobody had a right to look at Lily's flesh — not even him, not until he married her. And the minute he had her safe, the first thing he was going to do was find a preacher and make her his wife.

"Hi there, beautiful," he said. "Has anyone told you lately you're pretty enough to stop a man's breath right in his chest?"

A smile twitched at her lips. She wiped her hands on the satin of her dress as if she relished staining it and destroying the rich material. "Well now, for that kind of compliment, I might just have to give you a little reward."

She rounded the table toward him, swaying her hips with each step. The message in her eyes said she was playing along, that she understood that their charade was a matter of life and death.

Some of the men hooted, and others called out crude suggestions.

Despite the danger of the situation he couldn't keep from appreciating her beauty, the way her long, loose curls flounced about her face and on her bare shoulders, the darkness of her hair against the smooth creaminess of her skin, the sparkle in her eyes.

She stopped in front of him.

He scooted back from the table. Should he grab her now and make a run for it? He glanced at the large clock on the wall next to the bar.

He had nine minutes left.

Something flickered in her eyes — questions, urgency, fear. But she kept her face a mask of calmness. "Hmm . . . let's see, what kind of reward should I give you?" She walked her fingers up his arm to his shoulder.

He forced himself not to look at the door or the bouncers — not yet.

Instead, he fixed his attention on Lily. "How about sitting right here on my lap?" He patted his knees, urging her to draw nearer, to let him shield her.

Her brows inched higher as if she couldn't believe he'd willingly ask her to do something so scandalous, but with her palm she pushed him back and then plopped herself down on his lap.

The movement brought another chorus of catcalls and whistles from around the room.

The attention was just what they needed

to draw the bouncers away from their posts.

He slid his arm around her waist and pulled her closer, catching the lingering lavender scent that was uniquely hers.

"Mister, you're in luck," she said loudly enough so that all the men could hear. "First, I'm going to give you a big kiss."

"How big?" he asked.

"How big do you want?"

Her gaze didn't leave his. Even though her voice was light and playful, there was nothing but fear and determination in her eyes.

She was good at the charade.

He forced himself to grin, to play the dangerous game. "Let's see what you've got. Then I can decide if I want to fill up that pail and take you upstairs."

The saloon erupted into coarse laughter, and a few protests from the men who'd been vying to win her.

She leaned into him, hesitated for a second, and then brought her mouth to his. Her lips pressed into his boldly.

His lips melded to hers, the taste of fear propelling them together. And when she deepened the kiss, his hand moved up her back and into the thick strands of her curls.

He had to get her out of there.

Her grip tightened as if she would never let go of him.

All he could think about was how much he cared about her — how desperately and passionately he loved this woman. He couldn't bear to think of anyone hurting her, and he knew he could do nothing less than give up his life to save her.

The chorus of calls tapered off into a chilling silence.

Lily's lips froze on his.

A shiver slithered up his spine.

He broke their contact and pushed his lips against her ear and whispered, "When I stand up, I want you to get behind me and stay there."

She nodded imperceptibly.

"I love you." The ragged whisper came out before he could stop it.

She pulled back, her eyes wide.

It was then that he saw Carr. Only fifteen feet away. A pistol aimed at his heart.

"I was waiting for you, McCormick." His voice was soft and his smile cold. "I figured you'd end up as one of our guests tonight."

"Last I checked this was a free country." Connell stood slowly, setting Lily to her feet and maneuvering her behind him. "I guess I have as much right as any other man to come up here."

Lily huddled against his back.

Connell's hand slid to his side, to his knife.

The cocking of Carr's pistol echoed in the deathly silent room. "Keep your hands up, McCormick."

Connell knew he couldn't take any chances — not yet. He lifted his hands as if to surrender.

Carr started toward him, his boots tapping in slow, calculated steps that rang hollow. He was as immaculately groomed as always, not even a hair out of place.

Lily's fingers crawled under his shirt, skimming over the skin of his back.

For an instant, all he could think was that she'd picked a poor time to entice him with her touch. But as her fingers closed over his knife, he realized what she was doing.

She slipped the knife out of the scabbard the same way she had when he'd fought the wolves.

"I figured it was past time for you to learn a lesson or two," he said, hoping to draw Carr's attention away from Lily.

"And what lesson are you going to teach me?" Carr said, now only seven feet away.

Jimmy Neil trailed him, his gap-toothed smile laying claim to victory. And two bouncers flanked Carr — hopefully the ones from the outside gate and door so that the men could make it inside the Stockade quicker.

Connell glanced at the clock. Four minutes left.

Would he already be dead by the time the others stormed the place?

"For starters you need to learn that forcing young women into slavery is against the law." Connell stood straighter. "Our country fought a war to outlaw slavery twenty years ago. And I'm sure many of the men in this room had fathers who gave their lives in that fight for freedom."

"These women aren't slaves." Carr closed the distance between them and stood only a foot away, close enough for Connell to catch the stench of whiskey and cigar smoke that lingered on his breath. "They're down here because they agreed to it, right, Lily?"

"You're a lying piece of scum." Her voice rang with fierceness. "You would have killed me in that closet if I hadn't agreed to your demands."

She started to step out from behind Connell, but he took a step sideways to block her. "Anyone who's met Lily knows she'd never willingly step foot in your brothel," he said to Carr, praying Lily wouldn't do anything rash. "And I suppose now you're going to try to convince everyone here that Frankie agreed to work for you too."

"Of course she agreed. She came to Harrison solely for the purpose of working for me."

"The truth is, you wouldn't have had to lure her up here under false pretenses if she were so willing. And you most certainly wouldn't have had to beat her to death if she'd wanted this kind of life."

Lily gasped and her body stiffened.

Too late he realized the poor timing of breaking the news of Frankie's death to her, and he wanted to smash a mug over his head for his stupidity.

"Frankie's dead?" Before he could stop her, she slid out from behind him. "You murdered a poor innocent girl?" Her voice grew shrill.

In that one instant, Carr grabbed her arm and captured her. He jerked her against him and held her in front of his body like a human shield.

She screamed in fury and struggled against him.

Connell lunged for her, but Carr shoved the barrel of his pistol against his heart, stopping him.

At the sight of the gun pressed into Connell, Lily froze and her face paled.

"That's a good girl." Carr jerked her tighter. "You do as I say. Don't move. Don't speak. And don't cause me any trouble, and maybe I'll go easy on you later when I give you your beating."

"Let her go, Carr." This was exactly what he'd hoped to prevent. The scoundrel had to know that with Lily as his prisoner, he'd be able to get Connell to do just about anything he wanted.

"And what other lessons do you plan on teaching me tonight, McCormick? Go on. Do your best to *reform* me." The hard gleam in the man's eyes told Connell exactly what he thought of Connell's recent involvement in the Red Ribbon Society.

"I think you're going to find that there are a lot of people in this town, and even in this saloon here tonight, who are tired of your intimidation and the way you've been running this town into the ground."

"Is that so? I bet there's not a man here who would agree with you."

The room was silent except for a belch from a drunken shanty boy at the table next to them.

Carr's grin widened. "See —"

"I agree with McCormick" came a man's voice from the edge of the room.

Connell's heart roared to life. Was Stuart inside?

"There's a lot of us who are fed up with

all your bullying," another voice called out — a voice that sounded like Herb Nolan's, his foreman.

"We're sick to death of you breaking the law, Carr." The calls came from around the room, and Connell could only pray all the men had made it into the compound and were in position.

Carr's expression wavered, but the pistol pointed at Connell's heart didn't budge.

The grumbling around the room continued.

"Let Lily and Connell go," shouted Stuart above the din, "and maybe we won't tear your place apart right here and now."

"You so much as lay a finger on anything in the Stockade," Carr shouted back, "and I'll blow a hole through McCormick's heart faster than you can blink."

"If you shoot him," Stuart's voice rang out, "you might as well count yourself a dead man."

Once again the room turned into a silent tomb. Stuart pushed through the revelers, and some of the other men followed, pointing their guns at Carr and the bouncers who stood near him. Jimmy Neil's grin faded and fear flashed across his face.

"You're done, Carr," Mr. Sturgis said.

"We don't want you in Harrison any longer."

Carr didn't move. "If you don't put down your guns and walk on out of here, I'll make sure every single one of you lives to regret the day you stepped into the Stockade."

"Your threats don't scare us anymore."

"Nobody likes you, Carr." Mr. Sturgis spoke again. "You might as well pack your bags and get out of here, 'cuz your days are numbered."

Carr finally glanced around the circle of men who surrounded him. His clean-cut features hardened. "You all know that my business is what keeps this town alive. And it keeps the shanty boys happy and out of trouble."

Disgust rose swiftly inside Connell. Had he really once believed the same thing as Carr? That the taverns and brothels were a necessary evil in the lumber communities?

He met Lily's gaze and hoped she could see the remorse there.

Her eyes brimmed with a determination that sent a nervous shiver over his skin.

What was she planning to do next?

"We have evidence that you're behind the log thefts this winter." Herb Nolan stepped forward, his hunting knife unsheathed and pointed at Carr.

"You don't have any evidence," Carr snarled.

"A whole bunch of logs on the rollway down in Averill is plenty of evidence, especially because ain't no one seen you or your men doing any cutting this winter."

Several of the shanty boys throughout the room cussed and still others turned angry eyes upon Carr.

"After all the hard work these boys have gone through to cut and haul those logs," continued Herb, "they don't take kindly to anyone tampering with their profit."

Carr's hard expression flickered for just an instant, but it was enough for Connell to see that the man knew his days in Harrison were numbered.

"We don't need you, Carr." Stuart's gun was leveled on Carr. "We never have. In fact, this town will finally have a chance to prosper once you leave. We'll have law and order and maybe we'll get some decent families wanting to come here to live."

Carr took a step back.

The pressure of the steel pistol in Connell's chest fell away. Before he could take a breath of relief, Carr swung the gun around and pressed it into Lily's temple.

"No!" Connell started toward Carr.

"Don't take a step closer or I'll kill her."

CHAPTER 29

The cold metal jabbed into Lily's head with a pressure that would have given her a headache if she hadn't been so angry.

She'd had enough of Carr. He'd not only stolen the life and love out of Daisy, but he'd murdered Frankie.

Picturing the frail, sweet Frankie taking blow after blow from Carr's brass knuckles only managed to stir her anger all the more. The poor girl would have been terrified and in torturous agony.

"Don't any of you try to follow me," Carr said, dragging Lily backward toward the steps. "Or she's dead."

Maggie stood in the stairwell, the dark shadows hiding her. Even so, Lily could see the glint in the woman's eyes, the one that said she'd warned her not to try anything and now was going to pay for lying.

Panic raced through Lily. If Maggie got hold of her again, she wouldn't let her go.

She'd haul her back to that dark closet and lock her in there for good. She'd be as good as dead too.

Oh, God, her heart cried. She'd tried to trust Him throughout the awful evening. Could she *keep* trusting that He'd work out His plans for her?

She glanced across the room to Connell, to the haggard fear that crisscrossed his face. He'd come to save her. He'd risked his life for her. Again.

But he'd done everything he could. Was anything more possible?

As if sensing her question, he slipped his hand underneath his shirt. His fingers came back empty. His gaze darted to her hand, to his knife.

She clutched it, wishing she could toss it across the room to him.

First fear, then desperation flashed over his features. He glanced around as if looking for something he could use to stop Carr from taking her away. His focus landed on the sharp blade of the knife his foreman had drawn.

Connell nodded at the boss and then at the knife, indicating that the man should toss it to him. The foreman lifted his brow. And Lily was sure he was thinking the same thing she was — how could he toss Connell the knife without being seen and putting Lily in more jeopardy?

"You're all big fools for interfering with my business," Carr called. His arm around her waist was as tight as a chain.

She fought against his hold, but he only jammed the pistol until the pressure made her dizzy with pain.

The knife burned in her hand, turning her palm sweaty. Did she dare use it?

She curled her fingers around the handle.

Carr neared the bottom step. And Maggie's eyes above the scarf mocked her, almost as if she were smiling in anticipation of the torture she would lay upon Lily when she got her hands on her.

"No!" Lily yelled. With a burst of strength borne of all the anger, pain, and fear rolling deep in her heart, she raised the knife and swung it backward, making contact with Carr's upper leg.

He gave a scream of agony and fell away from her, releasing his hold. The gun slipped from his fingers and clattered to the floor.

She started to fling herself toward Connell, but fingers gripped the back of her dress and yanked her backward. She found herself falling against Jimmy.

In that instant of confusion, she saw the foreman slide his knife across the floor to

Connell. He swooped it up.

Lily strained to duck, to give Connell a target. And before Jimmy could move, Connell flung the weapon. It flew through the air with a speed that would have frightened Lily had she not seen Connell throw a knife before. The sharp tip sliced into Jimmy and embedded into his shoulder.

Jimmy shouted a string of curses and grabbed the smooth handle of the knife that had gone deep into his flesh. He shoved Lily away as if she were completely to blame for his pain.

She stumbled forward, scrambling across the distance toward Connell, her heart thudding with the need to reach him.

He was already halfway across the room. She launched herself into his arms, desperate for his help and strength.

"Lily," he breathed as he swept her up, lifted her into his arms, and cradled her against his chest. The warmth and power of his hold enveloped her, and she buried her face into him, needing to block out Carr and everything that had happened.

Around them the men roared to life. They lunged at the bouncers, fists swinging. The crash of chairs, the shattering of glass, and the shouts sent her heart racing with new fear. Would they make it out alive?

She wound her arms around Connell's neck.

He ducked as a bottle whizzed past them. A second later it crashed against the wall.

"Hold on tight," he said, focusing on the door. He plowed forward, knocking into some men who didn't seem to care who they were fighting, only that they relished a brawl.

One of the bouncers by the bottom of the steps shouted and began to make his way toward them. His eyes narrowed with a murderous glare.

"Hurry," Lily urged. She didn't know if she had the strength to fight anymore.

"I got him," Stuart shouted to Connell. "You get Lily out of here."

Connell hesitated.

"Go!" Stuart called again. Then with a cry, Stuart rushed at the bouncer, swinging the butt of his rifle at the man.

She could feel Connell's muscles tighten as if he resisted the idea of leaving his companions to finish the bloody battle. But the leg of a chair flew past them, and Connell put his head down, shielding her with his body. He barreled his way to the door and kicked it open.

A rush of frigid air splashed her. For once she didn't care that Michigan was so cold.

Indeed, the flittering snowflakes were like kisses against the bare skin on her arms.

He crossed the yard, and the dogs raced to the fence of their pen, growling and barking. But their fierceness didn't taunt her as it had in the past. She'd faced the dogs and won. And now she'd faced Carr and walked away from him too.

A fountain of unidentifiable emotions began to bubble inside her.

She'd lived through the horror of the past twenty-four hours, she'd stabbed Carr, and she was still alive to tell about it.

A ripple pushed up her throat and ended in a short sob.

Through the blackness of the night, broken by light streaming from the open doorway, Connell peered down at her. "You're safe now," he murmured, the worry in his eyes caressing her face.

She nodded, her throat too constricted to utter the gratitude she owed him.

He made his way through the unguarded Stockade gate and down the hill. Shouts and cries of the brawl followed them each step. She clung to him, knowing she should get down and walk but not sure her legs could hold her if she tried. He didn't stop until he reached the front step of the Northern Hotel.

His labored breath filled her ears with a strange feeling of comfort. He banged the door with his elbow. Immediately it opened and they tumbled inside, into the light and warmth of the hotel dining room.

Oren's hand shook against the door. His bushy eyebrows formed jagged arches above his red-rimmed eyes. At the sight of her in Connell's arms, his shoulders slumped and his face crumpled. Tears began to trickle down his cheeks. "Oh, thank the good Lord. Thank the good Lord."

The gurgling fountain of emotions rose in her. She wiggled to loosen herself from Connell's hold, leaving him little choice but to lower her. The moment her feet touched the ground she reached for Oren.

His arms folded about her, and he pressed her face into his shoulder. He held her tightly, as if he would never let her go. Silent sobs rose inside her chest, the sorrow and pain from all she'd lost and now all she'd gained. She clung to him as she would a real father.

She couldn't remember anyone ever crying over her. Anyone worrying about her the way Oren did.

Hot tears streaked her cheeks. Maybe she didn't have Daisy anymore. And maybe she'd have to give up her dreams of making a home for them. But God hadn't left her alone. He'd given her an unlikely family in this old man.

For all his gruffness, she didn't think a real father would have been capable of loving her any more than Oren did. And she was sure there were those, like Connell, whose fathers didn't love or respect them even half as much as Oren.

She had to remember to count her blessings.

Oren pulled back and tugged a hankie from the inner pocket of his coat. The checkered linen was crumpled and crusty, but he wiped the moisture from his cheeks and then blew into it, making the noise of a rusty bugle.

She swiped at the dampness on her face with the back of her hand.

"You didn't let any of them no-good boys lay a pinkie on you, did you?" He stuffed the hankie back into the tight pocket.

"Of course not." She smiled at him through her tears.

"Good." He took a deep breath, and his drooping shoulders rose like a weight had been lifted from them. "Then that saves me the trouble of having to go up there and start smashing heads together like rotten squash."

Lily caught Connell's gaze. The look told her what a struggle he'd had convincing Oren to stay back at the hotel during the rescue. She couldn't even begin to imagine what kind of threats he'd had to use to keep the man from barging out the door and striding into danger.

She nodded her thanks, hoping he could see how grateful she was for his protection of Oren.

He nodded back.

The door banged open and a gust of snow and cold swirled inside with Stuart. His brow was wrinkled, and he gulped for breath. "How's Lily?" He stopped at the sight of her next to Oren. "Are you okay?" His voice was gentle and his eyes filled with agony — the agony of a man in love with a woman he'd just about lost.

Her breath stuck in her chest.

Did Stuart love her?

She'd always sensed his affection. But the look in his eye went much further than normal concern.

"I'm doing fine now that I'm here," she said, avoiding looking directly at him. Had she somehow led him on? She'd tried to keep things plain and simple between them. She considered him a good friend and a companion in the fight for justice. But that was all.

She could feel his gaze probing her.

"Did Carr hurt you?" He took a step toward her.

"I would have died first before letting him defile me." She turned away from Stuart, knowing the gesture would hurt him but needing to tell him somehow they could never be more than friends.

Vera draped a quilt over her shoulders. "You don't know just how sick with worry we've been." Her eyes were puffy and red, and when she patted Lily's cheek, her lips trembled. Mr. Heller huddled nearby, his whittling abandoned in his chair by the fireplace. Even his face was full of worry.

Lily drew the quilt over the exposed flesh of her bosom. She couldn't keep back a shudder at the thought of how close she'd come to ending up like Frankie.

The sorrow of the girl's death squeezed Lily's heart and brought fresh tears to her eyes. How had she managed to fail so miserably to help Frankie?

Her head dropped. She'd lost both Daisy and Frankie.

How could she have been so foolish to think she could orchestrate everything by herself? Why had she ever believed she needed to be the one in control, that she knew more about what needed to be done than God?

Look what had happened when she'd finally relinquished her plans — God had sent practically the entire town to her rescue.

"Well, you won't have to worry about Carr anymore." Stuart twisted his hands together. "Maggie helped him to his office. And once he was gone, his bouncers stopped fighting."

For the first time, she noticed Stuart's sling and the lacerations on his face. Guilt threatened to choke her. She didn't need to ask him who beat him up.

"I think," Stuart continued, "the townspeople made it clear they don't want Carr or any of his men around anymore. It's only a matter of time before he moves out of Harrison."

"Good." But at the moment, she couldn't even take consolation from the fact that she'd had a part in the man's downfall. It all was too little, too late.

"Maybe with your help," Stuart offered, "we'll be able to close up a few more taverns."

She shook her head, fighting back the overwhelming emotions that threatened to make her start sobbing again.

"And we had twenty-three in attendance at the Red Ribbon Society meeting last night —"

"I can't stay, Stuart." She finally met his gaze. She was sure he could read the truth in her eyes, along with her regret at having to hurt him.

His kind eyes clouded.

When she looked over at Connell, at the haggard lines that drew his handsome features tight, she couldn't keep her heart from leaping at the remembrance of his whispered declaration of love.

He'd told her he loved her.

But had he meant it? Or had he spoken the words out of the desperation of the moment?

Surely he could see the questions in her eyes. The desire for him to declare his love for her again. To promise to take her away from this place and never return.

He shoved his hands into his pockets and didn't say anything. Even the depths of his eyes were murky and unreadable.

She dropped her chin, but not before she caught sight of the understanding on Stuart's face. He knew why she couldn't stay with him. His face acknowledged what her heart was afraid to admit — that she was in love with Connell.

"Lily needs some time away from this Godforsaken town," Oren muttered. "I'm taking her back home. At first light."

Home. The word was warm and comforting and wrapped around her like a fresh spring wind.

He was offering her something she'd never had. A home. With him.

She reached for Oren's hand and squeezed it. "You're right. I need some time — time to sort out my life."

He pressed back, his eyes promising her that he'd take care of her and give her everything she needed.

As much as her heart longed for Connell to declare his love for her again, to sweep her off her feet and take her somewhere where they could always be together, she was grateful for Oren and his offer. He was giving her a chance at permanence, at settling down, at belonging.

She didn't need Connell. Instead, she probably needed some time to get used to the idea of not taking care of Daisy anymore, of letting her go, and finding how she fit into the plans God was piecing together for her life.

Besides, hadn't she been the one to say that she and Connell were too different, that they should go their separate ways?

She smiled at Oren. "Let's go home."

If only her heart didn't already miss Connell.

CHAPTER 30

Glorious spring sunshine poured through the large windows of the photo studio and bathed Lily in warmth. She dipped her rag into the sudsy bucket of water and splashed it against the glass.

In the darkroom, down the hallway, she could hear the clinking of vials as Oren prepared the daily emulsion, dissolving nitrate of silver in a bromised gelatine. He'd taught her how to spread the mixture over the plates that would eventually go into the camera.

She didn't enjoy the process of preparing the plates as much as she did the actual picture taking, which Oren had started teaching her too.

She rubbed at the window, making it sparkle, the vinegar in the cleaning solution tickling her nose. The sunshine would make for a good day in the studio, providing the necessary lighting. Thankfully, their appointment book was full.

In the early morning, the traffic on Washington Avenue outside the shop was still slow. With the recent spring thaw, the streets were nothing but giant mud puddles. By midday, they would swarm with all the shanty boys who'd left the camps during the river drives and had come to spend their hard-earned cash in the taverns and brothels of Bay City.

She tried not to think that Daisy was somewhere in the middle of all the debauchery.

It was easier to pretend she'd gone somewhere new, somewhere to make a decent life for herself.

With a sigh, Lily paused her robust efforts of cleaning the window. She'd tried hard over the past month to accept that Daisy was gone and hadn't wanted to be with her, but the rejection still stung.

She hadn't been able to understand why Daisy had run away again. She wasn't sure that she ever would.

But she'd honored Daisy's wishes and hadn't gone looking for her. Although that hadn't stopped her from wanting to march down to Hell's Half Mile and search until she found her. And it didn't stop her from asking Mrs. McCormick if she'd heard from or seen Daisy every time the dear woman visited the studio.

But the answer was always the same: She hadn't seen Daisy anywhere.

Her sister had disappeared. And apparently not even Tierney knew where she'd gone.

And, of course, Mrs. McCormick always had news of Connell. She claimed he had approached his father with plans for reform within the company and had begun implementing some of the changes, even though Mr. McCormick had been opposed. It was clear Mrs. McCormick was proud of Connell.

Truth be told, Lily was too.

He hadn't walked away from the problems like she'd wanted him too. Instead, he'd done something even more courageous. He'd stayed and was fighting to make things better. He was discovering where God wanted to use him.

Lily dropped her rag into the bucket and walked over to the wicker chair in front of the plain gray backdrop they used for most of the portraits.

With a heavy heart, she plopped into the chair, drying her hands on the folds of her skirt.

She rested her elbows on her knees and

lowered her face into her hands. She was ashamed to think of how judgmental she'd been, of the accusations she'd leveled at Connell.

If only she could rewind time and take back the things she'd told him.

A painful ache lodged in her throat.

She'd been wrong to suggest that he leave his family business for her.

And now because of her foolishness, she'd lost him.

As much as she'd tried to tell herself it didn't matter, that she'd make a life for herself without him, she knew losing him would hurt until the day she died.

If only she hadn't been so proud. She wasn't as pure and righteous as she'd thought. Except by the grace of God, she too could have fallen into a sinful life like Daisy. Perhaps the first step in battling temptation was humility — recognizing that she wasn't infallible and needed God's help.

The bell on the door jingled, and a breath of the cool spring air rushed inside the studio.

Lily pushed herself up from the chair. "I'll be with you in just a minute." She quickly turned her head and tucked stray hairs back into the knot she'd only loosely tied.

"I don't think I can wait another minute."

At the sound of Connell's voice, her heart sputtered to a stop. Slowly she pivoted until she faced him.

She almost didn't recognize him. Gone were the shanty-boy clothes — the plaid mackinaw, the heavy trousers, and the dirty caulk boots. In their place was the apparel of a gentleman — an open frock coat that went down to his knees, revealing an embossed brocade vest, bow tie, and pinstriped trousers.

He took a step away from the door and lifted his hat off his head, revealing his clean-shaven face. He looked more like a banker than a backwoodsman.

Under one arm he carried a box.

But it wasn't his clothes, or his freshly groomed face, or his parcel that caught her attention. Rather, it was his eyes — the warmth of the pine green — that took her breath away.

"I've waited thirty-one days to see you." He pulled his watch out of the front pocket of his vest and examined it. "That's exactly 44,640 minutes."

Her stomach did a flip.

"I'm hoping I gave you long enough to sort out your life." He hesitated, almost as if he were restraining himself from charging across the room to her, as if he didn't quite know if she'd welcome him or send him away.

She wanted to tell him he'd given her too long, that she didn't expect she'd ever have her life sorted out, that maybe she wouldn't see the pattern God was putting together but she'd trust Him with the bigger design anyway. But the words stuck in her throat.

He took several steps toward her. In the empty studio, his footsteps echoed with determination. "If I didn't give you long enough, I'm sorry. But I really couldn't wait another sixty seconds."

"Are you telling me you're an impatient man, Connell McCormick?" Warmth spread through her middle, and she couldn't contain the teasing smile that tugged at her lips.

"I'm the prince of patience." He smiled back, his face visibly relaxing. "In fact, I think I deserve to be crowned king for all the restraint I've had when it comes to you."

There was something in the depths of his eyes that made the warmth in her stomach curl like ribbons. She couldn't help thinking back to the last time she'd kissed him, at the Stockade, when she'd sat on his lap and pressed her lips against his like a hussy.

Of course she'd only been trying to keep them out of trouble. Hadn't she? Even as she asked herself the question, the truth nudged her. She needed to learn more restraint.

She dropped her gaze, reminded once again of how weak she was.

"I was planning on giving myself more time to . . . to get my own plans squared away." He tapped the box under his arm. "But then I found this and thought of you."

"Should I be flattered that a wooden box made you think of me?"

His grin widened. He lowered the box to the floor and kneeled in front of it. "I found something that needs saving. And since you're the queen of rescues — I figured you might want to take a shot at another rescue."

"So now I'm the queen of rescues?" She kneeled onto the polished wood floor across the box from him.

"No one can pull off a rescue like you." The teasing glimmer in his eyes pulled the ribbon in her stomach tighter. "Although I won't ask you to promise that you'll refrain from any more middle-of-the-night rescues."

She smiled.

"Because I think we both know you won't be able to keep that promise."

She laughed softly. "Well, if you're the king of patience and I'm the queen of rescues, I guess that means we're both royalty."

"Maybe that means we're meant to be together." His voice turned soft, and his gaze captured hers with an intensity that made her breath catch in her throat.

What was he saying?

The look in his eyes drew her forward, like a magnetic pull. They were warm and wide and full of longing.

She found herself leaning across the box, closing the distance between them, wanting him, breathless for his kiss.

A muted cry within the box stopped her. Her heart started beating again, faster. "What was that?"

He sat back and pried off the lid.

As he slid it aside, her eyes widened.

There in a bundle of rags sat a dainty white kitten. It peered up at her with gentle blue eyes and gave a tiny mew.

"Oh, Connell." Lily smiled, speechless at the beauty of the helpless creature.

"I found her this morning in the stables."

She reached two fingers toward the kitten and ran them over the fluffy fur on its back.

"The stable hand said the mother cat died last week. The other kittens disappeared. This is the only one left, and she won't make it without some help."

Lily couldn't resist a second longer. She scooped up the furry bundle and brought it against her chest. She cupped it in one hand and stroked it with the other.

It gave another soft mew, one that brought tears to Lily's eyes. "Oh, you sweet thing. Of course I'll take care of you."

"I figured if anyone could save her, you could."

Lily pressed a kiss into the downy fur between its tiny pointed ears. She scratched the crook of its neck and was rewarded with a rusty purr.

It was motherless and homeless and needed someone with a heart big enough to care — someone like her.

She pulled the creature back and looked into its little face, with its wet pink nose, feathery whiskers, and big trusting eyes. "You're home, little one." She planted a kiss on its forehead and then cuddled it against her chest again.

Connell smiled.

"Thank you," she whispered through an aching throat. How had this sweet, loving man known exactly what to bring her? The kind of gift that would mean more to her than anything else?

"If you need something else to save — *someone* else to save — I have a lifetime project I can give you." His smile faded, and his eyes darkened.

Her pulse quickened.

"I'm a man with many faults, Lily." His gaze caught and held hers. "And I don't know that I'll ever leave the lumber business —"

She reached out her fingers and touched them against his lips to stop him from saying anything else.

But he took hold of her hand and slid it into his, intertwining his fingers through hers. His palm pressed into hers, and the warm moisture of his touch caressed her.

"I can't leave — at least not now."

She nodded. "I understand —"

"But I want you to know," he continued, "God hit me over the head, and I'm finally realizing how much work needs to be done to make some long overdue changes within the lumber industry. And I'm leading the reform."

Her heart swelled with pride.

"I'm investigating the efforts of reforestation in some of the camps. I'm putting into place policies that will help pay worker benefits upon disability."

"That's what your mother was telling me —"

"I've also begun looking at ways we can

improve working and living conditions — not just in the camps but among the mills too." He spoke earnestly, as if his life depended upon how well he could convince her of his merits. "And I'm doing some research into future business opportunities for Bay City, ways the city can survive once the lumber industry pulls out of Michigan."

If only he would be quiet for a second and let her tell him none of it mattered to her.

"The biggest battle's been getting my dad to agree. But in places where I've begun implementing changes, he's starting to see some of the payoff. Worker loyalty and output have increased by twenty percent."

"That's fantastic —"

"I'm fighting hard, Lily." He cut her off again. His brow wrinkled. "I might not be there yet, but I'm learning —"

She leaned across the open box and stopped his words the only way she knew how — with a kiss. She touched her lips to his, and his sentence died. Gently, she pressed her fullness into the softness of his, letting the warmth of his breath mingle with hers.

She wanted to increase the contact, to press harder, to taste of him deeper. But with new restraint, she lingered only an instant before pulling away.

"I love you," she whispered.

His eyes widened.

"I love you for who you are — not what you do or who you'll become."

Her face burned with the brazen declaration. The kitten mewed, and she scratched its head and followed with a kiss.

Connell lifted a hand to her cheek. His gaze met hers with wide-eyed marvel. His thumb caressed the edge of her chin and simultaneously brought her face back to his. "I love you too, Lily."

The words were a whisper against her lips.

His eyes promised her another kiss and a future full of them.

Suddenly he stopped.

"No one lays their pinkie on Lily and lives to tell about it." Oren stood over Connell and pressed the barrel of his rifle into Connell's temple. His gray brows dipped into a scowl.

"Oren, it's just me. Connell." He didn't look the least bit frightened. Rather, a spark of merriment danced to life in his eyes.

"I know who you are, and it don't matter one little lick."

Connell's lips twitched with a grin. "After all the times you've stuck your gun into my head, I'm surprised I'm still alive."

Lily had to bite back a grin of her own.

"You're just mighty lucky that I haven't made you eat lead yet," Oren mumbled, but his voice lacked conviction.

"Now, Oren." Lily smiled at the man. "You won't need to kill him. At least not today."

She exchanged a glance with Connell, and the light in his eyes told her that he shared the memory of the night they'd met, when Oren had threatened him for the first time. They both knew it wouldn't be the last. And they loved the old man for it.

"Look what he brought me." She held up the kitten.

Oren glared down at the animal. "What in high heaven . . . ?"

Lily laughed and stroked it. "I was just thanking Connell for the gift."

"You can thank him by getting off the floor and kicking his hind end right out the door." Even though Oren sounded grumpy, his expression was as soft as the kitten's.

Connell caught Lily's gaze. "Would it help to know that I'm planning on asking Lily to be my wife?"

Lily sucked in a breath.

The rifle wavered. "It might help."

Connell grinned.

And a thrill of wonder wafted through Lily. Did Connell really want to marry her?

Oren cleared his throat. "I suppose I can let you live this once."

Connell reached for her hand. "What do you say, Lily? Will you marry me and let me spend the rest of my life showing you how much I love you?"

She glanced at Oren. Beneath his overgrown mustache she could see the beginnings of a smile, the closest to a smile she'd ever seen from him. He nodded at her, and his eyes seemed to reassure her that no matter what, he'd always be there for her.

Lily reached for his hand and squeezed it.

Her heart whispered a prayer of gratefulness. She'd been a homeless orphan her whole life. And now God had brought her to a place where she had more love than she'd ever dreamed possible. Maybe it wasn't the family she'd planned. But God was giving her a chance at a family of her own the way *He'd* planned.

She smiled at Connell.

"Is that a yes?" he asked.

"Yes."

In the long dark winter of her soul, she'd never believed spring would come. But it had come at last.

CHAPTER 31

Six months later

Lily rubbed the back of the young woman as she retched miserably into a basin at the side of her bed.

"It won't be long," Lily said, "and you'll be feeling as good as new."

She'd seen enough over the past six months to know that alcohol withdrawal took about a week. Then after that, with enough healthy food and loving care, the girls would eventually stop their trembling and regain their strength.

Lily smoothed the girl's tangled hair away from her forehead and helped her lie back down against the plush pillows. She pulled the quilt up to the girl's chin, leaving a pale, drawn face with a greenish-purple bruise, an outward testimony to all the pain the girl had once endured.

"Thank you," the young woman whispered through cracked lips.

Lily smiled and rose from her perch on the edge of the bed. "I'll be back in a little bit to check on you."

A motion in the crack of the bedroom door caught Lily's attention.

She crossed the spacious room, her footsteps silent upon the lush carpet. Even as her gaze touched upon the soft print of the wallpaper and the elegant but demure colors she'd picked for the room, her heart pattered with amazement.

The house was hers. And she could do anything she wanted with it.

And she had. She'd done everything she'd ever dreamed of doing. And more.

With a smile, she pushed open the door and stepped into the dimly lit hallway.

Strong arms slid around her waist, and she suddenly found herself tugged into a fierce embrace. "There you are" came Connell's hoarse whisper against her ear.

Her belly quivered with a familiar warm tightness. "What are you doing here?" She feigned prudence, cocking her head away from him, making him chase after her ear.

He growled and found the hollow of her ear, placing a kiss there.

Her arms went around him, and her body melted against his.

She'd never expected, after several months

of marriage, that every time he touched her she'd long for more of him. She was grateful for the purity they'd both brought to their marriage and the way it had enabled them to enjoy and appreciate each other even more.

His kiss moved to the long stretch of exposed neck above her lacy collar.

"Oh, Connell," she whispered, closing her eyes, letting the sweet softness of his lips send trails of warmth throughout her body.

He pulled back so that she could see his mischievous grin, the one that said he knew the power he had over her and he delighted in making her melt in his arms.

She didn't care, because she knew when she turned on the charm, she had the same sway over him.

Connell still worked for McCormick Lumber, but he'd requested that he and Tierney split the traveling among the camps. As it was, most of Connell's business kept him in town, where he was able to work with other businessmen on a regular basis and push for the reforms that he was promoting.

"Have I told you yet today how much I love you, Mrs. McCormick?" His lips pressed against her ear again.

"Not enough. I think I could use a little

reminding." Her hand found his and intertwined through his strong capable fingers. With a smile, she tugged him toward a room that had been recently vacated by one of the girls who had found employment as a maid.

"Lily." There was something in his tone that halted her heartbeat and chased away the playfulness of the moment.

"There's someone waiting downstairs to see you." His gaze met hers, and something gently cautious in the depths of his eyes lit a flicker of hope in her heart.

"Is it — ?" She pressed trembling fingers against her lips, too afraid to say the name.

"Go see." He nodded toward the wide winding stairway that led to the front hallway.

With her heart galloping at top speed like an out-of-control carriage, she lifted her silk skirt, bunched it in her hands, and raced in a very unladylike manner to the stairs.

She nearly tripped as she rushed to descend the two flights. She was blind to everything about the luxurious home that Mr. McCormick had given to them as a wedding present. Of course, she'd wept when the stern, gray-haired man had handed her and Connell the deed — not because she'd been happy to have a place of her own, finally.

Rather, she'd wept tears of joy because she'd known she could fulfill her dream of opening a home for women who needed rescuing. Connell hadn't wanted her to feel any pressure to leave Oren, and when she'd suggested they turn their wedding present into a home of refuge, he'd willingly supported her.

And Mrs. McCormick had wanted to be a part of every facet of decorating and preparing the home for the young women. She'd poured her time and energy into doing everything she could for the young women who came.

They made a good team. During the times Connell had to travel for work, Lily found comfort in being with Oren and Mrs. Mc-Cormick, who had become the father and mother she'd never had. And through it all, she'd been learning to trust God to unfold His purposes for her life. He'd been doing so in amazing ways that she couldn't have planned, even if she'd tried.

She couldn't make her feet move down the steps fast enough. As she turned the last bend, she paused and peered over the railing. Mrs. McCormick was hugging a young woman, holding her against her bosom like a long-lost daughter.

Even though Lily couldn't see the face of the girl, tears stung her eyes and her throat constricted. Could it really be her?

Behind her, Connell's fingers brushed her arm, offering her a measure of support.

Slowly she descended the last several steps. As her slippered feet touched the polished hardwood floor of the entryway, the young girl pulled away from Mrs. Mc-Cormick. She swiped at the tears on her face with dirty fingers, leaving smudges on cheeks that were too thin.

Mrs. McCormick stepped back, giving Lily a full view of Daisy. Her hair hung in tangled, matted strands. Her satin dress — the same one Mrs. McCormick had loaned her all those months ago — was tattered and stained and barely recognizable. It hung from her emaciated body. Her skin had lost its lovely creaminess and had a yellowish tint. She covered her mouth and gave a harsh cough that bent her bony shoulders.

First shock, then sadness spiraled through Lily. *Oh, Daisy,* her heart cried. *What have you done? What has become of you?*

The young woman standing before her was only a shadow of the sister she'd once known. She was like the dress, worn and lusterless beyond recognition.

But when Daisy straightened, and her big

brown eyes met hers, her gaze was the same as it had always been — trusting and filled with hope.

Lily's heart pinched with a twinge of pain and love. She wanted to rush over to Daisy, grab her into a hug, and never let her go. Instead, she held herself back. She'd pushed the girl away once with all of her mothering and loving. She didn't want to do it again.

"Hi, Lily." Daisy's voice was soft and hoarse.

"It's good to see you." Lily smiled at her sister.

"I didn't know if you'd be happy to see me or not."

"I'm very happy."

"You are?" Daisy's eyes widened. Another coughing spasm took hold of the girl, bending her over with the force. Mrs. McCormick gently patted Daisy's back until the coughing ceased.

Lily's throat constricted and her eyes burned with painful tears. She wanted to rush to the girl, usher her upstairs to one of the rooms, and call the doctor.

Connell laid a hand on the small of her back, as if sensing her pain.

Once again, she forced herself not to move.

Finally, Daisy straightened. This time sadness etched the girl's grimy face. "I'm sorry, Lily. So sorry . . ."

Lily couldn't speak past the tightness in her throat.

"I've been so foolish," Daisy whispered so low that Lily almost couldn't hear the words. "So, so foolish . . ."

The ache in Lily's chest expanded, and it pushed the tears that were brimming in her eyes over the edge and down her cheeks.

"I was so miserable, I didn't think I wanted to live anymore," Daisy said. "That's when one of the other girls told me about your home. She said you were giving girls a fresh chance. . . . So I came, but I was too scared to knock on the door. I started walking back down the street, and that's when I met Connell. . . ."

Daisy fixed her gaze on the floor, on the tip of her boot poking out from underneath her skirt, at the hole in the leather that exposed her bare toe. Her lips trembled and tears pooled in her eyes. "I know I don't deserve your kindness or help, not after the way I treated you, the way I demanded so much of you and then abandoned you. But . . ."

She lifted her head then, and her eyes pleaded with Lily for a second chance, begged for her forgiveness, and beckoned her to love her again.

The pain pushed a sob out before Lily could stop it, and heartache propelled her across the distance to Daisy. She threw her arms around her sister and crushed her in an embrace that spoke of all the desperation and longing she'd buried.

To her surprise, Daisy flung her arms around her and buried her face against her chest. Sobs wracked the young girl's sickly body. "Oh, Lily. Oh, Lily. Oh, Lily."

Lily pressed her face against Daisy and breathed in the sourness of whiskey and cigar smoke and unnamed filth with every choked lungful. She let her tears fall upon the girl, washing her with a love that would never fail, ever. No matter how many times Daisy strayed, no matter how many times she failed, Lily knew she could do nothing less than open her arms to her precious sister.

"I love you, Daisy," she whispered. "Nothing you do could ever make me stop loving you."

Daisy's arms squeezed her tighter.

Lily planted a kiss against the tangled hair. A prayer of gratefulness erupted in her heart — gratefulness for God's bigger plans, for His higher ways, for His wisdom.

She wouldn't always be able to see what

He was doing, and maybe she wouldn't always have Daisy in her life. But she would cherish the moments she did have, and know that even if life didn't always make sense or go the way she wanted, God had opened wide His arms to her.

He was still in control.

And His love would never fail.

AUTHOR NOTE

In the 1870s through the early 1880s, lumbering employed more workers than any other industrial occupation in the United States. The white pine tree was considered "green gold" and netted greater profit than the gold rush of the West.

The lumber era of the north woods brought confidence and prosperity to the Midwest. It helped develop many of the cities in existence today. The era is often glamorized, and many legends, songs, and stories have developed out of the lumber camps and lumber towns. If you were to take a drive through Michigan or Wisconsin, you'd run across museum after museum (some devoted entirely to the logging industry) with excellent depictions of what life was like during the lumber era.

However, often forgotten in all of the lore is the toll that lumbering took not only on the land but also on lives. The philosophy of many lumber barons was to get all they could from the land, as fast as they could, and then to let tomorrow's people handle tomorrow's problems. In other words, as they moved their camps from place to place, they left behind barren land, often not even suitable for farming.

Not only did the lumbering industry devastate the land, but it also brought a plethora of moral problems — alcoholism, prostitution, and violence. In fact, the lumber era is credited with introducing white slavery (forced prostitution) into Michigan.

It is my hope in *Unending Devotion* to bring attention to some of the situations that existed during the lumber era, particularly white slavery, which, unfortunately, is still a problem within the United States (and throughout the world) today.

Harrison was a real town in central Michigan that sprang up during the lumber era. In the early 1880s it had a population of only two thousand people but had over twenty saloons.

James Carr was a real villain who took up residence in Harrison to prey on the shanty boys of the area. He built a two-story saloon and brothel on a hill overlooking the town and named it the Devil's Ranch Stockade.

Every night between fifty and two hundred fifty men visited the Stockade. So many men lost their lives there that eventually the hill outside the Stockade became known as Deadman's Hill.

When recruitment of prostitutes for his brothel ran low, Carr resorted to procuring women by any means he was able. He kidnapped young women off the streets of Saginaw and Bay City. And he advertised in downstate newspapers for chambermaids and waitresses for his Harrison "hotel." When unsuspecting young girls arrived in Harrison by train, Maggie, Carr's lover and whorehouse matron, would meet the girls at the depot and whisk them off to the brothel. Those who objected were beaten into submission. Most of those girls were never heard from again.

One girl did manage to escape from the Stockade. Her name was Jennie King. She was one of the young girls who answered the newspaper ad, expecting to work in Carr's hotel. Instead, she found herself enslaved at the Stockade. She fled but was recaptured and beaten. The brave and desperate woman escaped again, wearing only a nightgown, and this time gained help from a family in Harrison. Carr tried to get her back, but the family helped smuggle

Jennie out of Harrison and to a safe place.

Unfortunately, many girls didn't survive. Another prostitute named Frankie Osborne was beaten to death by Carr because she refused to dance for the shanty boys. While Frankie's death went unnoticed by law enforcement, the Clare County newspapers used the event to begin exposing Carr's evil deeds.

Through the demands for reform from the press, the citizens of Harrison and Clare County began to stand up and fight against the rampant lawlessness. When a pair of reform candidates came forward to run for sheriff and county prosecutor, Carr's men were voted out of office. The new district attorney vowed to clean up the county and made it his number one priority to get rid of Carr.

In 1885, Carr was put on trial for the murder of Frankie Osborne. Not even his highly paid lawyers could get him out of trouble. He was pronounced guilty of manslaughter and sentenced to fifteen years in Jackson State Prison. He died at the age of thirty-seven in a trackside shack on a straw pallet, penniless and drunk.

His obituary in the Gladwin County Record read in part, "James Carr, known throughout the state, and especially in northern Michigan, as one of the most notorious and wicked of its inhabitants . . ."

He hurt countless women, like Jennie King and Frankie Osborne.

They were the inspiration for this story — they and the many women like them, who are helpless, hurting, and abused.

May we never forget them.

And may we be like the characters in *Unending Devotion*. May we rise up, stand tall, and fight against the injustices that still exist today.

Perhaps we can't save the world (as Lily wanted to do), but neither do we need to sit back and let the evil go unchecked (as Connell first did). Maybe we won't have the beauty of a perfect summer. But neither do we have to endure the callousness of an uncaring winter.

Instead, we can all look for our own spring — we can discover where God wants to use us.

Do you hear your whisper of spring?

ACKNOWLEDGMENTS

I'm always amazed at the amount of work that goes into bringing a story from the kernel of an idea into a book that finally sits on the shelf. The labor of love involves many people in a variety of capacities.

As always, I must thank my husband for his unending devotion to me as I strive to write my stories. He ceaselessly believes in me and my abilities. And he faithfully supports me in the challenging task of writing books while parenting five children.

I also want to thank my mom for being a willing listener and encourager. She's always there to share both the joys and the sorrows of the writing journey, and I don't know how I'd survive without her.

I'm thankful for the blessing of working with the talented team at Bethany House. I'm incredibly grateful for the hard work and dedication of each person who had a hand in bringing my book to publication.

Thanks to all my online writing friends for cheering me on in my writing journey. And special thanks to Kelli Gwyn for her insightful feedback and excitement over the story.

I'm grateful to my friends Steve and Molly Black for sharing with me their wealth of knowledge about the history of Bay City and Michigan lumbering, for loaning me their *Bay City Logbook,* and for watching the kids while I toured the Historical Museum of Bay County.

Finally, I would like to thank you, Readers, for your support! I love hearing from you and knowing that you are enjoying my books. Your pleasure with each story gives me the motivation to keep writing.

Here are several ways you can connect with me:

Mail: Jody Hedlund
P.O. Box 1230
Midland, MI 48641

Website: JodyHedlund.com
Email: *jodyhedlund@jodyhedlund.com*
Facebook: *http://www.facebook.com/Author JodyHedlund*
Twitter: @JodyHedlund

ABOUT THE AUTHOR

Jody Hedlund is an award-winning historical romance novelist and author of the bestselling book *The Preacher's Bride.* She received a bachelor's degree from Taylor University and a master's from the University of Wisconsin, both in social work. Currently she makes her home in Midland, Michigan, with her husband and five busy children.